# RETRIBUTION

## WENDY MILLION

Stomill Books

# THE DONAGHEY SERIES

Retribution – can be read as a standalone

Resurrection – first book in a duet

Redemption – second book in the duet

For my mom, who always had a book in her hand.

# THE DONAGHEY SERIES

Retribution – can be read as a standalone

Resurrection – first book in a duet

Redemption – second book in the duet

For my mom, who always had a book in her hand.

# Chapter One

The phone in my front pocket vibrates. Checking it is the only thing I want to do right now. I shift in the metal chair and keep my hands clasped on top of the aluminum conference table that has seen better days.

The warehouse is deserted except for the six of us. It's a weird setup, but I learned a long time ago the right questions to ask and the ones to avoid. At least there's a table. This is a negotiation, not a confrontation. The table is important.

My heart thumps a violent rhythm in my chest, but I've gotten used to that too. The erratic heartbeat is my tell, and I'm thankful the people I work with can't hear it, even when it pounds in my ears. I've been well-trained for this double life, at least on the outside.

"Look," I let impatience seep into my voice. "Carys is going to be pissed when she finds out you guys are screwing her over." My first indication this meeting wouldn't be lucrative should have been the lack of heat in the building. It's so cold that each time I speak, I wonder if I'll see my breath. Teddy is too cheap to pay the prices we need to make this deal worthwhile.

"Next time, she comes to the meeting herself or we'll be taking care of business in a different way." The metal of Teddy's gun twinkles at me as he flips his suit jacket with false casualness.

I give him a mild glance and suppress my eye roll. Guys who have this burning desire to whip out their gun as a substitute for their dick piss me off. *You got a gun. Good for you. I have four.* The one up the sleeve of my leather jacket would nail him between the eyes before he even unholstered his archaic piece of crap. It's no wonder he's searching for an arms deal.

"I have a feeling she's not going to want to do any business with you after this stunt." I keep my features neutral. This is a wasted opportunity, and frustration eats at me. "Call me when you're serious about working with us. Maybe she'll still be interested." I nod to the two men who came with me, and they mirror my movements, ready to follow my lead.

"What's she paying you, Kim? I'll double it." Teddy readjusts himself under the table.

Ambling toward the exit, my throat fills with unease. My brain should be engaged in this conversation, but I can't stop thinking about the message on my phone. I call over my shoulder, "You couldn't afford me, Teddy. I'm above your pay grade."

"You got balls of steel." He chuckles when I keep walking. The warehouse is large and has too many of his steel products lying around which doesn't absorb his voice. His voice echoes, drawing my attention even when I'd prefer to ignore him. I'm not sure what he wants with Carys, but I doubt it has anything to do with guns.

Pausing before the exit, I shake my head, half turning back to him, flanked by Carys's two burly men. "I'd take a pussy made of diamonds over balls of steel any day."

Teddy's grin fades, and his chair screeches across the concrete when he stands. The two men with him are like shadows. "You want diamonds? I can arrange that."

"Forget you know my number." I push the emergency exit door, and it pops open. "Unless you have money for the deal."

The door slams behind my last man as we head to our black SUV waiting in the deserted gravel parking lot. The sky is blue-black, and the snow on the ground is melting, creating puddles in the potholes. Spring is on the way, but it isn't here yet. At some point, we'll get another blast of winter.

"What a waste of time." I pull out the phone in my pocket as it vibrates again.

"That Carys?" Jay raises his dark eyebrows as he opens the rear passenger door for me. His close-cropped brown hair is ruffled by a sudden breeze.

"Could be." I duck down, folding my almost six-foot frame into the car, but I don't take the phone out. Why am I being contacted? The FBI programmed the phone with a unique vibration for agency texts. When it went off in the meeting, I worried someone would notice my reaction. Creating suspicion in any of the people I work with could get me killed—shot dead without hesitation.

*Dead.*

The car jerks forward, and Jay mumbles an apology as I focus on my hands, turning them over.

*Dead.*

My pocket vibrates again, and this time when I look down at my hands, they're covered in blood.

"Kim?" He tries to catch my gaze in the mirror. "Carys is going to be ticked."

My head snaps up, and I tuck my hands under my thighs, sliding along the black leather, and release a dark chuckle. "I told Carys I didn't think there was any way Teddy was buying from us. He hasn't got enough money, and no use for guns." Carys making me the point person for the deal was a step in the right direction. So I didn't argue too much.

"He's got lots of use for you." Jay meets my gaze.

"He wouldn't be able to handle me." I ease back into the seat and stare out the window as Chicago zooms by. The skyline is one of the things I love about this city, and dusk brings it to life, the lights dancing across the lake's surface.

"You ever work for a man before?" Jay checks his mirrors.

The new guy beside him, whose name I can't remember, pipes up, "She's too much of a ballbuster to work for a man."

Jay gives him an annoyed look. "Carys will shoot you herself for chirping Kim like that."

"I'm perfectly capable of shooting him," I say, my tone mild. The cityscape outside the window rushes by. I can't stop thinking about my phone, but it's too risky to take it out right now. "Yeah, I've worked for some men. I try to avoid it. They're too preoccupied with their balls."

The new guy laughs, and Jay gives him another sideways glance.

"I can see why." He isn't getting Jay's silent message. Over the seat, he's scanning my dark ponytail secured near the top of my head down to my Lululemon pants. "What are you, anyway? You're like, exotic or something. I can't put my finger on it."

Giving him a cold stare, I say, "Your fingers don't belong anywhere near me." Compared to me and Jay, this kid is as pale as a ghost.

"You're getting fired, man." Jay shakes his head and adjusts his hands on the steering wheel as we merge into heavier traffic. "If you keep talking, you're going to end up in concrete shoes at the bottom of Lake Michigan."

The only bit of color in his face disappears. At least the new guy has the good sense to take Jay's comment seriously. He's probably in his early twenties, a kid looking to make a quick buck. Everything about him reminds me of someone I don't want to remember but can never forget.

"That's not a real thing." His voice quivers.

"They're all real things," Jay says. "You don't mess around with these people, Paul. The stereotypes, the rumors, the shit you see on TV—most of it is taken from someone's real life."

*Ah, a name.* Not that I'll need to remember it after the conversation we're having.

The car glides to a stop in front of my four-story brown brick apartment building. The trees lining the street are mature, hanging over the sidewalk and road. The streetlights work, and the front door has a security guard. Not that I need one of those. I chose this neighborhood on purpose. It's not too run-down, but it's not new and shiny either. Carys has offered to let me live with her outside the city. I can't, though. While it might make aspects of the job easier, it would make others infinitely harder.

"I didn't mean anything by my comments." Paul's voice is uncertain.

He isn't as big as Jay and, standing up, he and I are about the same height. I'm maybe ten years older than him, but that gap is massive right now. I've been on this job with Carys for almost a year, but in some ways, it's my whole life.

"You're not cut out for this, Paul. Quit before someone kills you." I'm half out the door when I turn to Jay and say, "Tell Carys I have some personal business. I'll be back in a few days."

"Your brother?" His brown eyes are full of sympathy.

"Yeah." I give a curt nod. "Anniversary of his death."

"I'll let her know."

I slam the door behind me and enter the building, waving to the security guard at the desk. In the elevator, I put my hand over the phone in my pocket. How much time will I have?

At my door, I slide the key in the lock. My steady hands belie my racing heart as I slip inside. I flip all the locks in place and tug the phone from my pocket.

It's been almost six months.

*Airport. Two hours.*

Glancing at the current time and when the text was sent, I'm pretty sure I can make it. It's going to be tight. Opening the entryway closet, I grab the prepacked bag and then undo the locks on the door.

I disappear into the night.

# Chapter Two

Malik likes meeting at the same hotel, same room, every time. It's a midlevel chain in a midsized city. Everything about the meeting is constructed so I don't have the run-in we dread. Being undercover and seeing someone from either version of our lives is one of the few things that makes people like me wake up in the middle of the night, covered in sweat, making sure there isn't a bullet lodged in our brain.

When I slip into the hotel room, the scent of stale cigarettes hits my nose. The rooms need to be renovated, but I never question Malik's desire to meet here. This is his area of expertise, not mine. He stops pacing when the door clicks shut behind me. His dark face and eyes soothe my unease.

He scans me from head to toe, assessing. "I wasn't sure you'd be able to make it."

"Your message didn't come at the best time. Carys let me take another meeting today. It was a waste of time though."

"Like the last one," he says, finishing my thought.

I shrug. "It'll come. She's giving me more and more authority."

"So that explains why you're dressed like a ninja supermodel." His smile is half-hearted. "What have you got for me?"

Twisting, I swing my black bag forward until I can dig into the pocket for the latest USB drive. It's full of whatever documents I've managed to get off devices in the office, screenshots of texts and emails, anything that might have a shred of evidence to build a case against Carys. I hold the device between my fingers, flipping it over and over.

With a sigh, I drop it into Malik's open palm. He doesn't say anything. I'm sure he knows. Carys is the kind of woman I like, and gathering information on her doesn't sit well with me. She's not a bad person, but sometimes she does bad things.

"I have some... news," Malik hesitates.

I glance up, trying to catch his attention, but he's not looking at me anymore. "Something I won't like."

"Maybe you will."

"Malik, seriously, you've been my handler for a few years." I let out a huff. "The way you started this conversation tells me I'm not going to be happy. Are they pulling me?"

"Yes." Malik sighs, his shoulders dropping. "Probably."

"I'm getting somewhere. It takes time." I've never been pulled off an assignment before, and it stings more than I expect. Time, that's what I need. She trusts me.

"It's not what you're assuming." He sits on the edge of the double bed. The white duvet cover is too pristine, too pure compared to the rest of the dingy room.

I sit next to him, and he takes my dusty-brown hand in his two darker ones. My body relaxes as though it's releasing a giant breath. I've been holding myself in for weeks. Being on high alert is exhausting. Here, with him, I can be me, Kimi. Out there, I'm Kim, and keeping my lies straight is like walking a tightrope. One wrong move, and I'm falling to my death.

With a side glance, I appreciate the familiarity of him, his broad shoulders, muscular biceps, and angular, open face. From the first time I arrived at a hotel room to find he replaced my previous handler, we've had an easy, steady relationship.

"For what it's worth, I asked them to keep you on this assignment. You might stay. It depends on whether you're picked or whether we can slot you in easily."

"Picked? Malik, you know I hate riddles. Out with it."

"Are you familiar with the Donaghey family?"

I frown, ticking through the operations I've been part of the last few years. "No," I admit. Something about the name is just out of my grasp. The name spins around my consciousness searching for the last time I heard it.

"Hmm. That's probably good. We couldn't find any direct employment connections even though you grew up outside Boston. You consistently use Kim which makes it easier compared to other undercover agents."

A name close to my own keeps me grounded. Some people need to divorce their normal selves. For me, weaving details is easier than inventing them, then remembering my inventions.

"What about the Donaghey family?" I remove my hand from Malik's to rub his thigh in slow circles.

"Brothers. Mafia in Boston. The head of the organization, Eamon Donaghey, their father, was murdered."

Now my brain latches onto what I saw on TV a while ago in Carys's office. She knew the brothers and liked them. Or she liked one of them. My eyes narrow, trying to remember what she said. Her wording was precise, as though there was more to the story. At the time, I wondered if I should pry, but it hadn't been information I needed for either job.

"The organization is fracturing. Lorcan and Finn are on the cusp of an all-out war."

"And?" How well would Carys know these men? Sometimes connections between people are stronger than they appear.

"The younger brother, Lorcan, has been low-key looking for a female bodyguard to add to his staff."

I freeze and remove my hand from Malik's leg. "They want to undo months of work on my part to make me a *bodyguard*? Are you kidding me? I'm practically the second-in-command with Carys. This is ridiculous. Off the top of my head, there are at least ten FBI women who could do this."

"Any of those women read, write, and speak Irish Gaelic?" He cocks an eyebrow.

I frown. "They only communicate in Irish?"

Malik's shrug is almost imperceptible while his dark eyes search my face. "Our mole says most top-secret communication happens in Irish Gaelic—emails, verbal conversations, text messages."

*Shit.* I can see why they'd want to move me. My father, after my older half-brother was killed, developed an obsession with Irish Gaelic. It was all he spoke until his death. I had to learn it.

"I guess that answers the *why me* part." I sigh and stand up, crossing to the minibar and plucking out a couple of bottles. I pour Malik a whiskey in a coffee cup and pass it to him and then pour one for myself. "Am I getting an introduction? Is there a plan?"

"You're not mad? You're okay with being close to home?" Malik eyes me while he takes a sip of his whiskey.

"I'm not thrilled." I put my own glass to my lips and breathe in the sharp aroma.

"You might be able to slip away and see your mom."

Tension radiates through me at the mention of my mother. On the wall is a painting of a lone boat in the middle of stormy seas. Each time we're in this room, it catches my eye. Something about it reminds me of my mother, or maybe it's me. She's all I have left.

"A plan?" I prompt again.

"We think Carys knows them."

I laugh, the tension easing out of me. The whiskey burns my throat when I take a sip. "Carys knows everyone. But she's not going to broker an introduction. Why would she hand me over or even consider giving me up?"

Malik grins and takes a long drink. "*How* do they know each other?"

"An arms deal makes sense." The conversation with Carys about the brothers refuses to resurface from the caverns of my memory.

"And yet, that's not it. Or at least we don't think so. What's near and dear to the heart of your beloved Carys?"

His tone is teasing, but it still pisses me off. I hate when he pokes my weaknesses like it's a game.

"Kids with cancer," I mumble. Carys funnels a lot of her money into charities which aim to treat or support childhood cancers. Her brother died from a brain tumor when they were in high school. A few months ago, we got drunk and traded dead-brother stories. Well, she got drunk. I pretended to be drunk.

"Lorcan also has a soft spot for cancer patients." Malik tips back the rest of his drink and stares into the coffee cup. "There's a cancer fundraiser coming up in Boston, on the cusp of being big, not there yet. We've asked them to highlight children's cancers and breast cancer—that's how his mother died. Lorcan has confirmed he'll attend."

"So I only have to convince Carys? Fly from Chicago to Boston on a whim?" That's a tall order without raising suspicion.

"Not quite. We've arranged for her to get an invitation. You need to give her a gentle nudge. If Lorcan and Finn do escalate into a full-on war, it'll be ripe for arms deals."

"If she doesn't take the bait?"

"I have no doubt you can be persuasive." He puts his empty glass on the TV stand. "We'll figure out a way to broker a meeting another way if you can't make it work. We have a substantial file on the father but not on the two sons." He nods to the duffel bag in the corner of the room. "I brought some information so you're not going in blind."

"The assignment goal? An arrest? War?" I stare into what's left of my drink, swirling it around.

"No, no war. We want to avoid that. Civilian causalities would be out of control. Both brothers are prone to escalation. An arrest is best if you can get the right information, but otherwise, try to keep the situation stable. We'll tackle whatever information you acquire."

"You'll stay my contact?" I glance up at him, worry eating at me. He knows and understands me better than anyone else at the bureau. His replacement would never be good enough.

"I will." Malik smiles.

I move to him, sliding my glass onto the table beside his. "Did you want another?" My voice dips low.

We're almost the same height, and the way I've lingered with my fingertips on the table means we're inches apart. His gaze flicks from my eyes to my lips and back again.

"I'll never say no to you." His tone matches mine.

I shift closer, my chest grazing his. "In case I die tomorrow, I'm going to live for today."

His lips lift into a half smile. "Have I ever told you how much I love your motto?"

"A few times." I take in his dark features under my lashes, enjoying the hunger I see. "What are you waiting for?" I murmur. "Make me feel alive."

It's the only invitation he needs before his lips dip to capture mine. His hand tugs the elastic out of my hair, releasing my long dark strands. I sigh, pressing my body tight to his, the parts of him that have come to life brushing against mine. We may only do this dance every few months, but I know each step by heart.

*Familiar. Easy. Safe.*

All the things I usually hate.

# Chapter Three

Hot pink. It's not a color I would choose, but it goes well with the darker coloring I inherited from my father. Carys insisted on buying my dress for this function. Convincing her to come was the least of my worries. I had more trouble talking her out of the ridiculous wardrobe choices for me.

"So, Native Barbie, are you enjoying the spectacle?" Carys clutches her champagne flute in her manicured hands.

I give her a sideways glance as I sip from my own glass. "Only *you* could get away with that."

There's a lot of lily-white in me, too, courtesy of my mother. People who need to classify me think I look odd, difficult to pinpoint. My focus skims around the high-ceiling ballroom and catches on the crystal chandelier that lends the majority of the light to where we're standing. I let the fingers of my free hand graze the gun attached to my thigh. For an event that was supposed to be small, it seems to have grown much bigger in the weeks since I met with Malik. Women and men in expensive dresses and tuxes mill around us, chatting in loud voices before wandering off.

"You go write your soul-cleansing check yet?"

Carys laughs. "And only *you* could get away with that." Her amber eyes soften when she gazes at me. "How's your dad?"

*Still dead.*

"Same as always." I give a slight shrug. "The anniversary of Chad's death is hard." Not a lie. At least the emotions aren't, but the details of his death are different for every job. The date, the place, the method of murder are fabrications.

"Well, I hope you and your dad can work out your issues someday. Family is important."

*Family.* The word echoes around my brain, bumping into memories I keep buried.

Carys flags a waiter to deposit her empty glass and takes another. She signals to me, but I shake my head. "First you insisted on a dress you could move in, and now you won't drink with me. I swear you think someone's lurking around every corner waiting to kill you."

I laugh with her, even though it's not outside the realm of possibility. "You like that I'm prepared."

Carys sighs. "It's true." Her hand nudges a piece of her blond hair back into its intricate braid. "I'm starting to think Lorcan's not coming. I should have called him and scheduled a meeting. You're right about the territory being ripe for deals if the two of them explode."

"Is it wise to pick a side?"

"Hmm. My side is probably obvious. At least this way it might appear like a genuine coincidence. The charities we support are here, and we happened to run into each other."

I'm about to ask Carys why her side would be clear when I catch sight of a blondish-brown head coming through the open doors of the ballroom. He's dressed in a dark-blue suit and a pink tie, not a tux like many of the men. Two men flank him, as tall and broad as the man in the middle, but their suits don't scream money. I tip my head in his direction. "Who's that?"

Carys glances over her shoulder, and her lips curve into a smile. "Speak of the devil."

"Lorcan?" It's him. Malik had photos. They didn't do Lorcan justice. In the flesh, the man is the kind of dangerous, rugged handsome which makes others glance in his direction without realizing they've done it.

"In the flesh," she says as though she can read my mind.

"Have you ever?" I force my focus to Carys. She's fifteen years older than me, which makes her ten years older than Lorcan. Time has been good to her. Well, that and she has a dermatologist and cosmetic surgeon on call.

Carys shakes her head, but her attention lingers on Lorcan. "Being a woman in this business, you have to be careful who you get into bed with—remember that, Kim. A man will get you killed."

"Not all men." My mind strays to Malik.

Carys stares at me before nodding at the bar. "It seems Lorcan's been waylaid by one of the organizers before he got to the bar. I know what he drinks."

She orders three whiskeys and then sashays to where he is talking to a petite blonde who is giddy with nerves or attraction. Either is possible. He is bigger and more intimidating in person. Above his head there might as well be a flashing neon sign that reads *Danger*. Tension circulates in the air, surrounding him, enveloping us.

"Lorcan," Carys drawls, allowing her Southern accent to pop out. Her hips sway in a manner she reserves for those she trusts. No one takes a woman seriously in this business if they seem too womanly.

His head whips up at the sound of her voice, and a grin splits his face. He sidesteps the overeager woman to embrace Carys. "I didn't realize you'd be here. It's been an age."

"A delightful coincidence." She flicks her attention to the other woman before focusing on Lorcan. With a slight bow of deference to Carys, the event organizer wanders off, hands clasped.

While he and Carys chat, I take in his features: the goatee, the slight dimple in his right cheek when he almost smiles, and his hazel eyes which are alight with surprised amusement.

"Who is this bright spot of loveliness behind you?" He nods at me. He searches my face, appraising, but his gaze never travels my body in an assessing way.

"This is Kim." Carys gestures with her hand flung wide. "She's the best at what she does."

As an introduction, I couldn't have hoped for better. The grin on my face is genuine while she slings an arm around my waist in a motherly fashion.

"What's that?" His voice carries a hint of an accent that isn't Bostonian. Of course, I know from the file his parents sent him and his brother to boarding school in Ireland.

"Everything." Carys beams at me.

"That's quite a compliment." Lorcan takes a drink and tilts it in my direction. "What do you think of that?"

"It's not much of an exaggeration."

He chuckles and again his gaze roves over my face as though he's trying to piece me together. My hot-pink dress is garnering little attention from him. Should I be pleased or offended?

"You got any mates? I'm looking for someone like you."

Carys tightens her grip on me and sips her whiskey. "She's taken. Keep your mitts off her."

He raises his glass, eyeing me over the top. "People who can be bought aren't for me, Carys. You know that."

She scoffs. "Not true, Lorcan. I *do* know you. I've played this all wrong. I should have told you she was thinking about leaving my organization."

"I *am* terribly unhappy." My gaze connects with Lorcan's, and I offer a mischievous smile.

An answering smile spreads across his face. "That so? Now, Carys, you need to treat *your everything* woman a touch better before someone swoops in and sweeps her away."

"As long as you aren't *the someone*, Lorcan." She glances at me. "I appreciate the effort, but I'm afraid once he's on the hunt, he can't be deterred."

"You make me sound terrible." Amusement pours out of him.

"I used to like you," Carys says. "Finn, on the other hand…"

"… is an acquired taste." Lorcan's grin fades. "One I've gone off recently."

She glances at me and then back to Lorcan. I've seen that look on her face before. She's trying to figure out the best approach.

"Sorry to hear that," I murmur, surprised by the sudden chill in the air.

His lips quirk up. "You wouldn't be sorry if you knew him." He empties his whiskey. "It's been a pleasure, ladies. Thank you for the drink. You know me well, Carys." With a nod to his men, Lorcan drifts into the crowd, leaving me and Carys to finish our drinks on our own.

"Shit." She sighs and taps her glass with a fingernail. "I should have left Finn out of it."

"Can't ask him if he wants a deal without letting him know there's a deal to be done."

"Their organization buys arms, just not from me." Carys purses her lips. "It should be me. It'd be a good time to slip in there. Maybe we can still salvage it later."

"Are you doing that or…"

"If you get a chance to ask, fine by me. Plant a seed, see if it grows."

Lorcan breezes through the crowd with his two burly security guards trailing behind him. He's a small fish in an arms world. Carys does much bigger, more ethically comprised deals than this. She hasn't let me near those yet. If I get out of here tonight with what I want, I'll never see them. I'm going to need to work fast to recapture his attention. His late arrival means there are two hours until this event finishes, and he's cut our conversation short.

"I'll see what I can do."

"You're not one to be charmed," Carys draws out the words, and I think she must be watching Lorcan like me.

I smirk and raise my eyebrows. "Is there a but?"

A smile plays on her lips. "No, I suppose there isn't."

"You've got nothing to worry about," I say. "If I can get him to consider a deal, I will. And, if not, it's been a pleasant evening. We haven't been to an event like this in a while." I knock back the rest of my whiskey and wiggle my glass at her. "Another?"

"No, I have people I want to connect with. Tonight is bigger than I expected."

"I'll be at the bar."

Carys and I move in opposite directions as she heads off to make or solidify her contacts. I sidle up to the bar and place my empty glass to the side. This end of the bar is for standing, but farther down, there are a number of stools with people perched on them, chatting away to each other. The ballroom is vast and airy, though the perfume and cologne circulating are enough to cause an asthma attack. Above the bar, pendulum lights are set low to match the rest of the mood lighting. Most of the charitable events I've attended with Carys have been dimly lit. It must seem too intrusive to ask for money with the brightness turned to full.

I'm waiting for the bartender, wondering how I can slip myself into conversation with Lorcan when a shoulder brushes mine.

"Be a shame for someone as talented as you to be unhappy with your employer," a deep voice says in my ear. His lilting accent is a sound I could get used to. It calls me back to the hours my father spent devouring anything Irish.

He's so close, Lorcan's hazel eyes are piercing in their intensity. The musky scent of his cologne floods my senses, and I'm glad for my training. Cool. Unaffected. "How do you know I'm talented?"

"Carys isn't one for bigging people up who don't deserve it." He turns away to signal the bartender with a finger. "Two whiskeys."

In this business, men are everywhere. But there's something in the curve of his shoulders, the slant of his jaw under the goatee, which makes him familiar. Part of his appeal has nothing to do with appearance and everything to do with the way he carries himself. Confidence seeps out of him, oozing over everything he touches.

The bartender passes the two glasses to us, and I pick mine up with my fingertips, swishing it around, letting the ice clink against the sides.

His back is against the bar railing, and his elbows are on the wood, so he can stare out across the wide expanse of the room. When he shifts toward me, his gaze connects with mine over the rim of his glass. "When are you heading home?"

"Tomorrow afternoon. Carys offered to show me some sites around Boston."

One side of his mouth twitches as though he's holding in his amusement. "Sounds grand."

"Does it?" I avoid looking at him directly, keeping my back to the room.

"Not quite as grand as coming round to mine for a meeting."

"What would we be meeting about?" I peer into my glass, hope rising in me.

"See if one of us can make the other an offer they can't refuse."

"I get offers all the time. I refuse them all." Our little game of cat and mouse amuses me, but I keep my features smooth.

"You never had one from me."

Somehow, I've managed to finish another drink. "I guess we'll see what you've got then. I'm a tough nut to crack."

He places his finished drink onto the bar. "I'm counting on it. Tell Carys to call me."

When I turn around, he and his men are gone.

# Chapter Four

The next day when we arrive at the gates of the Donaghey family complex, there's a chill in the air. Snow covers sections of the ground, but there are patches of grass. Before we get in the door, we're frisked within an inch of our lives. The first time it happened years ago, it was invasive, dirty. Not anymore.

They find every single one of my hidden weapons. I'll have to be more creative with the places I put them.

Their mansion is a sprawling bungalow masterpiece out in the suburbs. It's going to take me days to search the whole complex for evidence. The file I read gave me some details, but being here is cementing a new reality. At one time, the estate was isolated. The city has grown up around it. There's still a massive stretch of land in the backyard that looks like an empty farmer's field except for a shed in the far corner.

When the front door swings back, Lorcan isn't there. Instead, it's a man who is a little shorter than Lorcan but broad, muscular. His hair is so blond the strands are almost white, and his eyes, when they connect with mine, are a piercing blue, so pale they make me think of ice chips. *Finn.*

"Carys." His tone is dry. "We have an arms dealer. Shame you came all this way."

"Lorcan didn't tell you we were coming?" She feigns surprise, but she avoids making eye contact.

He shifts his focus, flicking his gaze up and down my body. "Who's this?"

Unlike his brother, he has no accent, not Irish, not Bostonian. He could have been raised in Pittsburgh given the inflection in his voice.

"Kim." She turns to me. "This is Finn."

"Kim," Finn says. "Are you the PA?"

"Sometimes." I keep my voice even. "I do whatever needs to be done."

He raises his pale eyebrows, gaze sharpening. "Whatever needs to be done? I like the sound of that. Assuming you actually mean it. Most don't."

"For me, she does." Carys tugs her purse higher onto her shoulder. "Lorcan's expecting us."

Finn steps back and makes a sweeping gesture with his hand. "If Lorcan is expecting you, I'll let you figure out where he is." He nods to a large man who is standing off to the side of the foyer. The front entranceway is long and wide, with high ceilings. The sun filters in from a skylight which brightens the dark décor. "Follow them. Don't let them touch anything."

Her voice is steel when she says, "A pleasure, as always, Finn."

Finn's laugh floats down the hall as he walks away.

"He's such a dick." Carys glances at the guard who reminds me of a former football player.

"Do you know where Lorcan is?" I ask.

"I do." His voice is a deep rumble.

"Kim." I thrust out my hand. "And you are?"

"Antonio." He grasps my hand in his large one, and his brown eyes meet mine.

"Can you take us? I'm guessing Finn's power play is to make us stumble around blind."

Antonio chuckles. "I'll take you. Makes my job easier anyway." He uses a radio to get someone else at the front door and then leads the way down the wide, tall hallway.

Finn went to the left before an oversize doorway which looks as though it leads to a kitchen, and we go right. Have they divided the house in half? Because of the layout, the space appears older than it is. Unlike modern homes, there isn't a whiff of an open concept.

We go down three or four doors before Antonio stops and presses an intercom button beside the heavy wooden door. Everything in the house is dark, rich, and expensive. Claustrophobia comes to mind.

"Yes?" Lorcan's voice comes out of the speaker fuzzy.

"Your ten o'clock is here."

The door releases with a buzz. Antonio opens it, and Carys doesn't seem surprised by the security measures. Given Lorcan's father died in a home invasion, I suppose the extra security is warranted.

When we enter the room, I'm struck by the difference in the décor. While the rest of the house is closed in, this room is much bigger than it seems from the outside, and the light-gray walls are welcoming. There's another skylight, and sunlight brightens the office, especially after the dark, narrow corridor.

Lorcan sits behind a large mahogany desk, but off to the side is a workout space. A small wooden conference table separates the two areas. He rises, and his jeans and T-shirt are in direct contrast to the formality of last night. The surrounding aura is still there. Calm. Confident. A touch of danger floats around the edges of him, but it's subdued in this room, as though being in his home softens his sharp corners.

"Carys." Her name rolls off his tongue.

Something inside my chest strains at the sound. Startled, I raise my eyes to meet his.

"Kim." His accent makes my name sound far more attractive than it ever has before.

Whatever his game plan is today, the charm is spilling out of him. I'm not sure if it's the accent, the more casual outfit, or being in his home, but I take an involuntary step toward him. A spark of desire almost catches before I snuff it out.

"Laying it on a little thick this morning, aren't we?" Her voice holds a hint of mocking.

He chuckles and comes around his desk to adjust the two leather chairs across from him. "Some ladies like the accent." Lorcan grins.

"Yes, well, I'm aware you're capable of speaking without it." Carys gestures for me to take one of the two chairs as he moves back to his own seat behind the desk.

"You're right." He smooths out his voice, any trace of an accent is gone, as he says, "You have to play to your audience." His attention strays to me. "Dressed as a princess last night and a yoga instructor today?"

I give him a half smile. "I don't like being restrained. This is pretty typical for me." Yoga pants and a flexible, lightweight shirt are my go-to articles of clothing. Carys mocks me for my lack of originality and makes any excuse to dress me up like a Barbie doll. Most of the time, I don't mind since she enjoys it so much.

"And last night?"

"Was for a good cause." I meet his gaze and stifle my smirk. Catching his interest was worth the pain of a pink dress.

"You're hoping for a deal?" He focuses on Carys. "I'm not sure I'm in the market for one."

"Finn assured us at the door *he* has a dealer."

"*We* do," Lorcan agrees with a grimace. Easing deeper into his chair, he steeples his fingers. "You understand the seriousness of what's going on in this house?"

"I do." Her face softens. "You're not going to war with each other. Finn's an asshole, but he's still your brother."

"There are things you can't possibly know. People change. Finn's mother and mine will be rolling in their graves." The hint of a lilting accent is back which makes me want to lean in, to hear more. Despite what she said, I think the accent might be real.

Carys isn't a mother, but sometimes, around some people, she gives off a motherly vibe. Like the hip sway, she doesn't let that side of her come out very often. Her connection to Lorcan and Finn runs much deeper than I realized.

"Can I help?" she asks.

Lorcan's stares at me before turning to Carys. "Possibly," he says. "I don't want an arms deal, at least not yet. I wanted Finn to understand I'm serious—my threats aren't idle—which is why I invited you here."

She shifts in her chair. "I used to babysit the two of you when our parents were in meetings. I know how close you and Finn are."

I try to keep my face blank as I listen to their exchange. Inside, my blood boils. I hate when the information I get from the bureau is wrong. The war on terror snags the best intelligence people, and those of us on the ground in other assignments get the leftovers. How many other details in the files aren't quite right?

"I'm starting to accept we're very different," Lorcan says. "I don't want to get into it with you, Carys. You'll end up in the middle."

"If you don't need arms from me right now, what's this meeting about? Are you simply sending a message to Finn? He answered the door."

Lorcan gives a sly smile. "I knew he would." He picks up a pen and taps on the desk.

I lean back in my chair waiting for whatever is coming next. Somehow, I need to find a way to ingratiate myself to him, or today is going to be a waste. How do I get back here if he's not doing business with Carys?

When I look up, he's gazing at me, his expression serious. "I want you to come work for me."

Carys sits up straighter in her chair. "You can't be serious."

He holds up a hand toward her. "I know what you said last night, and I've been thinking about it. All I've been doing is thinking about it."

Her lips pucker in annoyance. "Would you mind waiting outside? I have a feeling this conversation is about to go south."

"Are you sure?" My brain ticks through how I can make it clear I want to work for Lorcan without raising suspicion. Why would I leave her and her organization? In this business, she's a great employer, and it's taken me almost a year to get to a point of trust and mutual respect with her. Very pointedly, I give Lorcan the once-over as though I don't trust him, hoping my distrust might make Carys keep me in the room.

"I'll be fine." She waves a hand while gathering her purse closer to her chest.

I nod and open the door, slipping out into the hall. Propping the door open would be ideal, but he would notice. He can see the door from behind his desk. Outside, Antonio is standing guard.

"Slow day?" I take in his linebacker build. Carys has big men like this. Except for Jay, I have no use for any of them.

"Most of them are." He shrugs and tucks his phone into his pocket. "You guys finishing up in there."

"No idea," I admit as I count doors in my head, trying to set mental reminders about door codes and locations.

"You really do anything Carys wants?"

"Yep." I suppress a sigh. This line of questioning is familiar. We're at the point where he asks me questions and doesn't believe my answers.

"Ever killed someone?"

I avoid looking down at my hands and instead tuck them into the pockets of my black leather jacket. The blood isn't the stuff I've shed. "Of course."

"Huh." He mulls over my answer. "For money, status, retribution?"

My laugh sounds hollow to my ears. "All of those."

"More than one?" Antonio's eyebrows shoot up. His brown eyes are almost black when his gaze skims over me, appraising. "You got the build for it. Strong-looking, but not too muscly. You got that icy-cold attitude."

"Too muscly?" I give him a mild glance. "That's a thing?"

"I don't like my women to have more muscles than me."

My mouth twists in amusement. "I didn't realize this was an interview for a date. To be clear, I'm not interested."

"You don't like men? I wondered about you and Carys."

I shake my head, and for the first time, stare into his eyes. "I like men fine. As long as they aren't telling me who I am or what I can be, we get along." Guys like Antonio are a dime a dozen. They can't imagine their mere association with power isn't an instant aphrodisiac. It doesn't work that way, at least not for me.

The door behind us opens, and she signals for me to come in. She's not happy. Hope starts to surface in my chest. Has she given in?

As we cross the room to the desk, she snatches her purse from a chair. "I'm going to leave you with him to make his pitch. It's your choice. I'd never presume to tell you what to do. If you decide to work with him, you'll always be welcome to come back to me."

I raise my eyebrows, feigning shock. "You want me to listen to what he has to say?"

"I do."

Glancing at Lorcan, I narrow my eyes. "Is he pressuring you? I don't want to stay if he's making you do this." My insides are tap dancing, but I cover it over with suspicion.

"It's not like that. Listen to him. You and I will chat once you're done here." She strolls out of the room, her shoulders full of tension. Whatever went on in here, Carys isn't comfortable with some aspect. I focus on Lorcan as the door shuts behind her.

"Well," I say. "What's the offer?"

# CHAPTER FIVE

orcan's face twists with amusement. "I like that you're straight to the point."

"Why waste time?" I don't take a seat. "I'm happy working for Carys, so your offer needs to be something special."

"I've been seeking a female bodyguard—"

"Not interested." I twirl on my heel, a calculated risk. The more resistance I put up, the less likely he'll be to suspect me later. He'll have won me over.

"Wait," he says when my hand hits the doorknob. "I'm willing to go beyond the title for the right person. I understand you've been working very closely with Carys." The lilt in his voice is back again, and my shoulders relax. There's something in the cadence of his voice that could lure me straight into bed. Zaps the fight out of me.

"I have. I've earned my spot at her side."

"What'll it take to get you to come here, work for me?" In front of me now, he crosses his arms over his chest and gives me an intense stare.

"I like to feel important," I admit. "Central, needed."

He nods. "What I want you to do would do those things."

"If it's not a bodyguard, then what?"

His jaw tightens with tension. "You know my father was killed?"

"Yes."

"You know the circumstances?"

"Yes."

"Finn says it was a rival—the O'Malleys—they were hoping he and I weren't strong enough to run my father's territory."

I search his face, trying to figure out where he's leading this conversation. "Okay."

"I believe it was Finn."

I scan his face and posture for any indication he's bluffing. "Why?" Everything in the file we have at the bureau points in another direction. The information on Carys and Lorcan's connection wasn't right. Maybe the bureau's intel on who killed his father is also wrong. Keeping them from going to war might be harder than expected.

"I have my suspicions. Nothing I want to lay out right now. Would you be interested in helping me get to the bottom of it?"

"Why me? I'd think anyone who works here could help you."

"Carys speaks highly of you, said you're good at adjusting to changing situations quickly. Finn trusts very few people. He likes women. He likes strong, independent women. We don't have a lot of those inside the organization." Lorcan clears his throat. "And if he thought he was taking something I wanted, that woman would appeal to him even more." His words are deliberate, giving me a chance to mull them over.

"If I discover it was him?"

"We go to war."

"If it was the O'Malleys?"

"We go to war."

I scan bookcases on the right, reading titles, but not taking anything in. There's a series of filing cabinets behind Lorcan's desk I'm itching to explore, and there's a lockbox on the wall.

Of course I'm going to say yes, but it won't be easy to keep everything in order. If war lies in either direction, and my goal is to avoid it, creativity will be the key.

"Your life will most certainly be in danger." He rocks back on his heels. "In this line of work, that's a given, though."

"I'm well paid for that risk with Carys."

For a moment, silence sits between us. "I want what I want. I'll pay you the same, and I'll double it all if you find out who killed my father."

"That's quite an incentive. What sort of proof do you expect?"

"Let's go with the criminal justice standard, shall we? Beyond a reasonable doubt."

"The highest standard of proof. You're not going to make it easy."

"I'm not paying you like it's easy."

All this bartering is for nothing. Perhaps it's time I folded. The money doesn't matter to me. "I'm in."

His lips quirk up, and his one dimple peeks through. "Excellent."

"I'll fly back to Chicago today."

"I'll have you booked on a flight back to Boston for tomorrow. Does that give you enough time to pack up?"

"I travel light."

"Even better. You'll have your own wing of the house, and I'll set you up with tasks which look like responsibilities. But your focus will be figuring out who murdered my father." He meets my gaze, his hazel eyes intense. "Point the finger. Wage the war."

"I understand." There would be no wars if I could help it.

As Lorcan reaches for the door to dismiss me, he hesitates and gives me a sideways glance. "I implied this, but I want to be clear what you're getting involved in."

"You need me to pretend we're... something to each other."

"Yes, eventually. Finn will be more likely to take an interest if he thinks he's wooing you away from me."

"Why? Why would he want to do that to you?"

"It's complicated. Like all families."

My mind drifts to my father, to my half-brother. "We all have our secrets."

His face is grave before he opens the door. "Some secrets are best left in dark corners. Others, such as who killed my father, must come into the light." With one hand, he motions for me to pass through the door. "I'll see you tomorrow."

Antonio isn't in the corridor, but I remember how to get back to the front entrance. I weave through the house, and once I'm close enough, I hear Carys and Finn engaged in a heated argument. At the intersection between the halls, I peek around.

"Talk to your brother. Work together."

"You're not my mother, Carys." His gaze drifts up and down her body. "Though, you were an excellent tutor." Finn chuckles but it holds no humor. "Your voice means nothing in this house now."

Her jaw tightens. "It means something to your brother."

"He's a fool. He trusts the wrong people. Lorcan's going to get himself killed."

"You're impervious, are you?"

Finn steps closer to her. Moving from my listening spot, I call down, "Carys, thanks for waiting."

He turns sharply at my voice and runs one hand through his platinum hair. Glancing back at her, he says, "You don't know anything about me and my brother. Not anymore. Stay out of it."

Throwing up her hands, she snatches her bag off the floor and hitches it onto her shoulder. In a huff, she opens the main door then leads the way to the car. I follow her at a less hurried pace, mulling over what went on between her and Lorcan and why she'd bother trying to talk sense into Finn.

I slide into the back seat of the car beside her and stare out the window, waiting for her to start talking. Carys likes her mental space, and I like quiet. We're a good match.

"You said yes?" Her voice is soft.

"I did." I cock my head at her. "You knew I would."

"It seemed like something you'd have a hard time resisting. You've got a vibe that'll be a nice change in that house."

I laugh. "What's that mean?"

"You've got a moral compass. You don't make a big deal about it, but it's there."

"You're getting sentimental on me."

She peers out the window. "I've had a difficult time saying no to either of those men. Even when they were younger."

I take a moment to absorb her comment, thinking about her exchange with Finn. "You and Finn." Lorcan's remark about Finn liking strong women makes more sense now.

"He almost got me killed when I was in my late twenties, a bit younger than you. I went to Ireland for business and to visit them when they were in university. For some reason, the age gap never felt like much once we got to be a certain age. Finn and I had been off and on for a while—no one knew." She gives me a sidelong glance before returning her gaze to the window.

I wait in silence, hoping she'll continue without prompting. If she was drinking, she'd tell me, but sober Carys is much more cautious.

"I went out to a bar with him, someone offended him, called him Casper. A nickname, a stupid one he hates. Finn went off, out-of-control angry, and I was stabbed in the brawl. Only an inch from certain death." She fingers a place on her chest. "He never even came to visit me in the hospital. My parents cut ties with his family. I haven't seen Lorcan or Finn for years."

My intelligence person needs to be fired with a capital F. None of this should be a surprise. All of it is. "I shouldn't have suggested we come."

She turns sad eyes to me. "If I'd told you, I'm sure we wouldn't have. But it's been long enough. Sometimes we need to face our demons."

I tuck my hands under my legs. Boston passes by the window in a blur. "We call them demons for a reason. Sometimes they're best left in hell."

"You seem like a person who faces her fears instead of letting them eat her alive."

"Maybe." I shove my hands further under my thighs. "Why'd you give me the choice to leave?"

Carys sighs and focuses on the scenery out the window. "I know I seemed excited about the arms deal if they split. I wasn't sure I wanted to tell you any of this. The truth, the complete and utter truth, is watching them destroy each other would hurt my heart too much." A wry smile plays on her lips. "You know, what's left of it."

I offer her a half smile. Her iron facade isn't as pristine as she likes to think.

"I know them. I knew their parents. I can't sit back and watch it happen." She twirls one of the rings on her finger. "In the end, family is all we've got. All they have left is each other."

Unbidden, the memory of my mother's laugh rings in my ears. It never sounds the same anymore. For the first time, I wish I could be Kimi in this moment, confide, confess, and share my grief with someone.

"If you let them, they'll destroy you. Don't let it happen, okay? Keep your head in the game."

My mind snaps back into focus, and I wink at her. "My head's always in the game."

# Chapter Six

The next day when the door swings open to Finn, I curse Lorcan and his matchmaking skills. I sent Lorcan a text when I landed to let him know when I'd arrive at the house. He knew it would be me at the door. I step around Finn. The idea I don't understand how to seduce a man is laughable. Lorcan and I are going to have a chat. This isn't how I work.

"Carys must be a pretty shitty employer if you decided working for Lorcan is better."

Instead of turning to address Finn, I continue heading to the back of the house toward Lorcan's office. I offer Finn a wave above my head, not bothering to give him the satisfaction of a reply.

His deep laughter follows me until I round the corner. When I get to Lorcan's door, I press the buzzer like I saw Antonio do yesterday.

It takes a moment for Lorcan's voice to come through the speaker, and when it does, it's breathless. "Yes?"

"Kim."

The door buzzes, and I enter the spacious room. Shirtless, Lorcan runs on the treadmill at a full-on sprint. His stride is impressive. It's been a while since I've done the same, and my limbs ache with the remembrance of an unrelenting pace.

"Just be a tic," he calls to me before upping the speed on the treadmill.

I ease into a chair and cross my legs, watching him with mild amusement. His build isn't of a runner, more like a boxer or wrestler. As he slows, I say, "That's quite a pace."

"You never know when you might need to run for your life." He grabs a towel off a chair and wipes his face. With one last swipe at his neck, his gaze sweeps me from head to toe. "You work out?"

"Not much lately. I should probably get back into it." Fitness is vital for my job, but I'm athletic and don't worry about it as often as I should.

"There's a communal gym off the front entrance."

"Meaning Finn uses it."

"Maybe. I don't. I wouldn't know." He tosses his towel into a laundry chute by the workout equipment and crosses the room to perch on the edge of his desk.

"Pushing me on Finn isn't helpful."

Glowering at me, he runs a hand through his damp hair. "I know my brother. You don't need to worry how you appear. If I seem interested, he will be too."

I twist in my chair to face him. Gone is the charmer from the last couple of days. In his place is a man with a determined, edgy air.

"I need you to be ready in twenty minutes. I have a few errands to run."

"I'm ready now." I indicate my tight black yoga pants and my flowing black shirt. "Unless we're going somewhere special?"

He looks me over again before he rises and heads for the door. "What you're wearing is fine. I'll meet you at the front door in twenty. Go unpack, explore, whatever."

*Explore.* "Sure." The doors I passed on the way to this one showed promise. The best place to be is the office though. "I could wait for you here."

He chuckles and wanders closer to me. "I'm sure you could." He bends toward me, and his lilting voice purrs in my ear, "Unless you're *my a ghrá*, you don't get to stay here alone."

I close my eyes as the Irish washes over me. My father used to call me his *a chroí*. Neither of those will ever happen. I'll never be Lorcan's love, and I'll never again be my father's heart as he squeezes me tight.

"Want to know what it means?"

"No." I open my eyes and meet his gaze. "I like a bit of mystery. Besides, it clearly means I need to be someone you trust."

Opening the door, Lorcan's smile fades. "Front door."

"Twenty minutes. I got it."

He motions along the hall, shutting the door behind him. "Down there, to the left. That'll be your rooms."

"Rooms?"

"As many as you want. It's a big house. We've got staff but hardly any live-ins."

"Were there staff here the day your father died?"

"Place was empty save for him."

"Odd."

"Very." Lorcan gives me a curt nod and crosses the corridor to another door. "My bedroom—if you ever need to find it."

A smile spreads across my face. "If, huh?"

Amusement lights his hazel eyes. "Stranger things have happened."

"I've got bigger fish to fry," I say.

He chuckles and punches in his code without looking at me. "Oh, I doubt that fish is bigger." He winks at me before disappearing into his bedroom.

As soon as the door clicks tight, I ignore the tingling in my stomach and start wandering down the corridor trying each handle. After a few linen and broom closets, I realize he's only told me I can look around because anything worth seeing is under lock, key, and security code.

"Lost?" Finn calls from the end of the hall.

I frown, annoyance sparking in me. "You're allowed on this side of the house?"

He pushes his hands into the pockets of his light jeans and strolls toward me. When he gets closer, he gestures wide, his T-shirt stretching across his broad torso. "No booby traps or explosions. I guess I'm allowed." He stops in front of me. "Terrible manners my brother has. He should have at least shown you to your rooms."

I narrow my eyes at Finn. "I'm quite capable of finding them myself."

One side of his mouth quirks up, the opposite side to his brother. There's no dimple, and his icy blue eyes are piercing in comparison to Lorcan's warm hazel ones. "My brother is far too trusting."

The codes and locks on the doors say otherwise, but I stare at Finn, willing him to continue. He rubs the back of his head.

"I'll walk you to your rooms."

"No need," I say. "I have to meet Lorcan at the front soon, anyway."

"I'll walk you there." He strolls beside me in silence for a moment. "Your weapons are at the front."

Not all of them. I have one in the heel of my shoe. "Thanks."

"Not much of a talker, are you?"

"Should I be?"

"Most women are."

I cock my head.

"Yes, I realize the obvious deduction is you're not most women."

"Just like you're not representative of most men." I give him the once-over. Men in their position are suspicious by nature, but I hoped the introduction through Carys might have softened them both. "Were you in Lorcan's corridor to check up on me?"

Finn's gaze is steely. "I don't know who you are or why you're here. You're under my roof. My father died here. You can never be too careful when not even your own home is safe."

It's a reasonable response, but it's not the whole truth. "I'm here because Lorcan hired me."

"To do what?"

I give him a sly smile. "Whatever he wants."

Finn's eyes narrow as we enter the long, wide front entrance. His pace slows, and he faces me. "You were already doing whatever Carys wanted. I can't imagine my brother came up with a job title more impressive."

I take in the grand entrance, the high ceiling. "Titles don't matter to me."

"Ready to go?" Lorcan calls to me as he comes striding toward me down the narrow side hall. Two different burly guards, ones I don't recognize, are a few steps behind him. "*Deartháir mor.*" Lorcan nods at Finn.

"*Deartháir beag,*" Finn responds with a slight nod.

I raise my eyebrows at Lorcan, but he only shakes his head, taking my hand on the way past Finn. At least they're still addressing each other as brothers, even if the terms of endearment resemble battle cries.

"Anything I should know about?" Finn asks from behind us as we approach the exit.

"Checking on some of our assets today." Lorcan doesn't break his stride.

"Perhaps I already checked on them."

"Then they'll get another visit. I need to help Kim become acquainted with some of her tasks, people involved."

With my free hand, I scoop up my firearms off the table at the entrance. I'll have to put them on in the car. As Lorcan leads me out the door, I glance back at his brother. He's watching us, a frown marring his face. When he catches me staring, curiosity lights up his pale eyes. Is it suspicion or attraction in them?

Sliding into the black SUV, I risk one more peek at Finn, who is in the open doorway, hands thrust into his pockets, his expression pensive.

"Big brother is intrigued." Lorcan's lips are a hair's breadth from my ear. "Well done."

His face is close enough if I lean in a fraction, I could connect our lips. I lick mine, thinking about what it would be like to kiss him. He smells of oak trees and mints, and I wonder if the whiskey he drinks has fused with his skin.

"Men aren't tough to figure out. A hint of the forbidden. A touch of mystery."

Lorcan eases away from me, his back pressing into the leather seat. "Not me. I like my women to be what they seem."

"No surprises."

"Highly overrated."

Unable to resist, I say, "So what am I?"

A smile tugs on the edges of his lips. "You're *the everything* woman. Not a chance you're what you seem. I'm safe as houses."

Such a British thing to say, as though houses are safe. He should know better given what happened to his father. "Safe as houses, huh?"

"We're going to be good mates, you and me."

Out of the corner of my eye, I take in his profile. He may not be tempted by me, but I can't say the same for myself. That spells trouble for both of my jobs.

Distance. Detachment.

My head needs to stay in the game. If I still had a heart, I might have to worry about it too.

# Chapter Seven

The casino isn't much from the outside. It's a few sections of a strip mall with blacked-out windows, and in a part of Boston, were I anyone else, I'd never frequent. Once we go through the sliding doors, it becomes clear the business is nothing special on the inside either. Everything is faded and looks as though it came straight out of the seventies. Slot machines line every square inch of the place, and the stench of stale smoke envelops me.

"You own this?" My tone is far from impressed.

Lorcan gives me a sideways glance as he strides toward the back of the building. "It's not what it seems."

One of the security guards is in front of us, the other behind.

"Are you going to tell me more than that?"

"Not right now."

"Trust—"

"Is earned. You earned it from Carys, but you gotta earn it from me." He points his index finger, and his expression is full of determination.

His accent shifted to more Bostonian than Irish as soon as we entered the casino. The way he slips from one persona to another fascinates me. If he's aware he's doing it, he'd be an excellent agent. Lorcan's ability to blend into his environment or to stand out, depending on the goal, is impressive. Even some agents I work with aren't skilled chameleons.

"Watch and learn." Lorcan heads to the keypad beside a door at the back. Maybe an office? "Carys won't have handled business like we do." Over his shoulder, his gaze connects with mine before sliding away. "You gotta be okay with getting blood on your hands."

I push my hands deeper into the pockets of my jacket. Off in a corner, an elderly woman is chain-smoking and pressing the button on the slot machine, shoulders hunched. These places often have regulars, but there's something sad about knowing she's gambling away her savings. Slot machines are bad odds. "It wouldn't be the first time."

As soon as he enters the small room, the buzz quiets. The walls are bare, but there are tables packed tight in the space. The stale smoke smell is mostly absent in here, but there's a weird combination of too many perfumes. Women are everywhere counting money and packing drugs. For a moment, everyone freezes, then the buzz picks up again. A short, burly guy pops out of the crowd and comes forward, his hand outstretched.

"Danny." He nods at Lorcan while he waits for me to take his hand.

"Kim." I grasp his hand in mine, and it's damp with sweat. When I release his hand, I wipe my palm down the side of my pants.

"Did you figure out who it is?" Lorcan crosses his arms and scans the room, taking in the production.

"I think it's Bobby." Danny focuses on the workers, not on Lorcan.

"You *think*?" Lorcan narrows his eyes, his voice pitching lower. "You either know or you don't. If you don't know, you're no good to me."

"I know. I know." Danny's voice wavers. "He's skimming."

"Is he also the guy selling my product on the side?"

Danny nods.

"I need you to speak, Danny."

"Yes." Danny shuffles his feet.

*He's lying.* I glance at Lorcan and then Danny. He's clearly afraid of whatever comes next if he doesn't answer these questions. Why lie? He doesn't know, or he's hiding something. It's curious Lorcan doesn't pick up on the signs. Maybe everyone reacts to him and his demands with fear and uncertainty.

Stepping around Danny, I move through the room, watching the assembly line, the way they calculate the large sums of money. The women working with the drugs are in their bras and underwear. One woman who is clothed and sitting behind a folding table is counting money beside a dark-skinned kid who can't be more than twenty. Her focus keeps straying to Danny and Lorcan, biting her lip, only half paying attention to the money being counted.

"Bobby," Danny calls to the only other male in the room who does not appear to be doing any work.

The dark-skinned boy glances up, startled, and rises from his chair. "Yes, sir."

"Come here." Danny motions with his hand, waving Bobby toward us.

I trail Bobby as he heads to them, waiting to see what will happen.

"Office." Lorcan gestures to the door across the room with another secure entrance. He strides in that direction, and Danny, Bobby, and I follow.

Bobby looks bewildered, and he gives me a half smile. "You new?" he whispers.

"Ish." I try to read his features. He's either very skilled at keeping his emotions in check or he hasn't done anything wrong. "I worked somewhere else first."

"And you made it out."

As the door pops open, I grab it. "Sometimes you get lucky." And sometimes you get very unlucky. Bobby is the fall guy for the woman working beside him, but I'm not sure why. Danny isn't clueless, and that woman is nervous, anxious even.

"Who was the woman you were working with?" We slip into the room behind Lorcan and Danny.

"Megan? Danny's girlfriend." Bobby shoves his hands in his pockets, his posture more curious than afraid. Oh, to be young and ignorant.

A smirk touches my lips. "Of course it is."

"Do you think I'm getting promoted?" Bobby asks.

"Nope." My voice is clipped. "I think you're about to get screwed."

The office is little more than a desk and a massive safe. A large spot on the floor is a rusty brown, darkening to black in some places. That doesn't bode well for anyone dragged in here. Lorcan is perched on the edge of the desk, and Danny hovers by his shoulder. Bobby is frozen in the entryway.

Wandering to Lorcan's side, I lean close enough to smell the mint and oak which mingles on his skin. "Can I have a bit of leeway here?"

Lorcan's intense hazel eyes connect with mine, anger in their depths. "Don't go soft on me."

"You'll thank me." I give him a small smile.

One side of his lips quirks up, and he gestures for me to take the lead.

"Danny, can you get Megan in here?" My gaze bores into him, wondering if he'll spill the truth.

Danny's face loses color. "Megan?"

"Yeah, you know, your girlfriend."

"She doesn't have nothing to do with this."

Cocking my head, I say, "I like to have another woman in the room. What can I say?"

Lorcan raises his eyebrows and gives me an annoyed look, but he doesn't say a word.

Taking a deep breath, Danny shuffles to the door and opens it enough to stick his head out. "Meg, can you come here for a sec?"

When she appears, I realize my mistake. Behind the table counting money, it hadn't been obvious, but now it is. She's pregnant. Beside me, Lorcan recrosses his arms and settles more onto the corner of the desk.

I offer her a smile. "Congratulations on the baby."

"Thank you," she whispers, glancing at Danny, head down.

"When are you due?"

"Two months."

"It must be hard to afford the things babies need—cribs, car seats, clothes, diapers." I keep my tone gentle, understanding, as though what they've done is rational and not suicide.

Meg's focus flies to me before shifting away again. "We're getting by."

"Not without help."

Lorcan grunts beside me and runs a hand down his face. "Are you kidding me right now?"

Meg's face is ashen.

When Lorcan's hand drops, he towers above Danny. "Did you lie to me? You steal from me, and then you lie about it."

Bobby is slack-jawed by the closed door. "You thought it was me," he whispers, stunned.

"Danny told him it was you." I pop open the door. "It's your lucky day, kid. Get out of here."

Danny doesn't meet Lorcan's gaze. Instead, he's fixed on Meg. "Do what you gotta do to me, but leave Meg and the baby outta this. She ain't done nothin.'"

"Except steal from me." Lorcan brims with suppressed rage. "She's been stealing from me, and you've been covering for her." His fists are clenched at his side.

Danny doesn't say anything to Lorcan. His pleading eyes are focused on Meg. "It's okay, baby. It'll be okay."

Lorcan's elbow comes up and slams into Danny's face, knocking him back. "You don't steal from me."

I don't say a word, and I'm careful to keep my features neutral. I've witnessed people in my position lose their cool once the viciousness starts. Crying. Screaming. Begging. Not me. Living this life means I have to seem like I condone the violence. I understand it. Maybe I do.

Drawing back his arm, he drives his fist into Danny's cheekbone, and Danny hits the concrete floor with a thud. "You don't lie to me." An unconscious Danny is sprawled on the floor, and Lorcan whirls around, pointing his finger at a sobbing Meg. "You got twelve hours to get outta town before I send a cleanup crew. You take even so much as one more dollar out of this organization, and your family is dead. You hear me?"

"Y-y-y-yes." Meg is sobbing, and her agreement is almost impossible to decipher.

Lorcan throws the door open and scans the room, landing on Bobby. "Get my men in here."

Bobby jumps up and crosses the room to the other door, calling in Lorcan's two guards.

"Clean this shit up," Lorcan says to both of them. "Ian, you stay with me and Kim. Sean, you look after Danny and Meg. They got twelve hours to be out of Boston, or you can kill them."

Danny stirs on the concrete, and Lorcan gives him a swift kick to his ribs.

Up to now, Lorcan's been restrained, but when he goes to kick him again, I say, "Don't forget this kindness, Meg. You should be dead right now." My heart pounds in my ears, but my voice is even. Every time I'm in this situation, I thank the deities out in the universe my training is rock solid.

My voice brings Lorcan up short, and he rolls his shoulders, gathering himself. Bobby would not have gotten the twelve-hour grace; even Danny on his own wouldn't have. Assuming anything in my file is right, Lorcan's got a soft spot for mothers.

"Outta town. You never come back, you hear me? I catch a whiff of either you or Danny or your kid, and I'm coming for all of you."

Meg nods over and over, covering her face with her hands as each sob gets louder.

Lorcan opens the door to the office and jerks his head for me and Ian to follow. We both slip out behind him. Sliding my fingers inside my jacket, I brush up against the metal of a gun.

Once we're back in the car, Lorcan stares out the window, flexing his hand. "Did you know she was pregnant before she came into the office?"

"No."

"How'd you figure out it was them?"

"Danny couldn't stay still. Wasn't giving you clear answers without prompting. Reluctant. Bobby didn't care you were there. He was doing his job, like normal. He thought he was getting promoted. Megan wasn't doing anything but watching you. She should have painted a scarlet G on her forehead and then used an arrow to point at Danny."

Lorcan's mouth quirks up, but then he grows serious. "I would have killed Bobby."

"I know."

"For no reason."

I meet his look, and a spark of sympathy stirs in me at the sincerity flowing out of him. Many of the men I've known in his position wouldn't have cared.

"Thank you. I got enough on my conscience without adding to it." The lilting softness is back.

An uncontrollable urge to grab Lorcan's hand hits me. I want to touch him, solidify the connection. With a last glance at me, he focuses his attention out the window, and the moment passes.

# Chapter Eight

I spend the next few weeks trailing Lorcan around the city as he makes deals, leans on people, and accumulates more and more money. I'm never sure what Finn does with his days. Sometimes I see him, but most of the time it's like Lorcan and I are the only ones in the house. Finn is a ghost.

When my phone buzzes the familiar sequence, I'm sitting on the edge of my bed, contemplating the gym. I swipe the phone off the nightstand and catch sight of the innocuous message.

*Lunch is on me today.*

Malik.

Glancing at the clock, I realize I have two hours to make it out of the city to a dive bar in Newport, Rhode Island. I throw on my favorite outfit of black pants and shirt and secure my dark hair into a tight ponytail at the base of my neck. Grabbing my jacket off the chair where I tossed it last night, I head down the hall to ask if I can get the day off.

I ring Lorcan's office, wishing I could let myself in. We go through the usual pattern, and he buzzes me into the room.

"You should put a camera out there so we can dispense with the back-and-forth," I say as I enter the room.

Lorcan glances up at me from behind his desk. He's shirtless again, but he hasn't started his workout yet. Every single time he's like this, the pit of my stomach flutters.

"We're already at the stage where you can tell me my systems annoy you?" His tone is mild, with a hint of amusement flickering across his face.

"I think it's always best to say what you think in the moment." I smile.

Lorcan's face fills with disbelief. "No, you don't."

"You're right. I rarely say what I think. You should feel privileged I graced you with an opinion."

"Privileged."

"Yes." In my peripheral vision, the clock ticks, and it snaps me into focus. I should not be flirting with the guy I'm trying to take down. "Do you need me this afternoon?"

He snatches a pen from his desk and rocks back in his high-backed leather chair. "Not necessarily."

"I used to live in Newport, Rhode Island as a kid," I say. "I was wondering if I could borrow a car to drive there, look around."

Lorcan brings the pen to his lips and taps them. "Borrow a car. Drive to Rhode Island by yourself."

I bristle. "I'm not going to steal your car."

He chuckles. "That's not my concern. You've been all over the city with me these past few weeks. Your value is increasing, not only to me but to other people who might be watching my organization."

"You want me to take a guard."

"Will you?"

"I did when I worked for Carys. It's not exactly the trip I was hoping for."

"Or I can come with the guards."

I frown. "That would be worse." But also so much better. I've gotten used to having him near.

He comes around the desk and stops in front of me. "How confident are you that you can handle this trip by yourself?"

"Very." My mind is ticking away the minutes. If I miss the window, Malik will be gone, and this conversation will have been for nothing.

Lorcan runs a hand through his hair in a back-and-forth motion, mussing up his blond-brown strands. "You can go." With a couple of strides, he's at the lockbox that holds the keys to the cars in the garages. He plucks out a set and tosses them to me.

I catch them in one hand. "An SUV?"

"Good handling, bulletproof glass." He ambles to me, close enough for the scent of his musky cologne to touch my nose. No mint and oak today. "You're becoming an asset. I try to protect those."

When I glance up, I realize we're closer than usual. Any time Finn is around, Lorcan makes a point of standing in my personal space, gazing at me longer, but there's no audience here. It's just us. The air hums with a new sort of tension.

"I suppose I should be flattered," I murmur.

"I suppose so." His lilting accent is back again.

He must read my mind, or I'm giving something away in my body language. The dip in his voice, the intoxicating blend of his Irish and Boston accents, make my knees wobble. If only I could reach out to steady myself. If my skin touches his, our spark will become a flame, then a raging inferno will consume me. There are things I cannot want.

"Be safe." His gaze flicks between my eyes and my lips.

"Always." I rattle the keys in my hand, breaking the spell.

Lorcan opens the door and leans his shoulder into it. "When are you back?"

"I'll be gone for the afternoon."

"Any later than that—"

"I'll call."

His head nod is almost imperceptible.

I hurry out the door and down the hall. I wasted too much time in his office. I'm steps from the front door when I spot Finn.

"Where are you off to without my *dearthái beag*?" Finn calls to me.

"Out for the day."

"You're taking a guard?" He frowns. "People know who you are now." He's moving toward me, trying to head me off.

*No one knows who I am.*

"I'll be fine."

"Kim." Finn grabs my elbow.

I yank my arm away from him. "Touch me again and you'll lose some fingers."

He takes a step back. "This is a shit idea."

"It's not your choice." Inside me, a clock ticks. "Go do whatever it is you do."

As I beeline to the garage, I'm surprised Finn isn't following me. He doesn't like being defied.

Sliding into the vehicle, I open the garage door. Once outside, I cruise through the iron gates that block off their property from the ones surrounding it. The city has consumed them, and driving out of here is a constant surprise. The estate feels isolated even though it's far from it.

While I drive, I toy with the idea of stopping to see my mother. It would be out of my way, but might be my only opportunity to visit her for months. My presence never matters much. The good days are rare anymore. The sharp wit and intellect I admired in her as a child has leaked out, one memory at a time. My mother is no longer my mother. She's my last thread of family, and she's fraying so badly our tenuous connection is bound to snap at any moment.

A few blocks from the bar, I park and wander in and out of shops, keeping an eye on the time. Somehow, I'm here fifteen minutes early. Once I'm sure I'm not being followed, I zigzag through the streets until I get to the bar. Opening the door, I take a moment to let my eyes adjust to the dim lighting. The scent of spilled beer hits my nose as the bells overhead jingle. That smell must have seeped into the wooden floors a long time ago.

The bar is a place most locals, if they used it, would call a hole in the wall. There are a few tables, a bar top, and a bathroom at the back. The bar is well stocked, and I ease onto one of the stools. When I look up, it's as though Malik, dressed as a bartender, has appeared on the other side of the bar out of thin air.

He passes a whiskey to me and then pours one for himself. "You weren't followed?"

I don't answer, just stare at him over the rim of my glass.

"Any news?"

"I'm making progress. Lorcan's taking me around to meet a lot of people. I almost had to bring a guard today."

"Willing to give up assets to protect you. That's a good sign." He pours himself another drink. "The two brothers?"

"Things are definitely tense, but they mostly ignore each other. At some point, Lorcan is going to expect me to start investigating the death of his father."

"We know who did that."

"The file is shit so far. We might *not* know."

"Lorcan thinks Finn did it?"

"Yeah, he does. His second choice is the O'Malleys. Any outcome leads to war."

"Drag out the search—see if cooler heads appear in a few months."

"I'll do what I can."

"You going to stop in to visit your mom on the way back?"

Taking a sip of my drink, I catalog the dingy bar. The wood is painted black, and the stools are nicked, showing flecks of white at the edges on the high backs. The tables have seen better days. "You closing this up when I leave?"

Malik sighs and tries to catch my line of sight.

I focus on the whiskey in my glass, and the burning sensation rolls down my throat.

"The bar exists as a meetup for agency people, so yeah, I'll be closing. I might stay open for another hour or two after you leave. Better if the locals don't put two and two together." His hand covers mine across the bar, and he gives me a gentle squeeze. "You need connections in the real world, Kimi. It's too easy to get lost in Kim without them."

"You're my real connection." Even as I say the words, I realize they're not completely true. We sleep together, and he understands me very well. But I know the bare minimum about him beyond the job. We're friends, but I'm not sure how real that is sometimes.

"I like being someone you connect with. Believe me. But your mom isn't going to be around forever."

"The woman who raised me is gone, Malik."

"The last time I called the home, she'd rebounded a bit. Worth stopping in."

"I'll think about it."

When the bells above the door jingle, we both freeze. In the doorway, squinting into the darkness, his platinum-blond hair catching the only bit of light around, is Finn.

# Chapter Nine

Once his eyes adjust, he takes me in at the bar. Antonio enters behind him, his wide shoulders almost brushing against the doorframe. Malik cleans the bar, far away from me now. His ability to read and assess a situation in a heartbeat is admirable. A moment ago, he was holding my hand.

Finn frowns and shoves his hands in his pockets as he wanders to me. "All the way to Newport for a drink at some shitty bar?"

"It caught my eye." I gesture to the stool beside me. "Drink?" My heart hammers against my chest, reverberating across my ribs. He followed me. How did I miss that? The fact I didn't realize is more terrifying than having him here. These are the kinds of mistakes that kill agents, lead to bloodbaths.

Finn slides into the stool beside me. Over his shoulder, he calls to Antonio, "Guard the door."

"Whiskey?" I ask.

"Irish Car Bomb." Finn gives me a sideways glance.

Swallowing, I raise my hand to Malik who is at the other end of the bar. He saunters toward us as though he doesn't have a care in the world. His face and eyes are blank as he takes in Finn. Not a glimmer of recognition in him.

"One Irish Car Bomb, please." I take a sip of my whiskey. Does he think he's being funny ordering that drink? In Ireland, a reference to the IRA would get us chucked out of a bar. Or is it a warning? Does he know something?

Malik preps the request. He passes the shot filled with Baileys and whiskey to Finn and then pours him a pint of Guinness. Sweat trickles down my armpits. I lean onto the bar, letting my fingers slip inside my jacket to ease off the button holding one of my guns in place. More guns should be behind the bar. For Malik's sake, I hope the ammunition is well stocked. With Antonio at my back, I won't survive if this turns sour.

"Bombs away." Finn drops the shot into the pint. His Adam's apple bobs as he chugs most of the drink.

"Checking up on me?" I keep my elbow on the bar, leaning in so my fingers rest close to my gun.

Finn's lips quirk up as he sets his glass on the wooden surface. "You know the only person I trust?"

It should be his brother, but I suspect he doesn't even trust him. Both his parents are dead. "No idea."

"A dead man. That's the only person you can trust in this business. Anyone else, given the chance, they'll drive a knife into your back and not even think twice."

I give him a steady stare and try to keep my features neutral. "Very cynical."

"It's the truth, Kimmy." He draws out my name.

My name. He can't know. It's a common nickname. A wisp of panic threatens to take hold. *Calm yourself, Kim. Keep your head in the game.*

"It's Kim." I sip my whiskey. "Just Kim."

"Okay, Just Kim. What are you doing here?"

"Having a drink." I raise my glass. "It's been a long week or so."

He cocks his head and picks up the remnants of his own drink. "My *dearthár beag* treating you well?" He downs the rest and sets the empty glass onto the bar.

There's no menace in his tone. It's not what I think. He doesn't know. After releasing my held breath, I ease down my shoulders and take my hand out of my jacket. My heart calms in my chest, the sprinting done for now.

"You thought I was going to kill you?" His voice is tinged with surprise. He stares at the side of my jacket where I keep my gun. "Thought you could take me, did you?"

I give him a wry smile. "Your brother thinks the two of you are on the cusp of a war."

"If I was going to use you to start it, he'd never see it coming." Finn leans back in his chair. His pale gaze looks me over.

I shift in my seat so I'm facing him, an arm propped on the back of the stool, exposing one of my guns. "Perhaps you're the one who should be afraid of me."

He chuckles and with lightning speed snatches my gun out of its holster. I grin, pretending amusement at his quickness, his deft skill with a gun. Sweat trickles down my back. Very few people get the best of me. It scares me and pisses me off he's done it. *Stupid. Stupid.* In the back of my mind, I hear Carys say a man will get a woman killed. *Only if I let him.*

"The day I fear a woman is the day I quit this business." He checks the safety on the gun. "There's no quitting, Kimmy. The only two ways out are death or jail."

"You're warning me?" This time the nickname doesn't send my pulse skyrocketing.

"Nah." He offers me the gun handle. "You don't know enough yet. If you stay, someday you'll know too much, and then you'll be like me and Lorcan. No way out."

"I've been in this business, or a version of it, for a long time." I shove my gun back into its holster.

"Moved all around as a kid. Lived in Newport very briefly. Mother and father split up. You're not close to either one. One brother killed in a freak accident. You were a runner for an organization in Miami for a few years. Carys snatched you out of obscurity because she has a soft spot for tough, beautiful women. You've been working for her for about a year now, right?"

My jaw clenches. At least my backstory holds up. The lies roll off his tongue, but they hit me smack in the chest. Being confronted with them all at one time makes me unsteady. "Yes," I bite out, unable to say more.

"Why would you leave her to come work for Lorcan?" He gives me a side glance. "That's the question that's been circling."

"Your brother was very persuasive."

"I'm missing something. But I'll figure it out." Finn tilts his empty glass from side-to-side. "I like a little mystery."

"You drove all this way to check up on me, to figure it out?"

"Added bonus. I'm here expanding my empire."

He's focused on the alcohol lined up behind the bar, but he's clearly serious.

"Empire?" Does Lorcan know? Should I tell him? Or is Finn testing me?

"If we go to war, I need foot soldiers."

"Hours from Boston? You're bullshitting me."

He shrugs. "Maybe. Maybe not." Sliding off the stool, he opens his wallet and drops a twenty onto the bar. "See you around, Kimmy."

"It's Kim." I lean over my seat as he saunters to the door.

"Oh, right." He exaggerates the words. His back remains to me as he zeros in on the door. "I forgot."

My shoulders ache from the tension, and sweat has left pools on my skin. Maybe there's a shower in the back.

When he nears the door, he leans into Antonio and then gives me a look. "Antonio will stay to make sure you get back okay." His voice echoes around the empty bar.

"Wonderful." I raise the remnants of my drink.

Ian pokes his head in and prompts Finn. With one last glance, he leaves Antonio at the door and slips out onto the street.

Sighing, I swish my drink around. Any chance of speaking to Malik or showering is gone with Antonio standing guard in the doorway.

"Anything else?" Malik's voice is pitched loud enough for Antonio to hear.

"No," I say. "Just the bill." Twenty dollars sits between us. He hands a piece of paper to me. I leave the money and slip the paper into my pocket. Whatever it is, I'll have to read it later. "Keep the change."

"Have a good day." He uses the cloth in his hand to wipe the spot I vacated.

As I approach Antonio, his gaze travels over me. "You ever wear anything other than black?"

"Gray." I open the door. "I like gray."

"Seems kinda boring." He catches the door and then trails after me. "Pretty girl like you could use some color."

"Woman," I say over my shoulder.

"What?"

"I'm not a girl, I'm a woman. While I suppose it's nice you think I'm pretty, I don't need to hear it. We work together. We're not at the salon getting our hair and nails done."

I lead him through the streets back to my car, making sure to weave around the city in case anyone else is following us.

"You know, I'm here to protect you now. You don't need to take a stupid-ass route back to your car."

"I can protect myself."

He snorts. "Women think that until they get in too deep."

"I'm a good swimmer." Opening the driver's-side door, I slide in.

Antonio chuckles, climbing in beside me. "But you're shitty at picking up a tail. We followed you from the house."

My stomach drops. Have I become rusty and reliant on other people? With Carys, I was surrounded by bodyguards. When I needed to meet Malik, I left the city by plane. Now, meeting him a few hours away by car, I have to be more careful. Today's mistake can't happen again.

"He tell you why he followed me?" My seatbelt catches, and I release it to bring it across again.

"Finn don't tell me shit. I do what he says."

"Ever ask?"

"Asking gets you killed. He doesn't like curious people."

"You only work for him?" I put the car in drive and check my blind spot before pulling out into the busy traffic.

"I work for them both—mostly Finn lately." Antonio rubs his hands together and fiddles with the radio. He checks the mirrors and then glances behind him. "Truth is, I'd rather work for Lorcan."

"Why's that?"

"At least he'll ask you if you did it before he shoots you."

I flex my hands on the steering wheel and follow the soothing voice of the navigation system. It's set to an Irish accent—my choice when I got in earlier. Hearing it now, it's foolish. What must Antonio be thinking?

"You know the way back?" My hand is poised over the button to switch off the directions.

He gives me a sideways glance. "Yeah, I got you covered."

We drive in silence for a while. The note in my pocket is acidic, eating away at my clothes, burning my skin. Why did Malik want to see me? What's on the paper?

Antonio's phone beeps, and he takes it out of his pocket. "Boss wants us to meet him at The Cage."

"Finn?"

"Lorcan." He checks the clock in the car before texting him back.

How does he know Antonio is with me? Instead of asking, I stay quiet. Sometimes you learn more by not asking in this business.

"You got weapons on you?" He puts his phone back into his pocket.

"Always. Why?"

"The Cage is an O'Malley establishment. Lorcan's got a meeting with them."

I frown, pressing my foot on the accelerator to pass an old woman in the wrong lane of the highway. Nervous drivers on multilane highways piss me off. Stay home. Take a different route. Get out of my way.

"What's The Cage?" The Cage wasn't in the file, but according to my information, the relationship between the Donagheys and O'Malleys is strained.

"Underground fight ring."

"Is Lorcan trying to start something with them?" Maybe the intel is wrong, and Lorcan gets along with the O'Malley family. The crime syndicates in Boston need a road map to decipher the connections and old grudges. There's so much I don't understand yet.

Antonio laughs. "You think I know? He said come. We come. He said be armed. We make sure we're armed to the teeth." He eyes me with annoyance.

I'm asking too many questions. "The Cage it is," I murmur.

"Don't worry," he says. "I'll protect you."

His condescending tone grates on my nerves. Instead of correcting him, I drive the rest of the way in silence. Mentally, I tick through the ammunition I have, hoping it's enough for whatever comes next.

# Chapter Ten

Lorcan and ten other men hover around vans and SUVs two blocks from The Cage. Even though we've been running errands together for weeks, this area is new to me because it's in O'Malley territory. Being here causes my heart to beat an irregular rhythm. Sometimes I fear I'll have a heart attack from trying to control my outward appearance while my insides go haywire. I need to dump the note in my pocket. There's no way to know what it says with this many people near, and keeping it is too risky. Taking it out, I crumple it. On the way past a garbage can, I drop the paper in.

As we approach, Lorcan's focus homes in on me. He moves aside and jerks his head for me to position myself next to him. I slip in beside him and survey the others, wondering how to bring up Finn's sudden appearance in Newport.

As though he senses my unease, Lorcan's focus turns to me. "Finn followed you." His lips twitch with amusement.

I narrow my eyes. "You knew?"

"It's why I let you go alone. Figured my incompetence would lure him into action." He winks, and smugness leaks out of him.

Anger sparks in me, but I can't say anything. He doesn't know he could have gotten me killed. And, if he knew why, he'd kill me himself.

"Smart." I mirror his half smile. "He certainly fell for it."

He smirks at me and then focuses on everyone else. "Right." Lorcan raises his voice above the din of the men. "We're negotiating a joint venture. Do not shoot anyone unless we're fired on first. Does everyone understand?" His Boston accent is back in full force.

There are murmurs through the crowd, but no one dares to speak up. I frown as I listen to Lorcan organize the men according to weapons and skills. It's not an attack, but he's planning for the tide to turn. Considering the O'Malleys are suspected in the death of his father, this deal is unbelievable.

"Why them?" I ask Lorcan while the other men check weapons and talk amongst themselves.

"Money is money. Money. Power. They're the only two things that matter."

"This deal would be that lucrative? You think they might have murdered your father."

The intensity in his eyes sears me. "You're questioning me?"

I flush and glance away.

Taking my chin in his hand, he brings my face back to him. I grit my teeth.

"You don't question me."

"Understood." I push the word out. "Won't happen again." Knowing me, it'll happen several more times. Carys let me say whatever I wanted. Becoming the silent spectator without an opinion is going to be difficult, maybe impossible.

He releases my chin. Out of the corner of my eye, Antonio smirks. My fingers itch to reach for my gun and put him in his place on the ground.

With a sweeping motion of his arm, Lorcan gets us moving. We approach the door of the club like a mob. He's front and center. I'm on his right side, Antonio on his left, and everyone else placed behind us. Lorcan may not trust the O'Malleys, but he's still putting himself on the front lines. Is it impressive or stupid?

The door is black steel. Lorcan knocks, and a small door opens in the center. He passes through a piece of paper, and I mourn the note I threw out. If I'm searched here, having that paper could have been deadly. Malik isn't usually careless, but there's no way to be sure. Whatever was on the note is lost until I see him again.

Lorcan enters first. *Stupid*. It's not brave.

I follow close at his back, fingers hovering over the gun at my side that's easiest to access and best concealed. It's tiny, but it gets the job done if I have to fire in a hurry.

As soon as I'm through, the crowd of well-built men greeting us sets my heart racing. My gaze flicks around the entry, trying to take in as much as I can as fast as possible.

What the hell is this? In the middle of the warehouse is an enormous cage. The limp body of a slight, but muscular man is being dragged out of the fenced area by two men dressed in red with the words *Cleanup Crew* emblazoned on their backs. Is he dead or unconscious?

Hundreds of people are sitting in bleachers. There are tellers off to the right with a big sign indicating the fighters, the odds, and the bets placed.

"What's doin?" Derry O'Malley ambles to us out of the crowd.

His hair is thinning, and his stomach protrudes from his middle like a beach ball. He's not quite as tall as me, but he's broader, as though he might have been a fighter years ago. Definitely past his prime. While

Lorcan has an air of danger around him, Derry seems slippery, slimy even.

Lorcan rolls his shoulders and extends his hand. "Wicked busy night."

Derry takes his hand and peers over his shoulder at the cage. He smirks. "Business is good. Hope it's better after our chat." He acknowledges a few of the other men in the group, and then he zeroes in on me. "You bringing chicks with you now?"

I tense, prepared for Lorcan to be dismissive.

"Derry, this is Kim. She's my *everything* person, and you better give her the same respect you show my boys."

His emphasis on the phrase Carys used threatens to crack my stone-faced facade. I swallow the smile.

Derry's dark eyes skim over me again, narrowing. "Understood." Annoyance is clear in his tone. The O'Malleys are notorious for their terrible treatment of women. "All the same, I'd rather deal with you or your boys."

"You want a deal, you play nice with whoever the hell I send." Lorcan's voice is tight.

Derry grimaces and stares at his men behind him. "Follow me to the office, and we'll hammer this out."

I manage to catch Lorcan's gaze, and the dimple in his cheek appears when his mouth quirks up, as though he understands my nonverbal thank-you. Even if he's put my head on the chopping block beside his, I'm grateful I won't have to battle for my respect.

We're led down a wide hallway lined with photos. Across the top is the slogan *We Honor the Fallen* and at first, I think it's some kind of veterans' memorial. Except it becomes clear these are fighters who've died. Each flicks past, meaningless, until I latch onto a familiar face. My breath leaves me in a rush, and my body starts flashing hot and cold in alternating waves. I falter. The guy behind me runs into my back.

"Sorry, Kim," he mumbles as he squeezes around me.

Lorcan is busy talking to Antonio and doesn't notice I've fallen behind. When they get to the office door, Lorcan pauses and examines me.

I'm frozen to the spot. Too scared to see the photo again. Afraid it's real. Afraid it's not. I blink several times, not meeting Lorcan's gaze.

"Kim?" He gestures to the interior of the office.

"Bathroom?" I'm too stunned to get anything else out of my mouth.

"There ain't no chicks' toilet here," the biggest of Derry's brawny guards says. Using a thumb, he gestures around the corner. "You can use that one."

I shove open the door to the wheelchair accessible bathroom. The door clicks closed behind me, and I press on the soap dispenser over and over. Suds overflow my hands. Every time I glance down, there's a flood of red with flecks of gray across my hands, staining them. Impossible to get out. I wash them over and over.

Chadwick Lee. Chad. My half-brother. My *dead* half-brother. His face flickers in my memory, and I close my eyes, forcing it back.

How is his photo on that Goddamned wall? Did he work for the O'Malleys? Did they do it?

Bile bubbles into my throat. I only just get to the toilet before my stomach lets go, my whiskey lunch resurfacing. Seeing the contents of the bowl, I realize I haven't eaten anything today.

"You all right in there?" a male voice calls from the other side of the door.

I sink to my knees and close my eyes. "Yeah." My voice is weak.

*Get it together, Kim. Get your head in the game, Kimi. Deep breaths.*

The door opens without a knock. Why didn't I lock it?

"Kim?" Lorcan's words have the lilting quality that warms my body.

With the wall for support, I try to rise, but my legs almost give out. He rushes to my side and wraps a strong, sturdy arm around my waist.

"What the hell?" He examines my face, confusion and annoyance warring in him.

"I'm not feeling well."

Concern overtakes the other emotions, filling his hazel eyes, and his lips purse. "We'll reschedule."

"No." I shake my head. "I just need a minute." Easing away from him, I tug down my jacket and straighten my shirt. My hands are raw, red.

"Kim." His voice is pitched low. "I'm not putting you in that room if you're feeling rough." The bright color of my hands catches his attention, and he snatches one to examine. "What'd you do?"

"The soap." With my head, I gesture to the sink.

He watches me, curiosity tinged with anger dancing across his face. "Did my *dearthái r mor* do something to you earlier?"

I tug my hand from his larger ones. "No, no. I'm fine. I must have eaten something that didn't agree with me. It came on suddenly, but I'm fine now. I can do this. I'll be fine." Even as I say it, my hand shakes when I yank again on the bottom of my jacket.

"That room is full of men who could kill us. It's not the time for false bravado. Could you shoot a gun right now?" His voice is an urgent whisper.

"No."

"No?"

"No." Under my lashes, I can't meet his gaze.

He sighs. While he looks at me, his hands clench into fists and then relax over and over. "Come out when you're feeling better, or I'll have someone come get you when we're done. You hear shots, you get the hell outta here. Exit out to your left. You understand me?"

"Yeah, yeah."

I don't glance up until the door clicks closed behind him. At the sink, I press my hands into the sides of the vanity and stare at myself. Any credibility I've built the last few weeks is being destroyed the longer I'm in here. My black eyes peer back at me in a face that appears sun-kissed. I yank my hair out of the ponytail and redo it, trying to blank out my mind.

Chad. *My* Chad in that photo.

When I focus on my hands, Chad's sticky hair coats them, blood seeping between my fingers as I scream for help in a deserted street. My chest aches at the memory. With my eyes closed, I swallow, and my throat is scratchy. I pushed these memories down so far I didn't think they'd ever resurface.

It's been twenty years. Might as well be yesterday.

I will get answers. When he died, I was too young; I didn't understand. Seeing his picture on the wall is like having a window pried open in a hot, stuffy room.

I'm not closing it again.

War might be inevitable.

If the O'Malleys killed Chad, I'll be the one firing the first shot.

# Chapter Eleven

When I come out of the bathroom, there are fifteen sets of male eyes sizing me up. Some are part of O'Malley's crew and others are Lorcan's. One of Derry's men smirks at me, and he telegraphs his smart-ass comment before it ever leaves his lips.

"Morning sickness? Lorcan knock you up already?" He chuckles and checks the other guys for a reaction.

Witty responses light up my brain, and I sift through them, rejecting the ones that'll get me killed. "No, asshole. Food poisoning. Next time I have the urge to vomit, I'll aim at you, shall I?"

A few of his buddies stifle a laugh behind their hands. "Wouldn't be the first time a woman's puked at the sight of him," one of them says, laughing.

The door to the office swings back forcefully, and Lorcan storms out, Antonio and Ian close behind him. His focus sweeps over me before he says, "We're done here. The terms are shit."

Derry leans against the doorframe, arms crossed. Unlike Lorcan and Finn, his arms bulge from fat instead of muscles. Personal fitness must not be a priority. The men fall into formation behind Lorcan with me at the rear.

"Once you cool down, you'll know I'm right, Lorcan." Derry raises his voice to get in one last dig as we near the end of the hallway. "Don't be a fool like your old man."

Lorcan stops in his tracks, and I put my hand on my gun. When he turns around, his men rotate with him. "Watch yourself, Derry. Your idiocy is showing."

Derry's chest goes red, and then the color migrates to his face. "You're gonna have to come crawling back to me for this deal after that comment. On your knees."

"Not gonna happen. Hell'll freeze over first." Lorcan's arms are loose at his sides, and then he jerks his head for us to move out.

Derry's eyes narrow at me, and he sneers. "Collar your bitch, Lorcan. Hands on guns mean bullets start flying."

He's talking about me, but I don't move my hand. Derry could shoot me in the back. I don't want to be gunned down. I want to know why Chad was murdered. And once I know, people will pay.

"What'd you call her?" Lorcan spits out, his stride carrying him back down the hall. His hand reaches inside his own jacket and extracts his gun. Pointing it at Derry's face, Lorcan's rage is spewing out of him as he says, "You show her the same respect you show my men, or you'll take a bullet as proof I'm serious."

Five other men train their guns on Lorcan. There's a weapon in each of my hands, and I rotate them to different targets, trying to gauge who might be trigger-happy.

Antonio appears in my peripheral vision, guns raised. Ian's shoulder brushes mine as he takes his position beside me. The other men better have our back. If we're shooting our way out, this is going to be chaos.

The hallway with the bathroom is on my right. Escape is straight down the hall.

"Easy, Lorcan." Derry doesn't take his eyes off me. "She's not worth a war."

"It's not gonna be a war, Derry. It'll be a massacre. Yours." Lorcan readies his gun, his attention never shifting from Derry's face. "Apologize to her."

There's a cacophony of guns adjusting behind me.

Derry laughs. "This isn't about her. But, fine." He tips his chin at me. "I apologize for my language." He lets the end of the gun connect with his forehead. "We both know this is about your pride, and it's got nothin' to do with her."

Lorcan's jaw tightens, and he lowers his gun. "We're done here. You hear me, Derry?"

With a chuckle, he spreads his arms wide. "We'll see. You need what I got, Lorcan."

"You're not offering what I need," Lorcan says. "Stand down."

Guns clank back into holsters behind me. Easing down my hands, I slide my guns into their places, but I don't lock them in. What could Lorcan need from a sleazy man like Derry?

Without a backward glance, Lorcan strides past me and the rest of the men. When he gets to the steel door to outside, he slams his hands into it, forcing the door open at an abrupt speed.

On the way back to the vans, he leads the way in sullen silence. I'm still unsteady on my feet. When I weave, Antonio shoots me a look of annoyance.

"I need to eat," I say before lengthening my strides to catch Lorcan.

As we near the SUV and vans, he slows his stride. He whirls on the men and says, "I need a collection round. Everyone but Antonio and Kim, go collect from people. Protection, tariffs. I don't care what you gotta do. Money comes straight to me. None of it goes to Finn."

A couple of the men shuffle and squint at each other.

"Anyone got a problem with that?"

No one says anything, but it's clear the request isn't a normal one.

Antonio holds out his hand. I raise my eyebrows.

"Keys. You don't drive the boss. I do."

Taking the keys out of my pocket, I drop them into his hand. Do I sit in the front with Antonio who I'm coming to despise or in the back with an angry Lorcan? At least in the back, I might get answers before we arrive at the house.

Going around the SUV, I climb into the back seat. Antonio's unimpressed gaze meets mine in the mirror. Lorcan's still talking to a couple of the men outside.

We sit in silence until Lorcan gets in beside me. He doesn't acknowledge me. Antonio steers the vehicle away from the curb, and the SUV glides through the streets headed back to the house.

"You okay?" Lorcan's face is turned away, focused outside.

"Didn't eat enough today."

"Eat anything yet?"

Darkness is starting to fall on the city around us.

"No."

"Antonio, call ahead and see if Jackie can have something ready for me to pick up."

"Sure thing, boss." Antonio touches the Bluetooth device in his ear.

"Why are you knocking on doors?" I shift in my seat to see him better.

"I need capital."

"You're going to raise that through tariffs and protection money?"

"No," he bites out. "I was going to raise it through a deal with Derry."

"What happened?"

"He wanted the power and the majority of the money. I don't need that deal."

"A product or an investment?"

Lorcan's mouth twists, and he glances at me. "Product. People rise to the occasion for it."

I frown. "Drugs?"

A chuckle escapes him. "Viagra. Surprisingly lucrative. Men love their hard-ons."

"Isn't that the truth?" I give him an amused smile. "In my next life, I'm coming back as a guy. I need to understand the preoccupation with dicks."

He laughs and shakes his head. The tension seeps out of him. "Don't ever put your hand on your gun unless you're going to use it."

I don't bother telling him not only did he put his hand on his gun, but he held it to Derry's face.

"Guess I have a bit to learn."

"Self-protection is challenging to overcome."

"The Cage seems like an interesting organization. Do you know how it works?"

Lorcan searches my face. "No, I don't." He glances away, back out the window. "Finn used to fight for the O'Malleys years ago. He might be able to satisfy your curiosity. Course you'd have to be careful how you approached that."

"Finn fought for Derry?"

Lorcan tips his head. "Derry's dad. Needless to say, when our father found out, the shit and the fan connected quite quickly."

"He wasn't happy?"

"Finn was screwing around, but he could have got himself killed. The O'Malleys knew it, let him fight for a while then rubbed his record in my father's face."

"He didn't win very much?"

"Won all the time." Lorcan chuckles. "All the bloody time."

"He was making them money."

"Heaps of it."

I fall silent as we pull up to a house. Lorcan takes out some money from his pocket and passes it to Antonio. After sliding out of the car, Antonio disappears down the path of the modest townhouse.

When he comes back, he's cradling a take-out bag in his hands. As soon as he opens the door, the smell of stewed lamb hits me. The scent is so distinctive, earthy and animal. My stomach rumbles in response. Cooked vegetables and stewed meat permeates the SUV, and I'm not sure I'll be able to make it back to the house before ripping into the bag.

"Hope you like Irish stew."

"I'd eat anything at this point." I take a deep breath in through my nose. "That smells amazing, though."

"Jackie cooks it like my mum used to."

An image of my own mother laughing in our kitchen flickers to life in my brain. The city whizzes by the window, a blur of lights. "How old were you when she died?" The answer was in the file, but I'm not sure he'll tell me. Tiredness seeps into my bones.

"Fifteen. The year my life went to shit."

I jerk around, surprised at his honesty. "How so?"

"Nothin'. Nothin'. We're not trading best friend necklaces. No tales of our broken hearts. They ain't getting put back together."

The SUV glides through the gates and onto the property. Antonio stops the car outside the front door, and we climb out in silence. Lorcan leads the way back to the kitchen while Antonio stays behind to watch the door.

Once we get to the kitchen, Lorcan places the bag on the island and goes to the fridge. "Drink?" he asks over his shoulder.

"Water, please." I take a seat at a stool at the island as Lorcan dishes stew into bowls and downs a beer. He passes me a glass of water before coming around to sit next to me. His shoulder brushes mine.

With each spoonful of stew, I'm more like myself. I dip some of the crusty roll he gave me into the gravy goodness and almost sigh with contentment.

"I'll need you to go back to the O'Malleys."

Rearing back, I say, "Are you kidding me?"

"No." Lorcan grimaces.

"Why?"

"Finn controls the finances. If things go the way I think they will, I'll have no money. I'll be dead in the water."

"He doesn't know you're going to work with the O'Malleys."

"Nope. Would ruin the element of surprise."

"Derry O'Malley is such a prick."

Lorcan chuckles. "We're all pricks." His hazel gaze meets mine. "And don't say he's a bigger prick than me. I'll be offended."

"No one's bigger than you." I bat my lashes.

Laughter rumbles through his chest, and parts of my body warm in response. "I like the sound of that," he says. "I may need to get it recorded so I can play it back whenever I'm having a bad day."

"You'd be playing it an awful lot," Finn says from the doorway of the kitchen.

Startled, I glance up; my bubble with Lorcan popped. I almost forgot Finn could be around somewhere, lurking.

Wandering into the kitchen, he takes a beer out of the fridge and twists off the cap. He tosses it in the garbage and eyes our bowls.

"Irish stew. How quaint." He gulps his beer and stares at Lorcan. "Where'd you go today?"

"Out."

"So did I." Finn gestures to me. "Kim and I had a drink together."

"Shame you didn't feed her." Lorcan takes another spoonful of stew and raises it to his lips. "Would have saved me an inconvenience later."

I stir my stew while I listen to them spar, not focused on either of them. Nothing would have saved him the inconvenience. The reaction I had to seeing Chad's photo surprised me. The memory swirls in my stomach and bubbles in my throat.

Rising, Lorcan takes his bowl to the sink. Over his shoulder, he says, "Come find me later, yeah?"

"Yeah." My voice isn't much louder than a whisper.

Finn drinks his beer in silence, leaning against the counter. "What sights did my little brother show you this afternoon?"

Looking up from my stew, I say, "The Cage."

His pale eyes sharpen, and his jaw hardens. "The O'Malleys."

# Chapter Twelve

Finn pushes away from the counter and comes to lean across the island. "What the hell is my *dearthāir beag* doing taking *you* to the O'Malleys?"

I bristle. "You have a problem with me going to The Cage?"

"I have a problem with anyone associating with the O'Malleys."

"Except you used to fight for them."

"Means to an end at the time."

"What's that supposed to mean?"

"Means I had an agenda. Didn't work out quite how I wanted."

"Ah," I say, nodding. "Much clearer."

Finn chuckles, and his forearms rest on the granite island. "Please tell me my *dearthāir beag* isn't thinking about climbing into bed with Derry."

"Don't know. I wasn't feeling well." I raise my spoon. "Apparently, the human body needs food to sustain itself."

He drinks his beer in silence for a few moments while I finish my stew. His expression is impossible to read.

"How does The Cage work?" I scrape the last mouthfuls of the stew out of the bowl. My brother's name echoes through my brain. The picture on the wall of Chad, frozen in time, won't fall back into the recesses of my mind.

"Same as any of those underground things. Winning equals money and status. Losing equals no money and most likely death."

"Do all the deaths happen in the ring?"

Finn's sharp gaze tries to catch mine. "Lots of questions. Why do you ask?"

*Because my half-brother was gunned down in front of me. Because my family was never the same. Because I suspect the O'Malleys did it.*

"When we were there, the cleanup crew was dragging a guy out of the cage. He seemed like he was in rough shape."

"I'm sure all kinds of things happen. I was never on that end of a battle." He finishes his beer and opens the fridge for another one. "Drink?"

I shake my head. Pressing for more answers will cross the line from curious to intrusive. Lorcan and Finn can't realize what I'm up to on two fronts—my brother's killer and the FBI.

"You only drink whiskey."

"Everyone has their vice," I say.

"Hmm. Too true."

"What's yours?"

Finn slants his beer in my direction, a sly smile slipping onto his face. "You think I'm going to tell you that?"

"Never know." I take my bowl to the sink with my spoon.

He's so close to me his breath stirs the tendrils of my hair that have slipped from my ponytail. "Tell Lorcan if he gets into bed with the O'Malleys, he's going to need that arms deal. The truce we have right now won't last."

His paleness is even more evident when we're this close. He must be only a step or two from an albino. The Casper nickname is a kick in the teeth for a man like him. The tangy aroma of beer tickles my nose.

"What's your problem with Lorcan? You're brothers."

Finn looks away to take a pull of his drink. "Half-brothers."

"That matters?" Chad meant the world to me as a kid. I would have followed him anywhere, done anything to get more time with him.

"It does when your father had your mother killed to make way for his mistress and their bastard child."

My sharp intake of breath is loud in the quiet kitchen. "Finn." My gaze flies to meet his. That wasn't in the file. Someone needs to be fired.

"That's the first I've heard you say my name." His lips twist into an almost-smile.

"I'm sorry about your mother."

"It was a long time ago." He downs the rest of his beer.

"You're still punishing Lorcan for it."

Finn's icy focus locks onto me. "Careful, Kimmy. Careful."

I clench my jaw, fingers itching to shoot something, punch something. Do something. In a fit of temper, I push away from the counter. Finn grabs my elbow, leaning close.

Freezing, I say, "I told you—"

"I know." His voice is quiet. "You need to hear this. I entertained your questions tonight. You ask the wrong person the wrong question at the wrong time, and you're a dead woman. Especially with the O'Malleys."

With each word, his breath brushes against my ear. I suppress a shiver. "I'm aware of their reputation."

"You don't know shit, Kimmy." He lets go of my elbow. "Any deals made with them aren't worth the paper they're printed on. Lorcan doesn't need their money. Whatever he wants, he only has to ask me. Tell Lorcan he's a stubborn fool."

I face him. "Yeah, 'cause that'll go over well."

He gives me a steady stare. "I have no doubt you can be persuasive."

"He's not interested in my persuasion."

"Every man is interested—it's just the length of time he's interested that varies."

Part of me wants to slide up to him, rub against him, and see how long I can hold his interest. There's a hum building between us that I recognize. How far am I willing to take this to get the information I want? To maintain the peace?

"I'll keep that in mind," I murmur, one side of my mouth lifting. At the doorway of the kitchen, I pause and glance back at Finn. "Why don't you have an accent? Lorcan's got several."

Finn's smile is like the sun rising, inching across his face. "Lorcan wants to fit in. I have no desire to do that." He puts his empty bottle in the sink. "I didn't spend as much time in Ireland. My time was cut short."

Everything in me wants to stay and ask more questions. If Antonio is right about Finn, and I have to assume he is, I need to keep my insatiable curiosity in check.

Build the relationships. Tear the organization to the ground.

Lorcan's office is empty, and so is the gym. The only other place he is likely to be is in his room. My hand hovers over the buzzer. There are lines I don't cross. Living here, with them, is making me question where the lines lay. That can't happen.

"Ring the buzzer," Lorcan's amused voice comes out of the box on the wall.

My nerves of steel serve me well when I don't even startle. Searching the doorframe, I spot a tiny camera perched in the corner.

"I see you took my advice. That was fast," I say.

The door clicks unlocked, and I open it. His room is more like a hotel suite than a typical bedroom. There's a kitchenette, a sitting area, a king bed, and a few closed doors are probably closets and a bathroom. Unlike the rest of the house in darker shades, this room is in a soft gray with white accents.

"I liked your camera idea. When I see something I like, I take it." Lorcan swaggers over with two drinks. He passes me one. "You feeling any better?"

"Much better. Thanks. It was stupid of me not to eat today." Looking around, I realize there are no windows in his room. "This room cannot meet fire code."

Lorcan laughs and lifts his whiskey. "I don't play by the rules." He smirks at me before flicking a switch. Walls fall away behind his bed, and it's a vast expanse of glass between his room and the backyard.

"Impressive." I swirl my drink before taking a mouthful.

"And yet, you don't seem impressed."

I wander around the room, peering at photos of him with his mother, a few with his father, one of him with Finn. Physically, he's a lot like his dad. I suppose it means Finn favors his mother.

"What did my brother have to say after I left?"

"I told him we went to The Cage."

Lorcan snorts. "You're a terrible secret-keeper."

"I feed him info. He believes we're buddies. That's what you want, right? For me to get close."

A crease appears in Lorcan's forehead, and he swallows his drink. "I want to know who killed my father."

I understand that desire. Since seeing Chad's photo earlier, the urge to find the person who killed him is almost consuming. If there's a choice between this mission and finding Chad's killer, I'm not sure what I'll choose. "Why do you think it was Finn?"

"I guess if I want you to unravel this, I need to tell you something."

"It would help. I don't have to ask pointless questions if I already know everything you know."

"The day he died, the house was empty. That never happens. There's always staff or guards—someone. Finn inherited everything. Almost everything. This place is mine, but the rest is his."

"Unless your father was going to change his will, Finn would have inherited it no matter what, right? There'd be no need to kill him. Did they get along?"

"No. Not for years. The trouble between them began when our father caught wind Finn was fighting for Derry's dad. Before that, they seemed fine most of the time. Never overly close. My mum was the main parent. Father was too busy running his empire, killing people... not getting killed."

"When did you and Finn stop getting along?"

Lorcan's brow creases. "Hard to pinpoint." He throws back his drink and crosses the room to pour himself a second.

Lorcan must not be aware Finn thinks their father had his mother killed. Why would he tell me if Lorcan doesn't know? What game is Finn playing? "You two never got along?"

Lorcan takes a seat in an armchair and gestures for me to do the same. I wander to a chair and drop into it. A sigh escapes me, and I put my elbows on my knees.

Lost in thought, it takes him a few minutes to answer me. "We got along okay," he says, his voice soft. "Till my mum was dying. I was sitting beside her, her breathing labored. Only fifteen. A kid. So hard to watch someone you love die like that. Worse than anything, I wager." His voice is flat despite the painful subject. "Two people I worshipped the most speaking for the last time. And what does he say? He leans over her and says he wished she'd died instead of his own mother."

"Oh," I breathe out. I'm not sure I could imagine Chad ever saying something similar to my father.

Lorcan grimaces. "As you can imagine, our relationship started to sour after that. Twenty years later, here we are." He spreads out his arms. "Living in the same house but having almost nothing to do with each other."

"You weren't here when your father was killed?" I have the answer, or at least I think I do.

"In Ireland. Father was trying to get some deals going there."

"So why do you think it wasn't the O'Malleys?"

"Nothing to gain. Nothin-a-toll." Lorcan's voice has the lilting quality I've come to associate with his authentic self. There's a hint of an Irish accent, a little bit of a Boston one underneath. "Derry's a braggart. He wouldn't be able to keep it to himself, consequences be damned."

"You still want me to go there tomorrow?" I set my drink on the table beside me, reclining into my chair.

"No." Lorcan shakes his head.

But I want to go back. Chad's there. The truth is there, somewhere.

"We'll give it a few days."

"Then I'll go back."

Lorcan grins. "Yes. Definitely you. It'll piss him off." The grin fades. "Not alone, though. Never alone. Understood?"

"You don't trust me?"

"Trust is earned." He sweeps my glass off the table. "Still, it's not you. It's him. If he thought he could get the best of you, he'd do it in an instant."

"Kill me?"

"Among other things." The glasses clink as he drops them into his dishwasher.

I push my hands into the pockets of my jacket. "We're done?"

Lorcan nods and then meets me as I head to the door. He starts to key in the code to unlock it, and his eyes connect with mine. "Never alone. I'm serious."

"You know." I lean against the wall. "Despite what happened today with the not eating, I can take care of myself."

His hazel eyes soften, and he comes closer. "I like that you're tough, think you can handle anything. They're good qualities—things I value. But when you work for me, when you represent me, an attack on you is an attack on me. I don't want either of us in that position. He's a predator. Don't act like the prey. Be the pack leader, not the lone wolf."

My body yearns to wrap myself around him. The sincerity in his eyes, the lilting voice, the confidence, the power, the sense of family implied in his words—it's intoxicating. A lethal cocktail.

His fingertips graze my cheek as he moves a few stray hairs from my ponytail out of my face. "Understood?"

My gaze is locked with his. "Yes."

The door clicks open beside us, breaking the spell, bringing me back to myself. I could sleep with him. It wouldn't be the first time I found a mark attractive. These other things that keep bubbling to the surface need to be pushed under so deep I never feel the hint of wetness again.

"Good night." I slip out the door, head lowered, then stride to my own wing.

As soon as I round the corner to my set of rooms, I slow. Against my bedroom door is Finn, scrolling through his phone.

When I approach, he glances up. "Ah, there you are. I need you tomorrow."

I stop walking, keeping some distance between us. "What? Why?"

"You'll see. I'll clear it with Lorcan. Shouldn't be a problem though. I'm the one paying for you to be here."

Since Lorcan told me Finn controls the majority of the purse strings, his statement seems accurate. I'm not sure I want to go anywhere with Finn. "What if I don't want to?"

"Then quit." He kicks one foot forward to pop his back off the wall. He strolls toward me. "Because as long as you're living under this roof and taking a paycheck from our joint account, you're as much mine as his."

"I'm not quitting." I meet Finn in the middle of the hallway. "But I want to get something else clear. I'm not a possession. You don't own me. Lorcan hired me. If he asks me to go with you tomorrow, then I will. I don't answer to you."

Finn's lips twist, and he taps my nose. "You will, Kimmy. You will." Stepping around me, he wanders away, whistling a tune I've heard before. With a frown, I punch in the code to my room, my mind trying to grasp the song.

In bed, hours later, it still remains out of reach.

# Chapter Thirteen

The brisk knock on my bedroom door startles me awake. Instinctively, my hand grazes the handle of my gun secured under the bed frame.

"We roll out in fifteen," Antonio says through the door.

"Fifteen?" I ease my shoulders down, rubbing my face. Throwing the covers to the side, I check the clock. Somehow, I managed to sleep until ten in the morning. Of course, my brain didn't switch off until almost three.

"That's what you got left for your beauty routine. When Finn says wheels up, we leave whether you're in the car or not."

"Got it." I grab the gun I keep latched to the underside of the bed and put it on the nightstand. I rush into the bathroom. I brush my teeth with one hand while I comb my hair with the other. I strip off my pajamas and throw on another black outfit. *Screw you, Antonio.*

An alarm would have been helpful. Why didn't I set one? At least I showered last night.

Grabbing my gun, I tuck it into its spot inside my coat. I double-check each of my other guns for ammunition and ease of use before leaving my room. The hallway is empty, and I stride toward Lorcan's office.

Once again, I pause at the door, debating whether I should ask if he spoke to Finn. To take them down, I'll need information. To prevent the war between the brothers, I need them both to connect with and trust me.

I'm about to leave when the latch clicks unlocked. Glancing up, I spot another tiny camera above the doorway. With a huff, I open the door.

Lorcan looks up from the pile of papers on his desk. "You're right. This camera thing is quite handy."

I shake my head and roll my eyes. "Are you really loaning me out to Finn today?"

"Of course. I gave him a hard time about it. I was never gonna say no, was I?" Lorcan drops his pen and rocks back in his chair. "You've got a problem with that?"

I stare at him for a minute. "I gotta go." I rotate on my heel.

He is around the desk and in front of me before I reach the door. "You're mad. Why are you mad?"

"Your brother is a dick."

"I'm paying you to get close. The closer you are, the more information he'll reveal. I need to know." His voice dips low, racing along my spine, leaving goose bumps in its wake. My body warms at his proximity, the heat radiating off his body.

"I get it." I can't look at him. For a reason I don't want to examine, this arrangement bothers me, and it shouldn't. With my back to him, I grab the door handle.

"You're armed?" He takes the door from me as I open it.

"Yeah." My fingertips graze one of the guns attached to my leg. "Do you know where we're going?"

"No." His voice is tight. "He wouldn't say." He examines me, his gaze sweeping over my face. "When you get back, come see me."

"Got it."

"Kim," Lorcan calls. "Be safe. Be smart."

"I'm part of the pack today," I call over my shoulder. His chuckle echoes behind me.

When I get to the front entrance, Finn and five men are halfway out the door. I jog to catch them before the door shuts. He doesn't acknowledge my presence as we get into the car. He has a take-out container clutched in one of his hands. My stomach rumbles. How did I forget to eat again?

Once we're settled in the back, he passes the container.

"What's this?" I ask.

"That's your breakfast."

Easing the top off, the smell of eggs hits me. It's possible my stomach will reach out and grab the food before it hits my lips. There's an omelet, a set of cutlery, and a smoothie inside. "Oh." I glance at Finn who is gazing out the window. "You made this?"

"No. Someone else cooked me breakfast this morning. I asked her to make extra for you." He glances at me before focusing his attention out the window. "She's not much of a cook, I'm afraid. Her talents lie elsewhere." He sighs and then stares at me. "Since I'm sure you didn't get a chance to eat, it's probably slightly better than nothing."

His speech strikes me as funny. The idea of him eating a breakfast his one-night stand cooked him that tasted terrible is amusing. With the cutlery, I slice into the omelet and slip it into my mouth. "It's not bad. Just a bit bland."

"Sadly, that also describes her."

I choke and have to cover my mouth for a few minutes while I get myself under control. He's serious, and I can't decide if he's repulsive or humorous.

"Sometimes ready and willing is the best I can do on short notice." He slouches deeper into his seat.

"Poor woman." I unscrew the cap to the smoothie. Gulping back a mouthful, I catch Finn's grimace out of the corner of my eye.

"Poor woman? Poor me, you mean."

"That's not what I mean." I take another bite of the omelet. "Am I allowed to ask where we're going?"

"You can ask." He takes one of the berries beside my omelet.

"I think I just did." I polish off the final piece. It might have been bland, but it certainly did the trick. At least I won't be in danger of falling over today.

"Chinatown."

There's an up-and-coming Asian organization in Chinatown. The file didn't have them connected, but maybe this is something new. Taking a calculated risk, I play a card. "The Zhangs."

He raises his eyebrows. "Lorcan knows more than I thought."

I close the takeout container and place it at my feet. After swallowing the last of my drink, I say, "He doesn't know much." *Or anything.* "Why am I here?"

"Because I wanted you here."

The car glides up to the entrance of a strip club before I can ask any more questions. Unlike Lorcan, who is the first out of a vehicle, Finn waits for one of the guards to open his door, and then he nods at me to do the same.

A few of the guys go ahead of me, and Finn and a few others trail behind us. It's less organized than Lorcan, but being in the middle of the pack is safer than leading the charge.

Once we enter the club, it takes a few minutes for my eyes to adjust. The lighting is dim and, like in Vegas, there's not a clock anywhere. Losing time, as well as the money in the wallet, is the point of a place like this. Alcohol and sex waft toward me. The women on stage are moving to the music as though they're in quicksand, sinking further under. The walls and furniture are in shades of red, whereas the stage is bright white. The poles are dull, in need of a cleaning. While we wander through the club, the women are full of blank-eyed, dazed stares. Places like this set my teeth on edge. Outwardly, I can't afford to show my disgust. It's business, that's all.

Money. Power.

Nothing else matters.

We're led to the back by a security guard. In a room, before the office, is a gang of security guards who appear to be pressuring a drunk guy to go to his bank machine and clear it out. They're holding his wallet and a bunch of photos as ransom.

*Tell your wife what you did, buddy. One way or another she'll find out you're not a good man.*

When we get to the office, a slight Asian man and his willowy wife come out. She's draped across him like a shawl. People like her also cause my blood to boil. The women working here are selling themselves and not in the 'I'm putting myself through college' way but more of the 'this is my life, watch me crumble' kind of way. How do you see someone do that to themselves and not try to help? Instead, this guy's wife smooths over problems, escalates deception, and creates a false sense of understanding or trust. I've seen her too many times.

"Finn!" The man holds out his hand. "I'm so happy you came."

"Shen. Interested to see what you're offering," Finn says, his tone mild. "So far, it doesn't seem to be much."

Shen's smile falters, but he waves us into the office with enthusiasm anyway. "Drinks!"

We sit in a strained silence while we wait for the drinks to arrive. He didn't ask what we like, so I can only imagine what we're going to be obligated to consume. A waitress teeters back into the room carrying shot glasses and a bottle of *báijiǔ*. I'm not much of a vodka drinker, and depending on what they've used to make it, this won't be far off. Holding back a sigh, I take the shot.

Finn takes his shot and suspends it between his fingers. "Let's get this done, Shen. How much are you after?"

Shen reclines in his chair, any trace of nerves gone with the shot he took. Liquid courage is a real thing for him. "Five hundred thousand."

He doesn't bat an eye. "I give you that, and you give me what?"

"Any woman you want. Any time. A fifty percent cut in this establishment."

That deal would be good for me and my case against Finn and Lorcan. That sounds like prostitution, and it's clear the money trail isn't going to add up. Taxes might be another angle to work around this place. My brain keeps ticking along with other ways this deal might benefit me when Finn rises.

"I'll think about it."

Shen stands as well, pressing his fingers into his desk. "If not you, we'll go to the O'Malleys. They like making money."

Finn chuckles and narrows his eyes at Shen. "Don't threaten me, or I'll move my people in here and take over. I got the manpower to do that. You know it. You might want five hundred thousand, but you're not going to get it. I'll give you two fifty for a seventy percent stake."

Shen gasps and appears offended. "You're no friend of mine. I thought you were going to think about it."

"I did," Finn says. "I thought you were offering a shitty deal. Mine's better."

"Only for you."

"That's right."

"I'm not that desperate."

"You will be." Finn comes across the desk, getting into Shen's face. "Once the pressure starts, when the vise tightens, you'll think back to today and wish you'd taken my deal."

"I got other things going on." Shen's cheeks are full of color. "I don't need you."

"Give it a few days. You might be surprised."

Finn drops a card onto Shen's desk. It's for a heating and plumbing business, another one of their enterprises. They charge excessive interest rates to people who can't get credit elsewhere. When they can't pay, they lean on them in any way they can to squeeze money out of them. Blood from a stone.

As we're leaving, my stomach drops at what a waste of time this meeting turned out to be. I can't help any of these women; I can't act like I want to help them. Indifference. That's all I've got. At the light touch on my elbow, annoyance zings through me because Finn keeps touching me when I've made it clear I don't like it.

"Over there." He jerks his head in the direction of the bar. "Isn't that the guy who was tending bar in Newport?"

These are the kinds of moments I hate. The rush through my body isn't adrenaline or excitement but fear. Raw fear. Malik is tying a garbage bag by the side door of the club. He's not focused in our direction, and I don't know if it's because he grasps the seriousness of what might happen or he doesn't realize I'm here. My heart kicks in my chest.

# Chapter Fourteen

Telling him I don't recognize Malik makes me unobservant. Of course, saying yes brings other complications.

"Yeah." Feigning ignorance, I cock my head. "Yeah, I think you're right."

"Coincidence pisses me off. Go chat him up in the alley. I wanna know why he's here and not in Newport." As we step out into the bright sunlight, Finn scans the busy street. "Take Antonio with you."

"I can shakedown one bartender," I scoff.

He shoots me an annoyed look. "It's not a shakedown. I want information, not money."

Acting dumb is my least favorite stalling tactic. Sometimes it's the only option I have. "I know that." My words are clipped. "I can handle this. You want to watch? Be my guest. You brought me here. You might as well use me."

With his hands in his pockets, Finn observes the passing cars, his expression difficult to read. The other men shift their feet behind us, some of them lighting cigarettes. "You got five minutes to get me an explanation I can live with. Then I'm sending Antonio, and he'll get answers another way."

Finn and the rest of the men get into the waiting vehicles while I head down the narrow alley. I'm glad he's not watching, but I can't assume he won't show up behind me.

Malik is tossing another garbage bag into the bin when he glances in my direction. His attention flicks from me to behind me. He inclines his head in acknowledgement, his eyes saying things I understand because I know him so well.

"Can I help you?" he calls out.

"We met yesterday in Newport. You were the bartender at the Angry Irishman." The name made me smile the other day. Now, it doesn't seem quite so funny.

"Oh, yeah. My last day. Got a better offer here."

I stop not far from him, looking him over. The red shirt he's wearing highlights the richness of his dark skin. There are things I wish I could say, would have said yesterday if I'd known I might not get a chance. Instead, we are only feet apart, acting like strangers, talking in code.

The clock in my head ticks. Watching Antonio beat Malik isn't on my agenda for the day.

"Weird coincidence seeing you here."

"My girlfriend, Clarissa, got me in here—she knows Shen."

"Right." I file that tidbit away for Finn.

Malik peers beyond me before refocusing on me. When he speaks, his voice is even and casual, as though we're strangers chatting about the weather. "Reassignment. Dai Qing is in. I'm out as your contact. I'm here if you need me. It'll be tricky. But I would help. Backstory will cover me and Clarissa."

I nod, pushing my hands deeper into the pockets of my coat. "Whipped by a woman."

His dark eyes hold my gaze for an extra beat. "It was bound to happen."

"Something came up the other day. I have questions for you." I want to step closer, but I don't dare.

"Dai Qing." He shakes his head. "Not me."

"You. I trust you."

"It's a bad idea. I'm a last resort. I'm in with the Zhangs now. Contact is dangerous."

I hate we're having this conversation here, that our words are clipped, thoughts not quite complete. The clock ticks.

My watch beeps. I set it for three minutes. Finn might not be a down-to-the-minute guy, but I can't risk Malik to find out. "I gotta go."

"You okay?"

"I didn't read the note."

He grimaces. "I tried to tell you."

"I know. It is what it is."

Opening the side door, he holds my attention for an extra beat before saying, "Yeah, so Clarissa gets kinda crazy when I talk to other girls."

"I can see why," I purr and wink.

A woman pops her head out the door. Her long, curly brown hair is all I see. "Murray, Jesus. You're going to get fired on your first day." With her hand on his collar, she yanks him in the door. That must be Clarissa, his contact, his fake girlfriend.

I stride back to the cars and slide onto the leather seat beside Finn. He looks at me, eyebrows raised.

"He's Murray. Last day in Newport was yesterday. His girlfriend Clarissa got him in with Shen. Shitty tips in Newport and a jealous, possessive girlfriend."

"Last names?"

I shake my head. "Couldn't slip it in during the five minutes."

"I've worked with less." He focuses out the window. "We'll see what a bit of digging turns up."

"Do you want me to do that?"

He chuckles. "No. I have people who specialize in getting information."

My shoulders are tight with tension, and I tuck my hands under my legs, worry for Malik eating at my insides. If Finn didn't get anything true or suspicious on me, I have to believe Malik's backstory will hold. Hopefully, I'm insulated enough that even if they end up suspecting him, they won't start to question me.

The car glides through the streets, but it doesn't seem like we're headed back to the house. Instead of asking, I keep quiet. Soon, I recognize other things. When the car comes to a stop outside The Cage, my mouth goes dry.

"I hear this didn't go well yesterday." He glances at me with a wry smile.

"I wouldn't say—"

"You should." Finn cuts me off, his eyes like steel. "Don't lie to me. It's not worth lying to me. 'Cause I'm a digger." His jaw clenches. "I don't give up. When something smells rotten, I peel away the rot layer by layer. Once I have the truth, those who lied to me end up in pine boxes. You got me?"

I raise my chin, meeting his stare. "I got you."

"Mercy'll get you killed. Better someone else dead than me—woman, man, kid—don't matter to me."

"Consider me warned." My voice is even. My heart hammers against my breastbone, threatening to jump out and run away. It's not the first time my life has been threatened, not even close. It's one of the things I can't get used to, can't think of as a routine part of the job, even if it is.

"I'll give it to you, Kimmy. I've had bigger, tougher men piss themselves at that speech." Finn nods at me before knocking on his window. The door opens, and Antonio is on the other side with a few guys.

We climb out and approach the door, leaving the cars parked outside. Finn has Antonio knock and slip a paper through the open mail slot. When the door swings back, it's packed inside again. Does the fight club run all the time? Are there that many people interested in betting, fighting, and dying?

Derry ambles out of the crowd, but he doesn't have the same smarmy smile and attitude as he had yesterday. He's wary, unsure. More of Derry's men crowd around him, surrounding him, protecting him.

"Finn." His voice is strained. "What are you doing here?"

"You want to do this out in the open?" Finn throws his arms wide.

"No, no. Course not. Come back to the office." Derry glances over his shoulder at some guys, and they check their weapons.

It would make me laugh if he hadn't given me so much shit yesterday for touching my own gun. The same rules don't apply when Finn's here.

Leading the way back to his office, Derry keeps himself well-insulated with men. Pausing at his door, he surveys the crowd in the hall. "You and one other designate. No one else."

"Come on, now, Derry. You don't trust me?"

Silence greets us as Derry stares at him, uneasy.

"Kimmy." Finn checks for me in the crowd. "Come in with me. I know how much Derry loves looking at a pretty woman."

"Women are only useful when they're on their knees or bent over my desk." Derry smirks as his focus travels along my body.

Finn's eyes narrow. "It's my understanding my brother warned you about speaking like that to her." He cocks his head to the side, a puzzled expression on his face that I'm sure is fake. "Are you disrespecting my brother?"

Derry swallows. "No. No." He enters the room and sits behind his desk. "Come in, Finn." After a brief hesitation, Derry says, "Have a seat, Kim."

I lower into the chair beside Finn, but the air is so tense in the room, I can't relax. The door clicks closed behind us. Derry has five men around the back of him. This setup is very different from yesterday with Lorcan. Is it because Finn thinks Derry killed his father? Or is it something else?

"Lorcan was here yesterday." Finn slides a knife and a block of wood out of his jacket pocket.

Derry eyes Finn warily, and then his attention flicks to me, accusing. "He was."

Finn whittles away at the piece of wood, letting the chips fall to the ground as he takes his time continuing the conversation. "Your offer was shit."

Swallowing, Derry sits up straighter and puts his forearms on the desk. "What do you care? He's trying to get funds to go to war with you."

"We're not going to war." Finn glances up. "If that's not happening, then your shitty offer to him was actually a shitty offer to me." He digs into the wood with the knife. Something is starting to take shape, but I can't quite figure out what it is. "How do you think that makes me feel, Derry? To know you were fucking me over through my brother?"

A thin sheen of sweat appears across Derry's forehead. "I didn't know."

Finn blows on his carving, and I realize what he's doing. My lips quirk up, and I focus on the boxing photograph above Derry's shoulder to avoid an outright smile.

"Until bullets start flying in the streets, assume that when you screw over my brother, you're screwing over me. You got me, guy?"

It's the first hint of an accent I've heard from Finn. His voice is dipped low, menacing.

Derry's hand inches toward the edge of his desk.

"Your hand goes anywhere near your gun, and I'll blow your head off." Finn looks up at him, their gazes connecting.

Holding up his hands, Derry tilts back from the desk. The O'Malleys are too afraid of Finn to have killed anyone in the Donaghey family. It's so clear to me. I can't understand why he would even try to blame them.

Finn places the tombstone with the word *O'Malley* carved into it. "You'll notice I didn't put your name on it, Derry." His flinty blue eyes pierce the men in the room. "'Cause when I come for you, it ain't only you. It's your whole family—guilty, innocent, doesn't matter to me."

Shoving back his seat, Derry says, "I know how you work."

"Then I shouldn't have needed to come remind you."

"I thought I was dealing with Lorcan."

Finn's jaw tightens. "We're family, me and Lorcan. Until one of us is dead, we're a package deal."

"Not sure Lorcan got that notice."

Finn's lips twist. "I'm working on it. You keep your own house in order and stay outta mine." Tucking his knife back in his pocket, he rotates the tombstone on the desk and smirks. "Now, write up a contract that's good to us, and we got a deal."

Derry's mouth flaps like a fish suffocating. "I—I—it was a deal for Lorcan."

"Now it's a deal for me and Lorcan. I'll leave my Kimmy here to bring the paperwork back to the house. I got some other business to take care of around town."

Inside, my heart tap dances. Thrusting my hands into my pockets, I brush them against the lining to get rid of the sheen of sweat that pops up. Lorcan warned me not to stay here alone. Suggesting I need support makes me appear weak to both Finn, who may not care, and to Derry who'll circle me like a shark afterward.

The distaste on Derry's face says it all. He smacks his lips together. "I'll see what I can come up with. Your proxy can wait in the hall."

"That's a big word for you. You going back to school? Finally gonna graduate high school?"

Derry's hands clench at his sides. "I know what a fucking proxy is."

"Good. Then you'll know anything happens to her, it's like it happened to me. You got me, guy? You lay a hand on her—anywhere on her—you might as well be doing it to me."

With a curt nod, Derry moves to the door.

I exit first with Finn on my heels. He extends his hand to Derry. "Nice doing business with you."

Derry doesn't take his hand.

In the hall, Finn's icy stare connects with mine for a moment. "I'll see you back at the house. He lays so much as a fingertip of one of his fat, filthy fingers on you, you tell me. Ian will have the car waiting outside for you when you're done."

"Understood." I lean against the wall where the memorial photos end.

As Finn and the other guys wander the wide, well-lit hall, Derry closes the door to his office. I'm left in the hallway, alone.

# Chapter Fifteen

Like a magnet, I'm pulled down the row of photos to my brother's picture. Without anyone else around, I can let myself study him, remember him. Although this version of him isn't the one I knew. To me, he was my older brother, my mother's other child. Twelve years my senior, he looked out for me, took me to the movies, drove me to Tae Kwon Do, made silly jokes, teased me. This tough guy on the wall is a mystery.

"You like the look of that one?" Derry's voice startles me.

Inside, I curse myself. Getting caught up in my own thoughts here is a bad idea.

"Do they all die in the ring?" I glance at him, trying to pretend his presence isn't unnerving.

"Nah." His lecherous grin fades. "That one was shot down like a dog in the street."

"By you?" I raise my eyebrows. My mind races, straining for the truth.

"Not even. Wicked Wickie was our gravy, sweetheart. We woulda gone to war over his loss if we'd ever found out who did it. He was a hell of a fighter."

His loss is so much greater than a fighter. I keep my face blank. My hands inside my pockets are sticky, liquid oozing between my fingers. "Shame."

"Hell of a shame." He holds out an envelope. "I don't know what game you're playing, sweetheart. You're gonna get caught in the cross-fire."

I smirk. "I don't have a problem with danger."

Crossing his arms, he shakes his head. "I got no use for women in this business."

"Clearly," I say with a chuckle.

"I don't know, something about you seems kinda familiar. So I'm gonna give you some advice. Get outta that house. They'll tug you between them until they rip you apart."

"I don't break easily." I tap the envelope in my palm.

He scoffs. "Gives them more incentive to try harder. They ain't good people."

Coming from him, it's not much of a caution. Lorcan inferred Derry would have no trouble raping or killing me. Finn's warning before he left the building turned those ideas to concrete. Derry's a busybody who wants to feel more important in a situation that's out of his control.

"I'll take that into account."

"You should." Derry rests a hand on the wall and leans against it.

On another man, it might be an attractive pose. On him, it makes his stomach even more prominent. Given my height, his bald patches are obvious. A faint whiff of body odor hits my nose, and I school my features. It's not the pleasant scent that comes off men when they've been working but rather what happens when a man is sweating out his fear.

"I'd hate to think of a pretty little thing like you getting hurt."

The two things I wish I could do—make a puking gesture or roll my eyes—are out. Instead, I'm left with every woman's response when faced with a man who, for better or worse, wields more power. A saccharine smile is pasted to my lips. "Thanks, Derry. That's so sweet of you. I should get going, though. Ian is waiting in the car." I wag the envelope. "I've got what we came for."

"You might want to serve it with an Irish Car Bomb, soften him up."

"He's not going to like it?"

"Who knows with Finn. He works angles nobody else can see."

That tip is far more useful than his warning about the two brothers using me. Knowing Finn is impossible to figure out even for people who have known him longer, is a comfort. It's also scary. My life depends on me reading people to protect myself from any threat.

"See you around, Derry." I make a beeline for the front door.

"Hopefully not too soon. Take my advice."

I give him a wave above my head. Today, I'm not worried he's going to shoot me. Even though Finn isn't here, it's clear who carries the bigger gun.

When I climb into the passenger seat, Ian glances at the envelope. "We're good?" He puts the car into drive.

"Hope so."

We ride in silence, and I'm grateful for it. Derry's admission about my brother's fighting skills is surprising but also not that much. Chad always had pocket money and often slipped some to our parents. Chad's father was a deadbeat who never helped our mom. It was only when she met my father, Chad said things turned around for them. I met Chad's father a handful of times. He was never around. Stories about life before me and my dad was Chad's favorite thing to do with me over a burger and fries, sitting in a parking lot after he picked me up from one event or another.

Then it got blown to hell.

Glancing down at my hands, I shake my head a little. I can't afford to get lost in memories. Vengeance, yes. But not memories. Thinking about the disintegration of my family only leads to madness. My mother is the proof.

"You want me to deliver that?" Ian eyes the envelope as we cruise through the gates of the property.

"No." First, I need to slip away somewhere private, take photos of the contract, then send them off. "I'll take them to Finn after I use the bathroom. The O'Malleys don't clean their toilets."

Ian chuckles as he climbs out of the car. "Not surprising."

As soon as we enter the house, I duck into the two-piece bathroom near the entry. Taking out the contract, I snap photos, email them, and then delete everything off my phone. With a deep breath, I tuck the papers into the envelope and open the door. Finn is entering the house.

"You got it?" He extends his hand.

I pass it over, but he tucks it into his back pocket without checking it.

"He behave himself?"

"Yes." Except for some of his comments, but I realize that isn't what Finn means.

"You gonna tell Lorcan what I did?"

One side of my mouth twitches in amusement. "That's the point, isn't it?"

He chuckles and taps my nose. "You catch on quick. I might have to steal you away from my brother."

I bat at his hand, but I'm too slow. With a chuckle, Finn steps around me and heads for his rooms.

Over his shoulder, he calls, "You're going to have to be quicker if you intend to keep ahead of me."

As soon as he's out of sight, I search for Lorcan, but I can't find him anywhere. Back in my room, I pace. Derry didn't kill Chad. As sleazy as he is, he seemed sincere in that moment. It could have been another fighter, someone jealous of his success, someone who lost a bet or a great deal of money, a rival of the O'Malleys. The possibilities are endless again.

I need something to take my mind off of this. A run. A long one. Clear my head, figure out what the hell is going on in this house, with these brothers, and across the organization. Because I can't, I ache to talk to Malik.

As I'm getting on some running clothes, there's a sharp knock. "Who is it?"

"Your favorite Donaghey brother."

A laugh escapes me as I go to the door to open it. "You realize you don't have much competition, right?"

His hazel eyes are filled with amusement. "Thank God for that." Lorcan smirks at me. "Where are you off to?"

"A run."

"Not alone, I hope."

"Around the property." I make a looping motion with my hand. "I'll stay in the gated portion." Using my finger, I trace a cross over my heart.

"I'll come with you. We can chat about what you got up to today." Lorcan's lips quirk up in a half smile, and his dimple peeps through, charming me.

I suppress a sigh. A few minutes alone, the wind in my hair, darkness surrounding me, is all I wanted. "Sure."

"Walk with me." He gestures toward the hall.

"You're in a good mood."

"Very productive day." His smile is sly as he winks at me. "Thank you for that, by the way."

"You're thanking me?"

Raising his left hand, he waggles it. "While the right hand was out of the house, he couldn't know what the left hand was doing."

"You knew where we were going today?"

"Not necessarily. Probably best we chat outside."

He opens the door to his room and ushers me inside. I sink into a chair, tapping my knees with my fingers as I wait for him to emerge out of the bathroom.

When he does, he's frowning. "I was thinking."

"You don't look happy about that."

He chuckles. "Well, I'm not sure if you'll be annoyed with me. I was going to see if Carys wanted to come for a visit in a few weeks. Starting over somewhere is challenging, and the two of you seemed close."

My heart squeezes in my chest. Words stick in my throat. "That's... very thoughtful."

He shrugs a little. "'Tis nothin."

"Well." I stretch. "It's something to me. It would be good to see her." I'd also be able to find out if the agency managed to get Yssamae maneuvered into position in her organization. I couldn't do that introduction in case the dominoes tipped.

We head out of his bedroom together and wander to the back door, the one that leads to the pool and tennis court. Maybe I should have asked him for a game instead? Pounding a ball across a net might be as good as running, especially if I wasn't able be alone, anyway.

"You're not going to do any of the crazy sprinting, are you?" My training at the bureau was extensive, and we ran a lot, at a senseless pace with the understanding our lives could be on the line. Or someone else's life might depend on us getting somewhere fast. That wasn't what I wanted tonight.

At the edge of the backyard, I survey the vast expanse of lawn. The house is on a property more like a farm than a place in the suburbs. Still, that's exactly what it is. With the exception of a buffer zone, other houses peer into the field. Solar lights illuminate a trail along the fence line. There's a chill in the air, and a light breeze ruffles Lorcan's hair.

"Some sprinting is a must." He puts his hands on his hips. "We're training for real-life situations in this job, not just trying to keep from getting old and fat."

I laugh and admire his physique out of the corner of my eye. There certainly wasn't much fat on him. I grin. "Real life, huh?"

He brushes the stray hairs the wind has tugged from my ponytail. "How was today?"

"Okay," I say. "The Zhangs and then the O'Malleys."

He grimaces and glances away from me. "If you thought someone killed your father, would you do business with them?"

I gape. "That's pretty much what I already asked *you*. The answer, for me, is no. I'd kill them. No hesitation. There wouldn't be enough money in the world." Before me, out in the yard, my father's image rises into view in the darkness, wispy, infirm, dead. Chad's death was gory, real, in my face. My father's death was an accident. Something dumb. Nothing to avenge but stupidity.

"The answer for Finn is also no."

Understanding dawns on me. "You set him up."

"I suspected O'Malley would give me shitty terms, that he'd be an ass to you at some point. I wasn't sure how much I'd have to poke my brother to get him to step in. Not nearly enough."

If Finn thought the O'Malleys killed his father, he wouldn't become involved with them, or he'd seem reluctant to do it. He even warned me Lorcan associating with the O'Malleys was like declaring war. Then he swooped in and stole the deal, but not before sweetening it first.

"You knew."

Lorcan gives me a brisk nod. His whole body is primed with tension. Deep down, he doesn't want Finn to be guilty. "He's all the family I've got left." His voice is quiet in the night.

"Have you talked to him? I mean, actually asked him?"

Lorcan runs a hand through his hair and chuckles. "You don't understand him yet. Asking is as good as saying I think he did it. I do. He won't admit it if I ask. It's not worth the trouble it would cause."

"Then what am I doing here?"

He raises one hand and then the other. "Left hand, right hand. You're the distraction as much as the detective. He might let something slip. If he doesn't, he'll be so focused on trying to get the best of me through you he'll never know what I'm planning."

"Can I know?"

His mouth twists into a half smile. "No."

"Maybe I could help?"

"Finn would smell your lies a mile away. You can't know. Tell him what you like. Plan A and Plan B exist for every move."

The chilly air hangs around us, and I shiver. A strange, companionable silence develops in the darkness.

"Was Derry decent to you today?"

"Enough. I can handle myself."

His gaze roams over my face. The tenderness in the hazel depths unnerves me. "Shall we run?"

"Are you leading?"

"Sure," he says, amused. "I don't mind being chased once in a while by the right person." Lorcan smirks at me before taking off at a steady pace.

I fall into step behind him, letting the pounding of my feet on the trail lull me into oblivion. I was chasing him, and it wasn't only on the path.

# Chapter Sixteen

A few weeks later, I've managed to gather secondary information that might be useful in a conviction, but neither one of them has let me into the conversations they have together. Those seem to happen when I'm sleeping or off on another errand. My Irish isn't getting much of a workout. Otherwise, they dance around each other like two boxers, more preoccupied with defense than landing a direct hit.

I'm cooking myself some lunch when Finn strolls into the kitchen. "I hear we're having company tonight." He grabs a coffee mug out of one of the cupboards next to me.

"Yep," I say. "You got a problem with that?" Without looking at him, I drop more tabasco into the sauce on the stove.

"If I did, I wouldn't be taking it up with you."

"Ah, yes. You'd speak to your *deartháir beag*."

Finn raises his eyebrows as he pours himself a cup of coffee. "Ay, I would."

"It's not nice of you to mock his accent."

"He's my brother. I can do what I want. Just because it gets you all wet to hear it, doesn't mean it isn't a bit of a farce."

"You think he puts it on?"

"Come on, Kimmy. You're not dumb."

The full Irish accent and the complete Bostonian ones are certainly things he puts on like masks or costumes. But Lorcan's natural way of speaking, the lilt, the hint of an accent underneath is authentic.

"Well, I'm glad you think I'm smart." I twist his words. "Your brother has asked me to look into who killed your father. So he must think I'm pretty smart."

Finn stills beside me. "He what?"

"You're not deaf, Finn."

"It was the O'Malleys." He waves a hand.

"The same O'Malleys you're peddling Viagra with?"

He snaps his fingers in mock remembrance. "That does remind me, I need to sign that contract."

"You're not in business with them?"

Finn wrinkles his nose. "I went to the O'Malleys to screw with Lorcan."

"Yeah, I got that part. The deal must be decent?" I wave my wooden spoon around and set it down. When I was taking the photos of the contract, I skimmed it. It didn't seem like terrible terms or payout, all things considered.

"I don't like Derry. I made his family enough money years ago. They're a bunch of sleazy pricks who have no trouble getting into places they don't belong."

"What's that mean?"

"His father helped arrange my mother's death." Finn's icy eyes meet mine.

"That's why you fought for them?" Puzzled, I furrow my brow. Making them money sounds like the opposite of what I'd expect.

"I was trying to get information."

"Did you get it?"

"In a way."

I sigh. "Is that why you think the O'Malleys killed your father?"

"No." He takes the spoon off the counter, dips it into the sauce cooking on the stove, then pops it into his mouth. Finn's gaze connects with mine. "Certainly not bland."

"I like a bit of spice."

"As do I."

I roll my eyes and continue thinking out loud. "If the O'Malleys killed him, why aren't you doing something about it?" I take a new spoon out of the drawer and stir the sauce.

"You like wars, Kimmy?"

My focus flicks to him. "When they're necessary."

"Retribution isn't *always* necessary. When it is, the timing needs to be impeccable. No mistakes. No one left alive."

"That's your plan with the O'Malleys? Take them down?"

"Yes."

"Bullshit."

He laughs, the sound deep and full as it bounces around the kitchen. "I said you were smart."

"Actually, you said I wasn't dumb."

His laugh subsides to a chuckle. "That's not the same thing?"

"Not quite."

For the first time, his face is alight with something like genuine amusement, and my chest warms at the sight.

"What time is Carys arriving?"

"Before dinner." I remove the sauce from the stove and observe Finn, trying to decide. "I have enough for you, if you want."

"Ooh, yes please." He rubs his hands together as I dish out the rice, chicken from the oven then layer my sauce over it.

I pass the plates and then move around the island to a seat while Finn gets the cutlery.

"Where'd you learn to cook?"

"My mother." *A lie*. It was my father. My mother couldn't cook anything. She even burned toast.

He takes the seat beside me and holds his fork poised before his lips, ready to take his first bite. "You're not in touch?"

"No." Even though she isn't dead, the woman she used to be is dead to me, gone. She'll never be recovered.

Finn cuts a piece of his chicken and chews. "I don't remember much about my mother. Lorcan's mum was more like my mother."

"And your dad?"

Picking up his coffee, Finn takes a long drink. "My relationship with my father was complicated."

"Were you surprised he died?"

One side of his mouth quirks up, the opposite side to Lorcan. "I sure as hell hope so. Otherwise," he says, glancing at me, "it'd mean I had something to do with it, wouldn't it?"

When he says that, I look down at my plate, and it takes me a moment to meet his gaze, but when I do, I'm careful to keep my features neutral. "Would it?"

His eyes narrow, and he shoves another piece of chicken in his mouth. "Lorcan actually thinks it was me?"

There is no way I am answering that question. "Should he?"

Finn scoffs. "What did I gain I wouldn't have gained by waiting?"

"I don't know. Maybe the satisfaction of knowing the person responsible for your mother's death was dead?"

"I took care of that a long time ago. My father didn't kill her. He only ordered it."

"That matters?"

"It does when you're talking about family."

"You think it was the O'Malleys?"

Finn shakes his head. "No, I don't. I had to tell Lorcan something, didn't I? We were being attacked on all fronts, and I needed him to get back in the game. At least with someone to hate, he was focused for a while."

"Why not tell him that?"

"He's not going to listen to me. He thinks I did it. I've known for a while—but it's impossible to convince someone you didn't *do* something."

"You have to prove someone else did."

"That's the best way. I haven't had the time or energy to do that. I gotta keep this thing running. With Lorcan off making shitty deals, I have to clean up after him too."

"So," I drag out the word. "Assuming I believe you. Who else could it be?"

"Isn't that your job? I told you it's not me, and I don't think it's the O'Malleys, either. Now—Kimmy—work your magic." Finn waggles his fingers at me like he's doing a spell.

"Not even a list of suspects?"

"Everyone but me and the O'Malleys. There's your list. Ta-da!" He smirks at me. "I thought Derry was going to piss himself when we were in his office."

I laugh at the memory. "The stench of fear was real." Picking up Finn's empty plate and my own, I put them into the sink. "Seriously, though. Some kind of list of people you guys deal with? Anything?"

He crosses his arms. "Yeah, okay. I can get you a list of people we deal with."

My heart makes one loud, triumphant thump in my chest. That list will be gold for my investigation. But it's not going to help me figure out who killed Chad. "Do the O'Malleys deal with the same people you do?"

Finn's eyes narrow. "Why?"

"Curiosity."

"That'll get you killed." He points a finger at me. "Take the list I give you and start asking around. Keep it subtle. Accusing people we associate with of murdering our father is a big deal. It could get you killed and put us under fire."

"I understand that." My heart deflates a touch because he didn't give me a straight answer about the O'Malley connections.

"Today, I want you to go back to Zhang's for me."

My face screws up with distaste. "Why?" That strip club isn't high on my list of priorities. Of course, if Malik is working, I can ask him if the bureau knew anything about Chad or about the O'Malley fight ring. Getting him alone without blowing his cover might be tough, though.

"Zhang says he has a better offer. I'm not interested yet, but I don't want to be completely disrespectful. The Chinese like to save face."

I clutch my chest and lean back in mock shock. "You know something about Chinese culture?"

"Only what I have to know to do business." He comes around the island to stand next to me. "Are you game?"

"Alone?"

"Take Antonio, but he can wait in the car. He's backup."

I give a slow nod. "Okay. Bring the offer back here?"

"Yes." Finn searches my face. "Thank you."

A hint of a smile threatens. "For?"

"Being a good listener. It's rare."

The sincerity in his ice-blue eyes takes me by surprise. "Maybe you're not talking to the right people?"

He chuckles and taps my nose. "Maybe, Kimmy. Maybe." He turns on his heel and wanders out of the kitchen, whistling the tune that's been stuck in my head for weeks. I can't forget it, and yet, I can't quite remember how it got there. Before I can ask, he's gone.

Everything he revealed circles as I scrub the dishes. It seems likely he didn't murder his father. If it wasn't him, who? And why?

Then there's Chad's death. Maybe going to Zhang's will be good. Maybe Malik will have answers.

# Chapter Seventeen

It takes a moment for my eyes to adjust to the dimness of the strip club. The music playing isn't a fast tune; God forbid the girls actually have to dance. Their naked bodies sway on the stage. How many of them realize they're stripping? That there's a leering audience below them?

When I scan the bar, I'm grateful Malik is working. At least something is going my way today. Now, I have to figure out how to get him alone. He's at the end of the bar, serving the lone customer. The rest of the people in the place are camped out in perverts' row.

I'm so focused on Malik I don't notice when the bouncer approaches me. "You here for an interview?"

I give him a wry smile. "Not quite."

He frowns. "I don't get it."

"Finn Donaghey sent me."

"Does Mr. Zhang know you're coming?"

"No idea. Finn said to come here, so I came. You know how it is."

The bouncer gives a curt nod. "Enjoy a drink on the house. I'll track down Mr. Zhang."

This time, my smile is genuine. "Perfect."

Cutting through the tables and chairs, I take a seat at the bar at the opposite end to Malik's other customer. He strolls over to me and stares for a moment, neither of us able to say what we want. "Drink?"

"Whiskey."

"How are you today?"

"Full of questions."

"I'm sure Mr. Zhang will have lots of answers for you."

"Possibly." I lean back in my chair and throw one elbow over the top.

Malik passes the whiskey across. "You need the bathroom?" He raises his voice. "Behind you."

We've worked together so many times in so many situations this is normal and strange in the same breath.

"Thank you." I head for the toilet.

Once I'm inside, I check for cameras. Malik wouldn't have chosen this route if he knew surveillance was in here. Going into the only stall, I jam toilet paper into the toilet until I'm sure it'll clog. Who makes a woman's bathroom with a single stall? I suppose women aren't their clientele of choice. A minute later, I wander back to the bar. The bouncer is waiting.

With a small smile to him, I focus on Malik. "I'm sorry. I have to go to the bathroom, and it seems like the toilet is clogged."

"Oh, sure." Malik angles his head at the bouncer. "Cover for me?"

The big man laughs. "Yeah, I'm not so keen on unclogging a toilet. Stupid dancers keep putting too many tampons down it."

The dancers use that bathroom? God, this place is awful.

Malik comes out from behind the bar and trails behind me to the washroom with a plunger. I flip on the tap to mask our voices. He bends over the toilet, plunger in one hand, and I keep watch by the door, ready to bar it or make it inconvenient for anyone entering.

"Go." His voice is pitched low.

"Did you know Chad fought for the O'Malleys? His picture is on their wall." I match the volume of his voice, conscious of the door behind me. The bouncer didn't seem suspicious. In this business, it isn't possible to be too careful, too prepared.

There's a beat before Malik says, "You think they killed him?"

"Derry says they didn't. I believe him."

"Jesus, Kimi. You asked him?"

"It's not as bad as it seems. It came up in casual conversation."

"With Derry-fucking-O'Malley. You've heard the stories about him."

"Finn and Lorcan warned him to keep his hands off me."

Malik drops the plunger and comes to cup my face. "He catches a whiff of inauthenticity off you and you're dead or worse. You need to be careful around him."

I jerk my chin out of his hands. "I know the score, Malik. Don't patronize me."

"I worry about you."

"Yeah, well, with Dai Qing at my back, I worry about me. How the hell did you end up here?"

"I got an introduction. Zhangs are up-and-coming in child-and-sex trafficking. We had an in. I was tired of being on the sidelines. We jumped on it."

I press my fingers to my forehead. "I'm here to make a deal with these people for Finn."

Malik doesn't say anything. I'd probably punch him if he reminded me of my job.

I pick up the plunger and force it down into the toilet bowl over and over. "Sometimes I hate this job."

"Few organizations work in isolation anymore. Money is money."

"Who's your handler?"

"Dai Qing." Malik runs his hand down the steel of the stall. "She asked me to encourage you to see your mom."

I laugh. "She did, did she? Are you sleeping with her? My family problems become your pillow talk?"

"Kim." His dark eyes are pleading. "We gotta go back out there. I don't want to leave it like this."

"Who else could have killed Chad if it wasn't Derry?"

Malik looks away from me, annoyance tinging his face. "Russians, maybe? The fight club brings in a lot of revenue. You'd need to know who owed who money, who thought eliminating Chad was the way to serve a blow to the O'Malleys. I'm assuming he was winning?"

"I got the impression you were winning or you were dead."

"This isn't part of the job. Checking into what happened to Chad isn't your job."

"No one else has done it."

"Don't compromise this mission for something that can't be changed."

I lift my chin, defiance spewing out of me. "Yeah, I get it. Chad's dead either way. But he deserves to be avenged." My voice is pitched low, and I point my finger. "I'm *finally* in a position to do that."

"Kim." There's a warning in his voice.

In a surge of annoyance, I yank open the bathroom door and school my features. The bouncer is off to the side, ready to take me to Zhang's office.

"Murray is such a good worker." I force myself to use a chipper tone and point a thumb over my shoulder. "He should get a raise." I swipe my drink off the bar before following the bouncer into the bowels of the club.

My escort chuckles. "Maybe he'll get promoted out of unclogging toilets at some point. Not my decision."

"Fair enough." I gulp the whiskey. If Zhang has the paperwork, I want out of here as fast as I can. The fingers of my free hand slip inside my jacket and graze my gun.

When I reach the doorway of the office, Shen is behind his desk. It's dark and dingy in here, and I understand why Finn might not have wanted to deal with them. Nothing about this place screams moneymaker.

When he looks at me, the sour expression on his face is a sharp contrast to his charming persona the other day when Finn was here. "Where's Finn?"

"He didn't come." I'm at the edge of his desk, but I don't sit down. This won't take long. "Do you have the offer?"

"He sent you alone?"

I give him an impatient stare. "No. I have guards. Do you have it or not?"

From his desk drawer, he withdraws an envelope. Without a word, he passes it. I flip it over, seeing the wax seal across the enclosure. "Very trusting."

"No one sees that but Finn." Shen makes a shooing motion with his hand.

"I'm Finn's proxy." I wedge my finger under the seal. "He won't mind."

"I mind." Color rises to Shen's cheeks. "I mind he sent you. That he mocked my first offer. That he's wasting my time."

"Must be terrible, having to bend over and take it."

His face fills with outrage. "Finn will put you in the ground for screwing up this deal."

"Doubtful." He might bury me in the ground, but the reason won't be this deal.

"Someone needs to put you in your place."

I laugh. "I know my place, Mr. Zhang. It's well above yours." I walk backward to the doorway and then knock on the doorframe. "It's been a pleasure."

"Someday it will be. You're not making friends today."

"Your value as a friend is questionable. Let's see if you're any good as an enemy." My heart picks up its tempo in my chest.

Before I left the house earlier, Finn asked me to piss off Shen. So much for respecting Chinese culture. His motives are a mystery. I hope Finn's plan isn't going to get me killed.

Shen sputters as I leave. When I stroll through the open bar area, I avoid looking at Malik. My heart is racing from what I said to Shen but also from my conversation with Malik.

It's not until I'm sliding into the SUV my heart starts to return to normal. Someday I fear my heart will beat right out of my chest.

"Got it?" Antonio starts the vehicle.

I wag the envelope, the seal flapping open. "You bet."

Once we're driving, he looks at me out of the corner of his eye. "You broke the seal."

"I did." I meet his gaze. "Finn's orders." That's not quite true, but it's close enough. Opening the contract let me piss off Shen and makes it easier for me to take pictures before giving the contract to Finn. This evidence helps Malik as much as me.

Antonio's jaw tightens a fraction.

"Say it."

"Finn's pissing everybody off lately. He's gonna get me killed."

My lips quirk up into a partial smile. "You're only worried about your own ass?"

"Yeah. Who else would I worry about?" His hands flex against the steering wheel.

"Embrace the fear. It's never going to go away. You might as well enjoy the adrenaline rush." Boston zooms by out the window, one mile at a time.

"Adrenaline rush." Antonio gives me a disgusted look. "You've already been in their house too long."

"You don't like it, leave."

He shakes his head. "You don't get it. You don't leave. There are only two ways out—death or jail—Lorcan and Finn are serious about that."

"Which are you hoping for?"

"Neither. I got kids."

"Immaculate conception?"

"And an ex-wife," he says with an annoyed expression. "I don't care about her."

We're not at the point where I can ask him if he'd ever roll on Finn or Lorcan. This information certainly puts him in my crosshairs. I have to be sure I can trust him to take a plea deal if he gets hauled in by us. Otherwise, I'm putting a giant target on my forehead instead of his.

"Kids, huh?"

"There isn't nothing a good father won't do for his kids."

That was true of my own father. His hiking accident ripped another hole in my mother, left a gaping absence in me as well. That hole rotted and festered in each of us in different ways. I'm here, doing this. My mother? She's gone. Checked out. Both of us are searching for paths to reunite our family. Her way is less violent.

"Well, I hope you get your wish, Antonio. You never know. Sometimes life goes in an unexpected direction."

The roar of a motorbike penetrates the interior of the car. I glance over only to be met with a loud *pop* as a bullet hits the window. Like a web, the glass cracks on impact. Antonio swerves. Two other shots ping off the car. I reach for my gun, ducking low in my seat.

"Jesus Christ," I say. "Are the windows bulletproof?"

"Far as I know."

"How many shots till it fails?"

"No idea. We've never been shot at before." He jerks to the side, and our car picks up speed.

The motorcycle roars beside us, a driver and the shooter. With what they're riding, they'll be able to outrun us all day, every day. Speeding away from them isn't an option. He tries to swerve into them, but the driver of the bike is skilled and outmaneuvers him with ease.

There are two ways this ends. I can let them empty whatever ammunition they have into the car. Or I can roll down my window and fire back. There's a good chance Antonio will be killed if I do the second option.

Another bullet hits my window, and the web spreads wider. Some glass is five rounds, others three, and some even less. Doing nothing is as much of a risk as doing something.

My hand hovers above the button for the automatic window.

# Chapter Eighteen

Without giving it any more thought, I hit the button while Antonio swerves again. The motorcycle jerks to the side with us.

"Kim, what the hell!" he shouts above the thumping wind entering the car. "You're going to get me killed."

As they dip closer again, I take a deep, steadying breath. My heart beats so fiercely, I swear each pulse twitches my fingers. I fire a round into the leg of the driver. The motorcycle veers and rights itself. The shooter on the back readjusts and takes aim. Before they can fire, I shoot the rider in the arm. In the darkness, the gun clatters to the ground, and the bike falls back again before roaring up beside us once more.

"Aim for their Goddamned heads!"

"I'm trying!" *I'm not.* Killing people means a lot of paperwork with the bureau. These things are supposed to be preapproved.

The driver fires a rapid set of bullets at the car, but they go wide. This guy can't steer, aim, and shoot. The passenger is slumped over, clutching his arm.

"Ram them!"

Antonio swerves again, and the bike pitches to the left before crashing to the ground and spinning out of control.

He slams on the brakes, reverses with a squeal of the tires, throws the car into park, then flings open his door.

"What are you doing?"

"Finishing them off."

"Jail? Really? That's what you want?"

"They gotta find me first."

"My bullets in them. We're in a residential area. Someone's called the cops. Let's go. Get back to the house. Secure an alibi."

He stares in the direction of the crashed bike, and his face flashes with indecision. He slips the safety off his gun and disappears behind us. There are two consecutive *pop*s, then he climbs into the car, holstering his gun.

We cruise at a leisurely pace down the four-lane road. Drawing more attention to us or our vehicle is a bad idea. But the pace makes my heart pound. Sirens wail in the distance.

"You scared the shit outta me back there." Antonio glances at me. "But you did good. You shoulda hit 'em both in the head. We're not dead or in jail. So I'll call it a win."

My gun is tucked away, and I push my hands under my thighs. "Careful, Antonio. You might give me a big head." Earning his respect will make turning him against Finn and Lorcan easier. It's as much luck as skill. I could have gotten him killed.

"You don't seem like the big-head type. Maybe the bullshit type."

I laugh, but it sounds like tin. Gazing out the window, I wonder if those two people had families, if people will mourn them forever like I do my brother. "We've all got a bit of bullshit in us, don't we?"

"True dat."

When I glance at him, he's smiling.

—◦—

After I go to the bathroom and photograph the contract, I head for Lorcan instead of Finn. I'm almost at Lorcan's office when I realize Finn is coming toward me from my wing of the house.

"What are you doing?" He cocks his head. "Why didn't you come see me?"

"I wanted to talk to Lorcan." *Because I think you're trying to kill me.*

Holding out his hand, he stops in front of me. "How'd the meeting go?"

"Great." I pass him the unsealed envelope.

He chuckles as he fingers the seal. "This woulda pissed him right off."

"No doubt why he sent a crew to teach me and Antonio a lesson."

A smile plays at the edge of Finn's lips before he looks up under his lashes. "Oh, he did?"

The urge to punch him is almost too strong to control. He knew. He freaking knew what Shen would do.

"You're an asshole." I try to step around him. He steps with me.

"What are you going to tell Lorcan?"

"Nothing."

Finn frowns. "Why not?"

I roll my eyes and let out an exasperated breath. "Maybe because I'm tired of playing this stupid game. I'm not some pinball you two can fire back and forth." I lean toward him, crossing my arms. "You want to send a message to your brother, fine. Leave me out of it."

"Come on, Kimmy. You said you were game."

"Yeah, to talk to the Zhangs. Not to get shot at."

He gives an almost imperceptible shrug. "Part of the business."

"Yeah? When was the last time someone shot at you?"

His smile starts at the corner of his mouth and spreads. "It's been a while."

I sigh and rock back on my heels, arms still crossed. "You want me to tell Lorcan I was shot at today?"

Finn's nod is curt.

"Why?"

"He needs someone to hate. He cares about you. We'll be united in our vengeance." He smirks at me.

My first instinct is to deny Lorcan cares about me. I've only been working here a couple months, but when Lorcan hired me, he warned me we'd have to pretend to be something more at some point. I guess we're there already. I press my lips together to keep a denial from sneaking out.

Telling him might bring Finn and Lorcan closer. It might also start a mob war. "How powerful are the Zhangs?"

"We'll crush them, Kimmy." His light-blue eyes sparkle at the crack in my armor.

A child-and-sex-trafficking monster being crushed seems pretty good. But Malik's undercover there. How do I greenlight that knowing he might get caught in the crossfire? Admitting I don't want Shen to be put down is suspicious. He almost killed me today. "I'll think about telling Lorcan."

"He'll find out one way or another." Finn's shoulder brushes mine. In my ear, he whispers, "Antonio couldn't stop talking about how badass you were. I think you have a new fan."

Heat starts in my chest and spreads along my neck, up into my face. It's not embarrassment. It's the soothing sensation of my pride being stroked. Finn and I are mere inches apart. My focus flicks from his eyes to his lips and back again. "Who would that be?"

One side of Finn's lips quirk up. "Antonio." Our gazes connect. "But you're growing on me."

He taps the contract on my hip as he passes me, whistling the tune I still can't place.

Shaking my head, I start toward Lorcan's office door again. I'm almost there when the doorbell peals through the house.

*Carys.*

Turning, I jog to the front entrance, hoping I'll make it there before Finn. After what Carys told me, I'm surprised she can even look at him. Her voice echoes through the front entranceway followed by Antonio's. I'm not sure that's any better.

His voice is jovial as he says, "She rolled down the window real casual and took 'em both out like it was no big deal."

I wince and close my eyes. Taking the corner at a run, I skid into the hallway. "Carys!"

When she sees me, her face is pinched with annoyance. "I leave you with them, and you're already under literal gunfire. Are you ready to quit yet?"

Antonio chuckles behind her. "She's too badass to quit over that."

"If you can't take the heat." I wink at her and grin. It's good to see her. I've forgotten how nice it is to be in the company of another woman.

She shakes her head. "Get out of the arms race."

*Or the FBI.*

My grin widens. She circles her arm around my waist and draws me close to her side, her bag clutched in her other hand. "Somewhere we can chat?"

"I'll take you to my wing of the house."

"Ooh." Carys laughs. "Your very own wing. You're the gangster princess, are you?"

"Mafia," I correct her, raising a finger. "We're so much better than a simple gang."

Her laughter rings through the high-ceilinged entrance, and when I look away, Finn is at the crossroads to the two sides of the house, his hands in the pockets of his jeans. "You off for a gossip?"

Carys cocks her head. "Catching up on how Kim was almost killed today."

"An exaggeration, I'm sure."

"Oh." She fakes puzzlement. "You were there, were you?"

His lips twist into a partial smile. "Not quite. Antonio is prone to exaggeration."

Annoyance flickers in me. I have no interest in playing up what happened in front of Carys, but at least stick to the facts. We could have died because Finn wants Lorcan back on his side.

"We'll see you at dinner." I drag her around the corner to go through Lorcan's wing of the house to mine.

We're at the end of his hallway when his bedroom door swings open.

"Kim!" he calls. "Carys, so nice to see you." He strides down the hall, and something about his approach warms my insides. He gathers her into a hug.

When they separate, he scans me for a beat longer than normal. "You look happy."

There's a softness to his face I like seeing, as though my presence matters. Even though I know it's false, I can't help being sucked in by it.

"It's been a long day so far. But, yeah." I glance at Carys. "I'm happy now."

His face turns serious. "Anything I should know about? Are you okay?"

"I'm fine now. Everything is okay."

"I'll see you at dinner, yeah? The caterers arrive in about an hour."

"You're not cooking?" I smirk, knowing he rarely goes into the kitchen without a take-out bag.

He chuckles. "I fear she might have a higher standard than I'm capable of achieving."

"That's right," Carys says. "I keep a cook employed at mine." She takes in my figure. "Please tell me you're eating."

I laugh. "I'm fine. No need to play the mother hen." When I glance at Lorcan, his eyebrows are raised in assessment, but he doesn't mention my meltdown at the O'Malleys.

His phone buzzes in his pocket. He gives us an apologetic smile as he takes it out and checks the caller ID. "I gotta take this. Dinner, ladies. We have a few other people joining us. No yoga outfits, Kim."

I frown as he answers the call and wanders down the hall. My frown deepens when I realize he's speaking Irish to whomever called.

"Is that annoying?" She gestures toward him.

"What?" I lead her to my set of rooms.

"The Irish all the time."

I wrinkle my nose. "They don't do it a lot. Not that much, actually." It makes me doubly curious about who called.

She gives me a thoughtful look. "As kids, they used to use it to exclude people from their private conversations. I worried they were talking about me."

"Well." I cock my head. "The number of conversations I've seen Lorcan and Finn have has been limited."

"Must be a tad frustrating."

I make a noncommittal noise.

"You like to be in the thick of things."

"When they're using me like a Ping-Pong ball to bat between them, I feel plenty involved."

She drops her bag into a spare bedroom, and then we go into the sitting room which I use from time to time to read or watch TV. Running around for one of the men or working out consumes most of my time here. She eases onto a couch, and I take a plush chair.

"After Lorcan's mum died, Finn and Lorcan became more competitive than brotherly. I don't know if that makes sense, but there was a distinct shift."

That's what happens when one brother suggests the other's mother should have been sacrificed in favor of his own. How do you come back from that?

"I'm sure they had their reasons." I pick at the material on the armrest of the chair.

"How are you finding it? Lorcan seems to care quite a bit about you."

"He's a decent guy." *Understatement.* "Finn's a puzzle."

"Mmm..." Carys pushes a stray strand of hair into her braid. "Puzzle. That's a good word."

"One minute he seems kinda okay, and the next, I'm wondering why he has to be such a jackass."

She laughs. "He hasn't changed much." She gives me a wistful smile. "That was a lethal combination for me when I was younger. I could never quite get a beat on him. Did he like me? Did he only like sleeping with me?" She takes her lipstick out of her purse to apply another thin layer. "Then I almost died, and I realized figuring him out wasn't worth the pain."

"Should I trust Finn?" This question has been spinning in my head since I got home and realized what he did. Of course, I don't trust him, but I'm not sure whether I should be pretending otherwise or if suspicion is the right way to play him.

Her lips twist. "How so?"

"He set me up today."

Worry filler her amber eyes. "To be shot at?"

"He asked me to piss off Zhang. Then we got shot at when we left."

"Why?"

"Supposedly, he thinks it'll unite him and Lorcan against a common enemy." I can't tell her about Malik, but him being trapped between the two organizations is a consideration.

"Because he went after you." A frown creases her brow. "He thinks that'll set Lorcan off."

"I don't think it will, though. Lorcan's affection for me is partially staged." I'm so comfortable with her the words slip out before I moderate them.

"Partially staged?" Her eyebrows shoot up. "What the hell have you gotten yourself into?"

If she knew the layers on top of layers, her head would pop off. FBI; dead brother; dead Mafia don; dead mother; and Malik.

"I'm not sure. Lorcan has an agenda. I thought he told you, and that's why you agreed to let me leave?" It never occurred to me he might have given her a different version.

"He told me he didn't know who to trust since he thought his father's death was an inside job. He needed fresh eyes to help him catch a killer; protect him." Carys gives me a sly smile. "How could I resist?"

I laugh. "A man in distress."

"I know. I've got a soft spot there." Her eyes dance with laughter. "He looked so handsome when he asked, and you like that kind of crime-solving thing. You were keen to root out moles in my organization."

Only to deflect attention from me. Perhaps that worked too well. "You take on anyone new?"

"You're hard to replace. I've had a few moments when I considered calling and telling you to come back."

"No luck?"

"I didn't like the woman I hired. She was too nosy. Too into my business. I had to fire her."

"Oh." That must have been Yssamae. She hadn't been my first choice, but with my sudden exit, the bureau thought she'd be a good fit. "Do you want me to suggest someone else?"

"Do you know someone else?"

"I'll think about it." I wonder if I have the heart to set her up knowing how much I like her.

"Who else do you think is coming to dinner?" Carys tucks another strand of her hair into her intricate braid.

"No idea," I say. "It'll be a surprise for both of us."

She frowns. "I rarely appreciate surprises."

*Me neither.*

# Chapter Nineteen

Carys is applying another coat of mascara to my lashes when the doorbell reverberates through the house. I agreed to let her dress me up for old time's sake. I'm wearing a black dress that hugs the top half of my body but is flowing and sheer on the bottom. It's pretty but flexible, so it makes us both happy.

"Sounds like someone is here." She studies my face. "One more coat."

"I'll wake up tomorrow with raccoon eyes."

"No, you will not because you're going to take off your makeup like a good girl."

"You know I don't normally wear much makeup. I'll need a crowbar to take this off." I gesture to my face with a wry smile.

"I've hardly put anything on you. I wish I had skin like yours." She flicks the mascara brush and rocks back on her heel, taking in my face one more time. "Perfection."

Rising, I smooth down my dress. "You think these people Lorcan invited have something to do with you being here?"

"It's the only thing I can think of. He said he'd make the trip worth my while. I told him you were already worth the trip." She grins at me.

"Very flattering." I give her a sideways glance as I swish out the bathroom door. I am flattered. Not many people see this light, playful version of Carys. Her image has to be tough to run her organization. Being weak makes her a target.

We wander down the hall together, talking and laughing until we get close to the large, open living room and dining room on Finn's side of the house. The wood on the walls is dark, like the rest of the house, but the floor is lighter. It's only used for wining and dining people.

She presses her thumb and fingers together. She draws them from her forehead down to her stomach in a steadying motion. "Game face on."

"Let's go make you some deals," I whisper as we enter the room.

Lorcan and Finn are both in suits. Seeing Lorcan dressed like that will never get old. His tailor needs a raise. When I pry my focus from him to take in Finn, he's tugging on his shirt collar as though it's too tight. Then I realize there are five other men in the room, dressed in suits of varying style and color. They have reddish-brown hair, and each of them are a touch shorter than both Lorcan and Finn.

Carys puts a hand on my arm, and her face is alight with something like indecision.

"Carys," I whisper to her. The men haven't acknowledged us yet.

"Finn in a suit," she whispers back.

"Get yourself together, woman. You don't need another knife wound."

"Right." Carys gives a sharp nod. "Right." Her hand strays to the spot on her chest near her heart. If there's a scar there, I've never seen it.

Lorcan sees us first and comes over. He loops his arm around my waist as though it's the most natural thing in the world. Normally, I don't like being touched by a man unless I'm initiating the contact, but the warm press of his fingers through the thin fabric of my dress is comforting.

"Gentlemen," he calls to the other men in the room. "This is Carys." Using his free hand, he gestures to her.

As each man steps forward and shakes her hand, introducing themselves, their Irish accents are thick. They're either Irish from Ireland or they're recent immigrants. Lorcan mentioned he'd been trying to establish connections between their organization and someone in Ireland when his father died. Perhaps these men were from that faction?

"And this firecracker"—he gathers me tight to his side—"is Kim. She's my *everything* woman."

Every time he brings up that phrase, I can't help smiling. It's ridiculous. Each man shakes my hand. Liam. Gus. Jack. Connor. Thomas. As the names sink like stones in my chest, I realize I'm meeting the Byrne brothers from Ireland. My heart rate kicks up a notch. They're lethal.

"The Byrne brothers." Carys echoes my thoughts. "I'm honored."

Thomas laughs. "It's I who is honored to be in the presence of such fierce women. A woman should never be underestimated."

"Very true." Her gaze is assessing. "In town for a little business?"

"We were coming to meet with Lorcan and Finn. Lorcan mentioned you'd be here, and we thought we'd entertain any ideas you might have in how we could improve certain aspects of our business."

"I'd love to." She tips her head to Lorcan. "Did you want to do that first? Get it out of the way? Perhaps you can mull over what I can do for you over a few drinks?"

Thomas raises his pint. "I've already started without you, I'm afraid. Still clearheaded enough to talk business. Connor," he calls to his shorter brother, who is talking to Finn. "Quick meeting with the lovely Carys?"

Connor excuses himself from his conversation and wanders toward us. They switch to Irish, which seems rude with me and Carys there.

The two exchange a few brief comments about how they're going to approach their conversation with her. They don't say anything that raises an alarm in me. Otherwise, I'd be going into this meeting with her come hell or high water.

"You okay?" Lorcan's voice is quiet in my ear.

I ease down my shoulders, relaxing into his side. "Just wondering what they're saying." *Not true.*

"I wouldn't give Carys a meeting with people who'd screw her."

"Literally or figuratively?"

One side of his lips quirks up. "She wants to get into literal bed with any of them, that's up to her. But"—his fingers squeeze my hip gently—"figuratively speaking, I wouldn't steer her wrong."

For some reason, I believe him. I press myself closer to his side, and surprise flickers in his eyes. As Carys leaves the room with Connor and Thomas, Lorcan steers me to the other men.

"We speak a lot of Irish." In my ear, it sounds like he's apologizing.

"It's fine." I tilt my chin to catch his line of sight. "I can handle it."

"You know Irish?"

"A little."

Disbelief and confusion mingle in his eyes. "How?"

"My father's a bit of an academic. He likes odd languages. Taught me and my brother a few bits and pieces." *Not my brother—he was dead by then.*

"Full of surprises."

Half an hour later, Thomas, Connor, and Carys return, laughing. Part of me hopes she got a deal, but another part of me hopes maybe she didn't. If I manage to get enough evidence on Lorcan and Finn, she might be implicated by association. Agreeing to let her come here was a selfish mistake. I should have kept her out of this.

"Everything all right?" Finn looks between the three.

"She drives a hard bargain." Thomas gives Carys an admiring glance. "There's quite a brain in there."

Finn's attention lingers on her before shifting away and landing on me. He maintains his stony facade and takes another sip of his beer before something in the conversation beside him snatches his focus.

Carys approaches me and Lorcan, a martini clutched in her hand. "It's a good day. It's a good day."

"Went well?" The corners of his eyes crinkle when he smiles at her.

"Very. Thank you for setting that up."

My stomach plummets, and I take a big gulp of my drink. "Glad to hear it."

Connor's voice catches my ear as he exclaims, "The O'Malleys?"

Finn's interest flicks to our group and then back to Connor. Lorcan leaves my side to go to them. Right away, the men switch to Irish which means only Carys is excluded from understanding what they're discussing.

She starts to tell me about the deal she made with Thomas and Connor. I should be listening, but there's an undercurrent in the other conversation I'm desperate to catch. It's one of the times when I wish I could divide my brain in half.

Snippets of the conversation are clear, but I can't figure out the context. A caterer enters the room and whispers in Lorcan's ear.

"Gentlemen. Ladies. Dinner is ready." He gestures to the table.

I sit at the far end of the table. Lorcan is at the head on my right, Carys is across from me, and Connor is next to me on my left. Finn takes the other head of the table at the opposite end. Even at dinner, their inclination is to face off against each other.

Liam picks up the thread of the conversation as the soup arrives to the table. He glances between Lorcan and Finn and then says, in Irish, "I can't believe you're getting back in bed with the O'Malleys."

"We're not," Finn responds, continuing the conversation in Irish. "Pretty sure they're the ones who offed the old man. Not going down that road again."

Thomas laughs. "You made them enough money when you fought at The Cage. You went undefeated, didn't you?"

Finn leans back in his chair while his soup is placed in front of him. "I'm still alive, aren't I?"

"What was the name of that hot-shot fighter?" Connor raises his eyebrows. "Catchy nickname?"

He frowns and picks up his spoon. "You expect me to remember that?"

Coming to life, Jack snaps his fingers. "Wicked something, wasn't it?"

Gus swallows his soup and says, "Wickie, I think. Wicked Wickie."

My heart thumps, and I'm afraid it'll jump right out of my chest. My brother. They're talking about Chad.

Lorcan and Finn exchange a glance across the table. "Hell of a fighter." Lorcan sips his beer.

He knew my brother. Very carefully, I sit back in my chair and pick up my glass. My hand isn't shaking, but my insides are in turmoil.

Across from me, Carys is downing her drink and signaling for another. I'm longing to ask if they know what happened to Chad, and if they know who might have done it. Lorcan knows I speak Irish, but their conversation has been complex. Revealing I'm fluent is different from admitting I speak and understand a few words.

Instead, I lean into him and whisper, "Can you switch to English? Poor Carys must be bored out of her mind."

He notices Carys who is stirring her martini and checking her phone. A half smile touches his lips and then, in Irish, he tells the rest of them it'll have to be English only, so the ladies aren't excluded.

Thomas looks back and forth between me and Lorcan before nodding and picking up his spoon. "English, it is." He shoots a meaningful look at the rest of his brothers.

The night continues with a lot of banal conversations surrounding things I can't bring myself to care about, so I spend most of it drinking and chatting to Carys about her family and her business. It's late when the brothers finish off their drinks and organize security to their hotel.

We trail them out to the front foyer, Carys and I chatting, when I catch Thomas saying, "Next time, you'll have to come to Ireland."

Finn chuckles. His voice is low as he says, "It'll have to be Lorcan that does that."

"You still haven't been back?"

"No, too risky. I didn't know what I was doing then. A punk full of rage."

"That's her, isn't it?" Thomas indicates Carys.

I have an ear tuned to Carys and another to Finn's conversation.

His gaze strays to her, and he gives Thomas a curt nod.

"What happened?" I call out to Thomas, curiosity getting the best of me. Carys stops speaking beside me and focuses on the men's discussion.

Lorcan comes to my side and frowns. "An old story."

"About Carys?" I scan Finn and her.

Thomas chuckles. "Indeed. That lass there caused a whole ruckus in Ireland when she got herself stabbed in a bar brawl."

She raises her eyebrows, her voice steely when she says, "Got *myself* stabbed?"

Finn holds up a hand. "It's in the past. No point digging it up. Thomas—I can't come to Ireland."

"Why not?" Carys steps toward him. "It wasn't *you* who was stabbed."

His jaw tightens, but he doesn't focus on her.

"Apologies, Finn. Seems I opened a can of worms." Thomas pats him on the shoulder before he puts on his coat.

She's stiff with rage beside me. I link my fingers with hers. She squeezes my hand and chugs the rest of her drink before leaving for the kitchen.

The men head out the front door in a pack of laughs and backslaps. The way Lorcan and Finn behaved tonight, no one would ever know there was any tension between the two of them.

When the front door closes, Lorcan and Finn stare at each other for a moment.

"Are we pursuing that or not?" Finn asks Lorcan, his voice curt.

"Don't see why not." He eyes Finn. Wariness hums between them.

"Better book yourself a flight to Ireland, then."

"Will do." Lorcan's attention strays to me. "You staying up?"

"For a bit." I tilt my head toward the kitchen.

He presses his lips to my temple. My insides melt at the contact, and my hand strays to his chest. I shouldn't have had that last drink. When he draws back, his hand trails along my arm until he's out of arms reach and headed to his rooms.

"You don't mind mixing a bit of business with your pleasure?"

My attention snaps to Finn at his dry comment beside me. "Depends on the type of business and the extent of the pleasure." I glance over. "What are you doing?"

"One last drink before bed."

I purse my lips and raise an eyebrow. "You must love trouble."

He chuckles. "It calls me like a siren's song." He holds out his hands. "What can I say?"

He follows me to the kitchen where Carys is sitting beside an open forty-ounce bottle of vodka.

"Ah, going for some Russian relief?" Finn takes down a shot glass from the cupboard and passes it to her. He grabs another for himself but doesn't offer me one.

I remove a beer from the fridge while he pours himself, and then Carys, a shot. When she stares up at him, there is misery written on her face.

"What'd you do?" she whispers.

# Chapter Twenty

Finn throws back his shot and pours himself another one. "That's a silly question."

"I need you to tell me what you did."

"All these years, and you never asked anyone?" His searing gaze roams her face.

"I almost died. A hair's breadth from death." Her hand strays to her chest again. "Why would I want to relive that?"

I'm drinking my beer in great gulping swigs. I'm not sure I should be here while they're talking about this. Their conversation is intimate. There's a buzz between them that takes me by surprise.

"Thought you might have wondered why I never came back."

"Every day." Her voice is thick as her eyes fill with tears.

Finn's tough exterior slips. He pours himself another shot as though drowning himself in alcohol can ward off whatever is still between them. "Don't cry."

"I'm drunk. Of course I'm going to frigging cry." She wipes away her tears and holds out her glass to be refilled.

"I should go." I glance between the two of them. Chugging back the rest of my beer, I place the bottle on the counter. If I stay, I'm intruding, and I doubt I'd learn anything relevant to my case. Whatever is happening here is based on their shared history.

He stares at me for a beat, and then he focuses on Carys. "I'll look after her."

"You okay?"

"I'll be fine." She sniffs and fumbles in her purse.

I grab the box of tissues from on top of the fridge and pass them to her. She gives me a grateful half smile before turning to Finn.

With a brief rub to her back, I head out of the kitchen. As I'm leaving, she says to him, "What'd you do?"

I slow to hear his response.

"What do you think I did? I killed 'em, Carys. I killed 'em all."

It's not a surprise. Deep down, I knew that had to be what he did. The only logical reason he couldn't ever return to Ireland would be a crime like that. Still, hearing the way he says it to her, his voice tender and tough, causes a surge of longing to stir in my chest.

When I get to Lorcan's door, I don't have to knock before the buzzer clicks. There's no time for me to collect myself. Why did I suggest cameras?

In his kitchenette, he is pouring a drink. His tie and suit jacket are thrown across a chair. The sleeves of his shirt are rolled to his elbows. "Want one?"

"Not sure it's a good idea." My hands skim the paper-thin material of my dress.

"Finn and Carys getting into it out there?"

I frown. "How'd you know?"

"'Cause I know what he did. And I'm old enough to know women."

Suppressing a smile, I say, "Old enough to know women? That's a thing?"

Lorcan passes me a glass of whiskey. "Oh, it's a thing." He takes a sip of his drink, and he's so close, the light scent of his musky cologne mixed with notes of mint and oak drifts to me. I could bathe in that smell.

"So he can't go back to Ireland because he killed the people who stabbed Carys?"

"They got that far, did they?"

I tap a finger to my temple. "A bit of info, and my brains got me the rest of the way."

"Yeah, McCaffery family. No one in the immediate family—a few people in that circle. Finn can't set foot in the country."

"He killed for her."

"Wouldn't you kill for someone you loved?"

"Yes." To put a bullet in the person who killed Chad would be the sweetest feeling in the world. I'd do it a thousand times if I could. With my head cocked to the side, I examine him. "Have you?"

He swishes his drink around in his glass, staring down into it. "First person I ever killed was for my brother." Throwing back more whiskey, he avoids my gaze.

"For Finn?" That surprises me. They're so distant now, it's hard to believe Finn inspired that sort of loyalty.

"We didn't always hate each other."

"Must have been before his comment to your mother."

"After, actually."

I frown. "Why would you do that?"

Lorcan raises his eyebrows and wanders over to the couch and chairs. "In a misguided bid to win him over."

Win him over? It was Finn who offended Lorcan and his mother on her deathbed. That's a powerful sway if Lorcan felt he needed to make amends. It makes no sense to me. Of course, Finn's idea of winning over Lorcan involves manipulation and underhanded tactics like today's shootout. The situation is volatile.

I follow Lorcan to the chairs and take the one beside him. When I lower into the seat, our arms brush. The brief contact warms my arm, causing a spike of yearning in me. I stare into my drink, willing my body to sort itself out.

"You're not going to ask me about it?"

When I look up, his eyes are glassy from too much alcohol but also sincere. "Do you want to tell me?"

He frowns and turns his face away. With his glass to his lips, he takes a gulp of his drink. "Guy was a mechanic at a garage. He was working under a car after hours. I slipped in." He leans back in his chair. "Music was blaring. I disabled the jack keeping the car up." With one last swallow, he finishes his drink. "Crushed him like an ant."

The revelation should shock me, but I've seen all kinds. Something like that is nothing, a drop in the bucket. "Was that the first time you saw someone die?" I use a finger to circle the rim of my glass.

"'Twas the first time I was responsible for a death. Not the first time I watched someone die."

*Of course. His mother.*

"And you?" He raises his eyebrows.

There's a lie on the tip of my tongue. It's a familiar one, but there's something about him. The softness of his voice, the way he can't quite meet my eyes makes me want to be real in this moment. "I was ten. Drive-by shooting. I held him in my arms as he died."

"Ten." Lorcan's fingers skim my cheek. "A wee babe."

I ease my face into the palm of his hand like a cat arching its back for more contact.

"Did you know him?"

"Yes." Such a simple admission. It's the biggest truth I've given anyone in ages. My heart aches to say *my brother*, but I can't. It would blow my cover story.

But he doesn't ask. Instead, he rubs my cheek with his thumb. "I'd take that memory from you if I could. 'Cause there aren't any words that'll make that easier to bear."

A heavy silence sits between us as he tucks a few stray strands of my hair behind my ears.

"Are you going to Ireland?" My voice is too loud in the stillness of the room.

"No." With one last, searching glance, he goes to the kitchen to pour himself another drink. "Linking up with the Byrne brothers is only useful if Finn and I keep the organization together. We split, and that venture becomes a nightmare."

Finn's earlier request comes back. Do I tell Lorcan about the Zhangs trying to kill me and Antonio? My objective is to avoid a war. Malik would be penned in on the wrong side. No, no, I'm not saying anything tonight. I need a plan first.

"I should get to bed." I empty my drink and head for the door. "I can let myself out." This closeness we've developed in here needs to end. Outside this room, it's okay, it's needed. In here, it's dangerous.

"Kim." Lorcan follows me.

I keep my back to him. His familiar scent hits my nose before he gets close enough to touch. "Do you need to put in a code for me to get out of here?"

"What's the rush?" He ambles up behind me. His newly poured whiskey is cupped in his hand as he leans his shoulder against the wall.

"I'm tired." To make a point, I glance at the digital clock near his bed. "It's two o'clock in the morning."

He comes closer, and his body fills the narrow entrance to his bedroom. He leans across me to punch in the code, and then his hand drops to the door handle instead. "You don't need a code to get out." His breath stirs my hair, his lips close to my temple.

"The other night—"

"I was stalling."

When I glance at him, our faces are mere inches apart. "Why would you do that?" One side of his lips quirk up, and I long to brush the pad of my thumb over his dimple.

"Sometimes I enjoy the company of a smart, tough woman."

"Is this part of us becoming good mates?"

He searches my face for a moment. "Oh, I doubt that. If we were becoming good mates, you'd have told me you were almost killed today."

I take a moment to assess his reaction. He's angry, but it's restrained. "Who told you?"

"Antonio. You were rattled earlier. You faced down Derry O'Malley the other day without flinching. So I went digging. What puts a crack in Kim's armor?"

I cross my arms and focus on his bed.

"Antonio was quite happy to tell me about your adventure with the Zhangs." His jaw hardens. "Why didn't *you* tell me?"

I stare at him for a moment, wondering which version is the best one to put out there. "Finn set us up."

"What?" Lorcan growls, his posture tightening.

# Chapter Twenty-One

Meeting his intense gaze, I say, "Finn thinks you'll go ballistic about what happened. That it'll unite you two."

"Unite us?" Lorcan scoffs. "He killed our father. Nothing is going to unite us."

"You don't know that yet."

"I know it. I can't prove it." He points his finger at me, any hint of seduction gone. "That's your job."

"He says he didn't do it."

"Of course, he's going to tell you that." His focus bores into me. "I understand you're in a tough spot. Hold back or tell Finn whatever you want. With me, you give me all of it—whether you think it matters or not."

I purse my lips and stare him down. "Fine."

"It's not fine. You can't be keeping this shit from me."

"What are you going to do about the Zhangs?"

"What I have to do. My brother thinks he'll get a reaction, so that's what'll happen. I do nothing, and he'll know something is off." He looks me up and down. "I protect my own. Always."

My heart clenches at the emotion in his eyes when he stares at me. Valued. He values me.

"Did you see who shot at you?"

"Not very clearly. Both men, I think. I shot one in the arm, one in the leg. Antonio finished them off."

His hand wraps behind my head, cupping my neck. "You did good."

"I'm still alive."

Lorcan gathers me into his chest. "I woulda gone ballistic if anything had happened to you." His other arm, holding his drink, cradles my back.

I wrap my arms around him and, for a moment, let myself breathe him in. The mix of cologne, whiskey, and the familiarity of his own personal smell comforts me. "If you knew, why didn't you say something?"

"I wanted to see if you'd tell me. It's about trust. It's gotta run both ways, or this won't work."

In the end, it's not going to matter. Even if we get to that place, at some point, I'll be betraying him. That part is inevitable.

"Tomorrow morning when you and Carys go shopping, you take Sean, Antonio, and Ian."

"I don't need three bodyguards. You hired me as a bodyguard. I can take care of myself."

"It's nonnegotiable, Kim. I'm not playing around."

Reluctantly, I pull back from Lorcan. "We'll chat in the morning before I leave."

"I'm not going to change my mind."

"Maybe I'll change mine."

He chuckles. "About fighting me on it?"

With a tiny shrug and a playful grin, I let lightness take over. "I can be reasonable sometimes."

"Looking forward to seeing that side of you." He opens the door.

As I wander down the hall, the heat from Lorcan sears me. I'm not sure if he's still at the door watching me, but it feels like it. When I get to my rooms, I peek over my shoulder. He isn't there. Great, now I'm imagining things. Shaking my head, I see the spare bedroom door propped open, waiting for Carys. Either she's still talking to Finn or their talking morphed into something else.

After I punch in the code to my room, I strip and collapse onto my bed, glad I'm not leaving with Carys until ten in the morning. I'm about to drift to sleep when I remember I haven't checked my phone in hours. In the bathroom where I left it charging, a couple of messages are visible. At first, there's nothing important. Then, I see it.

*Sauce on the side.*

It looks like a text from a wrong number about a food order. But reading it causes a thin sheen of sweat to prick at the back of my neck.

Sauce on the side is an SOS. I need to see my mother as soon as possible. I may not like Dai Qing, my new handler, but that message isn't one she'd fake.

Tomorrow, I have to figure out how to ditch three bodyguards and Carys long enough to go check on my mother. Seems simple enough.

I awake with a start, drenched in sweat. When I look down at my hands, there's blood, and I close them again. Popping them open, the blood is gone. With a huff, I throw back the covers and sit on the edge of the bed, rubbing my face. It's still dark outside.

A few minutes later, I've showered, dressed, and I'm outside Lorcan's office door, full of indecision. There's a light under the frame, leaking into the hall. It's possible he forgot to switch it off, or he didn't go to sleep. The spare room is empty. Maybe no one is sleeping tonight.

Unlike normal, the blood on my hands when I woke up wasn't my brother's. I dreamed of my mother, drowning in a pool of blood, choking on it, sinking into it. Whatever is going on with her, I need to see her.

My house of cards might tumble down around me.

With my shoulders square, I knock on the office door. It clicks unlocked less than a second later. Across the room, Lorcan is sitting behind his desk, nursing another drink.

"Have you slept?" I shove my hands into the pockets of my coat.

"Not a wink." He studies me, assessing. "And you?"

I shrug. "I wanted to let you know I'm heading out for a bit."

He laughs. "Just like that, yeah? Just heading out." He swishes the alcohol in his glass and moves around to perch on the edge of his desk. "No."

Swallowing down the immediate indignation, I look away from him. "Last I knew, I was an employee, not a prisoner."

He slants his head toward the clock on the wall. "Where could you possibly need to go at five in the morning?"

"Female issues. Gotta do a little bit of shopping."

"Female issues." He pronounces the words as though they're preposterous. "Carys is here. We have other female staff. You can get what you need without leaving."

"I need to go out. Quick trip to CVS."

"Then I'll come with you."

My jaw tightens. "This lack of trust is getting old. Carys asked me to come back, work for her. Maybe I'll do that."

"You're not going to CVS at five in the morning. You haven't slept. I haven't slept. I know what's eating me. What's got you in knots?" He shoves off the edge of the desk, draining his drink in the process, and wanders closer.

"My mother."

Lorcan's eyebrows spring up. "Your mother? Doesn't she live in another state somewhere? Social worker or something?"

I almost laugh. So he checked my backstory. Thank the Lord it held up both times. "Used to be. She's moved into this area in the last few years. It's one of the reasons I agreed to take this job. She's sick."

He's impeaching on my personal space, but I don't mind. His hazel eyes are filled with sympathy. "Serious?"

"She'll never recover."

"Wouldn't wish that on anyone."

The tenderness in him almost undoes me. "She needs me. I have to go."

"Let me come."

"She doesn't make a lot of sense anymore. Rambles. Says things that aren't true. Half the time she doesn't even recognize me."

His fingers graze my cheek. "You don't have to be an island."

I lean into his touch. Saying yes is dangerous, insane. And yet... "You can't come into the room."

"That's a fair compromise." One side of his lips quirks up in that familiar way.

With my thumb, I brush the dimple peeking out of his scruff. "Lorcan," I murmur.

His lips brush my temple, and I close my eyes. He gathers me into his chest and sighs. The stench of whiskey is overwhelming.

"You sober enough to drive?" he asks. "Lord knows I'm not."

My heart beats a strange rhythm in my chest. The risk I'm taking right now is astronomical. I must still be drunk. "Yes." I step back. "I want to go before Finn and Carys get up."

Lorcan goes to the lockbox on the wall and takes out a set of keys. He grabs his wallet off the desk and shoves it into his front pocket. "She stay with him last night?"

"Think so." I shrug. "She's not in her room."

He nods. "Gonna make your job tougher with him."

"I think seducing him is off the table." Lorcan's scent still surrounds me. The idea of being with anyone else is the last thing on my mind right now. I want to forget about my job, my mother, everything, and lose myself in Lorcan.

"Perhaps Carys can be of some use." He places his hand on the small of my back, guiding me out of his office and down the hall.

Dragging her deeper into this isn't an option for me. "I'll figure something out."

"Resourceful as always." Lorcan looks at me, a half smile playing at the edges of his lips.

After we slip into the car, I put the key in the ignition. I half expect the car to explode, disintegrate, taking us along with it. I bite my lip and squirm in my seat. He's staring at his phone, absorbed in something else.

"What was eating you?" I start the car.

He examines me for a beat and then goes back to his phone. "You, Finn, my father, my mother... Once you fall down that hole, there's not much chance of coming back out."

I frown and put the car in gear. "What's that mean?"

He tucks his phone into his pocket and runs his hands along the thighs of his jeans. "I get enough booze in me, and I wish I could go back to when I was fourteen. Save the world." He gives me a wry glance. "You got a time machine tucked into your back pocket there?"

"Why fourteen?"

Lorcan crosses his arms. "So many reasons, Kim. So many. Can't go back, though. Gotta keep looking forward." Tiredness is written on his face. "Bit tough when you don't even know what that's going to look like."

"I'm trying." I squeeze his hand. "Finn's giving me a list of contacts to feel them out."

Lorcan frowns. "Let me double-check it when you get it." His fingers toy with mine as though he doesn't realize he's doing it.

My stomach flutters at the way his fingers skim along mine. I need to meet Malik in a dark alley. These pent-up urges will undo me.

We drive in silence for a while before I remember something else that's been bothering me. "What's the tune Finn whistles sometimes?"

Lorcan's focus turns to me. "He's been feeling quite pleased with himself, has he?"

"A few times."

"It's an old Irish ditty our father used to sing when he had too much to drink."

"Hmm..."

Lorcan raises his eyebrows. "Why's that?"

"I don't know. Something about it seemed familiar. I don't know why."

"It's not a popular tune." He releases my hand he's been playing with. He chuckles, but it holds no humor as he glances out the window. "Fellas at The Cage used to mock him with it."

I cock my head to the side and give him an encouraging look. Any mention of The Cage piques my interest.

"He didn't play any music when he entered. He whistled himself into the ring."

"Brave."

"Oh, Finn's all kinds of brave." One of Lorcan's hands skates through the back of his hair. The words are flattering, but his tone is not. "You lived round here for a while, yeah? It's possible you heard it on the street. He was a big deal in the underground circuit. You know any fighters as a kid?"

I shake my head while my insides flip, threatening to flop out my mouth. "No."

The word doesn't come out as clear as it should. Would my brother have mocked Finn? Sometimes I hung around him and his friends. Did they whistle that tune? Laugh about it? It wouldn't have meant anything then.

I drive into the parking lot of the care facility and find a space close to the door. "We're here."

# Chapter Twenty-Two

The building is a single story and appears more like an overgrown bungalow than a hospital or long-term care facility. One thing my job has afforded me is the ability to put my mother somewhere nice, even if she doesn't have a clue it's the best.

"You'll wait here?" I ask.

"Sure you don't want me to come in?" Lorcan's voice is soft, and his eyes sincere. "I got these big shoulders you can lean on if you like."

Without thinking, I run my hand down his arm. "Maybe later."

He catches my hand and gives it a squeeze. "You're armed?"

"Always."

"Anything seems off, I'm coming in."

"It's an old-age home. It's hardly a guns-blazing scenario."

He doesn't laugh at my joke. Instead, his eyes burn with more intensity. "I protect my own."

"It'll be fine." I rub his cheek with my thumb. "Promise." This place isn't part of my cover story. If he comes in, he'll learn more than he bargained.

He tips his chin in the direction of the building. "Text me if you want me to come in."

I nod and climb out of the car. At the door to the facility, I enter then stop at the front desk to check in. Mom hasn't been eating. The worker explains it's most likely the start of a severe decline. Her semi lucid days are numbered.

Although I don't come here often, her room is burned into my brain. Single bed. Dresser. Nightstand. All in a glistening white. Antiseptic but efficient and newer than lots of other facilities. The day I agreed to have her moved here was one of the hardest of my life. At that point, the best part of my mother was already gone.

I slip in, and I'm startled when a figure rises from the leather armchair in the corner. Fear pierces my heart as I glance over my shoulder. I hope to God Lorcan hasn't followed me.

"Malik." I shove my hands into the pockets of my jacket. "What are you doing here? It's dangerous."

"Dai Qing sent the SOS to me. I couldn't stay away. I know how hard this is for you."

"You shouldn't be here." My focus strays to my mother sleeping in the bed. Dai Qing would never come, and the fact Malik has, unasked, is both a blessing and a curse.

"I didn't like how we left things."

"Lorcan's waiting for me outside."

"What?"

"I got the SOS. I had to get here. They won't let me leave without an escort. Zhang came after me yesterday."

Malik crosses the room in a few strides. "Zhang came after you?"

"You must not be in deep enough if you don't know that."

Malik's brow furrows, and he reaches for me. I avoid his touch and shift closer to my mother's bed.

"I was at the bar when Zhang left his office. He didn't order anyone after you."

"Well, it happened." I yank my hands out of my coat pockets and throw them out wide. "I almost died yesterday."

"The Donaghey brothers—" He doesn't finish because my mother twitches in the bed.

I yank the wooden chair closest to her toward the bed and sit down, taking her hand in mine. "Mom?" There's no response, and her breathing goes back to normal. She gets into such deep sleeps. I rotate toward Malik, my mother's hand still clutched in mine. "It's all twisted up. Do you know what the bureau knows? I think Chad and Finn fought at The Cage around the same time. They knew each other. I'm sure of it."

"You're not there to dig for that. Going after that kind of information will put you in danger."

I laugh. "You think I'm not in danger? Jesus, Malik. The games these two men are playing. I have no idea who is telling the truth. Lorcan is convinced Finn killed their father. Finn tells me he didn't, offered to help me search for someone else. That's what I'd do if I was guilty. You don't hide. You offer. You direct. You manipulate."

Malik's brow clears, and he shoves his hands into his pockets. "It's what I'd do."

"Our file says it was the Russians, right? They aren't on the radar. I haven't even met them yet. Why does the bureau think it was them and Lorcan's not on that trail?"

"Maybe you need to set him on it."

I roll my eyes. "Yeah, with no evidence. That'll go down well. I might as well hold up a sign and ask them both to suspect me." A stray hair from my ponytail falls into my face, and I push it behind my ear. I'd give anything to talk this through with my mom or my dad. They were full of thoughtful advice as I grew up. Even unraveling this other side of Chad would be helpful. What did they piece together? Why did I know nothing?

"Of the two Donaghey brothers, which one is more likely to be honest?"

"Axel," my mother murmurs in her sleep. "Axel."

Malik's brow creases. "Your father?"

"Yeah," I say as she stirs in the bed. "She must still have some vivid dreams."

"Ho-Jun." She clutches my hand. "Ho-Jun."

"Who's that?"

"Chad's father." I smooth the black hair that's fallen across my mother's forehead. "Shhh." I run my fingers along her temple. "It's okay, Mom. It's okay." I squeeze her hand. "I'm here, Mom. Kimi is here."

Her eyes fly open. "Chad. Chad. My Chadwick." Her dark, wild gaze meets mine. "Where's Chad?"

"Are you hungry, Mom? They said you didn't eat."

Malik comes forward. "I can get the nurse, arrange for something to be brought to the room."

"Where's Chad?" She looks around us to the door.

My heart kicks up a notch in my chest. At any moment, Lorcan could come in. Malik needs to leave. "You should leave. Seriously. Lorcan was drunk. If he gets it into his head to come in, I can't explain why you're here. You work for the Zhangs, and as far as we know, they tried to kill me yesterday."

"Where's Chad?" She's louder now, more insistent.

"He's in the hall," I say in a tender voice, letting my eyes connect with her vacant ones. "Chad stepped out for a minute."

She relaxes into the bed and gives me a sad smile. "I had a dream he died."

"It was a dream," I whisper.

"Kimi." Malik comes closer, his hand hovering by my shoulder.

"Go, please. You can't help me anymore." The gulf that's opening up between us is starting to feel insurmountable. He knows things he's not telling me.

"You know where to find me." The door clicks closed behind him.

"Where's Axel?" Mom's body is a slight outline under the covers.

"He went with Chad, Mom." I grip her hand, willing her to come back, to push through one last time. It's been so long since she was here. "Are you hungry?"

"Axel's getting him out, you know."

I frown. "Getting who out?"

"Chad."

"From what?"

"Who are you?" She cocks her head and examines my face, but nothing registers. "Do we know each other?"

And she's gone again.

"In another life." I kiss her forehead. "In another life, you were the best mom."

"Well, aren't you sweet?" Her eyes drift closed.

Tears prick at the back of my eyes, and my attention is trained on the ceiling when the door clicks open again. I rotate, annoyance sparking in me. "Ma—"

"Sorry," Lorcan says, hands raised. "It was taking bloody ages. I wanted to make sure you were okay."

"Oh." I flush. Malik's name had been so close to slipping out. "I-I was about to leave."

"How is she?" He nods in my mother's direction.

"Lucid, sort of, for a brief moment. Mostly rambling about things I couldn't understand." I push my hands into my coat pockets and take a deep breath.

Lorcan comes closer to the bed, and her eyes pop open. She squints at him and then starts puffing and trying to raise herself up. But she's too weak. The monitors beside her go haywire, and a nurse comes charging in.

"You've upset her." The nurse rushes to my mother's side.

"We're leaving." My focus flicks between him and my mother. Something about him set her off, but he seems unperturbed. He watches the nurse calm her without a twinge of recognition.

"Get him out." Her gaze strays to Lorcan. "Out. Out."

He backs up, hands raised. "I'll go. I'll go."

My fingers are on his chest, backing him out of the room, and I follow behind him, listening to my mother's frantic calls for him to get away from her.

"Is she like that a lot?" We're headed down the hall together, and his brow is creased with concern.

"Yes." *Never. Not once.* He can't question what happened. If he's prompted to dig, I'm in trouble.

"Must be hard." His hand falls on the small of my back.

"Not going to get easier." At least that part is true. Even her moments of recognition are plagued with inaccuracies. It's impossible to have a conversation with her make sense. Sometimes I remember the last good talk I had with her, and I wish someone told me we wouldn't get to speak like that again. If someone froze time and said, *This is the last time you'll get to do this.* The moment would have been seared into my brain, savored for the rainy days to come when all I'd want to do is chat with her.

"The nurse at the front desk said it's early onset Alzheimer's."

Goose bumps rise on my arms, and I step away from the hand on my back. "You asked?"

He opens the entrance for me. "You're mad?"

"Of course. It's an invasion of my privacy. I brought you here as an act of trust. You snooping is... that's a violation."

"I wasn't snooping." His voice tightens. "I wanted to understand what I was walking into."

"You shouldn't have been walking into anything." I yank open the car door. "Because I asked you to wait in the car."

Lorcan climbs in beside me and gestures to the side of the building. "I was minding my own business, and then I saw a black guy exiting out the side of the building."

I don't miss a beat. "That's racist. Some black guy exits the building and you become suspicious. He's probably visiting family, or he works here."

"Call it whatever you want. It was suspicious, so I went in."

"I was fine."

"The nurse said the guy I saw wasn't a registered visitor."

My heart stutters in my chest. "An employee?"

"Not with how I described him to them."

"You've had a few drinks. Are you sure you saw what you think you saw?"

His gaze is like granite. "Drunk or sober, I can spot something off. That's my job."

"I don't know what to tell you. I didn't see him."

Lorcan focuses on the scenery outside the window. "I'll look into it more. It doesn't sit right with me."

A heavy silence sits between us for a moment. "I can look into it," I say. "They trust me here. I'm more likely to get camera footage and information."

"I can be quite charming when I want to be."

A half smile touches my lips as I start the car. "I'm sure. I would—I would rather Finn didn't know about my mom if that's okay with you. It's—it's something I keep for me."

He makes a sealing motion with one hand. "Your wish." He rubs my leg. "I'm sorry about your mum."

"Me too." I ease the car onto the highway. "Me too."

While I drive, I pray I've convinced Lorcan to leave the snooping. I can't have him discovering Murray or Malik. One leads back to the Zhangs and puts Malik in danger. The other leads to the FBI and sinks us all.

# Chapter Twenty-Three

Somehow, I make it through shopping with Carys without having a heart attack about Lorcan investigating Malik. When we arrive at the house to get her suitcases, I half expect the brothers to be at the entrance, guns poised to execute me on the spot.

"You okay?" She yawns as she drags her suitcase down the hall. "I'm the one who slept with Finn last night. God, I was so drunk. Such a dumb thing to do. You're acting like you're the one who did something naughty."

I purse my lips, wishing I could tell her the truth. She knows the undercover version of me better than anyone else. The inconsistencies in my stories would be glaring. "A lot going on in this house. You know?"

"Oh, I understand," she agrees. "Are you and Lorcan...?"

"Maybe?"

She rubs my back. "You could do worse."

"Are you and Finn together?"

"God, no. I can't do that again. I'm too old for his bullshit now."

"You don't think he's changed?"

"Oh, I'm sure he has. He's probably gotten worse." Carys winks at me as I swing open the front door. Antonio is beside the car, ready to drive her to the airport.

I tug her into a hug before she climbs into the back seat of the vehicle. "Thanks for coming."

"Of course." She backs up and pats my cheek. "Any time. I mean that. You need some more female influence, I'll brave it."

"You'll brave it?" My mind sticks on the legal ramifications.

"It would be so easy to be sucked into this again." She makes an all-encompassing gesture with her arms. "Too easy."

"Right." I give her another hug to disguise my uneasiness.

"Get some sleep." She slips into the car. "You're acting weird today."

If only sleep would solve my problems, I'd never get out of bed. "Hey, Carys." I come out of my head long enough for things to click. "Did you ever see Finn fight in The Cage?"

Her eyes light up, and she sighs. "Oh, yes. That's what started the whole mess between the two of us. Him fighting was only a secret from his father. Everyone else knew. Sweat. Muscles. So incredibly cocky. How could I not?"

"Do you remember anything about the structure? About who could fight when?"

She frowns and looks me up and down. "The O'Malleys don't let women fight. Do you need money? Is he being a shit about paying you?"

I stifle a laugh. "That's not it."

She shuffles further into the car and waves me in. "Ride with me. We can chat about hot men who fight in a ring."

I glance back at the house and catch Antonio watching me before I focus on Carys.

"I'll text Lorcan and tell him I talked you into it. Antonio is here to protect you."

She knows that'll seal the deal. "I hardly need him to protect me." I get in beside her, and Antonio appears in the driver's seat as the door slams.

"Got that right. She's a sharpshooter. Well, not quite, but still pretty impressive." He grins at me in the rearview mirror.

We drive out of the complex and onto the road.

"So why the sudden interest in The Cage?" Her fingers fly across her phone.

"Not sudden. I've been to the O'Malley's a few times. I saw their wall of dead heroes." My voice is full of derision, but this information is why I agreed to tag along for the ride.

"Ah, yes." She gestures to Antonio. "Do you understand how the whole thing works now? It's been years."

It's years ago I'm interested in, but I can't very well correct her. Doing that makes me appear suspicious or far too involved with Finn. Given she slept with him, it's not a great idea to appear as though I'm going in for the kill.

"Different hot-shot fighter every night." Antonio accelerates onto the highway headed for the airport.

I cock my head to the side. "Until the hot-shot fighter loses."

"Basically. You live and die in the ring. When you're fighting and winning, the O'Malley family treats you like a god."

"Money?"

"Anything you want. Carys is right though. They don't let women fight. Not that Lorcan or Finn would let you do it anyway."

"I got news for them." I focus on the scenery whizzing by the window.

He laughs. "There's a big fight in a week or two. Huge promotion going on right now. A couple of the weekend big shots going head-to-head.

It's rare. The O'Malley family doesn't like to double down on their best fighters. Maybe only once or twice a year."

"You going?" I meet his gaze in the mirror.

"Me? Nah. I ain't got that kinda cash lying around. I got kids."

"And an ex-wife."

Antonio frowns. "Yeah, her too."

Carys takes her eyes off her phone to glance at me. "I can get you a ticket. I'm sure Lorcan or Finn would take you."

"I don't know. We might be at war with the Zhangs."

She raises her eyebrows. "Lorcan knows they came after you?"

"He knows someone did." I'm still not convinced it was the Zhangs. Malik was so certain it wasn't, and he's good at his job. If there'd been an order after I left, he'd have heard something. A whisper. A word. An undercurrent that wasn't right.

"You're not so sure." She tries to coax me to make eye contact. "Your instincts are usually good."

"Keeping an open mind."

"It was the Zhangs." His faith is unwavering. "I told Lorcan it was the Zhangs."

I focus on Carys. "You can get me a ticket?"

Her lips twist into an almost smile. "I can. You got a thing for hot, sweaty men beating the shit out of each other too? Wouldn't have thought that'd be your thing." She raises her phone. "Leave it with me."

"It's not the hot, sweaty men." I'm lost in thought as I watch the blur of scenery out the window. I know myself well.

"Oh, no?"

"It's the danger. A life balanced on the edge of a knife. One wrong move, and they're done."

She grins and points her phone at me. "Now that, I believe."

From the front seat, Antonio chuckles.

I'm not home long when there's a knock on my door. At the intercom, I press the button wondering which brother is visiting me.

"Yes?" Sometimes I wish they gave me a camera.

"Housekeeping."

I frown. It is the day the house is cleaned, and the voice sounds familiar but out of place. For a moment, I stare at the door trying to decide if I should grab my gun. "Hold on." Their father was killed in the house. Better safe than dead.

Unsnapping the gun from under the bed, I cross to the door and ease it back, the gun poised in my hand.

When the petite Asian woman looks up, there's a smirk on her face. "I'm here to clean up your mess."

"Oh, I'm generally pretty tidy." Annoyance seeps into my voice.

"Not lately." Dai Qing slips into the room when I step back.

Closing the door behind her, I press my back into the wood. The risk she's taking right now sparks a touch of admiration in me. That'll only stick if she doesn't get me killed with this stunt.

"Do I need to sweep?" She's not scanning the floor as she checks the corners of the room for cameras.

"It's clean. I sweep it regularly."

She drops the pail with a clatter. "At least you're careful in that respect."

"Well, you coming here doesn't exactly help me out. How the hell did you get in here?" I hiss.

Dai Qing gives me a disgusted look. "Please. Petite Asian woman on a cleaning crew? No one batted an eye."

"If Lorcan or Finn see you, they'll ask or notice. I'm sure of it."

"We're covered up. No need to worry. As far as they know, I work for the company. I've even cleaned up some of their mess already. Might not be to the proper standards. What do I know? I have someone clean my own house for God's sake."

Annoyance flares in me, and I shove it back down. "Why are you here?"

"To clean up *your* mess. Seriously. Shooting people in a residential neighborhood? Do you know how many nosy people have cameras mounted outside their homes now? We got an alert when your face was picked up by a local police facial identification scan. We shut that shit down, but we shouldn't have to, Kim."

I stare at her, annoyed. "It couldn't be helped. I didn't kill them, just maimed them."

"Nonetheless, they're dead. You didn't tell anyone."

"I've been kinda busy. SOS. Malik. Carys was here. Finn and Lorcan are running circles around me with the games they're playing."

"You enjoy having men circle you."

"Sure, I'm the kettle, but that makes you the—"

"Your best hope at getting out of this assignment alive. You should treat me that way. I'm not your enemy."

"I can watch my own back. You worry about Malik. Don't get him killed."

"Why would that be happening?"

"Pretty sure we're going to war with the Zhangs at some point."

"Why?"

"Those dead guys? They were Zhang's men."

A smile blossoms on her face. "No, they weren't."

I freeze, and my gaze travels up and down her, speculating. "Finn?"

"Bingo!" Dai Qing makes a firing motion with her finger. "Yeah, looks like he hired them. I wonder why?" She taps the same finger to her lips in mock uncertainty.

"Because it'll fire up Lorcan." I shake my head. "I can't diffuse this without revealing I know what happened. There's no way I could know what you're telling me."

"You and I might not see eye to eye a lot of the time. But you're better than that, Kimi. Where there's a will, there's a way." She glances around the bedroom and picks up her bucket. "You can clean your own damn room."

"You risked blowing my cover to give me shit about bureau paperwork?" I roll my eyes.

"No, I came to see if you needed out. I wasn't sure what was happening with your mother. Malik said it was too complicated for you to meet me right now. So…" She throws out the hand that isn't clutching the bucket. "I came to you."

My heart softens at Malik's thoughtfulness. Even when he's not looking after me, he's still watching out for me. "Nothing has changed with my mom. She's still on the slow descent to checking out."

She crosses the room and places her hand on the door. "You need out, send an SOS or call the number. I won't come here if I don't have to." She sighs. "I'm off to clean one of the other gazillion rooms in your wing of the house."

"Dai Qing?"

She half turns to me before opening the door.

"Does the bureau have a file on me? On my family?"

Frowning, she faces the door for a beat before focusing on me again. "Of course. Files on everyone. They check everything before you're hired."

"I want to see it."

Dai Qing laughs. "Don't we all. Not possible."

"Then I want to see what the bureau knows about my brother."

With a deep breath, she looks me full in the face. "You don't want to be sucked down this hole, okay? Vengeance, whatever you want to call it, it's not going to bring him back. It won't make you feel better. What you feel isn't fixed by knowing."

"What do you know?"

She sighs. "You're asking the wrong questions. What happened to him wasn't because of The Cage, okay?"

"No, it's not okay. If you have information, I want to know." I point my finger.

A brisk knock on my door stops me short.

Her voice a harsh whisper as she says, "Leave it. Nothing good comes from you knowing these things right now, okay?"

"That's bullshit," I whisper back.

"Kimmy, I can hear you whispering in there. Who you got with you?" Finn's voice calls from outside my door.

Dai Qing glances up at me, her face draining of color. His reputation must precede him. Nobody wants to be on the wrong end of ruthless.

With a sweeping motion, I gesture to my bathroom with her cleaning supplies. The bucket in her hand, she scurries to the en suite. Sucking in a breath, I relax my shoulders and open the door.

"One of the cleaners." I school my tone to boredom. "She thinks I'm messy."

Finn peers into my room. With a glance over my shoulder, I confirm she's visible in the mirror tidying up my things.

"I'll have her fired." He's loud enough for Dai Qing to hear.

I stifle a smile. We may not get along, but her reaction to his statement would be similar to mine. Blind rage and defiance. The bucket clatters to the floor.

He tries to enter my room, and I place a hand on his chest. "Don't worry about it. I think she's a temp, anyway."

He frowns. "We don't allow temps." He hones in on Dai Qing, his eyes narrowing. "You a temp?"

She looks up, meeting his gaze in the mirror. "No, sir. Every Sunday, I come here. I clean."

Her accent is so thick, I have to strain to understand her. "Maybe I misunderstood." I shrug. "We're usually out on Sundays." My heart thunders in my chest, and for the millionth time, I'm glad he can't hear it. How often can I raise Finn's suspicion without pointing the finger at myself?

His icy stare scrapes over her one more time. "She seems vaguely familiar."

"Did you want something?" I keep focused on Finn as though Dai Qing doesn't matter. I'm sure she's laughing on the inside at how well she blends into the Asian cleaning company they have working for them.

"Lorcan came to see me." He smirks at me. "Wanna watch us plan a war?"

It seems like I was right about the impending conflict with the Zhangs. This will be as good a chance as any to see how their brains work. "If there's a war, I want a weapon and a say in how it's used."

"I thought you'd feel that way." He nods toward the hall. "Come with me."

With a last glance to Dai Qing, I close the door. She's safe. Now, it's Malik I need to protect.

# Chapter Twenty-Four

We're in Finn's office, which is a first for me. Unlike Lorcan's gray tones, his decorating tastes run much darker to shades of black and bloodred. It's not as big, either. There's no workout space, but there is a giant wooden table with maps of the city spread out across it.

Their makeshift war table makes me appreciate why Finn wanted Lorcan on his side. His mind works the opposite of Finn's. The ideas and tactics he's coming up with on the fly are impressive. Could I turn him? Someone like him at my back would make me a lot safer.

Finn rubs his chin and stares at the main map as Lorcan points out a few weaknesses of the Zhang organization. "I like that." Finn's focus rakes over me after he looks up. "You're being too quiet, Kimmy. It's unnerving. You've always got an opinion."

A half smile surfaces as I round the table. My shoulder brushes against Lorcan's. He kisses my temple. With my index finger, I circle the strip club. "This is home base, right?"

"It generates enough revenue to keep it. It's good for cleaning cash." Finn stares at me across the table.

"I like Lorcan's idea to draw them out. I think it's smart." Lorcan's arm snakes around my waist and tugs me tight to his side. He kisses my temple again. I also like that Malik might stand a chance of surviving this. Though I don't know what the brothers intend to do with any of Zhang's employees who are still alive when we're done dismantling the organization, I could guess.

"I'm more of a smash and grab man, myself," Finn says.

"Seems like a great plan if you want to end up six feet under. Come on, Finn." I cock an eyebrow.

"They tried to kill her. I think we should be more aggressive. Answer back harder." He stares at Lorcan, nodding his head at me.

Holding back an eye roll is almost impossible, but somehow, I manage it. "Having one or both of you dead isn't going to help anyone," I say before Lorcan can respond. "Least of all me." I glance up at Lorcan under my lashes, and he gazes down at me. Deep in his hazel eyes, I think I see a hint of amusement at the way I'm playing this.

When he turns to Finn, he switches to Irish. "You want action? We can do a roundup in a week or two after we understand the players."

He gives a sharp nod of his head. "I'll think about it. We need to come back strong."

Lorcan's phone goes off, and he takes it out of his pocket.

"You're both being rude right now," I say. "I'm right here. I'm part of this. Switching to Irish is a dick move." They've let me into this room, but the change makes me realize neither of them quite trusts me yet. It's unnerving. I'm never sure of Finn, but I would have bet money on my connection with Lorcan.

Finn laughs. "I never claimed I wasn't. Who's that?" He tips his chin at Lorcan who is engrossed in his phone.

"Carys. She's on about some fight at The Cage." He squints at me. "You want to go?"

"Is that a problem?"

Finn smirks. "Only if you turn up alone with Lorcan. It's a nonissue if I go."

"Perfect. So you'll both take me." Do I want them both there? Not really. But it will be a good chance to glean some information.

The brothers exchange a heated look. Finn smirks and then turns away, his lips almost forming a smile. "Just because you don't like it doesn't mean it isn't true, brother."

"If you hadn't fucked up my deal, we'd be fine."

"I sweetened your deal and then decided as an organization we didn't need shit from Derry. We can do better with those pissant Russians."

Lorcan stiffens beside me.

"You thought I didn't know about that?" Finn runs his finger along the edge of the table. "You might have the better tactical mind, but I put the fear of God in people. Apply pressure." He presses his thumb into the table. "You'd be amazed how quickly people talk."

Lorcan's right hand and left hand comment comes back in a rush. Was he meeting with the Russians while I was keeping Finn busy? And Finn knows? Does Lorcan suspect the Russians might have killed his father? My brain kicks into gear, churning out question after question as the two of them stare each other down.

"Are we done here?" Lorcan shifts away from me, his fists clenching and unclenching.

Finn shrugs as though he doesn't care. "That's up to you."

Lorcan's hand trails around my waist as he rounds the table and heads for the hall.

I sigh as the door clicks closed behind him.

"That seemed rather cold. He didn't even ask you to come with him."

*Because he has some weird notion you'll find me irresistible and tell me the truth.* "I don't get you." I turn to face Finn. "What the hell was that? You practically beg me to tell him the Zhangs came after me and then you almost blow the truce to shit."

Finn's jaw hardens. "There was no begging. I asked. You did it."

"Whatever. You need me to help win Lorcan back for some nefarious plan you've cooked up."

"You saw him. You understand why I need him."

"Not many people think like him, that's true. If you need him so badly, why are you determined to piss him off?"

"I want him in the organization, fully in. He needs to realize he's not in charge."

"Seems like he should be in charge."

Finn chuckles. "It would." He indicates the large map on the table. "But what I said is also true. He's smarter than me. No doubt about it. A strategist, corporate raider. He's your man. In *this* business though? People fear me. I hold grudges, chase people down, do the things no one else would dare to do."

"Including murdering your father?"

His attention snaps, and his posture stiffens. "We're back to that old chestnut?"

"You haven't given me a list yet. Why stall if you don't have a reason to hold back? Why wouldn't you want to know who killed your father?"

"I'm busy sorting out this other shit."

"Some of which you're actively creating." It's a challenge, but sometimes I can't help myself. My mouth runs away from my brain.

Finn comes around the table so he's closer. His icy gaze searches my face. "Why are you so interested in The Cage?"

I laugh, the tension going out of me. "That's your follow-up?" Inside, my stomach is doing somersaults. I need to back off, control my mouth, if my attitude is going to raise his suspicion even more. Having him grasp I'm the rot he needs to dig out of his house wouldn't be good. Before I go down, I need to understand what happened to Chad.

"Whenever you get a chance, you circle back to it. It's very curious."

"Fit men. Hot. Sweaty. Fighting for money and honor. Name a woman alive who wouldn't be interested."

"You sound like Carys."

"There's a reason we're friends."

He hums and narrows his eyes. "I cannot decide whether I trust you, Kimmy. My brother clearly likes you. Everything seems golden for a while, and then there's this moment where you're a little tarnished." He holds up the gap between his index and thumb to my eye level. "Something you say or do doesn't quite add up. And a voice in the back of my head whispers to me."

He's so close his breath stirs the tendrils of my ponytail that have come loose. Inside my chest, my heart races, and my fingers itch to release one of my guns. Fight or flight.

"Perhaps that whisper isn't what you think it is." I narrow the gap between us, my chest brushing against his. My gaze flicks to his, building an air of sexual attraction instead of letting fear win.

"That's why you're not dead yet." His voice is a hair's breadth from my ear. "I don't mind the whisper of danger. It keeps me on my toes. If the whisper becomes a roar, you'll be dead before you realize the volume has skyrocketed."

Pulling back, I offer him a lopsided smile which goes against every-thing inside me. "Save yourself a bullet. What you see is what you get."

His thumb grazes my cheek. "It's a very pretty package, I'll give you that. I highly doubt that's all that's underneath."

"You like what you see?"

Finn's lips quirk up. "Very much." He moves away, and cool air rushes against my body. "But I've screwed my brother too many times in too many ways to do it to him again regardless of how attractive the package might be."

Now he's farther away and my head is clearing, I'm not sure I like the implication behind his words. "I'm not some object you can pass around. I get a say in who I'm with and what I do."

He chuckles. "Oh, I'm well aware." He rounds his desk and shuffles some papers, organizing them. "I'm probably more than you could handle anyway."

"Not to mention you slept with one of my best friends last night."

"Wasn't the first time that's happened. Carys and I go way back."

"As evidenced by the scar on her chest."

He pauses his sorting and presses his fingers into the wooden desk. Looking up, his eyes are steel again. "What happened between us back then is none of your business."

"She's my friend. I look after my friends." Guilt pricks at my insides. I also gather evidence on them for an ongoing investigation.

"You've been spending too much time with Lorcan." He opens the top drawer of his desk and takes out a piece of paper. Handing it over, he says, "You know who I look out for?"

I take the paper from him, scanning the handwritten list of names and wait for him to continue. Sometimes I swear he likes the sound of his voice better than anything else.

"Me."

Glancing up, I frown. He's lying, and the only person he's fooling is himself. "And Lorcan. Whether you want to admit it or not, you care."

His bulky shoulders rise. "Lorcan needs saving from himself. He doesn't know when to let things go."

"You do?"

With a chuckle, he shakes his head. "Nah. If I was Lorcan, I would've killed me by now. He wants proof, vindication, to be right. Sometimes you gotta pull the trigger and deal with the fallout."

*The whisper doesn't always become a roar.*

"Watch your back. Some people on that list don't even like a whiff of trouble."

I nod and fold it several times, shoving it into my back pocket. I cross the room to the door and reach for the handle. Before opening it, I half turn to him. "You know, you see Lorcan's hesitation as a weakness. But he doesn't want to believe you killed your father. He doesn't want that outcome."

Finn laces his hands together and places them behind his head. "That's the thing. You can't let it be about what you want. You gotta let it be what it is. No emotion. Raw facts." Releasing his fingers, he says, "Go get him what he wants."

Yanking open the door, I start down the hall to my rooms. I need to photograph this list. Finn's words echo in my head. Part of me can't help wondering if Lorcan's right, if maybe Finn killed their father. Coming to that conclusion doesn't protect any of us. Given the impending war with the Zhangs, a split could kill us all.

# Chapter Twenty-Five

It's been almost two weeks of me checking into the people on the list, dropping by to check on deals, trying to ferret out how each connection feels about the death of the patriarch in the Donaghey family. Lorcan double-checked my names and confirmed Finn gave me plausible leads. While I've been doing this, Lorcan and Finn have been escalating the war with the Zhang organization. They've been sabotaging shipments, interfering in the transfer of women and children. The Zhangs haven't been able to execute any meaningful replies. The Donaghey brothers are a brutal force when they're working together.

When I enter Lorcan's office, his shirt is halfway over his head as he strides from the treadmill to his desk.

"What've you got for me?" He tugs down his shirt and drops into his chair.

I toss photos and notes onto his desk. "Pretty much nothing so far. No one seems overly sad or overly happy about the change in leadership here." What I don't say is how they fear Finn, his temper, his vengeance.

Lorcan laces his fingers together and taps his thumbs against his lips. "How much are you pushing?"

"Enough."

He makes a noncommittal noise, and his frown deepens. "At what point do I say, 'fuck it, he did it?'"

*If I can help it, never.* "It's only been two weeks. I haven't touched the Russians." In the two weeks I've been hunting down their leads, I've been trying to dig into the structure of The Cage as well. It seems like every family has a connection to the fighting ring. The web is vast, and it generates a lot of money for many of the families.

Unlocking his fingers, he reclines in his chair. "The Volkovs are last."

"Why?"

"I have my reasons."

"Would one of those reasons be you think they might have something to do with it?"

He chuckles. "It would not." He comes around the desk, leaning against the edge so we're close enough the scent of his cologne mixes with his sweat, surrounding me.

"Was Finn right? Were you making deals with them behind his back?"

"I was. Course, now he knows, he's paid them a visit, and that one's scupper too." Lorcan shrugs. "It's not the big one I've been working on, so it's no matter."

"The big one?"

"Secret project."

I ease forward so I'm between his legs and lean into him. "Too secret for me?"

The corners of his lips tip up as he loops a stray strand of my hair around his finger. "We're really going to The Cage to watch the fight tonight?" Releasing my hair, his hands fall to my waist. He touches me a lot in public, far less often in private.

"We are." Being this close is sending my body into overdrive. The tension between us hums, and I shift closer. He runs his hand along my waist to the small of my back.

"This is the kind of game you're supposed to be playing with my *dearthár mor*." His voice is husky, his gaze trained on my lips.

"What if I play it with him as well?" As the words leave my mouth, my lips graze his earlobe.

He tightens his hold. The effect I'm having on him is unmistakable. Desire stirs in my stomach and then travels lower so standing here is almost more than I can handle.

"Are you?"

"Wanna know my secret?" I murmur into his ear.

"What's that then?"

"I like you better."

Drawing back, Lorcan's hands come up to frame my face. "You're gonna be the death of me, you know that?"

*God, I hope not.* For once, my face must show what I'm thinking because Lorcan's hazel eyes soften in response. Inch by inch, I lean forward, sweeping my lips across his, giving him a chance to reject me.

When I ease back, his pupils are dilated, and he scans my face in earnest. "You sure about this?"

"You don't want it?" My voice comes from low in my throat and is filled with so much longing I almost don't recognize it. His body is certainly into this, and I want to push him until I get what I want, what I need. We've danced around each other for months.

With one last searching glance, Lorcan's lips descend on mine, and I moan into his mouth, pressing myself closer. He rises to his full height, his lips never leaving mine. His hand tugs my ponytail loose so his fingers can dive into the strands. Sexual frustration pours out of us. Before I can let my brain take control again, I yank off his shirt. He chuckles, the sound going into my mouth and filling my chest. With a gentle shove from him, my jacket falls off my shoulders and hits the floor. His big hands go up under my shirt, drawing it with him over my head, until we're half-naked, our lips locked together.

I've encountered few men who can kiss the way I like, a mixture of softness and firmness that's never quite balanced. Lorcan is nailing it. Heat pools in areas that have been vacant far too long. He walks me backward toward the table in the middle of the room. When my butt hits it, he lifts me onto the top. I run my hands along his chest, savoring the planes and angles which prove how much time he spends working out.

I'm so lost in him it takes a moment for the buzzer to penetrate my brain. Lorcan's lips tear away from mine to glance at the screen on the wall. My focus doesn't leave his face, willing him to ignore whoever is there.

"Finn." He glances at me, indecision in his eyes.

With my hand around his neck, I pull him into another kiss, pressing my hips forward against him. He groans into my mouth and deepens the kiss. One of his hands braces on the table while the other cradles my head, bringing me closer.

The buzzer sounds.

Lorcan's hands splay across my hip bones, and he tugs me tighter as he bends me onto the table. His lips graze my stomach, and I weave my fingers through his hair. He's at the waistband of my pants, and I am slick with need when a fist thumps repeatedly on the door, and then Finn lays on the buzzer without letting up.

I close my eyes and let my shoulders collapse onto the table. Lorcan is above me, hands braced on either side of my head.

"I'll handle this. Don't move." He brushes his lips against mine before he disappears.

The heavy door swishes back.

"I got news," Finn says.

"It can wait. I'm busy," Lorcan's voice is tight.

"You're not going to let me in?"

There's a brief pause where I picture them sizing each other up. With a sigh, I sit and run my hands through my hair. I have no idea where my elastic went.

"Kimmy, put on some clothes, will ya? We got things to discuss."

Jumping off the table, I snatch my shirt off the floor and get it on. His condescending tone sets my teeth on edge.

"It's fine." I mean about Finn coming in, not about being interrupted. The sooner we let him in, the sooner he can say his piece and leave. Once he's gone, I'll convince Lorcan we should pick up where we left off.

He comes back to me, grabbing my coat off the ground and putting it in my hands. His lips skim my forehead before he faces his brother.

"What's got you in a tizzy?" Lorcan raises his eyebrows, tugging me close to his side.

Finn's surveys the room for a moment, and he smirks. "Sorry to interrupt." His gaze lands on Lorcan. "Me and the boys did a roundup. They're in the basement." He nods toward the door. "Come down. Help me decide what to do with them."

Lorcan's hand sneaks up my back to the base of my neck. His lips stray to my temple, and he sighs. "Doesn't have to be right now, does it?"

"Kimmy can come too if that's the problem."

I run my palm across the small of Lorcan's back, wishing Finn wasn't such a persistent asshole. "It's fine." Glancing up at Lorcan, I give a half smile. "I'll come, see what we've turned up."

With a groan, he crosses to his desk and grabs his own shirt from the floor, bringing it down in a series of sharp movements.

"This is usually your favorite part, *dearthár beag*." He winks at Lorcan, and then his attention rakes over me. "You don't strike me as the squeamish type. I hope you've got the stomach for what comes next."

I raise one eyebrow and thread my arms into my coat. Shoving my hands into the pockets, I eye him for another moment. "My stomach is ironclad. Have no fear."

"Excellent. Maybe you'll get to play too." He rotates on his heel and leads the way out of Lorcan's wing without a backward glance.

I've been to the basement before but only on a brief recon visit when Lorcan and Finn were off running errands without me. Most of the rooms are innocuous storage areas, filled with things that had no meaning to me or any investigation. But there'd been a series of rooms that were secured with a small locked window on the outside of them too. Those must be the rooms we're headed to now.

Our feet thud down the stairs in an uneven chorus. In my chest, my heart booms with a touch of anxiety. So far, other than some shady business deals, I haven't witnessed a lot of violence from either man.

Finn comes to one of the locked doors and gives three brisk knocks. I take note of the depth and pitch of each rap, wondering whether I could repeat it if needed. The door swings back, and Antonio is on the other side, his knuckles bloody. Behind him are two of Zhang's men chained to metal chairs. Their chins rest on their chests, blood oozing out of various cuts.

"Jesus, Antonio. I said I'd be right back. I wanted them conscious," Finn says.

He shakes out one of his hands, and his shoulders rise. "They're not dead. As soon as you left, they started running their mouths in some language I didn't understand. I couldn't take the yammering."

Inside I wince at his unwavering simplicity.

"Well, guy. They're no good to me like this," Finn says.

"Hard to find out if Zhang was the one who sent men after me and Antonio when they're unconscious," I say.

Finn chuckles, but when he looks at me, his eyes narrow. "I didn't realize there was another theory floating around. Do tell." His gaze bores into Antonio. "You can leave."

I shrug and push my hands further into the pockets of my coat, and he closes the door behind him. "I like to be sure of things."

"The time to be sure." Lorcan drags a hand down his face as he surveys the bloody mess before us. "Was before we went to war. We're in it now. Whether we're right to be here doesn't matter anymore."

Finn mocks opening a book and pretends to flip pages. "Ah, there we are. Lorcan and I on the same page. Feels good, doesn't it?"

He shakes his head and glances at me out of the corner of his eye. It's brief but in that moment, I know what he's thinking regarding Finn.

"That recon rounded up two men?" Lorcan circles the chairs, unimpressed.

When Finn speaks again, he's switched to Irish. "Settle, brother. The rooms are full down here. We rounded up a dozen or so men."

I scan the room, taking in the stains, chains, and the methods of torture littering the small table in the corner.

"A dozen men?" Lorcan asks.

With a frown, I examine the corners of the room and turn to them. "You don't have cameras down here?" I saw the list of men they were rounding up. They were Zhang's heavy hitters. Twelve sounds about right.

Finn shoots me an annoyed look. "Yes, because we'd love to keep a record of what goes on down here."

"You also don't want people escaping."

"Anyone we bring down here isn't going to be running to the police," Lorcan says. "It doesn't work like that."

"What have you been doing with the sex-and-child-trafficking rings you've been disrupting? What about those women and kids?"

The brothers exchange a heavy glance. Finn winces. "We've been offloading them to someone else."

"Someone who helps them?" Even as I say it, I feel naïve. The exchange between them didn't suggest they were helping anyone but themselves.

"Maybe. Sure. Does that make you feel better, Kimmy? They're being helped. They're certainly helping us."

Rage boils in me under the surface. I try to get Lorcan's attention, but he's focused on the two unconscious men.

"Well, it seems like the two of you have this figured out. I'm going back upstairs. I don't want to see either of you anywhere near me until we're leaving for The Cage." I yank open the door.

As it slams shut, Finn's chuckle echoes behind me.

# Chapter Twenty-Six

The ride to The Cage is silent. Anger spills out of me every time I breathe. It's directed at them, but I'm angry with myself. My head is screwed on so crooked, I convinced myself we were doing a good deed by going to war with the Zhangs. We were disrupting the cycle, giving those women and kids another chance. Instead, Lorcan and Finn were lining their pockets at the expense of those helpless people.

"So far," Finn shifts in the rear, and I tense, anticipating a comment I won't like, "this is turning out to be a stellar night. Thanks so much for inviting me and Lorcan, Kimmy. So kind."

"Fuck you, Finn." I focus on the front passenger window as night falls across the city. "You invited yourself."

"At some point, you'll be thanking me for doing that."

"Doubt it."

"Leave her be, Finn."

Out of the corner of my eye, Finn points his finger toward me. "She's pissy because she had some Robin Hood fairy-tale bullshit in her head. Money and power. That's it. It's pretty simple. If we're not getting one or the other from a transaction, it's useless to us."

Attaching himself to Lorcan stretches my anger almost to the breaking point. Deep down, I realize he's right. Lorcan gave me the same money and power speech when I first started working for them. It shouldn't surprise me. But in the last few months, I've been lulled into a sense that, even if there isn't more to Finn, there is to Lorcan. He's not all bad. There's goodness in him. There isn't an ounce of goodness in what they're doing with the trafficking victims.

"I don't want to hear your theories on why I'm angry." The car butts up to the curb, and before anyone else can get out, I throw open the door. As I climb out, a hand grips my elbow with surprising firmness.

"You're angry." Lorcan's lips are close to my ear. "I get it. Being reckless on a night like tonight isn't good. Keep a lid on it."

Yanking my elbow out of his grasp, I tug my coat into place. "Don't touch me." I give him a cold stare.

He rears back, annoyance and hurt flash in his hazel depths. "Kim."

"I'm serious. Hands off."

Finn rounds the car, and his attention shifts between our two tense postures. He lets out a short bark of laughter. "Yeah, this is gonna be a lot of fun." Squaring his shoulders, he nods to the other guards we brought from another car.

We travel in a minipack now that we've attacked the Zhangs. Lorcan, Finn, and I are in the middle. Makes me wonder whether Lorcan's out-in-front stance when I first started was another facade he wore. Maybe he and Finn are more alike than I want to believe.

Distance. I need distance. I can't keep sinking into this life. We all have a role to play, and mine is to take them down and stop them from ripping each other apart. It isn't to get swept away by either of them.

As we're led to our seats, stale sweat, the sharp tang of fresh blood, and the overwhelming stench of too much cologne causes my stomach to roll. There are too many smells at once. The warehouse is packed with people dressed in a range of clothes from the very expensive and glamorous to something more akin to my yoga outfits as Lorcan likes to call them.

A burly man leads us to a group of three seats in the second row, close to the aisle and central to the action. Carys often surprises me with the people she knows and the things she can do. Rage-filled music is being pumped through the speakers, which is probably supposed to get the crowd in the mood for the bloody fists flying. As we file in, I realize I'll be stuck between Lorcan and Finn. There's no way I'm sitting next to Lorcan for the whole match.

Before I enter the aisle, I hesitate. "I'm going to the bathroom. I'll be back in a minute."

"They're over—" Finn tries to point.

"I know where they are." Moving past him, I head for the hallway as other people mill around me, taking seats, getting drinks, and placing bets.

I locate the accessible bathroom again, somewhat surprised there isn't a line up this near to the match. Once I'm finished, I open the door.

"The everything woman in my establishment, using my facilities. Whatcha doin' here?" Derry's dark gaze bores into me as he comes forward from his relaxed pose against the opposite wall.

His position forces me to either retreat into the bathroom or stand my ground. I'm not a fan of retreating. I clasp the edge of the still-open door. My free hand skims my side to where I concealed a small tactical knife in case I ran into trouble tonight.

"The fight." I tip my head in the direction of the action.

With a shove, Derry propels me into the bathroom. The suddenness catches me off guard. I stumble as he rushes in behind me. My fingers scrabble for the blade. Before I can latch onto it, his hand is around my neck, forcing me backward against the wall. My fingertips graze the hole in my pants where the knife is lodged, but I can't quite get it in this position.

"Did you know they were fucking with me? They never intended to do a deal."

"No." The word is pushed out as I calculate my odds and options of getting out of here in one piece without having to kill him. I could do it. The grip on my chin isn't strong, but it's still spiked my heart rate.

"Why are you here?"

"I wanted to see a fight."

His hold lessens when he comes closer to my face, his lips inches from my ear. In another man, it might even be a turn-on, but he smells like garlic and cheap cologne. "You're one of those women. You get hot and bothered by a bit of violence."

Am I one of those women? Maybe. But his brand of violence isn't the least bit seductive. I swallow and then smirk. "If I was hot and bothered about violence, you'd be on the floor right now."

He takes it the wrong way and presses his bulky body closer. Derry eases off enough on my neck my index finger manages to get purchase on the handle of the knife. I pull until it's almost in my palm.

"You know, the O'Malleys and Donagheys had a good relationship for years. Mutually beneficial. Then Finn had to find out about how his momma was done in, and it went to shit."

"Loose lips sink ships." Another piece of the puzzle.

"And fucking paper trails." Derry's lips graze my earlobe, and a shiver of revulsion goes through me. Again, because he's a clueless wonder who's had too many women with no choice but to say yes, he takes my shiver as excitement. "You like that?" he murmurs.

"Not even a little bit. Your garlic and cologne combination isn't working for me." I push the knife up my sleeve and try a less violent approach to getting free. In one sharp movement, I latch my hands onto his shoulders and slam my knee into his groin with as much force as I can muster.

He stumbles, cupping himself, groaning through clenched teeth, "You're gonna regret that."

With a flick of my wrist, the knife pops out into my hand. "Unless you're packing, I doubt it. You don't touch a woman who doesn't want to be touched. It's a lesson I hear you've yet to learn."

"It ain't gonna be a woman who teaches it to me."

The door creaks open, and Finn slips in. Derry's in such a rage he doesn't register Finn's presence. I keep my focus on Derry.

"If it was going to be a woman, I think she'd be the one to do it." Finn's tone is low and menacing. "If it needs to be a man, I'm happy to oblige."

Derry whirls around faster than I expect from a man clutching his balls. "Finn." His eyes are wild with fear. "We were talking."

"I think you were touching. And I'm pretty sure"—he holds up a finger—"I told you what touching her meant."

"I was just tryin' to find out why she was here. You're not on the list."

Funny, he didn't say a word about a list. I flip my knife around in my hand, content to let Finn lead this line of questioning.

"Didn't sound like it to me. We're on the list—Carys Van de Berg, party of three." His arms are loose at his side, but every once in a while, he makes a fist and releases it, as though he's warming up his hands.

"Van de Berg." Derry smirks. "Wasn't she the chick who almost got you deported to Ireland or some shit?"

Finn's right fist connects with Derry's face so fast, if he wasn't doubled over again, I'd wonder if it happened. He coughs and touches his face with his fingertips, grimacing.

"How many times did he touch you?" Finn asks.

"With his lips or his hands?"

Finn brings his fist around hard into Derry's side. "Sounds like at least twice."

"Oof." He falls to his knees, hands raised, bent at the waist. His breathing is labored. "I didn't mean any harm."

I snort. "You mean you couldn't do any harm." Rolling my eyes at Finn, I tuck my knife into my pants.

"I'm not getting into this with you anymore tonight." Finn's icy gaze watches him stumble to his feet. "I got a fight to watch. Don't think this is the end of it."

Derry clutches his side and limps out the door without saying a word. At least he knows better than to taunt Finn any more.

"Thanks," I say when the door clicks shut. "How'd you know where I was?"

"'Cause you headed in the wrong direction to the bathroom. The bathrooms for the fight are on the floor. You don't go down this hall unless you're doing business. Lorcan wanted to come, but I didn't figure you wanted his help."

I shove my hands into my coat pockets. "I didn't need help, actually."

Finn chuckles. "Can't give an inch, huh?"

"Would you?"

He eyes me with what seems like a touch of respect. "No." When I go to step toward the door, he steps with me.

"The fight is about to start." I can never read him, and it's exasperating.

"Are you pissed at Lorcan, or is this something you two engineered to create a rift between you?"

"Are you reselling those women and kids to someone else?" I stare at him, hoping I misunderstood.

He shrugs.

"Then I'm pissed. At both of you. Not just him. But mostly him."

"A leopard doesn't change its spots 'cause it starts banging a cougar."

"Nice, Finn. Real nice." I cross my arms and refuse to focus on him. "How'd your mom die?"

"What's that have to do with anything?"

"Oh, lots, I think. Derry brought it up."

"Any hack with Google can find out the answer." He ruffles the back of his hair. "I'm not sure if I'm impressed or annoyed you haven't bothered." He sighs. "Car accident. Faulty brakes." His voice drips with derision on the last two words.

"The O'Malleys had something to do with that?"

"They did. Look, Kimmy. It's complicated. It was a long time ago." His face is shuttered. "I got my revenge."

For the first time since we started talking, I lock my gaze with his. "Did it make you feel better?"

He chuckles but it's devoid of humor. "I'm probably supposed to give you some bullshit answer about how it wasn't what I thought it would be. Right? I think that's what you'd want me to say. But it felt *exactly* how I thought it would. I balanced the scales. I set things right."

*Balanced the scales.* Is that how I'll feel when I know who murdered Chad and why? Will killing whoever it is, assuming they're still alive, give me a sense of rightness?

This time, when I go around Finn, he lets me. He follows me out of the bathroom. "I know he hired you to get close to me."

I stop and whirl on him in the hallway. "Yes, Finn, because the world clearly revolves around you."

"I'm glad we agree."

Sashaying back, I trail my finger down the front of his shirt and pitch my voice low to say, "If that were true, I'd be doing a pretty terrible job. And I'm good at everything I put my mind to." I glance up under my lashes. "You see. If I were trying to get close to you, I'd have done it by now. I'd be like a second skin. Every time you took a breath, you'd breathe me in like oxygen. Every time you went to bed, you'd feel me pressed up against you. At night when you dreamed, you'd dream of me."

He angles his head so his lips almost touch my ear, like Derry's did earlier. Only this time, when the shiver races through me, it's not followed by revulsion.

"I know what you're doing, but I can't help being intrigued by you." He smirks. "My brother knows me well."

"What are you going to do about it?"

"The fight's about to start." Lorcan is at the end of the hallway, his voice echoing toward us.

I flinch as though scalded, and Finn chuckles. Tension radiates off Lorcan. Seeing him there causes an ache to spread across my chest. I want things I shouldn't.

"The fight." The words are forced out of his lips.

"Yeah." I turn from Finn. "I heard you. It's about to start." With that, I stride past Lorcan, avoiding his gaze. He tries to snag my arm, but I sidestep him.

"Come on, brother." Finn's mocking echoes in the corridor. "Is that all you've got?"

# Chapter Twenty-Seven

To anyone else, it seems like I'm focused on the fight in the cage, but I'm not taking in any of it. From time to time, Finn inclines his head in to murmur a bit of strategy in my ear, and I nod along while his words run right through me. The rage in me is bottomless, unending, and it's directed at Lorcan. It's irrational, I understand that much. But I can't figure out how to contain it. His face in the hallway, his part in reselling the women and children, the way he's so engaged in the fight as though what's happening between us doesn't mean anything—all of it keeps my anger boiling below the surface.

During every round, bar staff come to the first few rows to gather drink orders. The three of us pound beer after beer as though there's enough alcohol to drown out the tension.

When they cart the final unconscious, bloodied man out of the ring, Finn claps his hands in response to his betting prowess, and I stand up, ready to be done with it.

"What no autograph from the winner, a selfie, nothing?" His eyes laugh at me, and he chugs back the last of his beer.

I stumble, and Lorcan's hand snakes out around a seated Finn to steady me. With a yank, I free my elbow but almost fall face-first into Finn's lap. As he rises from his seat, he helps stabilize me.

"Easy, tiger." He drops his empty cup to the ground.

"I thought I was a cougar."

"Tiger, cougar." He makes a dismissive motion with his hand.

"What the hell are you two on about?"

"Private joke." I avoid Lorcan's probing gaze. Let him stew on that.

"You and Finn have private jokes now?"

"Seems like." I extract myself from Finn's grip and shuffle the few seats to the end of the aisle. The rest of the crew is watching the three of us with a mixture of curiosity and annoyance. Only Antonio peers at me with anything resembling concern.

When I get close, he leans in. "You all right?"

"No. I need to go back to the house and crash. Switch off my brain."

"You riding up front again?"

"Yeah."

The men scatter around, forming a barrier between us and anyone else. With a deep breath, I blink my eyes and force myself to focus. To be this drunk, I had to be too lost in my own head. I never get this blotto when I'm on the job. It's a bad idea. I couldn't defend myself right now even if I wanted to, and tomorrow will be an epic hangover.

The entire ride, I picture Lorcan and Finn sitting in the back, sizing each other up while I try to stay conscious, and Antonio drives with ease. As soon as we file in the door, Ian approaches Finn and jerks his head in the direction of the basement.

Finn examines me, his distaste evident. "Go sleep it off. You're no good to anybody like this."

As he strides toward the basement stairs, I yell after him, "I'm a person, Finn. I don't have to be good for anyone but myself sometimes."

Lorcan and I are left in the entranceway, staring at each other for an extra beat. There's so much I want to say, and none of those words can leave my lips.

"Bed. I'm going to bed." I step down the hall. Lorcan comes with me. "Alone."

Lorcan chuckles. "My rooms are this way."

"Don't." I wag a finger. "Don't turn on that accent like a faucet. It's not going to work."

"Pity. I was hoping it might dampen"—his gaze connects with mine—"your dislike of me."

"I can't talk to you right now."

"Tomorrow."

"No. Unless it's related to work, actual business you and I have together, we're nothing." I head to my rooms, half expecting him to follow me.

He doesn't.

At first, the pounding is part of my dream. As I try to puzzle out why there's a door in my beachy scene, my conscious brain kicks in, and Lorcan's voice follows the noise. I jolt awake.

Jumping out of bed, I expect there to be an emergency the way he's hitting the door. When I swing it back, the world is still fuzzy. The hangover hasn't kicked in, but I'm not falling down drunk. Buzzed. Much more acceptable. "Is the house on fire?"

Lorcan's muscular arms are braced against the doorframe. He smells like whiskey, and his attention trails over me, hot with desire.

Why is he staring at me like that? *Oh no.* I went to sleep in my bra and underwear. Drunk me is so classy. While holding up a finger, I grab a robe and throw it on, belting it. "So fire? Or police? Or...? Someone's dead."

"Oh, someone might be dead. Maybe several someones. Finn's been downstairs a long time. Not why I'm here, though." He slants deeper into the doorway.

"Well, if there's nothing work related." I start to close the door in his face.

"It's work related." He squeezes around me and the half-open door before I can think to stop him.

I cross my arms. "Okay." I squint at the clock. "What couldn't wait for another three or four hours?"

"Why are you pissed at me?"

"That's not work related."

"It is. I can't work with someone who is pissed at me."

"You work fine with Finn."

"He's not pissed at me. Least not anymore. I'm pissed at him. 'Tis not the same."

"It doesn't matter."

"It matters to me. It matters a hell of a lot when I see you sidled up to my brother like a horse in heat."

I scrunch my face, stuck on the visual. "Horses sidle up to each other when they're in heat? I didn't know that."

Lorcan lets out a grunt of frustration.

"You can't be angry with me about that. You hired me to do what I was doing in the hallway."

"Didn't think you were actually doing it."

"Of course I am!"

"I don't like it."

"Too bad."

"I hired you to do that, I can fire you from doing that."

"Suits me fine." I throw up my arms and go to the walk-in closet to pull out my suitcase. I toss it on the bed and unzip it.

"What are you doing?"

"You fired me." Taking a large armful of clothes from my dresser drawers, I chuck them into the suitcase.

"From seducing Finn, not from finding my father's killer."

"Well, if you're going to tie my hands in how I can get information, it's probably best you fire me."

"You're being irrational." Lorcan moves to the bed and flips the lid on my suitcase so when I throw the next load of my things in that direction they scatter on top of the suitcase and across the bed.

"A man's first line of defense and offense—call the woman irrational. You know what's irrational? Showing up at my door in the middle of the night to fire me. That's irrational."

"I'm not firing you from the job. I'm firing you from sleeping with Finn."

"I can sleep with Finn if I want..." I glance at Lorcan and then away. "Or not. My body, my choice."

We are mere inches apart. My breathing is heavy, labored as though I've been doing more than packing. His hazel eyes, when I look up, are darkened with desire. The things I wish for when I look at him can't be said aloud.

"Choose me," he murmurs.

"I can't." Everything in me strains to give in.

"Why are you mad at me?"

I close my eyes, unable to look at him. "I want you to be better. Better than you are. I know that's not fair. I thought maybe you were decent, and it turns out you're just like your brother." My voice is a whisper now, and the words spill from me. Saying this is reckless.

"I'll put a stop to the trafficking."

I open my eyes and our gazes connect. "Finn will be pissed."

"He'll understand why I did it."

"Ah." I take a step back, prepared to close myself off. "We're back to that again."

"No." His hand grips my elbow gently when I try to move away. "We're not. I was serious before."

"You're drunk."

"So are you."

"This is a bad idea."

"The worst idea I've ever had. And I've had some doozies. But I can't help myself. I don't want to anymore. At some point, the pretend became real."

I shake my head, my resolve cracking. "You and me—we're never going to go anywhere. It begins and ends with this job."

"Sometimes just for now is just as good."

I search his face, wishing I was more sober or rational or something for this conversation. Hell, possibly in life.

"Say yes, Kim."

Without a word, I lean forward, loop my hand around the back of his neck and tug him into a kiss. His lips taste like whiskey when they connect with mine, and he gathers me close in one fluid movement. As soon as I'm pressed against him, his hands are everywhere, and we are a wildfire, burning my defenses.

"I take it that's a yes." His teeth scrape against my earlobe.

"No talking." His lips trail along my neck, and a moan escapes me. Lower. Lower. "As a brief aside." I cling to his shoulders, loving the way his muscles move under my hands. "There was no way I wasn't going to sleep with you when you can kiss like this. What else can those lips do?"

My robe falls to the floor, and Lorcan angles back to stare at me. "When you answered the door like this, I thought I might collapse on the floor in front of you." His voice is deep and husky, blending my insides to mush. "You're gorgeous."

He tugs on the elastic holding my hair. Tossing it onto the dresser, he digs into my strands and draws me into another kiss.

My hands find the hem of his shirt, and I tug it over his head in one swift movement. Our lips only disconnect long enough for the shirt to clear his face. With a flick of his fingers, my bra releases, and it tumbles to the floor. I slide my hand into his pants and cup his manhood. His groan into my mouth is almost a growl. He murmurs my name over and over like a prayer as though saying it might save us both. When I press my body closer, his fingers peel off my underwear. Lorcan's hands slip under my thighs, and he lifts me onto the dresser.

His gaze locks with mine as he sinks to his knees and parts my legs. His tongue flicks and darts around my aching center. I grip his hair and show him how I like it. He adapts to my wordless directions, and I throw back my head, caught up in feelings I haven't had in years. The tension builds at my core, but it's not enough. I need more.

"Lorcan," I gasp. "I want you inside me. I want to feel you inside me."

He kisses his way up my body until he's at my lips. I push at the waistband of his pants and boxer briefs as he takes a foil package out of his pocket. It's happening so fast, but I can't bring myself to care. We've been on the cusp of this for months.

"Thought I was a sure thing?" I watch him step out of his pants, rip open the package, then roll it on.

Our gazes connect, and he kisses me again. Against my lips, he says, "Never. I sure as hell hoped."

One of his large hands brings my butt forward, his tip poised at my entrance. He digs his other hand into my hair, and we stare at each other.

"Tell me again," Lorcan says.

"I want you. I want to feel you inside me."

We kiss, and he slides into me. He secures my hips tighter to him, so each thrust rubs us together, drawing me closer to the edge once again.

"You feel so good," Lorcan whispers in my ear before he bites on my earlobe.

We move together, lost in a haze of sensations and kissing. The tension in me builds to a fevered pitch. I clutch his shoulders, wondering whether I can hold off.

"Lorcan." My voice is strained to my own ears. I'm so close. "Oh, God, this feels so good."

"Come for me, baby."

That's all it takes. The dam breaks, and wave after wave courses through me. His arms cradle my back, and with a few more thrusts, he follows behind me.

Languid and more relaxed than I've been since I arrived, I rest my head against the wall. His lips trail kisses across my shoulders and neck. "Come back to my room."

"Lorcan." I kiss his cheek, my hair falling around me like a curtain. "There's this and then there's that." Starting a pattern of sleeping in his room, cuddled up, isn't good. He may not realize it, but I know too well this won't end happily.

"I don't care."

"You might someday."

"In the moment, Kim."

With one finger, I trace the side of his face and along his jaw. When we lock eyes, I can't deny him. "Okay."

Such a simple word threatens to start an avalanche across my soul. This slope isn't just slippery; it might bury me.

# Chapter Twenty-Eight

The next morning when I wake up, my body aches. It's the good kind of ache, the one you only get from achieving maximum pleasure in a short period. Once we came back to his room, we spent more time exploring each other, releasing the pent-up desire that's been building for weeks. With one hand, I reach out for Lorcan, but the bed is cold beside me.

Then it dawns on me I'm alone in his room for the first time. Sitting up, I press the heel of my hand to my pounding forehead. On the nightstand are two aspirin and a glass of water. With my headache, I'm not in the mood to search his room. I don't allow my thoughts to drift to the other reason why I don't want to snoop right now. Tomorrow, I'll get my head back in the game. Today, I'll let it pound away. A note beside the aspirin says *basement* in Lorcan's familiar scrawl.

With a sigh, I pick up the pills and toss them back, chasing them with lukewarm water. He must have been gone a while. Throwing back the covers, I search the room for my robe and find it hanging on the back of his door. I certainly can't go to the basement wearing that. I have no idea what I'm going to find there.

At the entrance, I scan his room as I tighten the belt around my waist. As soon as I leave, I'm locked out. Should I take a look around?

My temple throbs in response, and that's enough of an answer for me. Exiting his room, I wander down the hall to my wing. As I round the corner, someone is scrubbing the floor outside my door.

It's Sunday. The cleaners are here again. Until Dai Qing showed up, I never paid much attention to anyone from the cleaning company. Now I know she has an in to the property through them, I give them all a second glance. When I get closer to the woman kneeling on the floor, she looks up. It's not her.

"Sorry." I point to the door next to where she's kneeling. "I need to get in there."

"Sure, sure." She shuffles sideways, hauling the pail with her. "I'll be here, scrubbing the floor."

Frowning, I punch in the code. "Okay. Thanks."

When the door opens, the smell of disinfectant is overwhelming. My head pounds again, and my heart rate accelerates. On the bed, my suitcase sits zipped closed, but there aren't clothes everywhere. Someone has been here. The hairs on my neck rise in response. I'm not alone.

In two strides, I'm at the bed, unsnapping the gun as someone comes out of the en suite bathroom. Whirling, I point my gun, willing my skull to stop its deep throbs of complaint.

"It's me." Her hands are raised. "I put Yichun on the door in case anyone walked in while I was searching."

"Searching?"

"I came in and saw your suitcase on the bed, clothes strewn everywhere, your phone left charging in the bathroom. No sign of you. I know they're in the basement. I was getting ready to call it in."

"Call it in?" My gun is still raised. Something is off with Dai Qing, but my headache pounds so hard I'm having trouble putting the pieces together.

"I was starting to think *you* were in the basement. That maybe you'd be the one screaming next."

"You thought they found out who I was." I lower my gun and ease myself onto the edge of the mattress.

Her focus flicks over me. "Lorcan's room or Finn's?"

Placing the gun beside me, I massage my temples. "Lorcan."

"You trust him?"

I shrug. "Can anyone be trusted?"

"No. Not right now. I'm not sure you're being very smart."

"When was the last time you were in the field?" I narrow my eyes at her.

A few years ago, one of Dai Qing's agents died a public and violent death at the hands of the people she was investigating. That agent was the person who trained me. I liked her, respected her. The bureau cleared Dai Qing of any wrongdoing. I never did.

She flushes but holds my gaze. "I can tell a dangerous situation when I see one."

I let out a bark of laughter. "They're all dangerous. I haven't been on an assignment yet that didn't put my life on the line every single day."

"You love it."

"I don't hate it, or I wouldn't do it." Dropping my hands into my lap, I'm thankful my aspirin seems to be dulling my aching brain. "Why are you here?"

"Malik," she whispers.

My heart kicks against my rib cage, reverberating to my skull. "What about him?"

"He's missing. We were supposed to meet last night."

"You tried the protocol? The checks?"

"Yes." She straightens her maid's uniform. "He said he had info for me, that the Donaghey brothers were rounding up Zhang's men."

"He wasn't on the list." My head sinks into my hands. "I checked the list. He wasn't on it."

"Would they have given you a complete list?"

The way they switched to Irish the other day when I was in the room, the way Finn says one thing and then does another, the glances the two of them exchange sometimes are loaded with messages I don't understand tell me I could be in trouble.

"The list came from Finn. It's possible it wasn't complete or he added names later."

"Malik could be in the basement."

Closing my eyes, I nod. "I can find out." I run my palms down my face and sigh. "If he is and he's still alive?" The ache in my chest spreads. Finn was in the basement when Lorcan came to my room. If we were... and Finn was... and Malik is...

Dai Qing frowns and runs her hand along the top of the dresser. "I'd suggest an extraction if he's still alive. It could blow up in our faces." She hesitates. "In your face."

"I can handle myself."

She worries her bottom lip between her teeth. "We're here until later this afternoon cleaning. You have to get the information before then."

"You don't think he's hiding out? Waiting for the roundup to clear?"

"No. You know Malik."

He doesn't hide. The thought of him in the basement, being tortured or dead is enough to make my stomach roll. He's like family to me, one of the few people who manages to keep me grounded when the insanity of a job threatens to drag me under.

"He might be fine. If they pulled him in last night, he might be one of the last."

"Finn was already suspicious of him. He saw him at the bar, then at Zhang's. I tried to play it off as a coincidence, but he doesn't believe in those."

"Get dressed. Find me later. We'll figure out what to do."

I ease my hands along my thighs.

Dai Qing passes me on the way to the door. "Oh." She half turns back to me. "I almost forgot. I looked at your file."

I straighten to my full height. "You did?"

"When you find me later, I'll tell you what I can."

"So there *are* things to tell?"

"Your file is weird. I'm still trying to figure out some of it. I can dig around once you and I have chatted, okay? If Malik is in danger, that comes first."

"Agreed. Of course. Yes." Before she opens the door, I say, "Thank you."

Dai Qing smiles. "Just doing my job." With that, she slithers out.

As fast as I can, I get dressed. At the last minute, I throw on my leather jacket. It's cool in the basement. Taking a couple of deep breaths, I steel myself before opening my door. Even if he's there, I can't give anything away. Whatever happens, I have to play my part.

Each step to the basement knocks at the door to my emotions. He's the only person left in the world who knows me, the successes, the failures, what keeps me up at night. I've taken our connection for granted. It doesn't matter what I have to do. If he's in the basement, I'm getting him out.

At the bottom on the stairs, Antonio is in the hall on a chair, playing with his phone. I wander toward him, grateful he can't see my heart beating against my breastbone.

"Where's Lorcan?" It's Finn I'm worried about, not Lorcan.

He doesn't look up, just points his thumb over his shoulder. "In there. Came to see what his bro's been doing and discovered someone he recognized." When he looks up, he squints at me. "Some guy's been following you?"

Bile rises in my throat. "What?"

"They got some black guy in there. Finn said he was suspicious, and then when Lorcan saw him, he said the guy'd been following you. Wouldn't give any other details." Antonio shrugs. "You wanna go in? It's probably a mess in there. Lorcan was fired up. He doesn't play around when he's mad."

I swallow the acid bubbling up into my throat. My first instinct is to rip open the door, fly in there, and drag Malik out. Lorcan might not kill me for it, but Finn would in an instant. I lick my lips and push my hands so deep into my coat pockets my fingers could burst through.

"Let me in." I tip my chin at the door. I want to press the heel of my hand into my torso to calm my insides, but I don't dare. No tells. No indication this is anything but routine curiosity.

He rattles his key ring. Then, he seems to think better of it and knocks on the door. "Kim's out here."

I wish he opened it. What if they don't let me in?

The entrance pops open faster than I expect. Finn is in the doorway, covered in blood splatter that makes my stomach heave again.

"You sure you got the stomach for this, Kimmy?" He eyes me then smirks.

"I think you know the answer by now."

"I thought I did, then you went soft on me yesterday about the women and children." His voice drips with mockery.

My gaze rakes over him. "I see you've been having fun."

"Indeed, I have. Watching those fights got me fired up."

*So you decided you'd come beat and torture defenseless people?* The words are close to tumbling out. I press my lips together.

He eases the door open to reveal Lorcan, blood coating his hands. My jaw tightens. I can't look at Malik. There's so much blood, and Lorcan's face is thunderous.

"Lorcan." I run my hand along his tense back. His cheeks and forehead are covered with red splotches.

Nodding his head in Malik's direction, he says, "He works for Zhang. It was no coincidence he was there that night, Kim." His bloodied hands are clenched at his sides.

I search his face. "Maybe not."

"There is no such thing as coincidence," Finn chimes in from the table where they keep the various tools for torture.

"Has he told you anything?" Already I know Malik hasn't given me away. Neither of these men is good at acting. Finn's enjoying this, and Lorcan's doing it out of a misguided attempt to protect me. If Malik wasn't a complete mess a few feet from me, it would be almost sweet.

"He hasn't been conscious often enough." Finn riffles through the tools on the table, searching for something before producing a pair of tweezers. "Ah-ha."

Whirling on him, I keep my hand on Lorcan's back, hoping it'll ground him. "Have you slept?"

"Nope." His icy eyes are bloodshot.

"Maybe it's a good idea to take a break. If you're not getting any information out of him, what's the point? Don't we want to know why he was following me? Who put him up to it?"

"Zhang." He shrugs. "Done."

I push back. "Or maybe I'm too close to your father's killer and someone hired him to follow me."

His eyes narrow, and he grows still.

"Seems like a reach." Lorcan guides his hand around my waist. It's the first hint of softening since I entered. Malik's blood is probably smeared across my waistband.

"You don't know if you can't ask." Pursing my lips, I glance at Malik and then wish I hadn't.

He's almost unrecognizable. One eye is swollen shut. Amongst the blood on the floor are fragments of teeth. The sea of red makes it hard to decipher what else is wrong with him. Unconscious, his chin rests on his chest. My throat is in a vise, and I'm not sure I'll be able to speak again. I'll never forgive Lorcan if he kills him, but that argument is impossible to make.

He turns to his brother, and there must be something on his face because Finn drops the instrument he found with a clang.

"I knew you didn't have the stomach for it, Kimmy." He takes two quick strides toward me and Lorcan comes between us. Finn points his finger at me. "You know that tarnish I was talking about? It's all over you right now. What the fuck do you care what we do to this guy?"

"It's not good business," I fire back. "If anyone looks suspicious here, it's you. Why not question him? Why not find out why he was following me? Huh? Or maybe you already know, Finn. Maybe he's been following me because you organized it."

He chuckles, but tension is leaking out of him. "Why would I do that?"

"You knew this guy was driven by money. It's why he went to work for Zhang. You were *supposedly* investigating him. Then, suddenly he shows up somewhere only Lorcan and I know about? I mean, come on." I throw up my arms. "Maybe he wasn't even following me. Maybe he was following you, Lorcan." I stare at Lorcan, letting my anger flow out of me.

His hazel eyes seek the truth in my face. I've played this game before, and it's never mattered more than now. I can navigate this.

"You think I hired this guy to follow my brother?" His voice is full of contempt.

Clenching my jaw, I refuse to back down. "It's possible. Why would you be so keen to off this guy without even questioning him?"

He takes another step forward, and Lorcan tenses in front of me. "I got every man in this organization in my back pocket. Everyone is a spy. I have no use for people with questionable loyalty."

Lorcan's fist clenches, and he leans into his brother. "I better be reading this wrong, *dearthái mor*. You don't threaten her. You got me, guy?"

With a chuckle, Finn rocks back on his heels. "That's all it took? One drunken fuck and you're choosing her over me?"

Lorcan's fist slams into his face with enough force for Finn to stumble back a couple of steps. He laughs as he wipes his nose, a trickle of blood running to his lips. "You get one, *dearthráir beag*. One. You hit me again, and brother or not, I'll fuck you up."

"From now on"—Lorcan secures my hand with his—"you stay away from Kim."

Finn puts his arms out, palms to the ceiling. "But you brought her here for me. I think it's only fair I get a turn."

He releases my hand, and his other latches onto Finn's neck, backing him up against the wall.

"One, brother," Finn says, the words squeezing out around Lorcan's hand. He holds up a finger. "You hit me again, and the gloves are off."

"You don't talk to her like that. You don't think about her like that. Even if you didn't kill our father, I'll never forgive you if you touch her."

Finn's gaze finds mine across the room. "What if she touches me?"

Lorcan gives Finn a violent shove, and his body thuds against the wall.

"Lorcan, let's go." I run my hand down his arm until I can link our fingers together again. "This isn't worth it."

"You're right." Finn yanks his shirt back into place. "It's not worth it." His gaze connects with mine, and Lorcan tries to escape my death grip on his arm again.

"Come on," I murmur. "Let's get you clean. Grab something to eat." Everything about this conversation is unnatural with Malik unconscious in the room. I have to find Dai Qing, but I can't trust Lorcan to keep a lid on his temper.

Never taking his focus off his brother, Lorcan opens the door.

"You're staying here?" I ask Finn.

"Oh, no. I'm moving on. I wouldn't want my *deartháir beag* to think anything you said had a point to it." Finn sniffs. "You smell that, Kimmy?"

I narrow my eyes.

"Rot. Eating away at the foundations of this place. I'd best root it out."

I roll my eyes even as that muscle I'm starting to loathe begins to pound once more. A heart attack is imminent. "Sure, Finn. You root out that rot." With that, I close the door behind us.

# Chapter Twenty-Nine

I insisted Lorcan shower before I'd have anything to do with him. He tried to coax me into joining him, but I only have a narrow window to find Dai Qing, tell her about Malik, and get whatever information she has from my file. Before rushing out of Lorcan's room, I tell him I'm going to change. I've got blood on my clothes. Malik's blood. It makes my stomach clench every time the thought crosses my mind.

I'm running down the hall when I see Yichun dusting my wing. Popping my head into where she's working, I say, "Please get Dai Qing as quickly as you can."

She gives a curt nod and dashes off while I punch in the code to my room. The light burns red, and it beeps at me. I missed the numbers. When I raise my hand again, it's shaking. With a deep breath, I steady myself. This won't do. I can't fall apart. Finn knows nothing. Malik needs my help. *Breathe*. I input the code again.

As I'm yanking off my shirt, there's a brisk knock. At the door, Dai Qing is there with her bucket of cleaning supplies. She comes in and drops everything with a clatter. The door clicks shut behind her.

"He's there." She takes the words right out of my mouth.

"Yes. It's bad." I discard my pants and search my drawers for other clothes. "When can you extract?"

"Maybe tonight. I don't know how much warning, if any, I can get you. Stay out of the basement. Try to keep at least one of them away from there. Fewer people means less likelihood of exchanging fire, setting off alarms, getting anyone killed."

I nod and pull a shirt over my head. "Noted."

She points to my cheek and frowns.

In the bathroom, I see a spot of blood. Over and over, I pump the soap and wipe my face. When I look, my hands are covered in blood. I scrub and scrub until she places her hand on top of mine.

"They're clean."

I look at her in the mirror. "Are they?" Tears pool in my eyes. "I'm screwed. Finn's suspicious. Malik—" My voice cracks on his name. "He's here because of me."

"We'll get him out."

I brace my hands on the counter and stare in the mirror. Hungover and haunted is not a good look on me. "My file?"

Dai Qing sucks in a breath. "I'm not sure right now is the best time for that."

"I want to know. When will we get a chance again? It's getting dangerous. I don't want you to end up in the basement at some point."

The color drains out of her face like a faucet running dry. "The deaths connected to you were ruled as suspicious, did you know that?"

I frown. "Deaths? There's one. Chad. Well, two, actually. My father. But he died in a hiking accident."

She shakes her head. "Three deaths, all with the phrase *possible Mafia involvement* and a question mark. It's odd. I mean, usually that's investigated before you get hired. Especially for your job. I mean, if you were an accountant, I could understand it. Even if you were someone like me. Or like an analyst or... security at the agency. But you, you're—"

"Dai Qing." I cut off her rambles. "There haven't been three deaths. There've been two." My watch starts beeping, and there's a soft knock on the door. He'll be out of the shower now. I need to get moving.

"Kim," Yichun says through the door. "Lorcan is calling for you."

He's probably worried Finn's after me. God. This is so messed up. I exit the bathroom and grab pants from a drawer and put them on. "Who else?"

"Chad's father. Ho-Jun."

My mind flashes to my mother murmuring those names when I visited her. Then, I remember the violent way she reacted to Lorcan. My skin begins to crawl. Shaking my head, I don't let the thought take hold. With some force, I gather my hair and loop an elastic around it over and over as tight as I can. "I don't understand."

"I'll try to dig. I don't know when I'll be able to get that information to you."

"Understood." I stride to the door and open it.

Without another word, I call for Lorcan, pushing my misgivings aside. I might not be able to keep Finn out of the basement, but I intend to do whatever I can to keep Lorcan away from there. If they come to extract Malik, I don't want Lorcan caught in the crossfire.

Lorcan's lips trail along my body, and I thread my hands through his hair. We've spent most of the day in a tangle of limbs, breathless sighs, and drifting in and out of sleep. As much as possible, I've tried to keep my mind off Malik in the basement.

Dai Qing showed up at Lorcan's door before she left under the pretense of cleaning his room. It was already done, but it gave her enough time to mouth they'd move in around three in the morning.

"Would you ever leave?"

Lorcan's lips freeze on my stomach, and when he lifts his head, one side of his mouth quirks up. "Leave?"

I lick my lips. "Organized crime."

His eyes narrow. "Seems like an odd question." He braces his elbows on either side of my body and crosses his arms over my stomach, resting his chin on top. "You're in this business. That question from another woman? Maybe. But you? You might not enjoy all of it, but you seem to enjoy enough."

"Never mind." I push on his shoulder with my hand, trying to dislodge his position. There's a chance all hell is going to break loose tonight, so more sleep is probably for the best. This conversation is stupid.

He shifts off me and comes back up to the pillow beside me. We're both quiet for a moment, and then he rotates onto his side, cradling his head in his hand. I don't look at him though. Instead, I stare at the ceiling, wondering what I'm doing in this bed with him when Malik is downstairs, possibly at death's door. What would Malik do if the situation was reversed? What I'm doing now. He's cool and calculated which is why I trust him more than most. My only hope is Finn got bored and went to bed.

"What are you thinking about?"

"My mind is a blank slate."

He chuckles. "I doubt that very much." He collapses onto his back and pulls me into his side. "What's eating you?"

"What was it you said once? You fall down that hole and there isn't much chance of coming back out."

He squeezes me tighter. "Must have been drunk. That sounds like drunk Lorcan."

"I've been thinking maybe when we figure out what happened to your dad, I'll do something different."

"Yeah?" His face fills with amusement. "You going to go work for some Hollywood starlet? Keep the paps from taking pics up her skirt or something?"

I punch him in the arm. "Or something. Seriously, did you always want to do this?"

Lorcan grows quiet beside me. "When I was younger, I didn't want anything to do with it. My father, his friends, some of the bodyguards—I was afraid a lot. My mum was protective, maybe too much. I dunno. Then she got cancer when I was fourteen. And I..." He makes a spiraling motion with his hand and then flattens his palm on my shoulder. "I scuppered any chance I had of doing something different." His shoulders rise and fall. "I wasn't afraid anymore of my dad or his friends. I understood the violence in a way my mum never wanted for me."

"Then by fifteen..."

"I'd killed a man, yeah." He ruffles his hair and eases his palm behind his head.

"You did it for Finn?"

"I did. Fat lot of good that did me. He wasn't grateful. He was angry. At the time, I didn't get it. I'd done him a favor. But Finn loves his revenge. Not sure there's anything he loves more than settling a score."

"It was a mechanic, right?"

"'Twas."

"Finn told me his mom died because of faulty brakes."

"And I denied him the privilege of avenging her death."

"At some point, you two must have gotten back on even ground?"

"We did, I suppose. 'Twas never the same. Our father had his mother killed—part of a transaction with the O'Malleys—because my mum asked him to put her first. When Finn found out, everything fell apart. She was dying... and I felt like I was dying too. It..." He shakes his head. "Terrible. 'Twas a terrible time."

I drape myself across him as though I can somehow shield him from those memories. I kiss his chest and slip my hand under the covers.

He groans. "Again?"

"Can I talk you into it?" I murmur against his chest.

"Talking probably isn't going to do it."

Rolling on top of him, I straddle him. "Well," I purr, flicking my tongue across the skin under his ear, "let's see what else these lips can do."

Lorcan grips my waist. "I've got a few ideas."

"You do, do you, big guy?"

"All I heard was the word big. Go on." His amusement is clear.

I slither along his chest. "I guess we'll see how big those ideas are."

"Bigger than average."

"Your ego certainly is," I say against his stomach.

"And other parts to match. A perfect set."

A laugh escapes me.

"I love that sound."

I glance up. "You do?"

"Yeah. Feels like I've won something when you laugh." He threads his hands through my hair, spreading it across his stomach. "It's so rare it's like a prize."

My heart thuds in my chest. "I like the idea of being a prize."

"You are. To me."

I crawl back up his body and push my lips against his. He meets my kiss and weaves his hands into my hair. Then we're falling again, sinking deeper into each other. I'm already so far down, I'm not sure how I'll see my way out.

# Chapter Thirty

The shrieking alarms are deafening. I wake with my heart thumping in my chest, adrenaline rushing through me. Lorcan's already out of bed, putting on his pants.

"What is that?" I ask.

"Alarm system. An intruder."

"Could Finn have set it off by accident? Someone else?" I don't want him to go downstairs. It's 3:10 a.m. They might still be there.

"Have you heard it go off even once since you've been here?" Lorcan's voice is impatient as he strides to the walk-in closet and parts his clothes.

Climbing out of bed, I yank on my shirt and pants to follow him. He's unlocked a gun safe and is taking out guns, adding ammunition to pockets like we're going into battle. "I want you to stay here."

"If you're going, I'm going."

His worried gaze meets mine. "I don't want you caught up in this."

"If you stay, I'll stay. If you go, I'm going." I rub my thumb over the dimple that's almost concealed by his goatee. "I don't want you caught up in this either." Same words, a different meaning.

He kisses my forehead. Then, he presses a gun and ammunition into my chest. "You understand how to use those?"

I glance at what I'm holding. "Yes." Nothing unusual.

Lorcan goes to a panel on the wall near the door and hits a few buttons. "The alarm was triggered in the basement." He frowns.

"What? Why does that matter?"

"You can't trigger it unless you're inside the house."

"One of Zhang's men escaping." Malik didn't look good enough earlier to be doing this on his own. Could someone else? Is it the bureau, or is something else going on?

"Possibly. If not, whoever it is, they know what they're doing."

*Let's hope that's true.*

Lorcan goes to the door, gun raised, and pops it open. He peeks outside, checking in both directions before signaling for me to follow. The alarm is so loud I'm not sure we'll hear anyone approaching, anyway. With light feet, we race down the hallway, guns at the ready. When we get to the stairs, he signals for me to go slow and follow him.

"I'm your bodyguard," I say into his ear above the blaring alarm.

"Now is *not* the time for jokes."

We whirl, guns raised at the heavy footfalls approaching behind us. It's Ian and Sean.

"Ian, take the perimeter. Sean, search the rest of the house. The alarm says basement, but I want to be sure," Lorcan calls out the instructions in a terse voice above the wailing siren.

Tension radiates off him as he watches the other two men leave. Adrenaline courses through me. We're both so tightly wound, I worry we'll make a mistake. Is Finn already there? Has anyone been hurt?

We creep down the stairs, Lorcan in front, me close behind. At the bottom, he peers around the corner.

"Antonio is down." His voice is pitched low, and I'm not sure I've heard him. "No sign of Finn or anyone else."

"I'll go to the right," I call back. "You take the left."

The hall is wide, and there are cells on either side. When I was here earlier, the doors were closed. Now, they're thrown open, some of them hanging on their hinges. At the wall, he punches in a code, and the alarm cuts out.

"What the hell happened?" he mutters to himself as we advance.

A couple of the rooms have bodies, left for dead or already dead. It seems like anyone who was conscious and able to leave fled the property. The double doors to the backyard are wide open.

"I'll keep searching." He gestures at Antonio who is sprawled at the entrance to a room. "Check him."

I cross the hall and place the gun on the ground. There's a lot of blood and a bullet hole in his forehead. Still, I check for a pulse. If there's one thing I've learned, it's you never know what people are capable of surviving. It's the only thing giving me a whisper of hope for Malik. "No vitals."

Lorcan looks in the last room and comes to my side. He presses his fingers into Antonio's neck and then tries to find a pulse on his wrist. There's a slight edge of desperation in his movements, as though he doesn't want to believe it's true.

"What do you want to do?" My shoulders fall at the realization Antonio didn't make it out alive. His poor kids.

"There're dead bodies strewn all over. I need to call in a crew." Lorcan pinches the bridge of his nose. "Who could have done this?"

"The Zhangs are the obvious choice."

"We've dismantled and disrupted enough of their activity. I know they're too scattered. This takes organization. Planning." He scans the area, shaking his head. "Inside information."

"The alarm was going off for a while." I head down the hall, peering into doors again. There's no sign of Malik except for his blood on the floor. I send up another silent prayer to whatever god might exist he makes it through this. "Where is Finn?"

Lorcan presses the heels of his hands into his forehead. "Maybe he's not here."

Neither of us is privy to Finn's comings and goings, but something about him not being here tonight feels wrong. He was enjoying his prisoners far too much to leave them unattended.

Ian pops his head in the double doors that were left wide open in the escape. "There are a couple bodies out here. Want me to check them out?"

"Yeah." He glances at Ian before focusing on Antonio. "Have you seen Finn? Did he go out?"

"Haven't seen him. He doesn't go anywhere without someone with him. Antonio's here, Sean's here, I'm here. The people working tonight are accounted for."

I stare at Lorcan and whisper, "Bodies in the field."

Both of them race out the double doors to the field, and I'm at the rear. Did the bureau kill him? Take him in? Leave him for dead? We head to different bodies, guns drawn in case the person isn't dead or seriously injured.

There's a chorus of "no" across the field as we each realize Finn isn't among the people left for dead.

"His room?" I call to Lorcan.

He nods and tips his head at Ian. "Go find Sean. See if he's found anything." Ian jogs back into the house. "Kim?" Lorcan heads for the side door.

"I'll follow you in. Just going to check for any identification on these bodies." They're dressed like Zhang's men, but I need to be sure.

He gives me one last look before disappearing into the house, feet pounding on the concrete floor.

After I've checked the three bodies, I pause in the middle of the field, staring at the garden shed at the back of the property. Did Ian check it? Something about it calls to me, and uneasiness slithers along my spine.

Drawing my gun again, I head to the shed, keeping alert for any signs of movement. The closer I get, the more my heart thumps in my chest. I'm not seeing anything out of the ordinary, but it's dark, and that inner voice is whispering something is very wrong.

When I get to the shed, I open the door, gun poised at the ready. It's empty, not even any lawn maintenance equipment in it. As I'm backing out, a shuffling to my right kicks my heart up a notch. I whirl, gun raised.

"Kimmy," Finn drawls, his shoulder pressed into the corner of the shed. His hand cradles his stomach. It's too dark where he is to see him clearly.

I ease my gun lower. "Finn. What are you doing out here? Zhang's men are gone. Someone broke them out."

He chuckles but there's an unusual strain to it. His shoulders rise and a dry, hacking cough follows. "Someone? The FB—fucking—I."

"What?" I glance behind me, wondering if Lorcan will follow me out here. "The FBI? I don't understand."

"You know the only person they dragged into their helicopter back here?"

"Not you, obviously."

"Murray." He coughs again. "Or should I say... Malik."

Even though my insides are squeezing me, pushing me to do something rash before he pulls the trigger, I laugh. "The one you hired to follow Lorcan was an FBI agent? You sure know how to pick them. Are you hurt? You don't sound good."

I step forward, but he raises his gun. He's still leaning on the edge of the shed.

"You know what he said." Finn coughs. "As he was being dragged into the helicopter?"

Unwilling to answer, I stare at him.

"He said, 'Don't leave Kimi behind'."

"He knows who I am, Finn. We met at the bar, again in the alley. We had a whole conversation in the room yesterday when you two took a break from torturing him. He said my name. Big deal."

He gives a sharp shake of his head and wipes his mouth with his hand. A smear of blood appears on his face. He's bleeding. With narrowed eyes, I see where he's been clutching his stomach is dark, too dark.

"I can help you, Finn. You're injured. Delirious."

"It was the way he said your name. Kimi." Another round of hacking coughs erupts in the darkness. "It's not how I say it." His breathing is labored. "It's kinda how Lorcan would say it if he called you that. Like your name *mattered*."

"You're going to bleed out. You want to talk about how one of Zhang's men had a crush on me?"

With a grunt, he pushes himself off the edge of the shed and shuffles forward, gun raised, but far from steady. "Not—not Zhang's man. FBI." He takes another faltering step. "Him. You. FBI."

Raising my gun is the smart move, but I can salvage this. I know it. He's barely conscious and shaky on his feet.

"No, no." My voice is level. "Maybe him. Not me."

Finn wobbles. "Coincidence—" The light catches his eyes when they roll back in his head.

As his body crumples to the ground, there's a moment where I could break his fall.

But then, his head bangs against the flagstones with a *thud-thud*, and the moment passes.

# Chapter Thirty-One

I stare at Finn's unconscious body. No one would know if I left him out here. Ian was supposed to have searched the grounds. He'll bleed out. There's already so much blood.

"Kim?" Lorcan's voice travels across the field, and when I scan behind me, he's silhouetted against the double doors.

Thoughts flick through my brain, almost too brief to catch. He'll see me walk away. If Finn killed their father, I could get away with leaving him to die. We don't know for sure. Could Lorcan forgive me? Would he understand?

*Time's up. Make a choice.*

"Lorcan!" I scream. "Lorcan!"

He breaks into a run, and I drop to my knees beside Finn. Cradling his head in my lap reminds me of my brother and makes it impossible for me to do anything but sit there, staring at the blood leaking out of him and across the flagstones.

Once Lorcan reaches my side, there's a flurry of activity as he struggles to staunch the bleeding while calling an ambulance and then a cleaning crew to collect and dispose of the other bodies. I want to tell him Antonio has kids and an ex-wife, and he needs a proper burial, but the words are stuck in my throat. I can't stop staring at my hands covered in Finn's blood. So much blood.

"Kim? Are you hurt?" Lorcan's voice sounds like it's underwater. "Kim, my love, you're in shock."

He grabs a first aid kit from the shed, and as he tries to patch up Finn, he yells at Sean and Ian to get the other bodies in the house, lock everything up; keep suspicion and the cops out. "Kim? Are you hurt? Do you know what happened?"

I shake my head.

It's forever and only moments before the ambulance drives onto the lawn, arriving beside the shed. How did they get back here? I don't ask; I can't ask. Every time I look down, I don't see Finn, I see Chad, and I can't figure out how to make it stop.

Lorcan lifts me into his arms, and we trail the paramedics to the ambulance. As they put Finn in, I wonder if this is the last time I'm safe. He knows. An extraction, now, while I still can, is the best idea. Then he shifts me in his arms, and his distinctive scent settles around me. Can I walk away? Am I capable of that anymore?

In the car, he drives while I sit lost in thought in the passenger seat.

He taps his fingers on the steering wheel as he works out what happened. "Someone we rounded up was valuable. To who? And why?"

"Maybe the same someone who did in your father." My words are sluggish, pushed out for no reason other than habit.

"It's the same level of organization, that's true..." He examines me before focusing on the road. "You okay?"

"I don't understand what's wrong with me." Except, I do. I'm trapped. Unwilling to give up, not even sure what I'm fighting for anymore.

"We all have our weaknesses." His hands clench and release around the leather-encased steering wheel. "Even Finn."

"Oh yeah? What's his?"

"A certain blonde arms dealer."

"Carys?" It shouldn't be surprising. Maybe it's not. The way his voice dipped as he told her how he killed for her reverberates in my mind.

"Aye."

At that, my brain clicks in and ticks through the sequence of events so far, everything that's led to this point. "When you invited us to the house and had Finn answer, it wasn't about the arms deal, was it?"

His lips quirk up, and he peers at me. "Seeing her at the benefit after all those years was a nice surprise. I'd been wondering how to nudge him. Let him realize he didn't hold all the cards."

"You were showing him you could lure Carys into this war."

"I was."

"The second time you invited her because of me, it wasn't for me."

"Well, that's not completely true. I wanted you to be happy. The fact her presence served a dual purpose wasn't so bad."

"You wove her into your business through the Byrne brothers."

"Not directly connected, no. Connected enough he knows she trusts me."

"What about me? Why me?"

"You reminded me of a younger Carys at the fundraiser. So cool and collected with this hint of danger." He winks at me. "I thought you'd be irresistible to him." His gaze rakes over me. "Turns out you were irresistible to me."

Warmth spreads through me. I press my back into the seat and look down at my hands. Chad's blood is gone, and what's left in its place is Finn's. "Did he ever say anything to you about Carys?"

"No. He'd never want me to know for sure. But there was something about the way he was with her. And then, again, at the door talking to Thomas about what happened in Ireland."

"You understand Finn well."

"Spent a lot of years studying him, wanting to be like him."

"You wanted to be like Finn?"

"He's my older brother." Lorcan frowns. "I don't have the stomach for it, though. I can do the hard things if they must be done. I don't get pleasure from it, and it's easier to do those things if my heart is in it. It needs to feel justified."

An image of Lorcan, standing above Malik, fists clenched, surfaces.

I blink, forcing the memory out. "You're taking what's happened to your brother better than I might have expected."

He glances at me and then rubs my leg. "That's the life we lead, isn't it? We're a single mistake away from death."

If he survives this, my mistake will be letting him live, not putting that final bullet in him. What was it Finn said once? Mercy will get you killed.

When we get to the hospital, there's a petite blond woman waiting to take us to a private room to wait for news about Finn. We're no sooner seated across the room from each other and the door closed when I turn, my curiosity piqued. "How are you getting the red-carpet treatment?"

"You mean because I'm a lowly mobster?"

I purse my lips. "That's not what I said. But—" I shrug. "Might not be far off from what I meant."

He chuckles and flexes his hands as he puts his elbows on his knees. "My mum."

I raise my eyebrows.

"When she was dying, she was here at the last. She didn't want to die at home." He tilts back in the chair and focuses on the ceiling. "Didn't want the place tainted with death. My father thought the facilities here were barbaric. He donated a lot of money." He focuses on me. "Now, I think it was probably inhumane watching my mum die. That's how it felt to me. Like we could've done better somehow."

The grief still so raw on his face stirs my losses to the surface. Without letting myself think too much, I cross the room and crouch, hugging him tight.

His voice is gruff in my ear as he says, "Where've you been all my life?" His arms circle me, tugging me onto his lap.

There's a muted knock on the door.

"Come in." He tightens his grip, preventing me from moving away again.

It's the same woman. Her gaze bores into us before she clears her throat. I don't like the way she lingers on Lorcan. "They're doing a full assessment. I'll come back when I have more information."

"Thanks, Fiona." His hand squeezes my waist as Fiona ducks back out of the room.

"She comes in here to brief you?"

"We pay her salary."

I stare at Lorcan and run my thumb over his dimple. "How?"

"Not every deal is shady. We have some legitimate interests. We use that to pay for Fiona's services and other things that sometimes come in handy."

"She's like your own private nurse."

One side of Lorcan's lips quirk up. "More of an attendant. She helps with the police too." His mouth twists in amusement. "Your line of questioning is rather curious."

"The way she looked at you was rather curious."

"I'm an attractive man."

I laugh, and he grins. "Ah, there's my prize."

"Your brand of cockiness is sometimes a little endearing."

"Only a little? I like the word 'big' used in reference to me."

"Then I guess you'd better up your game so I can use it."

He laughs, and the light in his eyes when he gazes at me almost makes me forget I'm hoping Finn doesn't last through the night. If he dies, though, the only person left to take down is Lorcan. Do I have it in me?

"What are you thinking about?" His face clouds, and his fingertips brush my cheek.

"Whether Finn's going to make it. There was so much blood."

"We're a match. I'll give him some of mine if they need it. Wouldn't be the first time."

"You're not worried?"

"Worry doesn't change the outcome, just makes the wait harder."

While true, I can't believe he's this calm. The thud of his brother's head bouncing off the flagstones lingers with me, replaying over and over below the noise of everything else.

Was it enough?

# Chapter Thirty-Two

We're knee deep in the second game of Settlers of Catan as we wait for news. Lorcan remembered the game was hidden in a cupboard from a previous wait. When I asked, he grew quiet and said he and his father used to play it, then later Antonio agreed to take part while waiting for news during some other close calls. The idea of him playing this game with Lorcan is both endearing and heartbreaking. It's tough to imagine he was any good at it, but it feels wrong to think it now that he's dead.

Still, I'm grateful for the distraction from Finn's condition and Malik's extraction. I'm trying to take Lorcan's strategy to heart. The outcome won't change for either man with my worry alone.

When I glance up from the board, Lorcan is watching me.

"Want some help?" He smirks, the familiar glint of amusement dancing in his eyes.

"I think I can manage."

"'Cause you have options."

"I see them." I tip my head at the board, fingering a card in my hand.

"I wouldn't want you to lose again."

"Don't worry. It won't become a habit. I like winning."

His face is lit with mischief. "As do I."

There's a brisk tap on the door, and Fiona enters with a doctor. As he approaches the table, we get to our feet. With a sigh, the doctor rubs his eyes.

"We're pretty sure he'll pull through," he says. "Multiple stab wounds, a head injury, a lot of blood loss."

"Stab wounds?" I'm not sure what I expected. Bullet wounds, maybe? It's implausible Finn would let anyone be close enough to knife him without doing damage himself.

"Only major injury from those was a collapsed lung. Except for the blood loss. He must have been unconscious for a while."

It wasn't the unconscious part that caused the blood loss; it was the staggering around like an idiot that did it. Lorcan and I haven't discussed how I found him.

He takes my hand and squeezes it. "When can we see him?"

"As soon as he's awake, I'll have Fiona come escort you." The doctor hesitates at the door, Fiona at his shoulder. "The head injury is still under assessment. We suspect a measure of memory loss. We don't know how much or for how long that'll last."

My heart kicks in my chest, and a spark of hope strikes in me. "How certain are you about the memory loss?" I glance at Lorcan. "It would be helpful if we knew who did this." But so much more helpful if Finn *never* knew.

The doctor purses his lips. "It's not uncommon with an injury like his. Difficult to say until he wakes up. We'll run more tests at that point."

No sooner have they left then there's another knock on the door, and she pops her head back in. "One of your men is here?"

"Let him in." Lorcan waves his hand.

Sean slips in, appearing harried and exhausted. Lack of sleep for all of us is taking its toll.

"What do you have for me?"

"We're still not sure. Maybe the Russians? There're the only ones we think have the manpower to pull this off. The only other thing that's kinda troubling is well, um, a helicopter might have landed? Does that make sense to you?"

Lorcan looks at his feet for a brief moment and then stares at Sean. "Might have landed? We're not in the land of *might* here, we're in the land of surety."

"It's the pattern on the ground." Sean raises his hands. "I don't know. We tried to google the pictures we took. Our best guess is a helicopter landed."

Lorcan nods, and my gut twists. I wanted Malik out, but a helicopter landing on their property isn't an easy thing to explain. And the fact we didn't hear it means the FBI used a stealth chopper. Impossible to ignore.

"After I've seen my brother, I'll come home and look myself. We can't chase down what we don't know for sure."

With a nod, Sean ducks out the door, and both of us stare at the game. I sink into my chair and gather the game pieces. My fingers toy with my cards. I should be thinking about whose turn it is, but all I can focus on is the inexplicable helicopter. It's a massive complication.

"Was he unconscious when you found him?" Lorcan hasn't sat down.

My heart booms, and my brain ticks through what to say. Whether Finn remembers could sink me based on which version of events I tell. "Yes."

"Does this helicopter business make sense to you?"

I shake my head and stay focused on the game board between us. When I look up, I'm confident I've shuttered my emotions. "Who has those sorts of resources? Not the Zhangs, not the O'Malleys, not the Browns, or the Simmons. Would the Byrne brothers interfere?" The names I'm rattling off are impossible culprits even without my inside information. None of them have the funds.

Lorcan puts his hands on his hips and rubs his lips together. My fingers itch to smooth the crease across his brow. "There are two legitimate options I can come up with and both spell trouble."

"And those would be?" I toss my cards onto the table and rise so we're almost eye to eye.

"I'd rather not say."

"I can't help you if you don't share your logic."

"I'm not asking for your help with this."

I straighten, not even having to feign offense. It's genuine.

Lorcan stares at me and then away, his hands still on his hips. "It's not whether you're capable of helping or trust or... any of that. I don't want you dragged into either scenario."

"I'm here, with you. I'm in it already."

He shakes his head. "You're not. You're really not. I've been careful about what you've seen, the things you've been party to."

"Because you don't trust me."

"Because I swept you away from Carys to do one thing. One thing. Find out who killed my father. I didn't do it so you could wind up in jail or dead." His voice booms out in a sudden burst, his hand making a sweeping motion.

"Both are still likely. Finn's already arranged my near-murder once. Keeping whatever you think from me does nothing except drive a wedge between us."

When he doesn't say anything in response, I throw up my hands, a noise of frustration escaping as I head to the door. Before I get there, he catches me around the waist and backs me up against the wall. His forehead presses into mine, and our gazes lock. We breathe in sync before his lips descend. I wrap my arms around him, meeting his kiss, wishing things could be simpler between us.

One of his arms is braced against the wall while the other circles my waist, tugging me closer. Once we break apart, we stare at each other again.

"Why won't you let me help?"

"Because I feel like I'm being ripped in half. Part of me is consumed with figuring this out, what happened, and why. The other half is absolutely desperate to keep you safe. I can't—I don't know how to do both and let you help."

"The best way to keep me safe is to keep me informed. If I understand the risks and dangers, I understand when I need to watch my back."

"I want you to do something for me."

I stare at him, not sure I want to agree outright without knowing what it is.

"Once Finn's awake, I'll see if he recalls anything. Then, I'm going to the house to check the marks. If it's a helicopter, I'm chasing the two leads. You understand me?" He slants his head to maintain my attention when I turn my face from him.

"You're not going to tell me."

"I want you to keep an eye on Finn, keep things moving at the house while I'm doing what I need to do to figure this out."

"Well, if you haven't told me your various shady dealings, how can I possibly keep things running?" My tone is mockingly sweet.

"My office. I'll give you the code."

My gaze flies to his. I would've given almost anything for that number months ago. Now, the notion of having a large chunk of unsupervised time sends a chill through me. My job dictates I take advantage, but my heart isn't in it anymore.

"Are you sure?"

"You don't think I trust you? You can have the keys to the throne." His lips graze my forehead. "Course, if there are no marks in the field, the offer of the code is rescinded."

"Seems fair." I smirk. My stomach is a stormy sea filled with the knowledge as he keeps me afloat, I'll be sinking him.

Our lightheartedness evaporates when our gazes reconnect. "I've put something in motion." He searches my face. "I'm not sure I can stop it now. If this raid is what I think it is."

I know it's not what he thinks, whatever that is. His cryptic comment doesn't help the unease spreading through me. What has he done? What is he going to do?

"Are *you* okay?" A different sort of fear grips me, one I haven't felt since my family disintegrated. I shouldn't be feeling this way about him, about anyone. It's dangerous.

He brushes his lips across mine. "Only time will tell."

There's a sharp knock at the door, and Fiona's voice follows. "Lorcan? Finn's awake."

He pulls away from me, but he's laser focused on the connection between us. I glide my hands along his arm until I can link my fingers with his.

"Be there in a tic," he calls to Fiona. He's memorizing my face, searching for something I can't give him.

"I'm coming with you to see Finn." It's a bad idea. Might be the worst idea I've had, and so far, I'm setting new records in that category. There's a sadness, a desperation in him that wasn't there before Sean arrived. The helicopter has him rattled.

"You wait outside the room with the guys till I've had a chance to talk to Finn alone. Then, you can come in. I wanna see if he remembers anything."

*Me too. Me too.*

With his free hand, he opens the door and nods to the guards as we wander down to Finn's hospital room. Lorcan lifts our joined hands and kisses my palm before letting our hands fall again.

This is the moment of reckoning. Staying with him through this will either be the smartest thing I've ever done or the dumbest.

# Chapter Thirty-Three

While I wait for Lorcan to emerge from Finn's room, I try to stay as still and calm as possible. Inside, I want to fidget, jump up and pace around, anything to release this nervous energy.

When the hospital door swings open, Lorcan pauses at the threshold for a minute, scanning the hallway for me, and I almost collapse in relief. His expression is the one I've come to recognize so well. There's no rage or confusion anywhere. Whether Finn remembers or not, he didn't say anything to his brother.

"He wants to see you." Lorcan nods at me.

We're toe-to-toe and he still hasn't moved from the doorway.

"You okay?" I ask.

A wisp of a smile flits across his face before it vanishes. His lips brush my temple as one of his arms circles my waist. "I'm headed home. I'm leaving one of the guys here to come with you." He gestures to a man whose name I can never remember. Felix? Jorge? It's strange to think how much I relied on Antonio. Lorcan's hand slides away, and his footsteps retreat behind me, brisk, determined. Closing my eyes, I realize I forgot to mention telling Antonio's family.

The metal door handle is frigid against my palm when I push on it. Finn's icy eyes snap open and zero in on me. Unlike Lorcan, I can't read him. I have no idea whether I'm in trouble or in the clear.

"How are you feeling?" I shove my hands into my pockets as the door clicks shut behind me. I hover inside the room, balanced between staying put and fleeing at the first sign of trouble.

"Like I was stabbed a bunch of times and left for dead."

"Is that better or worse than normal?"

He chuckles and then coughs. With a breath in that appears uncomfortable, he says, "I heard you found me."

With that, the tension drains out of me. He's not going to grill me. He doesn't know anything. I take my hands out of my pockets and inch closer to the end of his bed. "I did, yeah. Lucky find, I guess."

"Thank you."

A smile blooms in me, even as the sound of his skull connecting with the flagstones rings in my ears again. "You don't remember?"

"Last thing I remember is kicking the shit out of Derry in the bathroom because he was putting his paws on you."

That means he doesn't recall any of the interactions with Malik either in the basement or before he got in the helicopter. I couldn't have asked for a better head injury. "That's what you told Lorcan?"

"Yeah. You didn't tell him Derry was after you?"

I freeze. "No, no I did not."

"Well, he was fucking pissed. Looks like we might have more than one war to worry about now. Not that I mind. It knits us together tighter."

I run my hands down my face. "I should go talk to him."

"Do you or Lorcan know who did this? He said he didn't, but his face told me another story."

"He has an idea, but he won't tell me."

He smirks. "Keeping secrets from you? How dare he."

"What's your prognosis?" There are the obvious bandages, and I wonder what else happened to him I can't see.

"I'll be out of here in a week."

"According to?"

"Me, of course." When he shifts in the bed he winces. "I'm a liability here. Get home. Get the ol' memory jogged. Go after whoever did this."

"The doctors think your memory will return?" I clench the bottom of his bed.

"They don't know shit." With a grunt, he squirms in the bed again. "Can't get comfortable. They need to start giving me the good drugs."

My mind drifts to the last time I was seriously injured. It was a few years ago; I woke up to Malik clutching my hand.

"How'd you find me?"

I give my head a quick shake to clear the memory and devote my attention to Finn. "It *was* luck. Ian was supposed to have swept the exterior. We checked the dead bodies for ID or anything else. We thought you were missing. And I don't know. I was standing in the field, and something about the shed called to me. So I went to look."

"And there I was."

"And there you were." *Leaning against the side of the shed, pointing a gun at me.*

We stare at each other, time ticking between us, but I can't determine what he's thinking. If he was Lorcan, I'd ask, but Finn would never tell me, even if I begged.

"Well, I'm glad you're okay." Part of me actually means that; I hope it isn't the part that gets me killed.

"My *dearthair beag* says we're not trafficking women and kids anymore. I'm guessing that was your doing?"

"Bad for business."

"That *is* the business. If you're going to stick with my brother, you need to realize that. 'Cause whether me and Lorcan go our own way"—he pulls his hands apart and then laces them together, resting them on his stomach—"or we lock ourselves together, neither one of us is any Robin Hood. We've killed for each other. We're bonded by blood."

*Except there's good in Lorcan.* "I don't have a problem with your lifestyle."

"Not much you can do about it, even if you did."

A smile threatens to burst onto my face, and I glance away from him before it can take hold. Just because he can't remember doesn't mean he can't figure it out again. "I should go. All hands on deck while we figure this out."

"I want you here tomorrow with a status report."

"There might not be anything to report."

"Then come tell me that."

"Whatever you want." I open the door.

In my room, on the dresser, is a note from Lorcan indicating he'll be out of town for two days, with the code for his office scribbled beside it. I gape at the numbers for a while, surprised he gave it. Maybe he'll change it to something else as soon as he comes home. That'll be the true test of how much he trusts me. Does he leave me with the code beyond the next couple of days?

Although I didn't need to see the marks in the field, I made the trek out there for show as soon as I was on the property. It's important to keep up appearances, especially now.

When I pick up my phone off the nightstand, there are two messages. One is from Carys and the other is from Dai Qing disguised as another random text. This time it's a doctor's appointment.

Frowning, I stare at the text for a few minutes. They're calling me to headquarters for a meeting. While it would be nice to see Malik, the timing isn't great. I need to speak to Dai Qing before I leave for the airport.

I dial Carys's number and hold the phone to my ear.

She answers on the first ring. "Oh, God, Kim. Is he still alive?"

"What?"

"Finn. He called me early this morning or late last night. I was in a meeting, and so my phone was off. But he left this rambling message on my phone because he was dying." Her voice catches on a sob.

"He's alive, Carys." What else did he say in that message? She's calling me, so he couldn't have outed me as FBI to her, or she'd be here shooting me herself. "What did he say in his message?"

Carys takes a few steadying breaths. I picture her worrying a wad of tissues as she talks. "Some personal stuff."

"He has a phone in his room, if you want to call him. But—" I purse my lips. "He won't remember calling you. His memory of last night is completely gone."

"Oh," Carys breathes out the word in a rush. "He's okay?"

"A lot of injuries. Nothing that's going to kill him." Finn calling Carys when he thought he was dying softens me again. I can't imagine receiving that phone call and being too far away to help. How would I feel if Lorcan called and left me that sort of message?

"Will he—is he likely to remember?"

"The doctor wasn't sure." There's a heavy silence on the phone. "Look, Carys, if you need to see him, come. I can get you on the list at the hospital."

"No." Her voice is quiet. "No." Her resolve hardens. "There are more reasons I shouldn't. I have to go. Thank you for calling me and letting me know he's okay." Before I can say anything, the dial tone rings in my ear.

I stare at my phone, a little glad she's not coming. It would be another complication I don't need right now. Pushing my phone into my rear pocket, I head out of my room. I need the payphone—the one the FBI makes sure is within a few blocks of an operation for emergencies—to call Dai Qing and find out what's going on before I hop on a plane. While Lorcan and Finn are too tied up to wonder where I've gone, it doesn't seem like the best time to disappear, even if it only ends up being for a few hours.

Dai Qing answers on the third ring. "DQ, go."

"You want me to come in?"

"Kimi." There's silence for a moment, and I picture her scrambling around her office to double-check our connection is secure. "I want to talk to you about your file. And we need to talk to you about something else that came up."

"You need me to come there? After your sledgehammer subtlety last night, I have fires to put out here."

"I thought you might want to check on Malik." Her voice is quiet, but there's a hint of reprimand in her tone.

I worry my bottom lip between my teeth. "Dare I ask?"

"You should ask."

"How is he?"

"In a medically induced coma. I—it's—do you realize what they did to him?"

I swallow. "Some of it, yeah. I told you it was bad."

"You remember where to meet the plane?"

"I need to be out and back today. The turnaround needs to be quick."

"Noted."

"I'm serious, Dai Qing."

"I'll do what I can to make it happen."

"Finn wants me in his room tomorrow. I don't know exactly when Lorcan will be back. I can't create more suspicion in anyone right now."

"I understand. I'll do whatever I can to minimize that."

I hang up in a burst of annoyance. It's not directed at her. Part of me is afraid I care too much about the wrong people right now.

Going to the head office when I'm on assignment feels like I'm standing too close to an open flame. The stench of burned hair follows me around as though I'll burst into flames at any moment.

When I check in, Dai Qing has left instructions for me to meet her at the interrogation rooms closest to her office. That can't be good. Did they take Zhang's men with them when they left? Releasing everyone was a good initial strategy to keep Finn and Lorcan from knowing which person was valuable, but are they trying to force people to flip?

When I enter the room, Dai Qing is in the corner, her back to the door. There's a file laid out in the middle of the table. Without saying anything to her, I flick it open.

"When do I get to see Malik?" I glance up at her.

She cocks her head. "When we're done here, before you head back."

"What's this?" I tip my chin at the file. It's already obvious it's mine. I can't believe she's giving me access to it.

"Parts of your file. Not all of it was necessary for what you wanted, so I kept some of it." She crosses the room and places her hand on the top before I can riffle through.

"What?" I meet her dark gaze.

"There are clear connections in here to people you're currently working with."

"So what?"

"Kimi, reading this, it might make it impossible for you to keep pretending with them. Are you sure you want to do this now?"

"Are there definitive answers in here for Chad's death?"

"No." She takes a deep breath. "It raises questions in my mind. First, why you were ever allowed to become an agent. I mean, it was pretty clear the other day you've got unresolved PTSD, and there are serious Mafia connections floating around you."

My memory sparks again with the reaction my mother had to Lorcan. Not him. Not him. Anyone but him. "To the Donagheys?"

"Mostly the file points to the O'Malleys. But as you know, they're in bed together in one way or another."

"I know Chad was connected to the O'Malleys through The Cage. Who else?"

"Chad's father, Ho-Jun."

"He died a few months before Chad. An accident, right? I was so young, and then Chad died. I didn't ask a lot of questions."

"It was labeled an accident by the cops investigating. Ho-Jun worked at a garage as a mechanic. He was working after hours, and the jack holding up the car he was working on was faulty. He was—"

The blood leaves my body in a rush. Darkness floats around the edge of my vision. "Crushed."

# Chapter Thirty-Four

Blindly, I reach out for a steel chair and sink into it.

"You knew?" Dai Qing's brow furrows.

"No." I shake my head. "No. I was too young."

Her frown deepens. "But you know something now."

I swallow the bile rising in my throat. If Lorcan killed Ho-Jun, could he also be responsible for Chad? Finn said they killed for each other, and Lorcan told me about Ho-Jun's murder. Finn fought with Chad in The Cage, and Chad was good, one of the best. Could Finn have done it? Did they do it?

"If you know something"— she taps the folder—"you need to tell us."

"I don't know anything." I glance up at her and then away. "I was only ten. What would I know? I didn't even realize Ho-Jun worked as a mechanic. He was a deadbeat. We had nothing to do with him. I'm—" I scramble for the right phrase. "Surprised he died like that."

Dai Qing sinks into the chair across from me and drags the folder close to her. She riffles through it for a minute before extracting a paper. "The bureau also considered your father's death suspicious."

I frown and take the sheet from her. On it is the medical examiner's report. I scan it, using my FBI training to make sense of the jargon. So many injuries. It hurts my heart to read it.

"He was beaten before he sustained his fatal injuries." Stones drop and sink into my stomach, one by one.

"What did your mother tell you?"

"He went for a hike." My voice is so quiet I don't recognize it. Each word causes the image of my father to surface, alive, happy. "He loved being outside in nature." I gather the loose strands of my hair off my face. "It was foggy. He got off the path. Wandered over a cliff. The impact killed him."

"The last part is true."

I rub the paper between my fingers and pass it to Dai Qing. "The real truth is he was probably followed into the woods, beaten to semiconsciousness then tossed over the edge of the cliff."

"Yes." Her dark eyes are full of sympathy.

"So Ho-Jun was killed, most likely by—" I swallow. Lorcan's name bounces around my skull, on the tip of my tongue. I can't do it. "Someone from the O'Malley family. My father was most likely killed through some kind of Mafia connection."

Dai Qing closes the file and stares at me for a moment. "He learned Irish after your brother was murdered, right?"

I give a curt nod.

"The Donaghey family speaks primarily Irish for their business purposes."

"I haven't seen much evidence of that."

"It's common knowledge."

"I suppose."

"You understand where I'm going with this."

"My dad asked me to go on that hike with him. Father-daughter bonding time." I lean into the chair and cross my arms. "I didn't feel like getting dirty. I was an asshole at fifteen."

"If you'd been there, you'd most likely be dead. You know how these things work."

"That's twice, you know that? Twice I've beaten death."

"I'd guess it's more than that. You've beaten death on every assignment so far."

"How many lives does a person get? How many close calls, al-most-deaths?"

"None of us knows the answer to that."

I stare at her. "You think my father might have been working for the Donaghey family?"

"What do you think?"

"Don't turn this shit around on me. I don't know what to think. My head is spinning." Part of my head feels far too attached to my heart to make the leaps that need to be done right now.

"I don't think your father was working for the Donaghey family. There's nothing in your file to indicate anyone with the FBI suspected that either. But he learned Irish for a reason."

"To avenge my brother."

"Is that something you see your father doing? He wasn't Chad's bio-logical parent. He would have already known the dangers from Ho-Jun's unexpected death."

In my head, images of my father laughing and embracing Chad, cheer-ing him on at sporting events, passing him an ice pack from the freezer, sitting at the kitchen table and helping him with his homework, floats up to the surface. "It never mattered to my dad. He loved Chad like he loved me." My stomach rolls and sweat pools under my armpits. *My father. My father.*

"I don't know who killed Chad. Based on the information in this file, I'd say you're looking at someone in the Donaghey family as the likely culprit." Dai Qing shakes her head. "It's unbelievable you're in this position."

"I didn't work the Mafia circuit until the job with Carys came up. The intelligence from the bureau indicated she'd be likely to hire someone like me. Then I landed the Donaghey job because I can speak Irish."

"I mean, anyone who looked at your file could figure out there was a connection there." She flips the file closed with force. "Malik should have fought to keep you off this job."

Considering what Malik's done for me and his current state, there's no way I'm blaming him. If I hadn't seen the photo of Chad in the O'Malley's hallway, I might never have known any of this. Half of my brain turns over the possibility Lorcan shot my brother in cold blood right in front of me. Closing my eyes, I push my memory to that moment, but other than the blood, so much blood, I don't recall anything else.

"I wish I could remember."

"There's a reason you don't. Seeing that at your age would have been incredibly traumatic." She purses her lips. "Did your parents ever get you help? Like professional help?"

"Yes. I'm sure that's in my file."

Dai Qing raises her eyebrows. "I sort of wondered if you fudged that."

"Nope. Passed through those sessions with flying colors." I pace the room.

"Even then you understood how to become someone else."

I lean against a wall. "I'm good at slipping into someone else's skin. It's easy. Lately... ever since my mom had to go into a home." I thrust my hands into the pockets of my coat and can't quite meet her gaze. "Layers are peeling away, one after another."

"We should get you out, get you into counseling again."

"No." I straighten. "The one thing I'm sure I can do is my job. I know who Kim is."

"But you're not too sure about Kimi." She slides the folder off the table into her hand. "As handlers, we're taught the importance of a real-world connection for people who are undercover. If you don't have a life to go to when the job is done, the job becomes your life, and boundaries get crossed, things get fuzzy."

"Nothing is fuzzy." My mind drifts to Lorcan, the way his hand skates across the small of my back, the quirk of his lips when he finds something amusing, the soft lilt of his voice in my ear just before...

Dai Qing scans my face, probably seeing far more than I'd like. "I'm going to take you to see Malik, but first we have another stop to make."

I check my watch. "I need to get home soon. Finn cannot be suspicious, or he'll kill me. That's not hyperbole. I'll be dead."

"I understand. It won't take long, but there's one more thing you need to know before you go."

We exit the room and head down the hall in tense silence. She doesn't believe I'm okay. Maybe I'm not, but I don't care.

"I'm not sure where Lorcan's gone," I admit as we enter a two-way mirror room which looks onto an interrogation area. It's been a while since I've been in these. I forgot how dim the lighting is kept.

"Oh," she says. "You don't need to worry about him beating you home." She indicates the window in front of us.

Ice freezes my veins. Lorcan is deep in conversation with Zahir, a senior agent at the bureau. My hand touches the glass, and I can't stop staring at Lorcan, taking him in.

"What is he doing here?" I whisper.

"He knows it was us who landed on his property."

"Oh, my God." I look at her, stunned. "I can't go home."

"He doesn't know about you."

"Then how is he here?"

She sighs. "After we planted you in his organization, we arranged a bump to see if he had any interest in informing on his brother or other Mafia organizations he's connected to."

Lorcan's comments about his secret project, that Finn didn't realize the big deal he was working on, and his comment about setting something in motion he wasn't sure he could stop, flare in my consciousness. "No one fucking told me?"

She snaps the folder onto the table behind her. "And risk you blowing your cover? You already seem too invested in him. If you knew, you'd have blown your own story."

I shake my head even as a tiny voice wonders if she's right. "I should have been told."

"We couldn't risk it. He turned us down. He said the only way he'd give up Finn was if his brother murdered his father. Any other scenario and it wasn't a deal." She gestures to Lorcan in the other room, who is now leaning across the table at Zahir, who sits with an impassive expression on his face, hands loosely clasped. There are other agents in the room observing, hands not far from their guns. "You can imagine he's just a little bit pissed we were at his house."

"What'd you tell him?"

"That when he turned us down, we put an agent in Zhang's organization. When they went to war with Zhang, they rounded up an agent."

I rock back on my heels and dig my hands into the pockets of my coat. "It's true. Also, plausible. So why is Lorcan still here?"

"We're chatting with him."

"He should have a lawyer."

She purses her lips and glances at me. "From what I understand, he's only incriminating himself against future crimes so far."

I frown. "What does that mean?"

Dai Qing hits the button that lets us hear as well as see them. "There have only been two issues since he got here. I'm sure he'll circle around to one or the other again."

Lorcan tilts back in his steel chair and eyes Zahir. "You won't tell me which of the people we rounded up was FBI?"

"That's correct." Zahir's voice is silky. "That's not going to change no matter how many times you ask."

Lorcan looks up at the ceiling and then stares at the mirror. "Who's watching?"

I freeze, afraid to look at Dai Qing. Lorcan's eyes are piercing in their intensity. He's so angry, and I yearn to go to him.

"A stenographer. We have someone taking notes to protect us both."

Lorcan snorts. "Oh, I'm sure." With another appraising glance at the mirror, his eyes give him away. He's put something together. "Your agent was the black guy. The one following Kim." He shakes his head, the rest of his body tight with unreleased tension. Even here, behind the glass, the room seems to vibrate with his rage.

Zahir says nothing, just continues to watch.

"If you've planted an agent in *my* organization and I find out about it, or Finn finds out about it, they're dead."

"I suppose it's a good thing we haven't done that then." He picks at a piece of fluff on his suit and then glances at Lorcan. "We asked you to turn on your brother. That offer is still open."

"After you come onto my property, kill one of my men..." Lorcan's voice cracks, and he clears his throat.

My heart aches at the thought of Antonio.

"I'd never do a deal with you people."

Zahir regards him for a moment before rising. "I understand you're angry with us. We could have handled the extraction of our agent a little more cleanly. I won't deny that. We're checking into procedures." He sighs. "Don't be naïve. Whether we come for you today or tomorrow or next week or in a month, we'll be knocking down your door, dismantling your organization. It's only a matter of time."

"I don't know what you're talking about." His jaw is like granite. "We're clean as a whistle. Come looking. You won't find shit."

Zahir chuckles and rebuttons his suit jacket. "You realize we don't only come for you and Finn, right? We come for everybody."

"I already told you—" He clambers out of his seat, fists clenched. The other agents in the room stir in anticipation.

"And I'm telling you, it doesn't work like that. We don't exclude anyone. You only get to negotiate if you're at the table with something to bargain with, and you've brought nothing."

Dai Qing hits the button on the wall with a click as Zahir exits the room. It only takes a second for the door to our viewing area to pop open. My focus is glued to Lorcan whose elbows are digging into the table as he runs his hands along his face. I don't want to be in this room; I want to be in his.

"You caught that?" Zahir comes up beside me.

"Enough," Dai Qing says before I can speak.

"Yes." I focus like a laser on Lorcan.

"You understand you cannot tell him who you are."

"I think I could turn him."

"I think he would kill you."

Through the window, he starts pacing around the room, running his hands through his hair. My gaze strays to him again. "What if Finn did kill their father?"

"Our intelligence says it was the Russians."

My smile is tinged with bitterness when I give him my attention. "I got news for you about your intel. It's not always right."

"We aren't created equal. Some of us get the job done better than others."

"I can get this done. I can turn him. I know I can."

He searches my face. "Perhaps. The reason you want to turn him isn't the reason we want him turned. Don't let your emotions cloud your judgment. He and his brother have done awful things, truly terrible things for each other, to protect their organization. We've never had enough proof to haul down the house of cards, but there's a lot of anecdotal evidence about things they've done. They aren't good men."

I glance at Lorcan. "Sometimes circumstances turn good men bad."

"We are defined by the choices we make. It's that simple."

"People can't ever change? Make different choices?"

"Did it sound like he wanted to do that? Was that the impression he gave you?"

Another agent with Zahir whispers in his ear before I can reply.

"I have to go." He turns to Dai Qing. "I understand you're going to see Malik and then fly out?"

"Yes."

Refocusing on me, he says, "I can't keep you from telling him. If you tell him and it goes wrong, we probably won't be able to get you out alive."

"I don't think he'd kill me."

His gaze sweeps over me. "It's not something you want to go into half-assed. You have to *know* he won't."

As Zahir leaves the room, Lorcan paces on the other side of the glass. I want to go to him, talk to him, and figure this out together.

Dai Qing stirs behind me. "The truth is, Kimi, he could be the person who killed Chad. He could have played a part in your father's death."

Her voice is soft, but it hits my heart like a sledgehammer. I already know he killed Ho-Jun. What she's saying isn't a leap. Glancing at her over my shoulder, I say, "Don't worry. I'm not going to reveal myself until I understand what happened to my father, to Chad, and to Lorcan's father."

"Those are pretty big question marks."

"Hopefully, the answers fall the way I want." My hand strays to the glass again before I follow Dai Qing out the door, my thoughts drifting to Malik.

# Chapter Thirty-Five

Dai Qing's phone pings as we head to the medical building. "He's out of the medically induced coma and ready for visitors. Timing couldn't be better." She puts her phone into her pocket.

My stomach churns at seeing Malik and knowing Lorcan and Finn did the damage. Finn for fun and Lorcan in a misguided attempt to protect me. I run my sweaty palms along the sides of my jeans as we enter the building. He won't blame me, but there's a part of me that thinks I could have done better, somehow got him out quicker, realized Finn might round up people I heard nothing about.

"How are you doing, seeing him like this?"

She half turns and raises her eyebrows. "Of course I don't enjoy seeing him like this. I don't think that's exactly what you're asking."

"Well, I'm aware you two had a… relationship."

Dai Qing laughs. "Did he tell you that?"

"He implied it a few times. He never *told* me."

"Makes sense."

"Does it?"

"I mean, he's had a thing for you since you two first started working together. It's been pretty clear to me, probably to him, you didn't return those feelings." She glances at me. "At least not enough."

Unexpected heat climbs into my cheeks. "He's—I—I care about him."

"He knows. That's why he told you he and I were together. I was the buffer—the beard, so he never had to admit you were who he wanted. The only person he wanted." She looks at me out of the corner of her eye. "Not that I didn't try."

"So you and he…"

"I wish. But no. Never. He's been very focused on you." Dai Qing shrugs and opens the door to the hospital wing.

"I really wish you didn't tell me that right now." We come to a halt outside his recovery room.

"You cannot be so dense that you didn't at least suspect."

I stare at her for a moment, unable to say anything in my defense. Did I suspect? Yeah, sometimes. Malik played me the way I often play a mark. He expressed enough interest in me I realized the connection we had was mutual, but never enough to scare me away. I would have bolted if he'd told me what she's implying.

Knowing he was in love with me, letting myself love him back the way he wanted, would have ruined me as an agent. "That must have been hard for him."

She puts her hand on the doorknob. "It's going to be even harder for him if he ever sees the way you look at Lorcan." With that, she opens the door, and I have no choice but to follow her in.

Malik is only able to open one of his eyes when we enter his room. Two things object within my brain, at odds with each other. I want to know what happened in that basement with Lorcan and Finn. At the same time, I never want to know Lorcan's part in it. But knowing Finn's role might make it easier to kill him if it comes to that. It's impossible to get one without the other, so I stay silent.

"You came," he whispers. "Did they pull you out?" His eye strays to Dai Qing who says nothing. She's waiting for my lead.

"Yes." I lace my fingers with his. "They got me out."

His body sinks further into the mattress, the tension going out of him. "It was all I could think about. I didn't know what I said."

*Enough. Enough for Finn to know.*

"Nothing. You didn't tell them anything. I'm okay." I use my free hand to gesture to my jeans and T-shirt. "Perfectly fine."

He lets out a grunt as he tries to get comfortable. "That you are."

A smile plays at the edges of my lips. "How are you feeling?"

"Like I got run over by a train."

"Thankfully, not a train."

He squeezes my hand. "You sticking around for a bit?"

I concentrate on our linked fingers. "They've already assigned me somewhere else. You know, no rest for the wicked." My insides twist at the lie. Given how he looks and feels, he wouldn't understand why they'd let me go back.

His attention strays to Dai Qing. "You're watching out for her?"

"As well as she'll let me."

His nod is almost imperceptible. "As soon as I can, I'll get assigned to you."

I glance over my shoulder at her. "There's no rush. Work on getting better in the ways you need." When I turn, his good eye is focused on me with laser intensity.

"What aren't you telling me?" His voice is rough as though speaking is exhausting.

Dai Qing steps forward to come beside me. "We gotta get her slotted into place. You understand. Narrow windows of opportunity."

His eye doesn't leave my face. "Kimi."

"Nothing, Malik. I-I feel responsible for what's happened to you."

"My fault." He lets out a strangled cough. "Shouldn't have gone to see your mom. I blew my cover."

"I brought Lorcan there, and I shouldn't have."

She lets out a startled noise beside me. "You what?"

Ignoring her, he forges on. "I was in, you were in. I should have stayed away. I know better. Not your fault."

A nurse knocks on the door and pops her head in. "He shouldn't have visitors for too long."

"Of course," Dai Qing replies.

I take an extra moment to stare at Malik, really let myself see the damage Lorcan and Finn inflicted. His face is a mangled mess, and every time he speaks, his missing teeth make it difficult to understand him. The rest of his body is peppered with bruises and cuts. And there must be serious underlying issues for them to put him into a coma while they assessed him.

How can I be with someone capable of doing this? How can I *like* being with someone who does this to another human being? To Malik.

"We should go."

"Yeah." My gaze trails up to connect with Malik's.

"I'll be okay."

Tears prick my eyes at how he almost wasn't. And it would have been because of me. "I'm sorry."

He squeezes my hand. "I'm glad you're out."

"Yeah. Yeah." I extract my fingers from his grasp. "I gotta go, but I'll try to come another time to see you when you're better, when things slow down for me."

"The job comes first." There's no bitterness in his voice.

His words ring in my head. It used to be the job came first; I didn't think I had a reason to put anyone ahead of it. Now, I'm not so sure.

Once we're out of Malik's room and on our way, I say, "Am I going to make it home before Lorcan?"

Dai Qing takes out her phone, presses a few icons, and scrolls through. "Yeah. They're detaining him under some bullshit reasons. It's weird he isn't lawyering up."

"It's not weird." I push my hair off my shoulders, wishing I'd put it into a ponytail. My fingers fumble for the elastic I keep on my wrist, but it's missing. "If he lawyers up, Finn will realize he was here. Lorcan thinks he can beat the system, keep other people out of it."

A chuckle escapes her. "Confidence for days."

A wry smile twists my lips. "Neither of them has a self-confidence problem."

"Will Finn be an obstacle for you?"

I ease my hands into the back pockets of my jeans as we come to a stop where we'll part ways, so I can catch my flight home. "Only if he remembers." I rub my cheek. "I need to play him better. He's tough to get a beat on."

"SOS as soon as it looks like it's going south, okay? Malik will drag himself out of bed to murder me if you're hurt."

Tears spring to my eyes again, and I glance away from her.

"We can still pull you out. You'll disappear."

I shake my head, scooping up the couple of tears that manage to sneak out. "No. No. I'm fine. It's been a long few days."

She observes me for a moment. "I will trust you know what you're doing here." She shakes her head.

"I know what I'm doing." With that, I push open the door and head for the landing strip to catch a ride to Boston.

It's late when I get back to the house, and Sean is at the entrance to greet me.

"I'm going to pretend I know where you've been because Lorcan will be pissed if he finds out you went out on your own without protection."

"I was hired as a bodyguard." I dig my hands into my pockets as I wait for Sean to open the front door.

"You know that doesn't matter to him at this point."

"Anything come up while I was gone?"

"Still don't understand exactly what happened. Finn is holding steady at the hospital. Ian is off running down a lead. I've been here. Where were you?"

"Checking into what kind of helicopter could have landed, who might own one, and so forth. Nothing dangerous, don't worry."

Sean snorts. "I'm not worried. You're cold as ice under pressure, but I don't like lying to Lorcan when he calls in. Next time, take a guy with you or tell someone what you're doing."

"It's been a bit hectic since last night."

"No shit." Sean stops at the juncture between Lorcan's wing and Finn's.

"I'm going to Lorcan's office to take care of a few things. Come get me if anything changes." I'm headed down the hall when Sean's phrasing twigs with me. "He called you?"

"Yeah, maybe an hour ago? He's on his way here. Should be home in the morning."

"Did he say where he'd been?"

"Chasing a lead. Like you, he doesn't tell me much."

I give a curt nod and head down the hallway to Lorcan's office door. For a minute, I replay the numbers I memorized. Am I doing this? Before I can second-guess myself again, I punch in the code and enter the office.

The distinctive scent of Lorcan, a mix of tangy cologne and sweat hits my senses. I take a deep breath and close my eyes, letting myself soak it in for a moment. Snapping my eyes open, I force myself into agent mode. Even if I'm not intent on turning him in, I need to know if he had a role in the deaths of Chad or my father.

For months, I've been eyeing a series of filing cabinets behind Lorcan's desk on the right, pushed up against the wall. Derry's comment about a paper trail sinking the relationship between the O'Malleys and the Donagheys plays in my head. Would there be something on paper for either murder? Seems unlikely, but other than outright asking Finn or Lorcan, I'm not sure how else to get the information.

Opening a filing cabinet, I see it's coded according to business deals. I understand Lorcan's short forms for the various different operations, and if I was still looking to dismantle his organization, this would be a gold mine. There are more pressing things to have answered now. Once I've checked the drawers in that one, I move to the next one.

This cabinet is in alphabetical order. I scan through the Ls for Lee. Ho-Jun or Chad would be listed under that name. There's nothing. Almost afraid to look, I let my fingertips dance to the Hs. Henhawk, Axel. My breath catches in my throat at his name. My father.

My hand covers the folder, and I stare at the gray wall for a moment before pulling it out. Whatever is in here could change everything. Sinking into Lorcan's desk chair, I set the file on the desk's wooden surface, leaving it closed. I lock my hands together and then unlock them, squeezing my fingers. With a deep breath, I flip open the first section. The file is full of photos of my father, my mother, and a single photo of ten-year-old Kimi. I was fifteen when my father died, not ten. For some reason, Lorcan's family was watching mine for a while.

As I flip through the photos, it's clear they checked in with us once or twice a year. It's unreal there are photos of me up to the age of fifteen in this file and neither brother realized it. At thirty, I haven't changed enough for these photos to be unrecognizable.

I keep flipping, hoping I'll come to information other than surveillance photos. There, on the back, is a handwritten note. I don't recognize the scrawl, so it's not from Finn or Lorcan. It lays out my father's efforts to learn Irish and their suspicions he was trying to gather intelligence on them even as they gathered it on him.

Bile rises in my throat. My father knew the Donagheys were involved in Chad's death, and he was seeking his own brand of vigilante justice. Did my mother know? Did she support this foolishness? A lone man, unconnected, unprotected, after a Mafia organization. It's almost laughable.

Except it got him killed. So he must have been on to something they didn't want uncovered.

The final note is the recommendation. *Elimination.*

My heart thuds in my chest at that word. Underneath it is an amendment. *As per family policy, eliminating the daughter and wife is also recommended.*

A shiver runs through me, and goose bumps spring up across my arms. Tucking my hair behind my ears, I read it again.

I'm not dead, and neither is my mother, so what happened?

# Chapter Thirty-Six

I thrash around all night, my brain unable to process I should have died along with my father and brother. How was I spared? Why?

When I manage to quiet those thoughts, my mind strays to Lorcan. Is he home yet? Will he come see me? What am I doing with him?

Fed up, I throw off the covers to take a hot shower. More exhausted than I've been in years, I get dressed and head for Lorcan's rooms. On the way past his office, light shines under the door. For a minute, I wonder if I left it on. But I was careful about replacing everything as I found it.

After only a moment of hesitation, I punch in the code Lorcan gave me. The light flashes red and beeps. Frowning, I raise my hand to input the code again when the door buzzes open.

He's home. He already changed the code. I guess that answers how much he trusts me. Disappointment lodges in my throat as I walk into the room. Behind his desk, he sits with a glass of whiskey halfway to his lips.

"Anything I need to know?" His chair tilts back as he examines me from a distance. He doesn't rise or come forward like I expected.

"No." I cram my hands into my pockets. "I thought I might have left a light on."

"Just me." He lifts his glass, draining it, then pours another drink from the bottle. Beside him sits a shredder and as he talks, he drives a second stack of papers into it.

"How was your trip?"

"Not what I hoped it would be."

"Do you have an idea what went on? Any leads you need me to track down?"

Lorcan's gaze trails over me. He takes another sip of his whiskey. "You're fired."

"What?"

"I'm firing you. Pack up and be out of here by the afternoon. Go work for Carys or... I don't know... Try out that second career you were talking about. You're not welcome here anymore."

"Lorcan." My heart drops, but there's also an unexpected queasiness in my stomach. "We don't understand what happened to your dad yet. Why would you fire me?"

He sighs and downs another shot. "I have my reasons. I don't need to share them with you." Without looking, he pushes a third stack of papers through the shredder.

Leaning across the desk, I snatch his bottle of Jameson before he can pour himself another drink. "Why are you firing me?"

"Taking my alcohol isn't going to help. It's going to piss me off."

I meet his look and take a big swig from the bottle.

"Drinking my alcohol is definitely going to piss me off."

"Tell me why you're firing me."

When he doesn't say anything, I knock back more of the bottle.

He comes around the desk and crowds my personal space. With a yank, he removes the bottle from my grasp and sets it on the desk. "I don't want you here anymore."

"Tell me what's going on."

His jaw hardens like granite. "I'm done checking into my father's murder. Your job here is finished."

"Job's done. We're done?"

"It was always just for now. *Now* came sooner than you thought."

"You don't mean this." I ease my thumb across his cheek. "Lorcan, you don't mean this."

His hand grabs mine and brings it between us. He doesn't look at me; he's focused on our linked hands. "Don't be one of those women who doesn't know when to let go."

My heart squeezes in my chest. Yanking my hand out of his grasp, I step away. I shake my head, at a loss, before turning on my heel and walking out of his office. *One of those women.*

As soon as I'm in my room, I get out my suitcase and start packing. Half of me is tuned to the door the whole time, expecting Lorcan to show up, to explain or to apologize.

But he never does.

Ian sits outside Finn's room when I arrive at the hospital. Even though Lorcan's fired me, I promised Finn I'd come to see him today with a nonexistent progress report. I understand what Lorcan believes and can say nothing to Finn or Lorcan himself. Even as I packed, I wondered what I was going to do now. Give up? I'm so close to finding out what happened to Chad, to my father, even to Lorcan's father. I'm on the cusp of so much.

"Any improvement in his memory?" I ask Ian.

"No, nothing. It's still a blank hole."

"That's too bad."

"You're telling me. Guy's a bear. Better watch yourself. Nothing Finn hates more than being stuck doing nothing in a crisis."

I should tell him Lorcan fired me. I can't bring myself to say the words. It's too much like admitting defeat. Part of me wonders if Lorcan suspects me and if it's easier to let me walk away than to ask the hard questions. The answers to my questions are equally hard and just as impossible.

"Good to know." I turn the handle and open the door.

Finn's watching an MMA fighting program when I enter. He clicks it off and actually smiles at me. He must be bored if he's happy to see me. "Finally, someone with news."

"No news I'm afraid." I give him a partial smile. "Well, that's not entirely true. This will be my last visit."

He scowls. "You don't get to decide that. I do. I pay your salary."

"Your brother terminated my contract. So I guess you're not doing that anymore. What kind of severance do I get, anyway?"

"My *deartháir beag* fired you?" Finn's voice drips with disbelief.

"He did."

With narrowed eyes, he drums his fingers on the edge of his bed. "Why?"

"Don't know. He went to track a lead yesterday and came home last night. I saw him this morning. He was getting drunk. I asked if there was anything he wanted me to chase down about the attack on the house, and he fired me."

Finn's face morphs from frustration to delight. "Ah, makes sense. You're rehired."

"He fired me. Told me never to darken his door again." Not what he said, but close enough.

"Move your stuff to my wing of the house. Tell him you're a free agent, and I snatched you up." He chuckles. "God, I wish I could be there to see his face."

"This is funny to you?"

"I need to amuse myself somehow." Finn shrugs. "I'm stuck here. Being able to fuck with my brother while I'm in here is an unexpected bonus."

"You don't even know why he fired me."

He holds up a finger. "I do know."

"I don't even know."

"Then you aren't that bright."

I let out a frustrated noise. Pursing my lips, I try to think through moving to his side. It'll be difficult to avoid Lorcan, but getting closer to Finn might help me slot the missing pieces into the puzzle. If he remembers... "I don't know."

"We've established that. Not that bright."

I roll my eyes and give an exasperated sigh. "He doesn't want me there."

"I do." He holds up a hand when I try to speak. "What I want takes precedence over everyone else. Always."

"You can't intimidate me. Certainly not from that hospital bed. I can walk if I want to." That's mostly true. I'm afraid of him but in a much more abstract way than is good for my survival.

His expression grows dark. "I should scare you, Kim. Most people know better."

"You make working for you instead of your brother sound so appealing." Every time he calls me Kim instead of Kimmy, a frisson of unease snakes along my spine. He hasn't called me Kimmy once since he lost his memory. What does that mean?

"Move your stuff. Lorcan will stomp in here raging. All will be right with the world."

"He fired me for a reason."

A shadow passes across Finn's face. "We don't fire people. We terminate people. Do you see what I'm saying?"

I straighten up at the implication. "You're saying he can't fire me, he can only kill me?"

"I'm saying him firing you isn't how we do things. Read into that what you will."

I shove my hands into my pockets, contemplating what Finn is implying. The shredding Lorcan was doing, the conversation I overheard with Zahir, the way Lorcan couldn't look at me when he accused me of being *one of those women* adds up to him trying to distance himself from me.

Still, it pisses me off he didn't tell me the truth. "What would I do for you?"

"Find out how the fuck I ended up in here for starters. Once that's done, you can do whatever you were doing for my *dearthái beag*. He'll be over his tiny fit of rage by then." Finn gives me a sly grin. "He comes around to my way of thinking, eventually."

"Always?"

He raises his eyebrows. "We're brothers. That comes before everything else, everyone else."

I scan his face, but he seems sincere. For whatever reason, Lorcan's love for his brother doesn't supersede his love for his father. When push comes to shove, where will Lorcan's loyalty lie?

"I'll go move my stuff. I'm already packed, anyway." I head for the door. My hand is on the knob when I remember Ian is outside and Sean is at the house, not to mention the others I didn't know as well. "What do you want me to tell the rest of the men?"

He smirks. "Nothing. Act like you're in charge of my business. They'll fall in line or ask me. Probably fall in line."

Antonio's warning rings in my ears. Finn doesn't like curious people. Was that only a few months ago? Feels like years. I've gotten away with asking a lot of questions. Not without raising suspicion. I need to be more careful. "And Lorcan?"

"He gives you a hard time, you send him here."

I search Finn's face for a moment, trying to figure out why he's pulling me in. He'd be so much better off letting me go. Lorcan might not, but he would be. If someone is going to go down for these crimes, I won't let it be Lorcan.

"Thanks, Finn." Before he can say anything in return, I slip out the door.

# Chapter Thirty-Seven

I'm not sure where Lorcan is as I wander back and forth between his side of the house and Finn's suite of rooms. The décor on this side is depressing with its dark woods and walls of varying shades of black or red. Where Lorcan's side is brighter, at least inside the rooms, Finn's wing is claustrophobic.

Sean raps on the door as I slot the last piece of my clothing into a drawer. Part of me is tempted to keep my bags packed. If Finn remembers, I'll be fleeing from here. If he never remembers, he'll notice at some point I didn't unpack, and it'll raise his suspicion. In the end, I'm probably better to abandon everything, anyway. I'll be starting over somewhere else.

I glance up. The men realize what's been going on with me and Lorcan, so I half expect a slew of questions.

"You here now?" Sean's brow is furrowed.

"I am."

"Lorcan know?"

"No."

"You want him to know?"

I shrug. "Does it matter? He'll figure it out soon enough."

He gives a curt nod. "I wasn't sure if this was some sort of power play or if he fired you."

"He fired me."

"I wondered if he would."

I narrow my eyes. "You wondered if he'd fire me?"

"Yeah."

"Okay." As the final drawer shuts, I take a deep breath. I hope I'm doing the right thing. Probably not. I let the silence stretch between me and him, willing him to leave without me having to tell him to go.

"Lorcan's not like Finn. He cares about people."

"You think he fired me because he cares about me."

"Yeah." He shuffles his feet in the doorway. "Why didn't you go? Things are nuts right now."

I catch his gaze in the mirror above the dresser. "I don't like leaving things unresolved." Turning on my heel, I face Sean. "Has anyone been to see Antonio's ex-wife?"

He shakes his head. "Not as far as I know. She wouldn't want to see any of us, anyway."

"She needs to be told."

"Lorcan will send her a check and a note."

I purse my lips. "His kids. With everything going on, who knows when he'll remember to speak to her. Antonio's kids. They need to be told. His ex-wife should know."

Taking out his phone, Sean glances up at me. "Want me to get Lorcan on it?"

"Will he go see her?"

"No. Last time he went, she told him never to come back. 'Course, he was trying to talk her into sticking it out with her husband. Probably, she felt intimidated. Lorcan's a big guy. I was there too. Antonio was pretty upset about the divorce."

I frown, thinking of when my father died. It was so hard. I couldn't imagine not getting that message face-to-face. "We'll do it. You have her address? I'll tell her. Something should be said in person."

He hesitates. "I don't mean no disrespect. But should you be going around Lorcan and Finn like this?"

"Finn said I was in charge. This is what we're doing."

With a nod, Sean backs out of the doorway. "I'll meet you in the car."

The house is a modest bungalow on a quiet residential street. It's not what I would have expected, given Antonio's earnings working for the brothers.

"You want me to come with you?" Sean jiggles the keys in his hand.

I laugh. "No. Definitely not."

"All right. I'll wait out here."

Steeling myself, I open the passenger door and head up the pathway lined with summer flowers. It's a well-maintained brick house, and I picture Antonio walking this same path, excited to see his kids, to spend time with them. Tears prick at the back of my eyes, and I suck in a deep breath. Showing up with a tear-stained face will send the wrong message to Antonio's ex-wife. This is a business call. It's not personal.

I ring the doorbell. It reverberates throughout the house, the pleasant tone spilling out through the front door.

When the door opens, a curvy Latina woman narrows her brown eyes at me. "Who are you?"

"My name is Kim." I try for a kind smile. "I work for the Donaghey brothers."

"What, they hiring prostitutes to make house calls?" She skims her gaze over me. "Antonio's not here. He doesn't live here."

"I'm here to talk to you about Antonio, actually." Somehow, I manage to keep my voice even. Josafina's assumption I'm a prostitute when I'm dressed in leggings, a leather jacket, and a fitted T-shirt seems ludicrous.

"The Donagheys are hiring women now? What do you do?"

"A little of everything. Can I come in?"

She blocks the door with her body. "Like a secretary or a wife or something?"

"Or something." I burrow both hands into my coat pockets and stare at her.

"I don't want nothing to do with that family. It's why me and Antonio split."

"Can I please come in? I promise I'm not here to cause trouble. I need to speak to you about Antonio."

Reluctantly, Josafina lets me in. There's a small foyer which opens into a modest living room.

"What's he done? He owes someone money? 'Cause I got two kids to feed, a mortgage to pay, car maintenance. I can't afford to give up any of my money."

"You might want to sit down."

She sinks into the nearest armchair. "This ain't about money."

"It's not."

Josafina's face falls, and tears fill her eyes. "He's dead, ain't he? Oh, God. He's dead."

"There was an incident at the house. He was caught in the crossfire."

"Did Finn kill him?"

My immediate instinct is to deny it, but instead, I wander to the couch and sink into it. "He didn't. Why would you think he was involved?"

"He's a hothead with no respect for life. The stories... When we got together, I loved that he worked for them. Wherever we went, people were afraid of that family. It was an automatic respect, you know? Mr. Donaghey, his sons, mostly Finn, though. They had this policy. Kill 'em all."

"That scared you?"

"Not at first. I was young and dumb. Married Antonio 'cause I loved him. Then we had our first kid and a second kid. He got deeper in the organization. He got shot. Not real serious. But it was enough to make me ask him to leave. He said people didn't leave the organization. They were eliminated."

"Death or jail."

"Yeah, exactly. Antonio said Mr. Donaghey and Finn were hardliners. They'd kill him if he tried to leave. He said he thought Lorcan might let him go. Maybe. Then I heard stories about him. His hands were far from clean. Finn has a way of talking people into doing things they wouldn't normally do. Gets under their skin. When Antonio came home one night, and I woke up to him weeping, I couldn't take it anymore. I told him I was done."

It takes a moment for me to follow her story. "You left him because he was crying?"

"I left him 'cause he said Finn made him kill some kid. A kid. Their fucking family policy says no loose ends." Tears stream down her face. "I didn't want my kids to end up being loose ends. Can you imagine? I love my kids. I love my kids so much. The idea I signed them up for that." She shakes her head. "I—it's—he's dead, and my heart hurts. A part of me is kinda relieved. I don't gotta worry about them being loose ends if Antonio screws up."

A chill goes through me. My mind strays back to the note in my father's file.

"How long have you been working for them?" She doesn't meet my gaze as she rubs her hands along her cheeks.

"A few months."

"So you know."

"Know what?"

"That no one makes it out alive, anyway. But we did. We'll be okay now." Her voice is thick. When she lifts her hand to tuck her long dark-brown hair behind her ear, it shakes. "I have to figure out how to tell my kids." Her voice catches. "He was a good dad." More stray tears streak down her face. "He was a really good dad."

"I'm so sorry. I know that's not helpful. But I am. I liked him." It's not exactly true, but it's not a lie, either. He certainly had a side I came to like.

She grabs a tissue from the box near the couch. "That's nice of you to say. I appreciate you coming. I don't know if it was Lorcan's idea to send you or what, but I'm glad it wasn't a letter and some money like he promised. I'm glad someone came."

"Do you need me to call anyone to be with you?"

She runs a hand over her hair. "No, I'll be okay. I gotta get myself together before the kids come home from school." Her voice catches again. "It just makes me sad, you know? We had our problems, but he didn't deserve this. My kids don't deserve this."

People like Antonio bring kids into this life. Could I do it? Would I even want to? It seemed both brave and foolish. My parents loved Chad and I more than anything. I felt it every time they looked at us, spoke to us, touched us. How do people bring children into the world only to put them in danger? Carys never had any kids. She said she couldn't imagine fearing for anyone more than she feared for herself. Kids were a liability. A weakness.

"It's not a life for everyone."

"You got that right. I'm gonna do whatever I can to make sure neither of my kids ever follow their father." She squeezes my hand. "I hope you get out."

"You don't need to worry about me," I say with a small smile. "I know how to take care of myself."

As I walk back down the path and get into the car beside Sean, I wonder whether it was Finn, his father, or Lorcan who decimated half my family. My heart wants it to be Finn or his father, but my head heard what she said about Finn convincing people to do terrible things. Lorcan killed once for his brother; who's to say he didn't do it two other times as well.

When the car glides to a stop outside the front door, Sean nods for me to get out. "I'll go repark it."

"Thanks." My thoughts are lingering with Antonio's kids. They're so young.

"I think you did the right thing. Going there."

"I know I did." I open the door and pause with one foot on the ground. "But thanks for saying that." Climbing out, I wander in the front entrance and nod to Ian on my way past. My mind is still mulling over everything she said, everything I learned about the organization, and I'm not paying attention to where I'm going. On instinct, I turn down my old wing.

"Kim?"

His voice, tinged with anger and disbelief, stops me in my tracks. Something in his lilt undoes me. I push my hands deeper into my pockets and straighten my shoulders. Going this way was a mistake. My heart races in anticipation.

"Lorcan."

"What are you still doing here? I fired you. It might be a new concept to you, but it means you're no longer welcome." Anger spews out of him, but he's using my favorite version of his accent, as though he knows how to seduce me even at this distance.

"It's true. You fired me. When I told Finn, he declared me a free agent." I take my hands out of my pockets and spread them wide before shrugging. "He rehired me for himself."

# Chapter Thirty-Eight

Lorcan chuckles, but there's bitterness in the sound. "Of course, he did. And you, you couldn't resist?"

I search his tense frame, contemplating which buttons will get me what I want. "Couldn't resist him or the job?" I tilt my head at the end.

"I don't want you here."

"He does."

"He can go fuck himself."

"You better tell him that. 'Cause I'm staying." I stare at him. "He wants me." I flaunt the words. "I've already moved my stuff into his rooms."

His jaw clenches, and his hands flex at his sides. "Why do you want to be here? We're done. The job is done. Working for Finn is a death sentence."

"I've beaten death before. I don't like loose ends." My words are a deliberate nudge.

Lorcan comes so close I feel surrounded by him. If he was anyone else, I'd be uncomfortable. He won't hurt me though.

Rage spills out of him, straining against his control to say, "You cannot stay."

"You fired me," I say evenly. "That's your choice. Finn asked me to work for him. That's my choice."

There's anguish in his eyes when they connect with mine. His hands frame my face with a mixture of tenderness and frustration. "He'll kill you, Kim." He touches our foreheads together. "You can't stay."

"He won't kill me." Unless he remembers, and then I'm one breath away from a bullet in the head.

"There are things going on. Things you don't understand. That he doesn't know about. I—you can't stay."

"Tell me."

"I can't." He swallows and closes his eyes. "I won't stand by and let him do as he pleases, putting you in danger because it amuses him."

"Maybe you were right," I whisper. "Maybe if he comes to care about me..."

Lorcan's grip on me tightens, and then his fingers tug my ponytail loose. He buries his hands in my hair but keeps his forehead against mine.

"No," he mutters.

"You don't want me anymore, Lorcan. Why does it matter to you?"

"Bloody hell. It's not that I don't want you." He presses his body closer, and I arch my back, seeking his heat, meeting his desire.

"Then what is it?"

"I can't keep you safe anymore. The idea of anything happening to you because of me—" His eyes close, and his jaw tightens. "It'd ruin me. I can't have you here."

"The only person who gets to decide the direction of my life is me. Just me."

"And you want to work for Finn."

"No."

One of his hands comes out of my hair and circles my waist. "What do you want?" His voice is gruff with an undisguised desire.

"You," I breathe out. "Beside me, inside me, all around me." I try to catch his gaze. "Always."

"God help me." His lips skim my temple as he breathes me in. His breath stirs the tendrils of my hair freed from my ponytail. "I tried. Remember I tried."

"It was a valiant effort."

His lips find mine, and I can't help the moan which escapes me. It hasn't been long since we touched, but the brief time where I wondered if it would ever happen again was devastating. Around my waist, his arm tightens, pulling me flush against him, every part of him hard against me.

Without breaking the kiss, he walks us backward to his room. When we get to the door, he pushes me against the wall, pressing his body against mine. He doesn't look at the keypad as he inputs the code. The door buzzes, and he almost kicks it open, dragging me with him, shoving my jacket off, his motions hurried, frantic. His hands on the hem of my T-shirt jerk it over my head, and my hair falls in a heap around my shoulders. This frenzy is as though, like me, he can't believe we're doing this, and if we pause to consider the wisdom, we might change our minds.

Being with him again is foolish. I'm spinning deeper into this web with him. And it's sticky, latching onto pieces of me I didn't realize existed anymore. When my family disintegrated, part of me thought I'd be alone forever. To love is to risk. From the moment Lorcan opened his mouth at that benefit, I've been sliding downhill without any brakes. Do I want them? Would I use them? So much of what's happening between us feels almost destined, as though he's exactly what I've been looking for.

His lips find my ear, and he's murmuring things that would make other women blush as we discard clothing in a rush. Once we're on the bed, the sensation of his body against mine is intoxicating. Will I ever get tired of this? Of him? Is it possible to feel too much for someone?

With my back arched, I mold myself to him, needing to experience every inch of him against me, flush with my skin.

"I missed you. I missed this," he rasps against my neck. Something in his voice bumps up against a memory. The tone, the pitch, but I can't quite catch it. For a moment, my brain forgets where I am, trying to snatch the fragment of memory peeking out at me.

"You okay?" He eases away and smooths my hair off my face.

It amazes me he caught the subtle change in my mood. He's come to read me so well. His gaze bores into mine, and I give a half smile. "Déjà vu."

One side of his lips quirk up, and his dimple appears. We stare into each other's eyes, and I rub my thumb along his dimple as he starts to move against me.

"I was that good in another life?"

A smile touches my lips. "I guess so."

"I like the sound of that."

I clutch onto his back and try to shut off my brain. It wasn't déjà vu, but I'm not sure what it was.

Lorcan's hand skims along my side, leaving goose bumps in its path. With his other hand, he brings the sheets up higher to cover me.

"Finn told me going to work for him would win you around."

Lorcan stills, and then his hand resumes its leisurely exploration. "Did he?"

"He said you come around to his way of thinking, eventually."

While I wait for his response, I listen to Lorcan's even breathing. I almost think he's fallen asleep when he says, "I suppose that's been true in the past."

"I know about the mechanic. Have you ever killed anyone else for Finn?" I'm not sure I want this answer, but I have to ask.

Lorcan sighs. "I might have done. Does it matter?"

A tense silence settles over us. I should dig further, push deeper. I may not like what I find. "I went to talk to Antonio's ex-wife today."

"Ah, I see. That was kind of you."

"Do you think?"

"She's not the easiest woman."

"Women are supposed to be easy?"

"I plead the Fifth." He secures me tighter against his side, as though he's worried I might try to slip away. "I don't need easy. Reasonable will do."

I laugh. "I notice you didn't say logical."

"There isn't much logic in what we're doing right now." His other hand brushes the hair off my shoulders, making it fall against the pillow. "Feeling the way I do about you, in the situation we're in—it's dangerous. That people realize I care is doubly so."

"Finn would use me against you?"

"In a heartbeat. As would others."

Silence sits between us for a few beats while my thoughts return to Josafina. "She said she was sad about Antonio, but also relieved."

"Relieved?"

"The family policy."

Lorcan sighs. "Finn's policy."

"You don't share his penchant for killing an entire family?"

He shifts on his side, and I face him. "That surprises you?"

"No," I whisper. "She also said Finn can be persuasive."

His knuckles trail across my cheekbone. "He can be. Doesn't mean I can be persuaded to do something I don't believe in. I wasn't lying when I said I needed the violence to be justified. I might look like my father, but Finn's the one who inherited his heart, his ability to flip the humanity switch. I've never figured that part out."

"Never? You've never killed someone who didn't deserve to die?"

"Who knows?" His thumb strokes my cheek. "Not intentionally. Sometimes I even managed to talk Finn and my father around. Rare, that was, though. Like piranhas at the hint of blood."

"They didn't give you a hard time about that?"

"I learned early to pick my battles. They both loved me in their own way." He scans my face over and over. A smile plays at the edges of his lips. "I don't know what brought you to me. Destiny, maybe. Do you believe in that?"

Did I? If I believed he and I were fated to meet, doesn't it also mean my father and brother were fated to die?

"No," I murmur. "We make our own luck, our own opportunities. And we make our own failures."

He grins. "I shoulda known."

"I want to prove Finn killed your father."

Lorcan's grin fades. "What kind of luck do you think that'll bring you?"

"Closure," I say. "For you."

He rotates onto his back and looks at the ceiling. "Then what? I drag you into a war with my brother."

"Or maybe we walk away. Do you even want this, Lorcan?"

He faces me. "We'd both become celebrity bodyguards, saving the honor and modesty of countless starlets?" His tone is teasing, despite the seriousness of my request.

"We could, or maybe become whatever we wanted, together."

"I like that last bit. The first bit? I'm not sure it's possible. I've done things. A lot of those things make me a liability for you. You're good. I'm—I don't know what I am. But I don't think I'm good. The man I am when I'm with you—I like him. I like him a lot." He chuckles and gives me a sidelong glance. "You think I'm better than I am. I wanna be that man, the one you see."

For a time, we lie together in silence, looking at each other. I don't know if a future is possible. But I don't want him to approach this situation as though he's trapped, doomed to stay in this life. If I can turn him, maybe the FBI will go easy on him. "What if we can prove your brother killed your father? What then?"

"I had a plan, but it got shot to hell. Quite literally."

"Is it salvageable?"

His face turns serious, and he is focused over my shoulder at the wall. "I don't know."

He might not, but I do. "I think we should act like it's still possible, like that plan is still viable. Then, we can adjust."

On his back, he rubs his hands across his face. "You don't even know what the plan was. Truth is, I'm not even sure I can trust those people to keep their word."

We're dancing around the edges of what we're not telling each other. If I keep going with this, I'll say something I shouldn't. "You've been keeping me from the Russians. Why?"

"They're the one organization in Boston who isn't afraid of Finn. Not even a little bit. It's why I was in discussions with them initially without Finn. Going to them is tricky."

"Could they have killed your father? I mean, if they're not afraid of any of you."

"Possibly. Doubtful. But possible." His head falls to the side, so our gazes connect. "Semyon's not very well going to admit it, is he?"

"I read people pretty well. Take me with you to visit him."

Lorcan sighs. "You enjoy inserting yourself in the most dangerous situations."

"Occupational hazard." I give him a small smile.

He plays with my hair in silence. "All right. I'll organize a meeting. It might take a few days. You cannot tell anyone we're going. You understand me? It'll be you and me, no one else."

Easing myself up his body, I kiss his jaw. "Whatever will we do while we wait?"

Lorcan chuckles and tugs me under him as his lips trail kisses along my body. "I've got more than enough ideas to keep us busy."

I've never been good at waiting. Especially knowing Finn's mind ticks, one lit fuse of memory away from blowing everything sky-high.

# Chapter Thirty-Nine

Lorcan circles me in his room before he faces me and gives a curt nod. "They'll still search you."

"One of us needs to have some sort of weapon on them."

"Can you sit with that knife against your thigh?"

Striding to a chair by his kitchenette, I ease into it.

"You look as though you're a hundred doing that."

I laugh. "Well, you keep him talking while I sit." I wink. "It'll be fine. This isn't the first time I've concealed a weapon for a meeting."

Lorcan's expression turns heavy, and he shakes his head. "It's the first time I've given a shit if someone gets caught."

Rising, I cross the room and put my arms around his neck. "I doubt that's true."

He doesn't meet my gaze and instead brushes a kiss across my forehead. "I think I should go alone."

"You're not going alone. You need someone to watch your back."

"It's not my back I'll be worrying about."

"I can—"

"Yes," Lorcan says, pulling away. "I'm well aware that you can take care of yourself." He raises one eyebrow and rests his hands on his hips. "This is—it's new to me. I've never been with a woman who understood the business and who was…"

"Amazingly competent?" I arch my eyebrows, a teasing smile playing at the corners of my lips.

Unease and humor war in the depths of his eyes. "Experienced."

"What sorts of women do you normally sleep with?"

Lorcan purses his lips and looks at me under his lashes. "Did you really just ask me that?"

"Why not?" I move to the kitchenette and pour myself a glass of whiskey. "I suppose I should know where your parts have been before."

"Does it mean I get to ask you that question?"

I sip the drink and angle the glass at him. "Answer mine first, and we'll see."

He chuckles and comes forward, plucking the glass from me and swallowing a taste of whiskey before returning it. "I like uncomplicated women. I told you that."

"And yet?" My thumb caresses his cheek.

"And yet I seem to have fallen in love with an amazingly competent woman who is incredibly complicated."

My stomach dips. "All I heard was amazing and incredible."

"Ay." A smile touches his lips, and when one side of his mouth quirks up, his dimple peeks out. "You're *my a chroi.*"

*His heart.* My own heart squeezes. My father called me that. Words bubble up into my throat, but I can't say them. They're there. Until he knows everything, I can't say it. I need to be sure. There's a chance he aided in the murdering of my family. Can I get past that? Would I want to? Even if I did, can his love for me overshadow his love for Finn once he knows the truth?

"I like the idea of being your heart." I glide my hand to his chest.

His eyes light. "You know that one?"

My throat is tight, and I clear it. "My dad used to call me that."

"Used to?"

My mistake causes a frisson of fear to shoot through me. It's a slip but not dire. I can salvage it. Careless mistakes will get me killed. I'm losing sight of too many things.

"We've drifted apart." Glancing at the clock above Lorcan's shoulder, I say, "We should go. Don't want to be late."

"You're sure about that knife." His hand rubs my thigh and the almost imperceptible groove left by it.

"I'm sure I don't want to be defenseless if they're as ruthless as you say." If anything in my files at the start of this was true, the Russians aren't going to be impressed with our questions.

It's a sprawling estate on the opposite side of Boston. The house sits low and squat surrounded by huge iron gates. While Finn and Lorcan's place is also gated, it doesn't have the grandeur and the sense of luxury spewing out of every nook and cranny. The Russians don't mind flaunting their fortune. I half expect to see the onion domes protruding from the roof, but they haven't gone to that extreme. The giant balls on the stone pillars around the gates are the closest they come to that level of decadence.

"Impressive," I mutter.

"You know"—Lorcan gives me a sideways glance—"size isn't every-thing."

I laugh and squeeze his hand. "Don't worry." I bat my eyes. "I find you far more interesting than their big balls."

When we advance into the circular drive, a guard comes out. He leads us into the house to an area where we're patted down. Lorcan keeps a careful watch on the guard's hands but because the knife is on the inside of my thigh, the male guard skims it. I wink at Lorcan. Sometimes spandex and secret pockets are the best inventions ever.

We follow the guard through the interior to a brick-and-tile outside space with immaculate landscaping. A fire roars, and beyond it, like the Donaghey house, is a vast field. The sun is starting to sink, and the blaze of the fire matches the colors warring in the sky.

"Lorcan." Semyon comes forward, his hand outstretched. "Nice to see you again."

So far, he's not intimidating. He's not as tall or broad as Lorcan, and his round face is almost jovial. The graying hair sprinkled throughout his dark locks makes me think he's close to the age my father might have been.

"Appreciate you taking the time."

"Of course." He gestures to a couple of seats at the edge of the fire and settles into his. A bottle of vodka and two glasses rest on the table beside us. "Have a drink. The vodka will put hair on your chest."

"This is Kim." Lorcan takes the seat closest to Semyon and obscures any view of me as I ease into the chair.

Except for the guards on the surrounding edges, the conversation feels friendly.

"Kim. Kim." Semyon taps his chin. "You seem familiar. Have we met?"

I shake my head. "I get that a lot." I offer a fleeting smile. "One of those faces, I guess."

His expression is pensive as he drinks his vodka. "No, that's not it. I have a thing for faces." He circles his own face with his free hand. "We've either met or I've seen you somewhere before."

My brain starts rapid firing on any the occasions when he might have come across my photo or interacted with me. I'm drawing a blank. It doesn't seem possible. Whatever he thinks he's putting together, I can't grasp it.

"She's been working for us for a few months." Lorcan's hand slides to my knee. "She's good at her job. Maybe you've simply caught wind of her."

Semyon nods, but I can tell he isn't buying Lorcan's explanation. The problem is I have no idea why I'd be familiar to him. It doesn't make sense. Maybe an arms deal with Carys? Did we sell to them? I've never been to this house.

He focuses on Lorcan. "What is it you were after?"

"Information."

"Sometimes free, sometimes costly. Which sort are you looking for?"

"You might not even have the information we need," I add.

Semyon perks up and gestures to the vodka again. "Drink. Drink. I insist."

Lorcan pours us both a glass and passes me one.

"So you're fishing?" Semyon sips from his glass as the fire pops and crackles in the middle of the pit. A piece of charred bark floats in the air for a moment, burning bright red against the darkening sky.

"We're casting a wide net looking for information on my father's death."

"His murder?" Semyon sits forward, a smile playing across his face before vanishing. "Ah, you're the good son? Worried about honor and family." He smirks. "If it was my sons, they'd party in the streets because they were in charge. The little buggers think they know better than me."

Lorcan meets Semyon's stare without a hint of unease. "Do *you* know anything?"

We'd both been nervous for this meeting. Every angle had been discussed and debated. Did we need Sean or Ian? He didn't trust either of them the same way he had Antonio. So we're here, armed, praying we get out without a serious confrontation or creating waves between the families that rage out of control.

Semyon frowns and upends the last of his drink into his mouth before pouring another. "I know nothing." His attention returns, narrowing. "You have family in the business? There's something about you."

Frowning, I avoid looking at Lorcan. "No, no one in the business."

We sit in silence for a moment as Semyon's focus keeps shifting toward me and then away again. "Both my boys are single. You're very attractive. Clearly, you understand the business."

Lorcan tenses beside me.

"That's a lovely thing to say." I smile and hope it doesn't look like a grimace. "I'm taken." Women as a commodity sets my teeth on edge. I widen my smile, hoping the distaste in my mouth can be overcome with false enthusiasm.

Loran squeezes my knee and then returns his hand to his own lap.

Semyon follows the action, and a sly grin emerges. "Information isn't cheap, you know."

"What is it you'd like in exchange?" His tone is mild, but his posture is tense.

Another moment passes, and the fire crackles. We stare at it, waiting for Semyon to come out with it. I realize what's coming. It won't be the first occasion a man has thought he could buy me. It's one of the reasons why I've found things with Lorcan so easy from the start. For the most part, he's treated me like an asset, a person, someone with value. To him, I've never been a commodity.

"You want to know about your father. I want Kim on loan to us for as long as it pleases us. There's something about her. No term. No contract. Open-ended."

Lorcan takes my hand in his, and I rise with him. "She's already said no."

"Has she?" His attention returns, lingering. "What do you say, Kim? Want to work for a real organization?"

"I quite enjoy where I'm at." I square my shoulders. "If that ever changes, I'll be sure to get in touch."

Semyon heaves himself out of the deck chair and stands close to the fire, pensive for a moment.

Lorcan tenses and grips my hand. It's the signal to get out the knife, but I don't spot any reason to give ourselves away yet. I squeeze back.

The firelight catches Semyon's features, and the true menace I didn't see before is startling.

"I'm going to let you go," he says. "But don't come back here fishing. We don't have a relationship where information is free. You don't want to pay my price, you have no business being here."

I open my mouth to speak, and Lorcan almost crushes my hand.

"Understood." His nod is curt. "I appreciate your time."

"You were foolish to come here with no men." He takes a poker from beside his chair and prods the flames. With a pointed glance at Lorcan, he says, "Finn doesn't know you're here."

Lorcan straightens. "We're both seeking the truth in our own ways."

Semyon chuckles, but it holds no humor. "You're much more civilized—more your mother's child. Finn is like your father, like me. Take what you want and damn the consequences."

"You didn't stay at the top with that mentality all the time," I reply.

He grins at me. "Very astute. Some things are worth it, others are not." He shrugs. "It's why you're leaving in one piece. A war isn't worth it. Not right now. Even if your organization is stretched a bit thin." He swings the poker in his hand back and forth. "My men will show you out."

The drive to the house is silent. I'm certain Semyon knows something about Lorcan's father's death. The only way to get information is by trading myself. A few months ago, I would have done it in a heartbeat. Now, the thought of having any of them lay a hand on me sets my skin crawling.

"I don't care what he knows." Lorcan looks at me when the car is parked in the garage. "You're worth more than anything he could ever tell me."

I swallow. "If it's the only way we can access the information, get you closure." *Get you off the hook with the FBI, give us a chance beyond this.*

"Another avenue will turn up." He gets out of the car and comes around to take my hand, leading me into the house.

"What do you think he knows?"

"Finn did it. Somehow, he convinced them to help him cover it up. Semyon knows something. What else could it be?" Lorcan brushes his lips against my temple. "Other than me, Finn's been the one who has benefitted from our father's death. It's the only thing that makes any sense."

As we near the front door, Sean comes out and nods at me. "You've got a visitor."

I frown. "Who's that?"

"Carys Van de Berg." Sean shrugs. "She showed up about an hour ago, looking for you, Kim."

Releasing Lorcan's hand, I hurry in the entrance. It's odd she didn't tell me she was coming. Carys is a planner. "Where is she?" I call over my shoulder.

"Your old rooms."

The night Lorcan asked me not to work for his brother, he helped me take my stuff to his wing of the house. Instead of moving it into my rooms, he'd insisted on putting everything in his bedroom. When I told Finn the next day, he laughed and clapped his hands, clearly entertained. That had been almost a week ago now.

Heading down the hall, I leave Lorcan trailing behind me. When I reach my old sitting room, Carys is perched on the edge of the couch, scrolling through her phone. She glances up, and relief floods her face.

"Oh, thank God. I was starting to worry I wouldn't see you before I have to fly out again." She brings me into a hug.

"Is everything okay?"

"I've been agonizing over something. I tried to investigate it myself, but I ran into too many dead ends."

Lorcan's footsteps stop in the doorway behind me, and Carys stiffens before moving away from me.

"Nice to see you, Lorcan." Her posture makes me wonder if she means it.

"You all right?" His brow furrows.

"Fine. Fine. Needed Kim time. You understand what it's like." She winks, but something is off.

"I'll be in the office." His hand grazes my arm, and a shiver runs down my spine. "You staying tonight, Carys?"

She shakes her head. "I have to catch a plane out in a couple hours. No rest for me."

"Well, you're always welcome."

She nods, tension leaking from her.

"Have you been to see Finn?" I close the door to the hallway.

"No. No. I can't do that. Seeing him... I just... It's a bad idea. I—I'm worried about him. I can't shut it off."

"Okay." I frown and clasp my hands. "Can I help?"

She presses together her lips and pushes her phone into her purse before dropping it on the couch to wander the room. "I can't decide if I should tell you." Carys glances at me and then paces. "But I trust you. I trust you."

From my spot on the armrest of the closest chair, I watch her, not saying anything. I earned her trust through the work I did for her, but I certainly don't deserve it. She might end up in jail thanks to me and the information I collected.

"What's going on? You're worrying me."

"When Finn called me, the night he almost died, he—it—it wasn't all personal." She sends me an anguished glance. "He told me the helicopter was FBI."

I suck in a sharp breath. "Oh my God." She's telling me, so he mustn't have put it together when he phoned her. At what point did he figure out I was also FBI? That Malik's slip wasn't a coincidence or misguided feelings for me? Had he known for sure? Or had it been a guess?

"I know, right? So I tried to dig. Why the hell were the FBI here? I mean, besides a bust. But they didn't bust any of you."

"Finn doesn't remember any of this."

"I realize that. Someone needs to be told. I don't—I'm not sure it should be him. You understand what he's like. Is Lorcan mixed up with the FBI?"

I hesitate as though thinking it through. Instead, my mind is racing, trying to calculate how to ease Carys's concerns without raising suspicion.

"The organization rounded up some of Zhang's men." I close my eyes as though I'm putting the pieces together. "Maybe—maybe they scooped up an undercover agent?"

Carys snaps her fingers. "That makes sense. That makes sense. I knew you'd have an idea."

A zing of pride zips through me because she thinks so much of me. Her opinion shouldn't matter to me. "I don't know if it's the right idea. We knew about the helicopter but not who. God—that's—that's unbelievable."

She gives me a worried glance. "Do you think Lorcan has anything to do with it? He's on this mission to find out who murdered their father."

"He wants closure." I cross to the window at the rear of the room and stare at the edge of the field. "I can understand that." More than most, I get it.

There's a heavy silence in the room, and I face Carys. There's a glimmer of indecision in her eyes. She's holding back. "What else?"

Her hand slides an invisible strand of hair into her intricate braid. "If I tell you something, can you keep them from going to war?"

I go still and stare at her. There's only one thing she can be talking about right now. "He did it?" The words barely make it past my lips.

"The night we slept together, we were talking, and he didn't come out and say he did it. He didn't admit it. Not completely." She's rambling which is unlike her. "He said he never realized how angry Lorcan would be over their father's death. And the way he said it… the context…"

"Made you think he miscalculated his plan."

"I didn't ask. I couldn't ask. For me, being around Finn—it's like an inferno. He sucks out the oxygen in the room. I can't be pulled back in."

For the first time in my life, I understand what she means. Lorcan is a version of that for me. What he said about destiny echoes through my brain. Whether I want it to be true or not, it feels as though I was fated to meet him, like my life was leading me to him. It doesn't make any sense, but from the moment he showed up at the benefit, he's been my home, a home I didn't even realize I wanted.

"You can't tell Lorcan."

"I don't have any proof anyway." I press my fingers into my coat pockets. "What he said to you isn't enough."

Her shoulders relax. "You'll help me keep them together."

"You know me." I give her a reassuring smile. "I'll do whatever needs to be done."

She takes a deep breath and releases it. "If it looks as though Finn's in trouble..." Closing her eyes, she sighs. "I want to be told, okay? Even if I don't do anything, I want to know. Can you do that for me?"

"Of course."

Eliminating the distance between us, Carys draws me into a hug. "Coming to you was the right thing to do. I knew you'd help me figure it out."

I squeeze her tighter, even as I consider when and how to tell Lorcan what Carys revealed. It doesn't matter if Finn admitted it. What's she's told me is enough to sink him. Lorcan already suspects him, and once I tell him what Carys said, her instinct will be a deadweight, sinking Finn to the bottom of Lorcan's affections.

First, I need answers about who murdered Chad and my father. If Lorcan had something to do with either murder, I'm not sure what I'll do.

## Chapter Forty

The next morning I'm sluggish. Semyon recognizing me, Carys revealing Finn's part in his father's murder, and my uncertainty over what to do about any of it don't give me the headspace for a restful sleep. In the middle of the night, Lorcan tugged me flush against his body and whispered in my ear how much he loved me. Now that he's said it once, it spills out of him at every opportunity. His voice, half-asleep murmuring those words in my ear led to even less rest.

He's gone off to check on a few of their interests and left me in charge. Finn's coming home this morning, so Lorcan asked me to stick around in case Finn wanted an update on anything. There's nothing to report, and I'm worried as soon as he arrives there will be rapid progress in discovering who was responsible for his injury. The minute he remembers who I am, I'm dead. I know it, and I'm still here. There's a voice inside my head that sometimes wonders if I have a death wish, if the decimation of my family makes me incapable of caring about my own life.

I check my watch. "Sean," I call down the hall. "What time is Ian arriving with Finn?"

"Should be any minute."

My phone pings in my pocket. It's an SOS from Dai Qing. Her timing couldn't be worse. I can't answer it right now. Pushing my phone into my back pocket, I brush my fingers against my weapons. Dai Qing couldn't know whether Finn remembers. It can't be about that. Still, an SOS from her worries me with him on his way home. My life is on the cusp of exploding, and I'm not sure which grenade will have the pin yanked first.

Yesterday, when Lorcan went to see him, he said his brother was still a blank slate about the twenty-four-hour period around his injury. Neither of us wants him to remember. Lorcan thinks the helicopter leads to himself. Somewhere inside Finn knows it leads to me.

The front door opens, and Finn strides in. There isn't a trace of his injuries in the way he walks or carries himself. If there's one point I can give him, he's a warrior. Surviving those wounds and being out of the hospital within a week is impressive. And scary.

"Kim," he snaps. "I want you and Sean in my office. I want to understand why the fuck everyone here is so incompetent you don't know what the hell happened."

Rotating on my heel, I follow him down the hall. "Does that incompetence extend to your brother?"

He grunts. "No, it doesn't. That fucker knows something, and he's keeping it from me." He glances at me over his shoulder. "You got one hand on his balls lately. You need to get me information."

"To be fair," I say from a step behind him. "It's really a two-handed job."

Finn chuckles and stops suddenly. His gaze skims over me. "I don't want to see you again today until you have what I want. You can't get it? I'll find someone who can." He raises his eyebrows. "I almost died. Someone needs to pay. You got me? Someone will pay."

Unease races along my spine, but I hold eye contact with him. "Understood." My stomach flips. Maybe I need to tell Lorcan about my conversation with Carys sooner than I want. My back may be against the wall, but I'm not in a corner yet.

"Well." He angles his chin in the direction we came. "You can go. I'll chat with Sean about what you've been doing and where the gaps are. Maybe I should have put a man in charge."

I bristle.

Finn chuckles. "Ah, I thought that'd get you. I don't care what's going on between you and Lorcan. I'm paying your salary. Get me information."

"I will."

He motions with his hand for Sean to follow him, and I'm left in the hall, staring at their retreating figures.

When I get to the front entrance, my phone registers a missed call from a blocked number. My heart thumps in my ears. Lorcan's been gone for a while. A blocked number could be Dai Qing trying to reach me another way. It's dangerous to call me since she never knows what position I'll be in or who I'll be with when the phone rings.

Jorge nods as I head out the door. A pang pierces my chest at Antonio's absence. In the garage, I punch in the lockbox code for the spare keys to the cars. Lorcan took an SUV, but with Finn home from the hospital, the other is there again. Snatching the keys off their peg, I relock the box then climb into the driver's seat.

When I arrive at the payphone a short drive from the house, I ease out of the driver's seat and glance around. With a shaking hand, I dial Dai Qing's private number I memorized when Malik switched roles.

"Dai Qing here."

"It's me." I fiddle with the cord to the receiver. There's shuffling on her end, and her office door clicks closed in the background.

"Are you alone?"

"Yes."

Dai Qing takes a deep breath. "I—God—I wish I was there. It feels inhumane to say this on the phone."

"Malik?" I whisper.

"No, he's—there's an infection, but he's stable for now." There's another tense pause, and then Dai Qing says, "It's your mom, Kimi. She died this morning."

"What?" My knees buckle, and I place my hand on the thick plastic of the payphone wall. "What?" Last time I saw her, she was frail, but not close to death. "How?"

"She contracted pneumonia a few days ago. They—I guess no one updated them about Malik not being the contact anymore. It took them a couple days to get connected. And I tried to get in touch with you this morning. But they called me a few minutes ago to say she'd passed."

A sob catches in my throat. The lump feels immovable, but I swallow it. "Okay." Chills race across my chest and along my arms. I stare at my hand pressed against the plastic wall. "Okay. I need to—I should—what do I do now?" I ease my back against the wall, sliding until I'm crouched, the receiver clutched to my ear.

Dai Qing's voice is quiet when she says, "You can still go see her if you want."

I shake my head, and tears slip down my cheeks. "No." My voice is thick, almost unrecognizable. "No." There's more firmness in the word than I feel. "She's been gone a long time."

There's silence on the other end of the line. Dai Qing breathes in my ear. "Then you need to collect her things. The facility said it isn't much."

"Yeah, right. Yeah. Malik helped my mother pack up and get rid of any extras while I was on assignment." When I close my eyes, an echo of Lorcan whispering he loves me floats across my consciousness. I cling to it like a life raft. "I'm supposed to be finding fake information for Finn today. I'll go to the home now."

"Do you need me to meet you there? Or do you want me to get someone to meet you there? Or pick up the stuff for you? We can hold it for you until you're ready."

"No." I swallow the bile gathering in my throat. "I need to do this." My chest is tight, and I clear my throat. "I should have spent more time with her."

"Kimi," Dai Qing's voice is filled with kindness. "You were a good daughter. I have no doubt she loved you, and she was proud of you, of everything you've done with your life."

I choke on a sob. "I have to go." I push on the lever to hang up. Tears stream down my face as I press my forehead against the top of the payphone. Without giving myself a chance to second-guess my choice, I slip money into the slot and let my fingers fly across the numbers I memorized months ago.

"Lorcan Donaghey." The timbre of his voice is all business. He wouldn't have recognized the number. I should have called from my cell, but I'm not thinking clearly.

"Lorcan," I whisper.

"Kim," his tone becomes guarded, and the noise around him quiets. "Talk to me. Are you okay? Where are you?"

"My mom." I have to force the words out of me, and I can't say the rest.

"I'll meet you there," he says. "I'm on my way."

"Okay." My speech is thick with tears. My finger hovers over the lever to cut off our conversation.

"Kim?"

Silence sits between us, and I listen to him breathe for a moment, a sliver of comfort across a phone line. Tears fall unchecked. I sniff and wipe them impatiently with one hand.

"I love you, *my a chroí*. Whatever's happened, I've got you. I've got you." His tenderness eases over me like a blanket. An engine starts in the background.

I press my finger on the lever disconnecting the call before my traitor heart either says the words bubbling inside me or I collapse sobbing on the floor.

It takes almost no time to collect her things. I've signed the paperwork and picked up the two boxes before Lorcan even arrives. When he strides through the sliding doors, my heart leaps into my throat, and for the first time since I arrived at the facility, I'm worried I'm going to cry. Nothing seems real. Having him here is like being hit by a splash of water. It jolts me into the moment.

He doesn't say anything when he sees the boxes clutched in my hands. Gently, he takes them from me and sets them on the counter. He draws me into his chest and wraps his arms around me with the right amount of pressure.

"It's not going to feel real for a long while." His lips move against my hair. "Maybe never."

There's a familiarity to the crushing grief, but I don't have my mother to lean on. I push closer to Lorcan, and he tightens his arms more. His lips press against my temple. I'm grateful he doesn't tell me everything will be okay. When Chad died, and then again when my father died, it was a refrain people couldn't help saying. Be strong. It'll be okay. Time heals. It's bullshit. The ache might change, but it never goes away.

"Let's get you home."

*Home.* My mother is dead. *Home.* The last of my family is gone. *Home.*

I glance up, and his hazel eyes are filled with kindness. He brushes another kiss across my forehead. I sink deeper into his side.

With me tucked close, he slides the two boxes off the counter and juggles them until they are perched precariously under his arm. He leads me to his SUV. When I go to move away from him to my vehicle, his fingers dig into my hip. "I'll send someone for the car. I'll drive you home."

I don't argue. I'm not sure I should be driving right now. Waves of dizziness and nausea keep hitting me out of nowhere. He places the boxes in the back and helps me into the vehicle. I want to resent his help, but I can't. My body is numb, and my brain isn't too far off that.

On the way home, he holds my hand and doesn't say a word. Having lost his own mother, he knows there are no words, and he doesn't try to fill the silence with ones meaning nothing.

When we get to the house, he tries to guide me to his rooms, but I shake my head.

"I want to be alone." I take the boxes from him.

He searches my face, and then his hand comes up to graze my cheek with his thumb. "I'll stick around here for the rest of the day. You come find me if you need me, yeah?"

"Yeah." I wander along the hall to my old rooms. The code hasn't changed. After entering, I place the boxes onto the dresser.

Collapsing onto the bed, I stare at the ceiling. Finn pops into my head, unwanted. I don't have any information, and I haven't told Lorcan anything. There isn't an ounce of energy in me to deal with it though.

I peer at the boxes a few feet away. What would my mother have deemed worthy of keeping? Curiosity gets the better of me, and I take the first box off the dresser, setting it on the bed. I dig through old family photos and a couple albums. The thought of looking at them right now makes me want to vomit, so I put the lid on the box. I put it on the top of the dresser and grab the second box. It's smaller, lighter. With a finger, I flip the lid off and stare into a sea of papers. Frowning, I pick up the first piece. Chills run across my chest and along my arms like in the phone booth. It's my father's scrawl across the header. *Notes on the Donaghey family.*

I suck in a deep breath. "Oh, God."

With shaking hands, I spread my father's notes across the bed, putting them in order, sequencing his surveillance, his suspicions, and his mini-files on each member of the family. Every time I see Lorcan's name, I avoid reading too much of the page and add it to his pile. It's smaller than the others, but it isn't insubstantial. I was fifteen when my father died. So Lorcan would have been twenty. He should have been in Ireland going to university. Finn would have been home by then, twenty-five, done with the fighting, done with Carys, neck-deep in the business.

When the box is almost empty, I glance at the bedside clock. I've been at this for hours, sorting, reading, trying to piece together what my father stumbled upon that got him killed. It probably shouldn't be taking me this long, but it's hard to keep my distance when each letter, each note is in my father's familiar scrawl. The box is a glimpse into a history I knew nothing about. Near the bottom is a white envelope. I pluck it out and tap it against my hand. It's sealed, but no one is going to care anymore if I open it. Sliding my finger under the edge of the seal, I rip it open.

*Dear Kimi–*

*I knew I needed to write this before I couldn't remember anymore. We both realize that time is coming, and I guess if you're here, that time has already passed. I'm sorry. If I could have stayed, I would have. I wanted to. So much. But somebody somewhere had other plans.*

*You're smart, so you've probably pieced together some of this box. Your father never did figure out exactly who killed Chad. I wish I could tell you he didn't die in vain. The only thing I do know is the Donagheys had something to do with it. And while I can't prove they murdered your father, I'm convinced it was them. I know it.*

*So when I learned I was dying, I took a risk. I used the money from the house to put out a hit on Eamon Donaghey. Did you wonder where that money went? Why I had none? I used my funds to pay the Volkovs to take him out. I thought they would. They promised me they would. As of now, they've done nothing. At some point, I won't even remember I paid them.*

*I wanted you to realize I tried. I wanted your father's death, Chad's death, to count, to matter, for someone to pay for what happened to them. When I approached the Russians, it seemed like the most important thing, worth my money.*

*I'm sorry I never told you. You are your father's daughter. I didn't want to lose you, too, in this fruitless search for retribution. We were never going to win. The odds were stacked against us.*

*Maybe now, with your connections, you can finally figure it out. Lay it to rest. Maybe even find a path to justice for our family.*

*I love you—always, forever, no matter what. Even though none of us are there anymore in body, we're around you, watching you, loving you from afar. If there's one thing I know to be true, it's that. Not even death can sever our love for you.*

*With all my heart, Mom.*

The words blur as I read through the letter again and again. She's right. I am my father's daughter. My instinct is to dig, to dig so deep the truth has to surface. Did the Russians take her money and bide their time? Or did something else happen altogether?

Glancing at the clock again, I realize I haven't eaten dinner, and it's almost midnight. I'm not hungry, but sitting with these piles of paper, reliving my mother's anguish and my father's frustrations won't get me anywhere.

I toss the letter onto the bed and press the heels of my hands into my forehead. Crying has given me a massive headache. With a sigh, I exit the room and close the door behind me. I fiddle with the handle to make sure it's locked and then wander the hall to the kitchen. I've gotten used to eating in Lorcan's kitchenette the last few days, and it's strange to be going to the bigger space.

As I'm heating up milk, someone pauses in the doorway.

"Warm milk?" Finn's attention rakes over me. "You're feeling like a cliché tonight, are you?"

"No," I snap. "I'm feeling like I need a bit of comfort. I'm not in the mood. Go somewhere else for five minutes while I finish up here."

"Who pissed in your Cheerios?"

"My mother died." It's the first time I've said it out loud, and my voice catches on the last word. My bottom lip trembles, and I cross my arms and turn away from him.

Finn's quiet for a moment, but he comes farther into the kitchen to the island. "Saying I'm sorry to hear that makes me feel like an inadequate dick."

"Well, it's all about how you feel, I guess."

Finn snorts. "Still is, actually." He runs a hand through his hair. "'Cause I understand what it's like to have your mom die unexpectedly."

Tears pool in my eyes, but I don't want his concern.

"Do you want to talk about it? Does Lorcan know?"

"He knows. And no, I don't have any desire to talk about it with you."

"Fair enough." He eases onto a stool.

I lean against the counter. When the microwave pings, I grab my milk then take a long drink.

Anger is coursing through me, chased by grief. I'm so tired of dancing around the things I want to know. Giving him a calculating look, I say, "I want to talk about you."

Finn raises his eyebrows.

"When your mom died, Lorcan killed the mechanic who screwed with your mom's brakes."

With a sigh, he eyes me but stays quiet.

"Why'd you get mad at him?"

"'Cause it wasn't his fight. I shoulda had that satisfaction."

"What'd you do instead? You told me once you took care of it or something like that."

"Why do you care?"

"My mom died, and I want to know it's possible to feel better about it."

Finn's shoulders lift, and he grimaces, the first sign of any pain since he got home. "You're never going to feel better about it. Never. That ache? It'll be with you, a constant companion until the day you die." He tries to catch my gaze, but I won't let him. Silence rests for a beat. "You remember when you went to see Derry with me?"

I nod.

"What'd I tell him about screwing with my family?"

"That you don't just come after him, you go after everyone."

"Exactly. Exactly. Derry realized what I meant. It wouldn't have been the first time I did it."

"Who'd you go after with the mechanic?" I'm so numb from my mother's death, this conversation isn't sinking in. Finn's sympathy over my loss is making him more forthcoming than normal.

"I killed his son." He stares at his hands.

I suck in a sharp breath. "You killed his son." My hand reaches for one of my guns, but I took them off hours ago and left them in my room. Stupid. Finn could remember everything at any moment, and I'm unarmed.

"Shoulda killed the sniveling little kid who stumbled on the scene afterward." Finn searches my face.

I'm so far gone, I don't even care what he sees there. "Why didn't you?"

"Lorcan was with me. He doesn't like the 'kill-'em-all' policy, and I was feeling generous that night. He begged me to go, to leave it alone. It was pretty dark, but I wondered if it'd bite me on the ass. She saw me, plain as day."

"Probably too traumatized," I whisper. Even as he's telling me, I can't access the memory. It's gone which makes talking about it right now even more unreal. "Lorcan was there?"

"Yeah, why?"

"He stopped you from killing her?" He saved me. Lorcan saved my life.

"Yeah. That get you hot and bothered? Got a hero complex? My brother isn't a hero. He's got a smidge more of a conscience than me."

That smidge is the difference. I drain my milk, drop the mug in the sink with a clatter, then leave the kitchen without looking back. My heart races as I stride to my rooms, my vision blurry at the edges. I need a gun. Then, I'm going to Finn's room, and I'm ending this.

*Chad. Chad. Chad.*

Blood coats my hands, and they shake. I try to punch in the code to my room, and my hand falters. I'm on my third attempt before I get it to register.

When I open the door, I'm dumbfounded for a moment, wondering whether the world has toppled off its axis. Beside the bed, bare-chested, my mother's letter clutched in his hand, is Lorcan. He stares at me, and his tense posture signals the depths of his anger.

Rage bubbles out of him. "What the fuck is this, Kim?"

# Chapter Forty-One

My mind spins from the revelations hitting me in the chest. Lorcan saved my life. He'll realize my mother put a hit on his father. Finn killed Chad. The last one bounces around in my brain again. Finn killed Chad. Finn almost killed me.

Ignoring Lorcan, I stride to the dresser to grab my gun. He reads me with ease, and he snatches it before I can slip by. I roll off him and reach under the bed to grab the weapon I kept strapped there for emergencies. We circle each other, guns raised.

"You've been lying to me," Lorcan's voice is a growl deep in his throat.

"Yes." My lies are done. I keep the gun trained on him, but love and anger are warring in me for dominance. "You're no Boy Scout yourself."

"Never claimed to be." He holds up the letter in his free hand. "This was to get close to us?" He gestures to the bed and the scattered papers he's riffled through, but his focus on me doesn't waver.

My carefully constructed piles are a mess. He's so smart I wonder if he's pieced everything together quicker than me.

"Yes."

"Your mother put out a hit on my father? How is this even possible?"

"You understand as much as I do."

Confusion, anger, and finally love surface before disappearing. His eyes turn stony. "What the hell is going on?"

My gun, in his hand, is still trained on me. "It seems our families are jumbled together."

He searches my face, slotting in pieces, making the puzzle whole. "You're Chadwick Lee's sister."

I swallow the bile gathering in my throat.

"The shooting you saw when you were ten... It was him." His face softens around the eyes. He knows what that moment did, how much it haunts me. I've given him pieces of me no one else has seen.

I nod, and tears gather in my eyes. Pressing my lips together, I blink to clear my vision. The tears slip out. This could still go in so many directions, but I don't want to fight Lorcan. I'm not sure I could shoot him even if it came to that.

"He died in my arms," I whisper.

"Kim." The gentleness in his voice soothes me. He lets the letter fall to the floor as he raises his free hand and lowers the gun. "Can we—can we lower the guns and talk about this?"

"I don't know." I shake my head. "There's too much. It's too complicated."

"My brother killed your brother. Your mother paid for a hit on my father. Your mother had my father killed."

I keep my gun raised even as Lorcan lowers his. "I don't think she did. I don't think that's what happened."

He places his hand on the top of my gun, pushing my hand to my side. His proximity relaxes me, takes the edge off my sadness and anger.

"Their mistakes aren't ours." His voice has the lilting softness I love, and a shuddering breath escapes me.

"I think your father had my father killed." Except as far as he knows, my father isn't dead.

Lorcan frowns as he takes the gun from me and sets both on the dresser. His gaze rakes over me, and I wonder what conclusions he's making. A single thread tugged the right way is unraveling everything.

"There's only one explanation that makes sense. There's only one way your backstory checked out so completely, that your identity was sealed up so solidly."

I hold his look but say nothing. Anger touches the edges of his features again. Anything I do at this point is risky. At least we aren't pointing guns at each other anymore.

"I saw you there talking to Zahir."

His posture tenses, and space opens between us. "FBI."

"You were willing to work with us if Finn killed your father."

"Us," he scoffs. "I told Zahir I'd kill any agent he planted."

"I know."

We glare at each other for a moment. My palms are moist, and a trickle of sweat slithers along my side. I refuse to acknowledge the gun on the dresser. Lorcan won't hurt me.

"I suppose that deal is dead since your mother had the Russians kill my father. It would explain Semyon's behavior the other day."

"I think the Russians were involved. But I think Finn was too. I think you were right about him all along."

"Convenient now for you to agree with me."

I purse my lips. "When Carys came to see me, she said Finn pretty much told her he had something to do with your father's murder."

"Pretty much." Lorcan raises an eyebrow, skepticism coating him.

"He didn't admit it, but Carys felt he said enough to suggest he did it or had a part in it."

"When were you planning on telling me any of this? I tell you I love you, and you keep this shit from me. I guess this explains why you don't feel the same."

"I was worried you'd kill me," I whisper.

Lorcan's jaw turns to granite, and disgust passes across his features. "Were you? You're still here. What does that say about you?" His annoyance bores into me like a drill. "I'm not Finn. I don't work that way."

"Unless you feel justified." I raise my shoulders in a tiny shrug. "This wouldn't feel justified?"

"Maybe. If it were anyone but you."

I search his face, trying to figure out where this conversation is headed. He's not full of rage anymore. The new emotion spilling out of him might be worse. His disappointment in me is clear.

"It's fucked up." Lorcan's fingers tuck a few tendrils of my hair back behind my ear. "Your father. Who was he?"

I gesture to the mess of papers on the bed. "You didn't get that far in your snooping?"

He raises one eyebrow. "Your mum died today. I haven't seen you for hours. I was worried about you and came looking." With a frown, he glances at the bed. "I didn't expect this."

"How could you? I didn't even know it existed."

"So you coming here, it wasn't for revenge?"

I rub my forehead. "I didn't realize we were connected until I saw Chad's picture in Derry's hallway. Then I started digging, and things slotted into place, connecting our families in ways I would never want."

"Who is your father?"

"Axel Henhawk."

Lorcan frowns, and then his eyes narrow. "Name doesn't mean any-thing."

"You have a file on him in your office."

A spark of surprise strikes Lorcan's face. "Not the only one snooping." He takes my hand and links our fingers together.

A sigh escapes me, and we stare at each other for a minute.

"What the hell are we gonna do?" Lorcan asks.

"I want you to tell me what happened to my father. I need to know. I... If you see the file, do you think you'll remember?"

"Maybe. What then? I've done things, a lot of things. And you work for the FBI."

"They were willing to make you a deal."

"If I turned on Finn."

"You've got your confirmation."

Lorcan frowns. "I need to be sure."

"Or else what?"

"I help you get out, and I go down with the ship. I can't let him take the fall for all of it."

"Why does it matter so much whether he killed your father or not? He's done so many terrible things." I'm almost pleading. I can't be a party to Lorcan's prison sentence.

"Family is everything. You know that." He examines me. "If he can kill our father, regardless of the reason, someday he could kill me. For the rest of my life, I'll be waiting for the knife in my back from the one person I should trust the most."

"Your father had his wife killed, and you trusted him."

"My relationship with my father was complicated. It's not an easy thing to explain. I've always known I could count on Finn. Always. The way my father died, it's made me think there's a side to Finn that can't be trusted." He looks at his feet before glancing at me under his lashes. "I won't live like that."

We are toe-to-toe, and I wonder whether it's possible to make it out of this alive and with my heart intact. Lorcan laces our fingers again and leads me out of my room and along the hall to his office. There, he riffles through the files until he comes to Axel Henhawk.

He drops the file on the desk, and we are shoulder to shoulder as we sift through it. "This was in there the whole time?"

I nod.

His finger traces over the photos of me. "I'd know you anywhere."

"Do you remember what happened?"

He scans each note before putting it to the back of the folder. At the end, he checks the dates and glances at me. "This is—it's incredible."

"And Finn doesn't believe in coincidence."

"Feels like a warped version of destiny. The name meant nothing, but looking through the file, it's a bit more familiar. Your dad was poking around, offered to snitch to the police if he could get hired on with us. That's how you learned Irish, yeah?"

I nod.

"He pissed off my father. Approached a cop on the payroll." Lorcan goes back to the first paper in the folder. "We tried to pay off your parents after Chad died—hush money. They didn't take it."

"How do you know that?"

He points to symbols on the page. "These. Means surveillance started because a payoff didn't work."

I peer at the symbols again and wonder why I didn't see them the first time. This assignment has dulled my senses, weakened my instincts.

"I was home on Easter break from uni. By chance, I walked in on a conversation between my father and one of his men. They were talking about what to do with you and your mum." His pained eyes search mine. "I told him I was tired of the murders without reason, and I wouldn't be staying in the business if he didn't reconsider."

"Your dad was okay with that?"

Lorcan's lips quirk up. "I was twenty. I didn't give a shit what my father was okay with. I knew I could convince Finn to back me up. He hated our dad back then, anything to screw him over."

"Twice." I focus on the paper in his hand before gazing into his eyes. "You saved my life twice."

One side of his lips rises, revealing his dimple. "I've never been so grateful for my soft heart." He drops the sheet into the file, and his fingers weave into my hair. "I've lived this life because I was born into it. I've never wanted anything or anyone more than this."

The intensity of his gaze causes an ache to bloom in my chest. Tears pool in my eyes and overflow down my cheeks. "Lorcan," I say, my voice thick.

"Hey, hey. *My a chroí*. We'll sort it out, yeah? We're going to come out the other side." He wraps his arms around me and keeps me tight to his chest.

"How?"

"If Finn killed my father, we go to the FBI and turn him in. We'll see what'll happen to me."

"If he didn't?"

"We'll sort it out."

That's not good enough for me. It doesn't matter what I have to do, I'm going to prove Finn played a part in his father's murder. I've lost everything else. I don't intend to lose Lorcan.

He frames my face and kisses me, and I deepen the kiss, pressing my body to his. I might not be able to solve anything tonight, but I can find an escape in him, relish in the connection, the fact we're alive. Against the odds, we found each other.

He knows what I've been doing. And I'm still here. Triumph blooms across my chest. I wasn't wrong. He loves me enough for the details to be a speed bump and not a roadblock.

In the morning, I'm paying another visit to the Russians. This time, I'm not leaving until I have the answers I need to seal Finn's fate.

# Chapter Forty-Two

Lorcan can be a light sleeper, so when I slip away from under his arm the next morning, I'm not sure I'll make it out of the room before he wakes up. The longer I stay curled up with him in bed, the less likely I am to do what needs to be done. If I can't prove Finn had something to do with Eamon Donaghey's murder, Lorcan won't be safe. According to Finn and Antonio, the only ways out of the business are death or jail. Antonio has already proven one of those true. It won't be Lorcan who proves the other.

Before leaving, I head to my old room and clean up the mess of papers strewn around. I'm still surprised he let himself in yesterday, and if he's capable of doing it, then I know for a fact Finn wouldn't hesitate. I put both boxes in the closet and change the code on the door to one number off Lorcan's birthday. Let's see him figure that out.

I slip out of the house through a side door to avoid anyone seeing me leave. I'm through the front gates and headed to the Volkovs' when my phone pierces the silence in the car. I glance at the display. *Lorcan.* There's a pang of unease in my chest. If I answer, he'll realize something is wrong. If I don't answer, he'll think there's something wrong anyway.

My hand hovers over the green button on the display, but I never press it. My phone pings with a voicemail message. Almost immediately, it rings again.

With a sigh, I answer.

"Kim, where are you?" Lorcan's voice is laced with a hint of anger.

"I'm okay. There are a lot of arrangements to make for my mom. Funeral, burial, and so forth." Flexing my hands on the steering wheel, I hope my mother, wherever she is, doesn't get angry at me for using her death as an excuse. She told me, in her letter, to make it right. This is the only way I know how to do that.

Silence hangs in the vehicle, and I picture Lorcan weighing my words, trying to decide. "I want to be done with the lies."

My hands tighten on the leather wheel. If I tell him where I'm going, he'll follow me. I'll never get the information. It's a particular version of Kim who is needed today, and I can't be her with him around.

"Christ. I want to order you to come back. Fall in fucking line and don't do whatever you're off doing." Silence stretches across the phone line again. "It doesn't work that way anymore. I know. So I'm going to decide to trust you. I don't know if you're telling me the truth. If you were here, I might be able to figure it out. The fact you snuck out..." There's another tense silence.

I keep quiet, willing him to continue so I don't have to lie.

His voice is rough when he says, "You're *my a chroí*. My heart, Kim. Whatever you're doing, make sure you come back to me."

"Always." I barely get the word out. "It's nothing. It's mom stuff."

"You need me, call, text, whatever. I'll be there. I'll come. You understand me? Don't be a lone wolf."

Three words are on the tip of my tongue, and they almost topple out. I can't say them on speakerphone while I'm lying. I can't.

"I'll see you back at the house in a bit." Each word leaves a bitter taste as it exits my mouth.

"Be safe." His voice is rough again.

After he disconnects, I stare out the windshield, a weight settling across my chest. Lying will be worth it if I can nail Finn's involvement, give Lorcan his proof.

When I get to the gates, a guard is posted there the same as the other day. "Name?"

I hesitate, and then I take a chance. "Vivian Lee."

He speaks into his walkie-talkie. Turning from me, he talks a bit longer and then comes to my window. His phone is directed at me, either taking a picture or giving whoever is on the other end a video.

He touches a button on his belt, and the gates ease open. "Someone will meet you at the door."

My heart beats against my breastbone, but I give the guard a brief smile. "Excellent. Thanks."

As I drive the car up to the circle driveway near the door, Semyon appears flanked by two guards. He grins at me as I put the vehicle in park.

Sliding out of the car, I stand by my door for a minute, debating the wisdom of coming here. It's too late now. I'm loaded to the gills with weapons, and no one has searched me this time. Semyon's opinion of women is they can't be dangerous. At least I have that going for me.

"Vivian Lee," he crows as I come around the car. "I knew I recognized something about you the other day." His focus rakes over me. "How do you know Vivian?"

"A distant relative." A small smile touches my lips. "She passed away yesterday."

His smile fades. "That's too bad. She was an exceptional woman." He waves his hand around his men. "Come in, come in. Lorcan and Finn don't realize you're here."

It's not a question, but I'm still tempted to lie. Having him think I have no backup is extremely dangerous.

"On the contrary," I say over my shoulder. "I told Lorcan I wanted to hear your offer in more detail."

He chuckles. "I bet that made him happy."

Half turning, I aim a sly smile at him. "What can I say? He likes me."

"Yes," Semyon says. "I bet he does."

His guards lead us into a sitting room without laying a finger on me. It's unbelievable they're this trusting because I'm a woman. Lorcan bringing me on as a bodyguard seems like a pretty smart move now. Derry underestimated me, now Semyon is doing it too.

"So." He pours me a glass of vodka and passes it. "How did you know I knew Vivian Lee?"

"I was under the impression you had a business arrangement. I only found out yesterday. She was on her deathbed. She asked me to come collect what was owed to her. Apparently, you didn't fulfill your end of the contract."

Semyon freezes and then chuckles. "You think you're so slick. I know Vivian's memory was not what it once was."

"Indeed. And, had she lived longer, it might have been true she'd forgotten. It wasn't her Alzheimer's that took her. It was pneumonia."

He screws the top on the bottle of vodka, his back to me. Resting my hands on my thighs, I take stock of my weapons and which of them I can reach the quickest, eliminate the most targets.

"Lorcan doesn't know you're here. Neither does Finn." He sighs. "I was hoping you'd be a good match for one of my boys. Or at least a pleasant distraction. Seems I miscalculated."

"Women aren't toys."

"The best ones are."

"I want Vivian's money. You broke the contract."

Semyon chuckles and whirls around, his men tense. "You come to my house to make demands? You may not be a toy, but you haven't got many brains in that lovely head of yours."

"You broke the contract."

"We had no contract. We slept together a few times. She paid me some money for my time."

I raise my eyebrows. "You're the prostitute in this situation?" My heart races, and a thin sheen of sweat coats my palms. Setting down my glass, I ease my hands along my thighs. Assuming he lets me leave, I need to be sober enough to drive out of here.

The thought of my mother sleeping with this man is repulsive. She should have told me what she was trying to do. I could have helped her.

"You think making me mad is going to get me to tell you something? No. No, that's not how this works. Honey works better than vinegar." His gaze roams over me.

He's not getting any honey out of me. "Did you fulfill your part of your agreement with Vivian?"

"He's dead, isn't he?"

"Did her payment do that?"

He looks at me for a minute and shakes his head. "What did I tell Lorcan about fishing?"

I lean back in my chair and stare. My fingertips brush up against my gun. "I'm not Lorcan. And I'm not fishing."

"What would you call this exercise, then?"

"It's a friendly conversation between Vivian's proxy, the executor of her will and estate, and a man who owes that estate money."

"I owe her estate nothing. Eamon Donaghey is dead. You cannot prove I did that nor can you prove I did not."

"So she got screwed over in more than one way by you."

His granite gaze meets mine as he throws back the last of his drink. "I liked Vivian. But she was two things I could not tolerate. Consumed by revenge. Consumed by disease. One of those, maybe. But both? No. No. She was a shell of a woman. A beautiful shell. She had nothing left to give anyone except death and destruction. Her family was dead, and she wanted to light the world on fire."

Hearing him speak about my mother that way is almost enough to call my bluff. It's too fresh. "That's rich coming from you."

"Maybe." He waves his hand in a dismissive gesture. "I'm done entertaining you now. My guards will see you out." Semyon tips his head at them. Before he leaves the room, he stops in the doorway, his back still to me. "Make no mistake, Kim. If you or Lorcan come back here seeking anything from me, one of you will not make it out alive. I'm done with your nonsense. Whatever you're after, you won't find it here."

Before I can say anything else, he's out the door and down the hall.

I pinch the bridge of my nose and stand to leave. The primary guard touches his ear and holds up a hand. "Wait a minute."

My fingers move to the gun inside my jacket.

At the door to the room, a familiar figure appears. I googled the whole family before coming here. This looks like one of Semyon's sons, a younger, fitter version of his father.

"Hagen." He enters the room with an almost catlike gracefulness.

"Kim." I ease my hand out of my coat. If I rub him the right way, I wonder if he'll purr for me. I keep my focus on him but don't say anything else.

"I saw you here talking to my father the other day. You're back again." His gaze trails my figure in a possessive, lustful way I used to enjoy seeing. Men with that attitude never think with their brains.

"I am," I reply breathily, giving him my best smile.

"Why exactly?"

There are a few things I could stroke right now which would draw the information out of him. Something in his eyes are both sinister and childlike. He'll enjoy seeming like the expert. Ego, it is. "Your father took cash for a contract kill and never did it."

"Eamon?" He raises an eyebrow. "We did it eventually." Hagen shrugs. "The initial money wasn't high enough. She needed to make a war worthwhile."

"That means you didn't fulfill the contract."

"That's not how it works."

"So what changed, then? She didn't pay enough, but you still killed him. That makes no sense."

"We had a guarantee of no retaliation."

"From who?"

Hagen smirks and bends forward. "From someone who could guarantee there would be no retaliation."

"Lorcan." I say his name as though he's the obvious choice. My heart booms in my chest, but I keep my shoulders lowered.

"Lorcan," Hagen scoffs. He eyes me for a beat. "Finn thought you'd get here, eventually. I guess I'd better call to let him know the jig is up."

"No need." A drop of sweat races along my spine. "I knew it was him. Carys told me. He told her. I told Finn I knew. We wanted to see if either of you would flip, if he could trust your family. He told me everything." It's a risk. If Finn knows I've been here before I can get back home, I'll be met at the door by a gun to the head.

Hagen chuckles. "That sounds like him. I doubt he told you everything. He plays the odds. Trying to figure out who's going to fuck him over. Guy's paranoid." He gives me a calculated look, and his eyes narrow. "You haven't told Lorcan? Finn said you had him by the balls."

"No one wants a war. I'm here to make sure one doesn't get started by accident."

He watches me for a beat longer than I'm comfortable with. "You'd better get out of here before my father changes his mind about letting you go. Or before I decide it's worth having you stay."

I'm not going to wait around for him to tell me twice. As I glide past him, his hand brushes my ass. "They're lucky men."

My instinct is to confront him, to stand my ground. I've spent years honing that instinct and tamping it down. In the grand scheme of things, I'm outnumbered, and he could do so much worse than grab my ass.

It doesn't take long to get back to the Donagheys' property. I'm lucky no one stops me for speeding. It's the last thing I need right now. Although Hagen appeared to buy my story, I can't be sure he hasn't called Finn to confirm.

When I stride in the front door, a sense of relief spreads through me. There's no sign of anyone except Jorge standing guard. With a wave, I head toward the kitchen. I need food before my stomach starts eating itself.

I'm buttering my toast when Finn wanders into the kitchen clutching his phone. The sight of him and his phone causes a sharp jolt of fear, and I straighten.

"I'm not sleeping worth shit." He grabs a mug from the cupboard above me.

It takes me a moment to register he hasn't said anything that'll lead to my murder. "In pain?" I take a bite of my toast and chew.

Maybe I should have gone straight to Lorcan. Every time I look at him, all I can think about is Chad, dead, blood leaking out of him and onto me. When that happens, part of me becomes so angry it's hard to see straight, let alone think straight.

"I got drugs for that." He shakes his head and runs a hand down his face. "My dreams. Or, I don't know, maybe nightmares. I'm waking up to the thwump of the helicopter blades." With a huff, his brow furrows. "Someone calling your name. I don't recognize the voice. He calls you Kimmy."

I pause before I take another bite. His back is turned, but his posture isn't tense. He's on the cusp of remembering, but he knows nothing yet.

"That's weird," I say. "You used to call me Kimmy, though. You haven't since you woke up."

He frowns and glances at me. "No?"

"Nope." I pop out the p. "I gotta go see Lorcan."

Finn nods. "You know why I'd hear someone calling your name?"

"Not a clue." A brief smile crosses my face. "Maybe it's your subconscious telling you to call me Kimmy again, even if I hated it. Or maybe you're taking too many drugs."

He smirks and rubs the back of his head as the coffee finishes brewing. Glancing at me, he says, "That's not it. It's a memory. I can't quite catch it."

"I'm sure it'll come." I dust off my hands. There's a sinking sensation in my stomach. Although my tone is casual, inside, a riot brews.

Before Finn says anything else, I leave the kitchen and head for Lorcan's bedroom. The door unlatches before I key in the code. He must have been watching for me.

"All sorted?" He eyes me from the kitchenette. There's a wariness to his posture I'm not used to seeing anymore. We're not back on even ground yet.

"He did it." I move closer to Lorcan. "I know Finn had a hand in your father's death."

# Chapter Forty-Three

Lorcan stares at me for a moment. "You went to see Semyon."

"I did."

He closes his eyes and bangs his fist on the counter. With a swipe of his hand, the glass beside him flies against the wall. His stormy gaze lands on me. "He could have killed you. You shouldn't have gone, and you certainly shouldn't have gone alone."

"I've been working for the FBI for quite a few years. You think this is the first time I've gone into a dangerous situation? Coming here, working for you and Finn is as dangerous as what I did today." I examine his tense, coiled rage. "If you love me, you have to love all of me. This is who I am. This is what I do."

"And if you gave a shit about how I felt, you wouldn't be lying to me still."

"I—I knew you wouldn't want me to go. That you'd either come with me or stop me from going. I wouldn't have been able to get the information."

"He came out and told you? Denied me the other day but spilled it to you."

"No," I say evenly. "His son Hagen couldn't resist rubbing his knowledge in my face. Guys like him love having little nuggets of truth to lord

351

over others." I cross my arms. "He said Finn figured I'd be knocking on his door at some point."

Lorcan presses his hands into the counter and doesn't look at me.

"He said, and I quote, 'I'll have to let Finn know the jig is up.'"

"I saw him this morning. He was complaining of headaches and bad dreams." Lorcan focuses on me. "What happened out by the shed that night?"

For a moment, I consider lying. Protecting myself is so ingrained, even though I understand I can trust him, my instinct is to hold back.

"I found Finn leaning against the shed, already injured. It's true. The FBI planted an agent in Zhang's organization. It's also true you rounded him up. Finn saw the helicopter, heard the agent call my name. He was already suspicious of me. Then he added the pieces together."

"I knew he was suspicious of you."

"You weren't?"

"I didn't *want* to be. 'Cause if I let suspicion take hold, there was only one thing to be done." He straightens and props his hip against the counter, crossing his arms.

I let my gaze travel over his features. At every crossroads, whether or not it's been a conscious decision, he's chosen me. So many things in my life have come to an awful end. What we have between us can't go that way. I won't let it.

"If he remembers..."

"He'll realize I'm FBI."

"I want you to stay in here for the rest of the day."

I open my mouth to protest, and Lorcan holds up a hand. "Whenever that moment comes, he's going to want to kill you. His sense of self-perseveration is stronger than any other instinct. He'll take you out right in front of me and apologize after. There's no mercy, no consideration for my feelings or your life."

I swallow.

"I need to talk to some people, make it seem as though business is carrying on as normal. Do you have an FBI contact?"

I nod. "Dai Qing."

He runs both his hands through his hair, frustration spilling out of him. "Am I really going to do this?"

"If he wasn't your brother, I'd kill him myself. My whole family, Lorcan... one way or another, they're gone because of him and your dad." I move between his legs, resting my hands on his hips. He gathers me tight with a sigh. "The reality is once Finn realizes we know about your dad, once he remembers I'm the rat, he'll take action. If we wait, we might end up dead."

Lorcan's lips graze the top of my head. "I get what he's done to you and your family. I understand why you'd want him dead. I would, too, if I was you. But for years, he's been the guy I wanted to be like, the man I wished I could somehow become."

The thought of him turning into Finn terrifies me. I press my palm into his chest, over his heart. "I'm glad you're not him. I'm glad you're a little softer, a little kinder, and a little more human." Our gazes connect, and I say, "I love you, Lorcan."

He sucks in a sharp breath and draws me tighter. "I wasn't sure you'd ever say it."

And then, because it feels as though the weight on my shoulders has eased, I say it again. "I love you."

"*My a chroí.*" His lips find mine, brushing against them and then deepening the kiss as he turns us around. Without breaking contact with me, he lifts me onto the counter. "I'm going to keep you safe," he murmurs against my lips. "I'll do anything to keep you safe."

To the soundtrack of moans and sighs, he proceeds to show me how loved I am.

⸻◆○◆⸻

The text comes in the middle of the night. My phone buzzes from beside the bed, and I snatch it off the nightstand. Lorcan shifts, and I hold my breath, hoping he doesn't wake. When I'm sure he's settled again, I glance at the display.

*Warehouse by the water in one hour.*

Finn.

My heart dips, threatening to fall to my feet. I stare at Lorcan's sleeping form as I clutch the phone to my chest, muting the bright light of the home screen. He looks peaceful and strong, and like all the things I never knew I wanted but can't imagine not having now. I ache to trace his features I love so much. It would wake him up, and I don't want that. It's the last thing I want.

These few months, Finn's asked me to do any number of odd things. But he's asked in person. Whether he realizes it or not, this lone text message tells me more than him coming here and beating down the door. I could ignore the message, pretend I slept through it. That only delays the inevitable.

I ease myself out of bed and get dressed. I cast a last look at Lorcan. If I make it out of this, he'll be pissed at me for not waking him up. There are a lot of things I'll sacrifice for my job, but not him. The idea of him being hurt or killed by his own brother or someone in his organization because of me is unacceptable. I love him. I won't lose him too. This time, I'm going to save him.

At the walk-in closet, I key in the code he used the night of the extraction. Everything had been so chaotic he hadn't tried to hide the numbers from me. Glancing at the bed, I gather as much ammunition and as many weapons as it makes sense to carry. There's a lock-picking set nestled in amongst the ammo, and I grab it. Never know.

I'm not sure what to expect from Finn. He's cocky enough to keep the meeting between the two of us and have us go head-to-head, but he's also smart enough to never underestimate people. I select one more gun and tuck it into my waistband before sliding into my jacket and striding to the door.

Once it clicks shut behind me, I head for the entryway. I send a brief text to the emergency extraction number and to Dai Qing. Things can't continue like this. It ends tonight.

Sean rises from his chair beside the door as I approach. Finn doesn't have him, but there are at least a dozen men who could be at the warehouse with him.

He checks his watch and frowns. "Going out?"

"Warehouse." I watch Sean's reaction. What does he know?

His frown deepens. "Finn took five or six men there a couple hours ago." He searches my face as I get closer. "Lorcan isn't going?"

So he didn't go alone. "How did he seem?"

"Pissed off." He shrugs. "That's normal for him lately. He's constantly mad about something. Mostly that he can't remember."

I nod and move to go past Sean and out the door.

"And Lorcan?" he asks.

Instead of turning around, I keep my back to him. "He doesn't need him for this." I disappear out the entryway and into the dark of the early-morning hours.

It's an easy drive to the warehouse. I've got time to spare, and the FBI is on the way. There's no point in going in early. Dawn is a cloak, and I park the car a few blocks away from the warehouse. A cluster of trees across the street keeps me hidden well enough to watch for any traffic coming and going from the building. To pass the time, I take out a few of my weapons and double-check they're ready to fire and easy to access in a hurry. I yank my hair out of its ponytail and then do it again but tighter. The last thing I need is hair in my face while I'm trying to take a shot.

I'm checking my watch again when a black SUV comes tearing around the street corner and whirls into the parking lot as close to the door as possible. Hopefully, whoever it is doesn't keep the vehicle there. It'll make it difficult for the agents to access the entrance. I step into the shadows until the driver's door swings open and familiar jean-clad legs and a brown-blond head emerge.

*Shit.*

My heart kicks up a notch as Lorcan exits the SUV and rounds the hood, pulling out one of his guns. I leave the safety of my spot, and I'm about to call out to him when the door to the warehouse blows open and a hand yanks him into the building.

A noise of distress catches in the back of my throat. I take out a gun from inside my coat and circle the building to a rear entrance. Finn has Lorcan.

At the door, I wiggle the handle. It's locked. Taking out my lock-pick set, I slide the pieces into place and listen to the lock tumble open. Easing down on the handle, I slip inside, gun drawn.

"Where the fuck is she, Finn?" Lorcan's voice booms through the empty warehouse.

Sean said Finn took five or six men. They could be anywhere in here. My senses are on high alert.

"For the second fucking time, she's not here. You're a paranoid fuck." Finn's voice bounces around, his annoyance clear. "Go home, little brother. This meeting's got nothing to do with you."

"Who are you meeting?"

"People."

"Bullshit. Where's the table? This isn't a meeting, it's an execution."

There's a brief pause, and I move along the hallway, trying to get closer to the open space beyond the block of offices without getting caught. Goose bumps rise on my arms at the silence between the two men. Something Lorcan said has got Finn thinking. That can't be good.

"Why the fuck would I execute Kimi?" There's a shuffling of feet.

*Kimi.* He knows. He knows something.

Lorcan's sigh is loud with frustration.

I need to get eyes on him, on this, before things go sour. He's tired of the lies. Confronting Finn when he's outnumbered six to one isn't smart. I pray Lorcan can keep his emotions in check. He can't admit to him he knows who I am, what I am, or else he'll be signing his own death warrant.

"Come on, *deartháir beag.* Tell me why I'd want to kill Kimi." Finn's voice is low and menacing.

There's not a doubt in my mind he realizes the truth. Now he's trying to figure out how deep the betrayal goes.

I check my watch. It's too early for the FBI to be here. But I can't let Lorcan sink himself.

Removing one of my guns and emerging out from the safety of my spot, I focus on Finn. "I have proof you killed your father."

He whirls on me, gun drawn. A dark chuckle escapes him. "What? No front door? You knew you were in trouble." He gestures above him with his free hand where a couple of men are stationed with guns trained on us.

Two men appear on either side of me and reach for my weapons. I tamp down my urge to fight them. Instead, I give in. One of them secures me with my arms behind my back. It doesn't matter. I can't watch Lorcan get shot, and if we descend into chaos, there's a good chance he'll get hurt.

Lorcan's nostrils flare. Fury licks at every part of him when his gaze connects with mine.

"I thought there was a chance Hagen would call you, yeah." I shrug. "The jig is up."

Finn's vision sweeps over me, and then he glances at Lorcan. "Something else came to me tonight. FB-fucking-I, Kimi. Ring any bells? 'Cause, I gotta tell you, it was like a fucking chorus of bells in my head this morning."

Whatever he's remembered, it's still not quite clear, or I'm pretty sure I'd be dead by now, whether or not Lorcan stands in his way. The men behind me tighten their grip.

"They landed on the property," I admit. "We've been checking into it."

Finn's smirks. "Checking into it. Easy when you're on the inside."

"Who are you accusing?" Lorcan's been silent to this point, but his gun is still gripped in his hand aimed at Finn. If anyone fires, we're dead. Already, it seems almost impossible we'll make it out alive.

"You go home, brother. You don't need to see this." Finn's attention is locked on me.

Lorcan keeps his gun trained on his brother, but he steps in my direction. "I'm not leaving. Not unless Kim's coming with me."

"She's rotten. Eating holes in our organization." His posture is full of menace as he shadows him.

"We ate holes through the fabric of her life years ago, *deartháir mor*."

I close my eyes, and my jaw tightens. "Lorcan," I say. "Don't." I snap my eyes open, but it's too late. He's put it together.

"You fucking knew?" His voice booms out through the warehouse. "You fucking knew she was no good?" He stalks toward him, rage etched in his features.

I strain against the men securing me.

Lorcan holds his ground, the gun steady in his hand. "You kill her, you might as well fucking kill me. 'Cause I'll hunt you down."

"I don't give a shit if we ripped her life to shreds years ago, brother. I don't care if she's got some sort of magical vagina that lures good men to insanity. And I don't give a shit if you're coming for me. 'Cause she'll already be dead. You don't keep a rabid dog as a pet, *deartháir beag*. You put it down. No matter how much you love it."

Finn's looking at his brother during his speech, but then he whirls toward me, gun raised. Lorcan's voice travels along a tunnel as he screams for him to stop. The gun discharges.

A searing white-hot feeling slices through my chest. When I see the burning spot, blood is spreading out from the wound. My knees buckle, but the men behind me keep me upright.

Everything is moving in slow motion as Lorcan shoots Finn, takes out two of the men above and then tries to make his way to me as he's fired on from above. He's sprinting and weaving as the bullets fly.

White-hot pain springs up in my foot and my thigh, and I realize I've been hit again. The men behind me tug me toward the offices. My instinct is to fight, but I'm sluggish, heavy.

Without warning, the pressure on my arms is gone, and I almost stumble face-first into the cement floor. But Lorcan's there, catching me around the waist, dragging me with him as bullets ping off every surface.

From behind, a flash grenade goes off. He jerks forward, collapsing onto the ground.

Somehow, he breaks our fall. We're side-by-side, and the shouts of the FBI echo in the distance. I need to tell them we're here. We need help. I open my mouth, but I can't force out any sound.

My head falls to the side, and I meet Lorcan's gaze. His eyes are glassy, dazed, unfocused. The black shirt on his chest appears wet, and I will my hand to touch him. But I can't.

My whole body is so heavy. And I long to close my eyes.

"Lorcan," I murmur.

It's the only word I squeeze out before everything goes dark.

# Chapter Forty-Four

I awake to the steady beeping of machines and the hum of a hospital. I haven't been hospitalized for a few years, but I'd recognize the sounds anywhere. And the smell. Antiseptic. Enough to sour my stomach on a good day.

It takes a moment for me to remember why I'm here, what happened. The room is empty of any visitors. *Lorcan.* Last time I saw him, he looked like he was bleeding out. A bubble of panic forms in my chest. I fumble for the call button and hit it before I lose my nerve. Closing my eyes, I wait for the whoosh of the door opening. *Please let him be okay.*

"Ah, you're awake." Dai Qing smiles at me as she makes her way to my bed. Behind her, a nurse comes bustling in.

She checks my equipment and then leans on the bedrail. "How are you feeling?"

"Lorcan?" I shift my focus between the nurse and Dai Qing.

"Alive," Dai Qing confirms with a small smile. "He was even more riddled than you. It's a miracle he survived. The doctors said he's a fighter."

"Are the meds managing your pain?" the nurse asks.

"Is he going to be okay? Really okay?" I try to read Dai Qing. Survival sometimes doesn't mean what we want it to mean.

"He woke up an hour ago. Started asking for you." Dai Qing raises her eyebrows. "That answer your question?"

Tension whooshes out of me, and I relax into the bed. Taking a deep, calming breath, I say, "Yes. Perfectly."

"Hit the call button if you need anything." The nurse checks my IV again before opening the door then vanishing into the hallway.

Dai Qing drags a chair up to my bedside and watches me in silence.

"You're not going to say anything else?" I ask.

"What would you like me to say?"

"What's going to happen to Lorcan?"

"He's cooperating with us."

I squirm in the bed and groan. "Where the hell did I get shot?"

"Where didn't you get shot?" She gives me a strained smile. "The bullet to the chest was the worst." She clears her throat. "You still had Malik as your next of kin, so I had to tell him what happened."

"Oh, Jesus." I can't meet her gaze. "Is he—is he in the hospital?"

"Yes. Though I was pretty sure he was going to check himself out and fly to Boston when I called him."

I rub my face, pressing my fingers into my eyebrows. "When I get out of here, I'll need to talk to him."

"It'll be a race to see who can heal faster to confront the other. Sounds fun."

I roll my eyes at the tone of her voice. "Did you want me to tell him about Lorcan when he was injured so badly?"

"No." Dai Qing wrings her hands. "Part of me wishes there was no Lorcan for Malik's sake, for the agency's sake."

Even without him, I'm not convinced I would have given Malik a fair chance. He was familiar, easy, and safe. Being with Lorcan will never be any of those things. "I can't help how I feel."

She sighs. "Ain't that the truth."

"I want to see him."

"When we're done extracting the information we think we can get, I'll get one of you wheeled into the other."

"Who's with him?"

"Zahir."

I frown. "He came here to talk to him?"

"He's the person who offered him the original deal."

"But Finn's dead."

Dai Qing shifts in her chair.

"Isn't he? I saw Lorcan shoot him. And..." I search my memory. "Finn collapsed on the ground. I'm sure of it. He went down."

"Yes, well, it seems in the chaos of the raid, we misplaced him."

I stare at her for a moment. Only Dai Qing would say the FBI *misplaced* a skilled and very deadly mobster who would love to see me laid low. "You're kidding me."

"I'm afraid not. We're trying to determine if Lorcan knew about his brother's extraction plan."

I purse my lips. "Finn's not a planner. Not like that. He's an opportunist." I pick at the blanket lying across my waist. "And I... Lorcan didn't know about the warehouse, about what Finn had planned."

"You put your career—your life—on the line, and you didn't trust him enough to take him with you?"

"That's—that's not it." Frustration eats at me, and I shift in the bed again. Another groan escapes me. They need to give me the good drugs.

There's a knock on the doorway, and Zahir is in the entrance, a tailored black suit clinging to his frame.

"You're awake." He wanders in, unbuttoning his jacket and pushing his hands into the pockets of his suit pants.

"How's Lorcan?"

He shakes his head and laughs. "Lucky to be alive. Much like you. Why the hell did you go in there? You knew we were on the way."

"Lorcan wasn't supposed to be there." It's not the professional answer, and he might take me out of the field for good after this. Playing these kinds of games has never been my specialty. "When he went in looking for me, I was worried Finn would do something to him to get to me."

He looks at me for an extra beat. "This whole assignment has fucked you up."

"I won't apologize for having feelings. For being human." I lift my chin.

"I'm not asking for an apology from you. I'm trying to unravel how you got into this situation in the first place. Your file..." He glances at Dai Qing. "Anyone could have drawn the conclusion this assignment wasn't good for you."

"Yet no one did."

"Dai Qing did, but it was too late by then." Zahir moves closer to my bed and scans me. "I'll get to the bottom of it, eventually. How are you feeling?"

"I've been better." All I can think about is seeing Lorcan.

"We're not going to bring you back into the fold for a while. Counseling, psych evaluations, and so forth, while you get healed up."

None of that appeals to me. Given everything that's happened, every-thing I've learned over the last few months, it might not be the worst idea. Now, with Finn out there somewhere, I'm not even sure undercover work is possible for me again.

"Then what?"

"We've done our best to obscure details, plant false ideas about what went down at the warehouse. If we can track Finn, and you want to go back out on an assignment, we might be able to make it happen. I'm not promising anything. Every single piece would have to click into place for that to occur."

"And Lorcan?"

Zahir's mouth twists. "We're in discussions about possibilities." His dark gaze searches me for a moment. "Like last time I spoke to him, his primary concern is you." He gives Dai Qing a pointed look before swinging his focus my way. "At least if you had to get yourself into such a mess, you did it for a man who seems to care about you just as deeply."

An *I told you so* is on the tip of my tongue, but I hold it back. Warmth fills my chest at Zahir's words.

Another knock on the door echoes through the room, and in the doorway is Fiona. She shuffles on her feet in a nervous manner I don't remember seeing last time we crossed paths when Finn was in the hos-pital.

"Sorry to interrupt. Mr. Donaghey was wondering when exactly you'd be wheeling Kim to his private room?"

"Who are you?" Zahir raises his eyebrows.

"Fiona, sir. I'm Mr. Donaghey's personal assistant."

She doesn't mention she only assists him and his family at the hospital.

He sighs. "Of course you are." A wry smile touches his lips.

"It's fewer resources if we only need to have guards for a single room." Dai Qing moves to Zahir's shoulder.

He raises an eyebrow at her and gives a small shake of his head. "You too?"

"She's been through a lot, sir." She adds, "And he did shoot his brother in an effort to protect her."

Zahir sighs. "Get it done. I'll see you both at Quantico when you're well enough to travel, Kimi. Physically and mentally." He points a finger at me before heading to the door.

Dai Qing waves Fiona over, and the two of them unlock my wheels and manage to take my equipment with me as well as rolling the bed. It's impressive. My heartbeat accelerates as we glide along the hall. I don't know what I'm going to find in Lorcan's room. He's well enough to talk to Zahir and order Fiona to come check on me. But Dai Qing also said he was lucky to be alive.

When we enter the room, his eyes snap open. One side of his lips quirks up in the way that makes my heart race for a different reason. The sight of him alive with a touch of humor in his eyes eases my soul.

"Right here," he says to Fiona, motioning to the far side of his bed. "Make it as though it's a big bed."

She hesitates and glances at the door. "Sir, you've been severely injured, and I'm not sure—"

"If that sounded like a suggestion, I apologize." He glances at me, and the humor is gone. "We almost died. I don't give a shit how injured we are. We're still here. Put the fucking bed right next to mine."

"Yes, sir," she mutters as she lowers a bedrail, pushes the beds together, and locks the wheels. She scurries out of the room while Lorcan and I watch her retreat in silence.

"I'm glad you're okay." I grasp his hand.

He searches my face, his expression difficult to read. "And I'm glad you are too."

"You're angry with me."

"You're fucking right I am."

"I'm sorry."

"Why didn't you wake me? Tell me anything?"

I swallow the lump lodged in my throat. "They're dead. My whole family. And…" I hold back the tears threatening to fall. "The idea you could be injured or killed, or you might have to kill Finn and never forgive me. I couldn't. It wasn't a risk I could take."

"You went there alone."

I shake my head. "I wasn't, though. The FBI was coming. I had to wait it out."

"So why didn't you?"

"Because you went storming in there. I didn't want him hurting you to flush me out."

Lorcan stares at the ceiling for a moment before letting his head fall toward me. "We need to work on our communication. Dying while trying to save each other's arses isn't romantic in real life. It fucking hurts."

A laugh escapes me, and his lips rise, revealing the dimple I love.

"My prize," he murmurs, and I trace his cheek.

"What do we do now?" I whisper.

"Zahir's given me a few options. Maybe you and I will try talking those out for once." He winks at me. "Not all of them send me to jail, but I doubt you'll like some of them, regardless."

"Where do you think Finn's gone?"

Lorcan's smile fades. "I don't know. Wherever he is, I'm sure he's a hurting unit. I got off more than one shot."

A brief surge of satisfaction floods my chest. I realize shooting his brother wasn't easy for Lorcan, and carrying around this residual anger at Finn and the rest of the Donaghey organization isn't going to help me or Lorcan in the long run. Even if Finn is out there dead somewhere, it wouldn't make me happy. No matter how much I've wanted to hate him, there's a part of me that understands the rage driving him. I've felt it for years.

It's time to work on letting it go. Maybe Zahir is right. "I'm sorry you had to do that."

Lorcan smooths my hair. "He's had it coming for years. 'Tis not your fault." His eyes lock with mine. "Doesn't matter what happens from here as long as we're in it together. You and me."

"Do you think that's possible? You and me? I mean, really?"

"Yeah, I do. I think somewhere, someone thought we needed each other. We've crossed paths too many times for it to be a coincidence. So I don't care what deal I have to make or what concessions I have to give Zahir. You're *my a chroi*. If there's one thing I know I can't live without, it's that."

It is true. Without the heartache I've suffered, I wouldn't have this with him. It's a bittersweet pill. Everything I've lost, everything I've gained.

"God, when did you get so good with words?" My eyes fill with tears.

He waggles his eyebrows at me. "These lips." He points to them. "Can do amazing things." Reaching out an arm, he helps me snuggle closer. "And as soon as we're healed up, I'm going to put them to much better use."

"I like the sound of that," I say as my eyelids grow heavy. Pressed up against his chest, I drift to sleep to the sound of his steady, familiar heartbeat.

**Read the next book in the series, Resurrection, here:**

**Bellerive Royals Series – Interconnected standalones**

Fake Crown

Scarred Crown

Heavy Crown

Fallen Crown

**Tucker Billionaires – Interconnected standalones**

Temporary Love

**New Adult Sports**

Saving Us

Fake Crown

**Donaghey Brothers Series – Romantic suspense**

Retribution

Resurrection

Redemption

**Little Falls Series – Small Town Romance**

Rival Hearts

Mending Hearts
Healing Hearts
Guarded Hearts

First Date Challenge – loosely linked to the same world – for maximum enjoyment, read after Book 2

**Adult Contemporary Romance**

When Stars Fall

Miss Matched

# ABOUT WENDY MILLION/W. MILLION

Wendy Million is a high school teacher whose award winning contemporary romances about strong women and troubled men have captivated her loyal readers.

Writing as Wendy Million, she is the author of the romantic suspense series *The Donaghey Brothers,* as well as the contemporary second chance romances, *When Stars Fall*, and *Miss Matched*.

Writing as W. Million, she's the author of the Bellerive Royals series, the Little Falls series, and the Tucker Billionaires series.

When not writing, Wendy enjoys spending time in or around the water. She lives in Ontario, Canada with two beautiful daughters, two cute pooches, and one handsome husband (who is grateful she doesn't need two of those).

# Acknowledgements

Thank you to Shanoff Designs for the newest covers for this series. Once I got my rights back from the small press, a rebrand was critical.

Thank you to my husband, Jay and my daughters, Hannah and Autumn. You've endured countless hours of typing as background noise; moments when I'm more lost in my head than lost in the moment; and nights when I stayed up way too late writing and didn't have quite enough patience the next day. I hope that you're learning that perseverance, hard work, and an unfailing desire to pursue a dream ultimately produce results. The three of you are the foundation upon which all my stories are built.

Mom, you're not here to read this, but I'm convinced that my love of reading came from you. You also taught me a deep sense of empathy which is so vital for creating good characters. I hope that wherever you are, you know that this book exists. Thank you for inspiring my love of a story well told.

Dad, you taught me the value of perseverance and pursuing my dream. I always felt like I could achieve anything because you never made me feel like I couldn't. That's been invaluable, not just in this endeavor, but in everything I've done while I lived under your roof and once I left (yes, Dad, I know the obvious joke). I love you.

Rich, you taught me the value of sibling relationships. I'll always be grateful that out of all the souls in the world, I got you as my childhood partner in crime. Throughout our lives, we've cheered each other on, and that is a gift not everyone gets. Thank you. I love you.

Gram, you taught me that creativity has value. You may not be a storyteller, but you passed along the sense that there's joy in the effort (and sometimes some frustration), but with enough practice, you can overcome obstacles or inadequacies to create something beautiful. I love you, and I cherish all the times I got to see you bring something creative to life.

Thank you to all my first readers: Jennifer Thompson, Karen Sampson-Venzon, Kelly Waldruff, Natalie Boersma, Sacha Delacourt, Natalia Britt, Elizabeth Gatzow, Grace Nomsa, Greydaygirl, Lynnette Macpherson, Iryna Barnas. Each one of you has given me such an incredible gift by offering encouragement, criticism, and enthusiasm for my stories when I've needed it most. I'm here because you stuck with me and made me feel like my work had value.

Thank you, Cole Lepley, my writing bestie. We've wiled away many hours talking about nothing and everything. I can always count on you for an opinion, and to be my biggest cheerleader when I think I've had enough. Go edit, so you can join me on this journey.